NOBLESSE OBLIGE

THE THIRD BOOK OF THE ANJOU TRILOGY

REX J. LIPMAN

PEACOCK
Publications

BY THE SAME AUTHOR

When All Else Fails, Read the Instructions. (1998)
ISBN 0-646-35947-9

Luck's been a lady (2000)
ISBN 0-9578019-0-4

The Quetteville Diaries (2003)
ISBN 1-876087-78-1

The Countess of Anjou (2004)
ISBN 1-876087-82-X

COVER PICTURES: The end of the battle of Waterloo.
The victorious Duke of Wellington (above).
The defeated Napoléon fleeing from the battlefield (below).

No part of this Publication may be reproduced, stored in a retrieval system or transmitted in any form by any means, electronic, mechanical, photocopying or otherwise, without first obtaining written permission of the copyright owner.

Published in Australia by Peacock Publications
38 Sydenham Road, Norwood, South Australia 5067
Copyright © 2004 Rex J Lipman
First published September, 2004
National Library of Australia Card Number & ISBN 1 876087 94 3
Designed and produced by Peacock Publications, Adelaide
Printed in Australia by Peacock Publications

Contents

Acknowledgements v

Family Tree of the Scott-Quetteville Family vi

The Anjou Trilogy ix

Part I   Bound for Botany Bay 1

Part II   The French Revolution 77

Part III   Napoléon Bonaparte 233

Part IV   The Battle of Waterloo 271

Epilogue 327

Bibliography 329

Dramatis Personae 332

Family Tree of the Scott-Quetteville Family – 19 June, 1815 338

For Christopher Hibbert, whose brilliant historical writings have given me much happiness – and a better understanding of the history of Georgian England and Revolutionary France.

Acknowledgements

In the first two books of the Anjou trilogy, *The Quetteville Diaries* and *The Countess of Anjou*, I gratefully acknowledged the writings of Christopher Hibbert, that have so brilliantly brought back to life the people and the events of the eighteenth century. That acknowledgement applies equally to this, the final book of the trilogy. I have identified in the bibliography those of his books that have been so valuable to me – and those of the other authors who have provided me with much of the material I have needed to enable me to give an accurate account of the historical events of the period. I must make particular mention of David Howarth's *Waterloo – A Near Run Thing*, Niall Ferguson's *The House of Rothschild* and Nils Forssell's *Fouché – The Man Napoléon Feared*.

In the production of *Noblesse Oblige* I have been singularly fortunate in having a loyal, capable and enthusiastic support group: Wendy Sutherland, whose experience and professionalism have been invaluable, Tony Baker, who has done his best to prevent my inexperience as an author from being too obvious; and Heather Fletcher, who has been a painstaking proof reader.

My special thanks go to Viki Bickerton and Alison Perkins, my conscientious and thorough assistants, who have spent hundreds of hours in research, editing and retyping the manuscript. Without them there would have been no *Noblesse Oblige*.

And finally, I must acknowledge the patience and forbearance of my wife, Eve, who for more than three years has had to put up with a husband whose mind – for too much of the time – has been two hundred years and half a world away.

Rex J. Lipman

Adelaide, South Australia
September 2004

FAMILY TREE — AT THE
THE QUETTEVILLES OF ANJOU

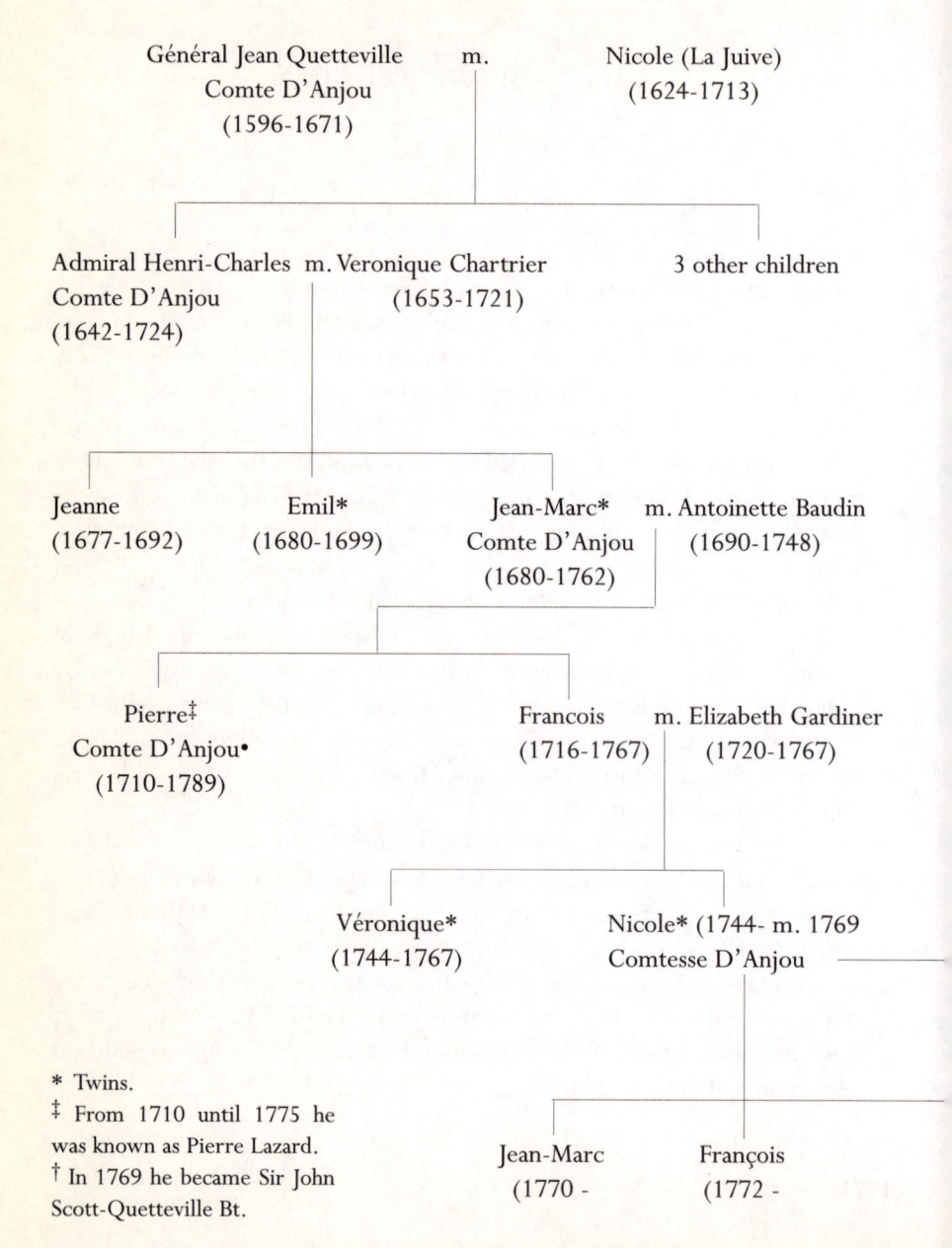

Général Jean Quetteville m. Nicole (La Juive)
Comte D'Anjou   (1624-1713)
(1596-1671)

Admiral Henri-Charles m. Veronique Chartrier   3 other children
Comte D'Anjou   (1653-1721)
(1642-1724)

Jeanne   Emil*   Jean-Marc* m. Antoinette Baudin
(1677-1692) (1680-1699) Comte D'Anjou (1690-1748)
                      (1680-1762)

Pierre‡   Francois m. Elizabeth Gardiner
Comte D'Anjou•   (1716-1767) (1720-1767)
(1710-1789)

Véronique*   Nicole* (1744- m. 1769
(1744-1767)   Comtesse D'Anjou

* Twins.
‡ From 1710 until 1775 he was known as Pierre Lazard.
† In 1769 he became Sir John Scott-Quetteville Bt.

Jean-Marc   François
(1770 -   (1772 -

BEGINNING OF *NOBLESSE OBLIGE*

THE SCOTT FAMILY

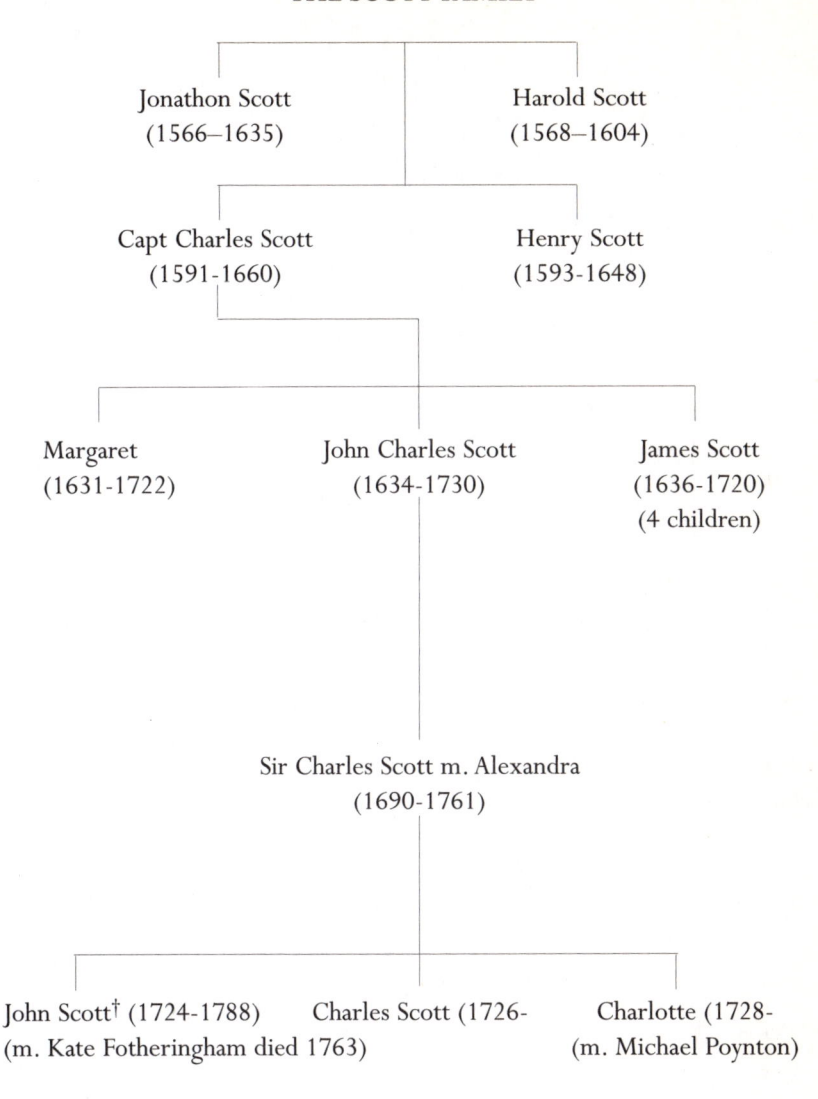

Jonathon Scott (1566–1635) — Harold Scott (1568–1604)

Capt Charles Scott (1591-1660) — Henry Scott (1593-1648)

Margaret (1631-1722)
John Charles Scott (1634-1730)
James Scott (1636-1720) (4 children)

Sir Charles Scott m. Alexandra (1690-1761)

John Scott[†] (1724-1788) (m. Kate Fotheringham died 1763)
Charles Scott (1726-)
Charlotte (1728-) (m. Michael Poynton)

William (1773 -

Dramatis Personae

To assist readers who have not read
The Quetteville Diaries, or
The Countess of Anjou,
for brief details of the
main characters,
please see pages 332–337

The Anjou Trilogy

PART I – THE QUETTEVILLE DIARIES

Jean-Marc Quetteville, le Comte d'Anjou (1680-1762), a former admiral in the French Fleet, lived – as a number of generations of his family had done – in Marseille. A few years after his death, there had been an attempt to assassinate his elder son, Marc. The assault had been badly botched and had resulted in the murder of his younger son, François and all his family except one of his twin daughters, Nicole. François was a brilliant surgeon who had studied at the Sorbonne and had taught at the famous College of Surgeons in London. Marc, on the other hand, a judge in Marseille, was both corrupt and perverted and was thoroughly despised.

A few weeks after the death of his brother, Marc, who had sexually abused and raped his daughter, Jeanne, tried to force himself on Nicole. She, a strong, athletic girl in her early twenties, was infuriated and, reaching for a dagger, she killed him and fled to London, where she worked as senior *receptioniste* in The Cloisters, one of London's most prestigious seraglios[1].

After meeting many members of the royal family and the nobility of England, and having been involved in the training and racing of Britain's greatest racehorse, Eclipse, Nicole married Sir John Scott Bt., the owner of the *Trentbridge,* the ship that had brought her to London. The family name was then changed to Scott-Quetteville. As well as being shipowners, the Scott family company was involved in Marseille's flour-

---

[1] High class brothels.

ishing soap trade and in a number of businesses in the American colonies.

Just before her wedding, in the autumn of 1769, thanks to Cardinal Bandini, a friend of her late father, Nicole learnt that the courts in Marseille had completely exonerated her for killing her uncle in self-defence and that she had inherited the family title.

PART II – THE COUNTESS OF ANJOU

During the first three years of their married life, Sir John and Lady Scott-Quetteville had three sons, Jean-Marc, François and William and, as the boys grew up, the Scott-Quettevilles appointed three brilliant young tutors to ensure that every aspect of their education and physical potential was developed to the full. These three graduates – Johann Freyberg and his sister Enika, and Franco Sattin – lived with the Scott-Quetteville family and, over a period of several years, they researched all the old count's writings and produced *Les Memoirs et les Écrits de Jean-Marc Quetteville – le Comte d'Anjou* – a task they found fascinating, and rewarding.

In 1784 the young Jean-Marc, who had spent much of his life in Marseille, was selected as a King's Scholar to study at *l'École Militaire* in Paris. He was in the same course as another King's Scholar, a young Corsican, Napoléon Buonaparte. The two became good friends and spent several vacations together.

François joined the Royal Navy and in 1787 went with the First Fleet to the penal settlement in New South Wales with Captain Arthur Phillip. The third son, William, whose ambition it was to be a banker, worked in Coutts' Bank in London and later in Frankfurt.

Lady Scott-Quetteville spent her time between France and England and, as well as remaining close to her sons, she built up the family businesses. In Paris she became a close friend of the unhappy young Marie-Antoinette, whose unconsummated marriage to the over-weight – and under-sexed – King Louis XVI, caused her sadness and misery. This situation gave the Paris lampoonists seven years in which they could – and incessantly did – deride their monarch and his Austrian queen.

Another of Nicole's friends in Paris was the Duke of Dorset, the

British Ambassador. It was at a dinner at the British Embassy that she met Prince Cardinal Louis de Rohan, whose life – and reputation – were later destroyed by the scheming strumpet, Countess Jeanne de Lamotte Valois.

On a visit to Frankfurt, as a keen numismatist, Nicole went to the Jewish ghetto in Judenstrasse where she met an almost unknown coin dealer Mayer Rothschild. It was during one of her several visits to his shop to purchase old coins that it was discovered that his great-grandmother and Lady Nicole's had been twins. The close friendship that developed between the two families was destined to last for several generations.

In 1775, by a curious set of circumstances, it was established that a Professor at the Sorbonne, Pierre Lazard, was, in fact, the elder son of the old Comte d'Anjou and that the dead judge, Marc, had been the illegitimate child of the wet nurse who was caring for the newborn son of the count, the two babies having been transposed when they were only a few weeks old. Although this revelation meant that Pierre Lazard was entitled to the Anjou title and its vast estates, the matter was resolved in a spirit of goodwill and understanding.

In 1788 Sir John, who devoted much of his time leading a research team that was involved in a project to adapt James Watt's steam engine for the propulsion of seagoing ships, conducted some trials in Paris, on the river Seine. Disaster struck when saboteurs exploded a bomb on the vessel concerned and Sir John, who was only a few feet from the explosion, was killed. His death left his widow grief-stricken.

Later in that year, there was a total collapse of the French economy and this – and a nationwide drought – caused such unrest and rioting throughout France that King Louis XVI decided to convene a meeting of The Estates General. Nicole, la Comtesse d'Anjou, was elected as a delegate to represent Marseille at the historic Convention that ensued.

The following year, just as the Revolution broke out, Nicole was gunned down in Paris by some paid thugs. Dying, she was rushed to the clinic at the Sorbonne by the British Ambassador. Although he thought it was too late to save her life, he was aware that two of Europe's greatest doctors, John Hunter from England and Jean-Marie Lassonne, were attending a meeting there. For the next twenty-four hours the two men battled against the odds to keep her alive.

It was not until the following year that her second son, François, who was serving in the Royal Navy on the other side of the world in the newly established penal colony New South Wales, learned of the tragedy.

Part I

Bound for Botany Bay

"…a solution to the problem of our much overcrowded gaols"
WILLIAM PITT *

1787 – 1788

---

* In a speech to the House of Commons 1787.

I

FROM THE BEGINNING OF THE eighteenth century many of England's wrongdoers were transported to the American colonies to serve out their sentences. This form of punishment was thought to deter would-be criminals and, at the same time, provide cheap labour for developing the southern American colonies. For a number of years the scheme met with general approval. The Government made money selling the convicts to their gaolers, the shipping companies made money transporting them to America and the gaolers made money by selling them for the term of their sentence to the plantation owners. The practice continued until the outbreak of the American Revolution, by which time some fifty thousand convicts had been transported across the Atlantic.

In 1776 the British Prime Minister, Lord North, informed the Parliament that, for a number of reasons, the practice of transporting convicts would cease. Rather than letting the Americans profit from this cheap labour, criminals would be housed on disused, unseaworthy vessels that lay idle in the nation's big ports and in some of the larger rivers, such as the Thames. Although living on these so-called hulks was cramped and uncomfortable, the convicts provided cheap local labour. As some politicians and reformers were sufficiently naïve to think that many of the wrongdoers would recognise the error of their ways and repent – and become useful members of society – they were all forced to attend divine worship every Sunday. This hope was pious and worthy – but unfulfilled. It was not long before the hulks were referred to as the Sodom and Gomorrah of England.

It was not long after the young William Pitt became prime minister at the end of 1783 that he summoned his home secretary to Downing Street to discuss the problem and find a remedy to what was becoming a national issue.

"Lord Sydney, in my opinion the problem of dealing with our criminals is rapidly getting out of hand. Although it is serious and cannot be ignored, I believe the newspapers and loud-mouthed politicians like Edmund Burke are blowing everything out of proportion."

"I agree sir. Nevertheless, what he said in the House yesterday was substantially true. The picture he painted, in his eloquent and convincing way, is not a pretty one. As you and I know only too well, there are now more than one hundred thousand wrongdoers locked up in our prisons and in the hulks – and that is far too many."

Pitt tried to goad the minister on.

"Almost every day there is either another pamphlet on the streets or another petition to a member of parliament – and I am not suggesting that these are escaping your attention. Although there is much hysterical nonsense being written, I am really interested to explore the proposal of that fellow, James Matra."

"Was he not on the *Endeavour* with Captain Cook?"

"Yes! And he was most impressed with a place in New South Wales that Cook named Botany Bay and he is strongly advocating the setting up of a penal settlement there. Would you please have the idea thoroughly investigated? I do not want to put anything before Parliament until we have worked out all the details – including the estimated cost."

During the two years that the Home Office was working on the plan to establish a convict settlement at Botany Bay, the practice of putting prisoners on hulks continued, amid louder and harsher criticism from philanthropists and do-gooders. They warned that these unhealthy vessels were destroying whatever moral values their inmates might have had and that the increase in the incidence of gaol distemper and smallpox among the prisoners was getting out of hand.

* * *

At the beginning of 1786 the prime minister and the home secretary introduced the legislation that led to the colonisation of New South

Wales. By the end of that year it had been passed by both Houses of Parliament and, during April of the following year, more than a thousand people were assembled in Portsmouth ready to embark and become members of what was later known as the First Fleet. Under the command of the Governor-Designate, Captain Arthur Phillip, there were two men-of-war, HMS *Sirius* and HMS *Supply*, six merchantmen and three store ships. Two hundred marines guarded more than 700 convicts, of whom 180 were women. In addition, there were the officers and crews of the ships and some wives and children.

François Scott-Quetteville, who had recently graduated as a midshipman from the Royal Navel College in Portsmouth, had been selected by Captain Phillip to go to Botany Bay in New South Wales. As a midshipman, François preferred to be known as Frank Scott and had been signed on under that name. In commending the young man for his good sense, Phillip informed him that, when he became a second lieutenant, he should resume his correct name.

The majority of the convicts going to Botany Bay were from the worst of the hulks and the remainder were some recently sentenced prisoners, the death sentences of whom had been commuted to "penal servitude in His Majesty's colonies".

One of the most extraordinary of these cases was that of a fine looking fifteen-year-old, Judith Hyams. Born in Boston she had lost both her parents. Her father, Judah, an English sea captain, had migrated to America in the 1750s. He had been the master of a ship owned by a Canadian shipping company that had vessels sailing out of both Quebec and Boston. His French wife, Nathalie, had died in childbirth when Judith was twelve years old. A writer and poet, Nathalie had educated her daughter at home and, during the summer months of each year, mother and daughter had always joined the captain's ship as he sailed from Boston to Marseille, Teneriffe, in the Canary Islands, or to London.

The loss of his wife had a devastating effect on Judah and, when his daughter pleaded with him to allow her to live on his ship with him, he more than willingly agreed. So that her education would not suffer, he had engaged a French-Canadian governess — a young friend of Nathalie — to sail with them. While living on board, Judith learnt much about shipboard life and the sea. Among her many other experiences, she had observed selected members of her father's crew – those who could swim – being trained in lifesaving and, on one occasion, she had witnessed the rescue of a drowning man in the estuary of the St Lawrence. At the time, she could not know that this learning experience would completely change her life.

By the time his daughter had turned fifteen, Judah Hyams realised that it was not in her best interests to spend the rest of her teenage years at sea. When he had discussed this problem with the wife of one of his Canadian friends, she suggested that her sister, who was married to a British army officer, Major Cornish, was looking for a young person to live in their Bond Street, London, home with them. She assured the captain that the quite mature Judith would fit well into this London household.

Exchanges of letters over the next six months resulted in a plan for the captain and his daughter to stay with this family for a few days while his ship was in port in London, to see how things would work out. With Judith very excited and looking forward to this new experience, they sailed from Boston in October 1786. Unfortunately, while they were crossing the Atlantic, Judah Hyams contracted pneumonia and died a week later. Following this tragedy, the first officer, who took over command of the ship, felt that the best thing he could do on his arrival in London would be to hand Judith over to the Cornish family, if they would be prepared to have her – and they were.

Mrs Cornish was a kind and gentle woman and she made her young American guest welcome. On her part, Judith tried hard to keep her sadness to herself and, with Christmas Day approaching there were a number of social engagements. However, as her parents were Jewish, Judith found Christmas a rather pointless celebration. Even so, her life was made as pleasant as possible by Mrs Cornish who, whenever the weather was sufficiently fine, showed her many of the historic sights of London.

During the first week of February Mrs Cornish had to go to Windsor to visit her mother and Judith was left in the house with the major and the servants. One evening, after she had undressed and had gone to bed, she was confronted by the major who was more than a little inebriated.

• PART I – I •

Without saying a word he removed his heavy, brocaded dressing gown and, stark naked, he proceeded to get into bed with her. Judith was shocked and revolted and, when he started to pull at the ribbons on the front of her nightdress and attempt to fondle her breasts, she became furious and ordered him from the room. He made no move to go and, although she found his slurred speech hard to understand, she had no doubt in her mind what he wanted. A nasty altercation followed, during which Judith, flaying her fists to keep the man at bay, hit him quite hard. When he still persisted, she jerked her knee so hard into his groin that he howled in pain. Swearing at her and livid with rage, he grabbed his dressing gown and still doubled up in agony, he left the room, muttering all kinds of threats.

Judith locked the door of her room and packed her trunk and her big travelling bag. She had had enough. As she was not certain when Mrs Cornish was returning from Windsor, she was determined to leave the house as soon as she could.

First thing the following morning, as heavy as it was, she took her luggage downstairs to the front hall, ready to depart. At breakfast she tried to be as civil as she could to the major. She thanked him for having her to stay and informed him that she was leaving as soon as she had said goodbye to the servants. His reaction appeared to be quite nonchalant.

"Where are you going?"

"I shall discuss my future with my late father's agent, Captain Duckworth."

The man shrugged his shoulders, stood up and, without another word, he left the room. Judith finished her meal and went to the kitchen where she knew she would find the servants having their breakfast. All but two of them were there. Ethel, the lady's maid, was upstairs doing Mrs Cornish's room – as she did every morning, in case she returned unexpectedly. The housekeeper, Mrs Earhart, was also upstairs. Judith asked Partridge, the butler, to say goodbye to them both and to thank Mrs Cornish for all her kindness. He was quite shocked that she was leaving in such haste.

"Miss Judith, could you not wait until the mistress returns? She will be very disappointed if you leave without saying goodbye to her."

"I'm sorry Partridge, but I really must leave at once. I shall write to

Mrs Cornish within the next few days. If you could get somebody to go out the front and look for a cab, I should really appreciate it."

"Certainly Miss – I shall go myself. Are you sure you have money and everything like that?"

"Yes, thank you, Partridge – I have everything. You are very thoughtful."

An hour later, her cab was pulling into the Thames-side office of the Quebec Shipping Company's agent. As she alighted, she was quite dumbfounded. There was Major Cornish, standing next to his carriage with a police officer at his side – and an empty cab. With a self-satisfied smirk on his face and pointing his finger toward Judith, he addressed the constable.

"I would ask you to arrest that young woman. I am sure that it is she who has stolen my wife's gold bracelet."

The policeman was polite but to the point.

"Excuse me, Miss, but I am afraid I 'ave to search you and your bags."

Judith was too shocked to say anything; but at that moment a man emerged from the shipping office. He was apparently a clerk. She asked him –

"Could you please ask Captain Duckworth to come out here? I badly need some help."

"I am sorry Miss, but Captain Duckworth 'as gone to Canada. The captain of one of our ships died and the captain 'as taken 'is place."

Before Judith could explain her situation further, the police officer interjected.

"Look 'ere, Miss, we must not waste the major's time. Do you want me to search you first – or your baggage?"

The major pointed to the big leather bag and the officer started to undo the straps. Within a few seconds he had found the missing item. He handed it to the major who, looking straight at the poor girl, barked –

"There's gratitude for you. Arrest her constable! Put her in the cab and take her back to Bow Street. I know the magistrate well and I know that a one-way trip to Tyburn is what this thieving young hussy will get from him." Cornish, with a feigned look of indignation, climbed into his carriage and tapped the roof for his coachman to drive off.

• PART I – 1 •

As Judith was not aware that, in England, people found guilty of theft were taken to the gallows at Tyburn, the major's taunt had no effect on her.

Judith burst into tears. It was too much for her. She knew full well how the bracelet came to be in her case, and that it would be difficult for her to prove her innocence. Trying to control herself, she appealed to the police officer.

"Somebody must have put that bracelet in my bag. I can honestly tell you, sir, that I have never seen it before in my life."

The officer was quite unimpressed.

"They all say that, Miss. Come along now and don't make any more trouble."

* * *

Judith had only been in custody a few days before she was arraigned before a magistrate with a number of other prisoners. Two old dears with whom she had been sharing a cell and who had been charged with vagrancy had warned her about him and advised her not to let him bully her. As he came into the big courtroom, it was not difficult to recognise him from their description – short and fat, with beady eyes, a small nose and a cruel mouth. With the reading of the charge out of the way, he soon made it clear that he had no intention of there being anything but a short trial. He even admonished one of the court officials for wasting too much of his precious time. He pretended to listen to the damning evidence of the constable; however, as the major was one of his friends, he already knew the details. The constable, not to be deterred, pompously recited his statement, detailing the visit to Bow Street of the major to report that his wife's gold bracelet had been stolen and had described the piece of jewellery in detail and how he suspected the accused who had been a guest in his house but who had suddenly departed. He then went on to describe the discovery of the bracelet in the baggage of the young woman standing in the dock.

"A cut and dried case," said the magistrate, as he dismissed the constable and turned to the major.

"I do not think it is necessary for me to inconvenience you by calling you to the witness box. The item in question is undoubtedly yours or your wife's. You described it accurately to the police officer and it was subsequently found in the possession of this young girl who had made a hasty, unheralded departure from your Bond Street home. She was already on the Thames wharf from which many of the ships going to America depart."

Although he knew that Judith was without a counsel, the magistrate then asked her who was representing her. She was more angry than she was frightened —

"I have no one to represent me, sir. I am an American and I have only just arrived in England. My father, who was bringing me here, was the captain of a ship and he died during the voyage from Boston. He and I were to stay in Bond Street with Major Cornish and his wife, who met me when our ship arrived in London and took me to her home. I left the house for personal reasons and I not only informed the major that I was leaving, I also told him where I was going. I would not, under any circumstances, take anything belonging to my host or hostess. I did not steal anything. As I told the police officer who arrested me, somebody wishing to do me harm must have placed the bracelet in my baggage."

The fat little magistrate turned towards her.

"Enough of your lies! I find you guilty of theft of a valuable gold bracelet and, although you can probably get away with things like this in America, in this country it is a capital offence."

He paused to let the full impact of his statement sink in. Looking over his gold-rimmed spectacles at the girl, he passed sentence.

"Because of your age — and, in this regard, I believe I am giving you the benefit of a very grave doubt when you say that you are only fifteen years old — you will be transported to one of His Majesty's colonies for a period of seven years."

Turning to the court officials, he continued —

"Take her down…Next case!"

Judith realised that, for the moment, there was not a single thing she could do but to accept her fate. As the two old ladies had said, the judge was an evil man and, irrespective of the evidence put before him, he had from the outset intended to side with the lecherous major.

She just stood there in silence until, prodded by a court official, she was pushed towards the stairs that led down to the cells. As she was going through the courtroom door, an envelope was thrust into her hand. It was not possible for her to get a good look at the woman who handed it to her as she was wearing a scarf that half covered her face and a hat with a broad brim. Although Judith had only a fleeting glimpse of her, she felt that she had seen her before.

The cells were dingy and the humid, smoky atmosphere and the pungent smell of stale tobacco and urine revolted her and almost made her vomit. She was longing to open the envelope she had just been given but, as there were three people in the cell, she felt it would be unwise. One of the three was a tall, coarse, heavy-bosomed woman of more than thirty. The other two were girls in their teens. Their faces were heavily made up and their clothing was gaudy. One of them welcomed her.

"I'm Amy and me friend 'ere is Alisha…"

Amy's welcome was interrupted by a sergeant who came to the cell door.

"This is a lucky day for yous four ladies. You are going a long way in life. Tomorra you are orf to Portsmouth where you will board a ship bound for New South Wales or New Holland. One or the other – I can't tell you which and I am not sure where either place is. But it is at the other end of the world."

Having made this announcement, he departed, leaving the inmates of the cell flabbergasted.

Amy was the first to break the silence; but before she had finished her speech of welcome, the big woman, who had made herself comfortable on a bench at the back of the cell, stood up. With her hands on her hips, she looked at each of the three girls in turn.

"Now let us all get a few things straight. To you young'ns, me name is Mrs B – and nothing else. We are goin' to be together for a long time, so I 'ad better tell yer 'ow things stand. I will expect yer three to do certain things for me and in return, it is my job to look after yer. There's nothin' for nothin' in this world but, as yer will find out, I will treat yer fair. As long as I am next to yer, the warders and guards won't lay a 'and on yer – nor will any of the men. You'll get lots of opportunities to earn the odd sovereign or two — but you will not go sleepin' with any Tom, Dick or 'Arry without me permission — yer understand? All that sort of thing will be 'andled by me. Now don't go worryin' yer little heads about me takin' 'arf yer money off yer. I won't, I promise yer. I can get yer fifty per cent more than yous can get off the men and all I'll take is a flat twenty per cent of the lot. So yer see, we'll all win. Won't we? And none of them slimy wimmen with their inquisitive little fingers and their 'ungry little tongues will dare lay a 'and or a tongue — or anything else on yer, neither."

She looked at Judith.

"And wot's yore name, Prettypuss?"

Judith had the good sense to play along with this experienced woman of the world. While Mrs B had been speaking, she had made up her mind that she had the right build and the right attitude to be a formidable ally — and an awesome enemy.

"I am Judy and I am American. Thank you Mrs B for explaining things to us — and for your offer of help. I accept it — but I'm afraid I won't be doing any sleeping about. I am engaged to a wonderful man and I would die before I betrayed him."

Judy held out her hand to her new protector, who was surprised at the strength of the American girl's handshake. The two other girls looked at each other before speaking.

Alisha, who had been standing a little behind Amy, let her friend speak for them both.

"Our trouble 'as always been gettin' paid. The bastards want the lot for nothin'. But if we are goin' to be on a ship, it'll be 'ard to find places that aren't too public, won't it?"

Their new protector tried to allay the girls' concerns.

"I've never been on a big ship, so I don't know 'ow things will work out; but I betcha there'll be plenty of it goin' on — more than yous two can cope with — there will be nothing else to do. Just do wot Mrs B tells yer and all will be well."

The two girls nodded their heads and smiled.

Well satisfied with the reception of her speech, Mrs B resumed her seat on the bench. With a distant smile creeping over her rather motherly face, she half stared at the dirty ceiling and, in a quiet voice, she added –

"And with all them fellas on the ship – the crew as well as the convicts – your friend Mrs B won't be altogether missing out neither. An ol' dog for a 'ard road."

Before the end of the week the four convicts were taken to Portsmouth and put aboard one of the ugly, over-crowded hulks and, a few days later, with many other women, they embarked on quite a big vessel, the *Prince of Wales*. Knowing she was only allowed to take one case with her, and being fully aware what would be useful to her on the voyage, Judy was able to sell the rest of her things to other convicts on the hulk. As they were a tough lot and without many scruples, she thought it better to let Mrs B handle everything for her. She was most impressed with the way her agent went about her business and felt that the commission she kept for herself was fair.

Although almost all the other convicts were older women in their late twenties and thirties – and some even older than that – there were a few in their teens, most of them prostitutes or petty thieves – or both. Judy realised that they were going to be together for a long time and made up her mind to keep as low a profile as possible – something quite out of character for her. When travelling on her father's ship, apart from working in the chartroom, she had always spent some time sewing and she thanked her lucky stars that she had brought all her sewing things with her.

* * *

It was not until they had been at sea for a few days that Judy found a place where she felt it would be safe to open the envelope that had been handed to her as she was virtually pushed out of the courtroom in London. It proved to be a really friendly letter from the Cornishes' housekeeper. The poor woman stated that she would like to have helped her but she knew it was more than her job was worth – and that, with a miscreant like Judge Roberts, her evidence would have had no effect on his verdict. Having read the letter several times, Judy realised that, if she could escape and show it to the American consul in Teneriffe – their first port of call – it could be very valuable. She would keep the letter in the same safe hiding place as some pieces of her mother's jewellery that she was guarding with her life.

The food on the *Prince of Wales* was anything but plentiful and there was no variety at all. Apart from having to clean up their sleeping area and the primitive lavatories each day, they were virtually in a state of constant idleness. Judy was highly amused at the ingenuity of Mrs B, who not only found customers for Alisha and Amy but also found partially secluded places for them to do their entertaining. As she had expected – and hoped – there was more than a sprinkling of older men, and this enabled her to establish a small clientele of her own.

Like all the other ships' masters, Captain Mason constantly preached good Christian living and, on Sundays, he exhorted the convicts to lead honest, chaste lives and redeem themselves. He warned the men, including the crew, that anyone caught in the parts of the ship occupied by the women would be flogged – and they were soon to learn that this was no idle threat. Even so, as is always the case, love – or lust – found a way.

As early as their second day at sea, it was common knowledge that there were going to be three ports of call on their way to New South Wales; Teneriffe in the Canary Islands, Rio de Janeiro and Table Bay in the south of Africa. Judith knew little or nothing about Brazil or South Africa but she had been to Teneriffe twice, as her father's ship had sometimes called there. She was well aware that the now independent United States of America had consular representation there. There was one other thing of which she was equally certain – she had no intention of being a convict in New South Wales, New Holland or anywhere else. To go to a new country as a free settler could be an exciting challenge, particularly as she had no ties in either Boston or Quebec. Besides, the stench of, firstly, the revolting hulk and now the crowded ship, the disgusting language of many of the women and girls – and the sordid nature of almost all their conversation – revolted her, and made her determined to escape.

As far as her relationship with Alisha and Amy was concerned, she had grown to like them and to understand that, coming from a pathetically poor and domestically brutal background, their outlook on life was quite understandable. Behind the tough façade of Mrs B, too, there was much to admire and even like. She was loyal and she was honest and she saw to it that nobody pushed her – or her three orphans – around.

From the outset when she became aware that the fleet would call in at Teneriffe, Judith made up her mind that she would jump ship there. She would make her way to the American consul and persuade him to help her get back to Boston where she knew she had assets – and money.

From that moment on, she did little else but think about the best way to escape, and the first part of her planning related to the timing of her exit from the *Prince of Wales*. This would have to be the last day in port – so that, by the time she was missed, the fleet would be well out to sea.

She clearly remembered the layout of the Teneriffe wharves. For a start there would only be room for a couple of ships to tie up there; the rest would have to be out in the bay and be serviced by lighters. She had little doubt that it would be the two warships that would be moored, as the danger of prisoners escaping from the other vessels would be much less if they were anchored off shore.

She felt that being tall and with a strong physique, it should not be hard for her to disguise herself as a member of the crew of one of the lighters; that is, if she could lay her hands on some suitable clothing. Realising that to plan and execute an escape completely by herself would be virtually impossible, Judy decided to put her trust in Mrs B and to give her, as a reward, those of her possessions that she could not manage to take with her – and that would probably be almost everything. Having done some sewing for one of the sergeants of the Royal Marines, Judy learned from him that they would be in port for about a week and that there would be a number of the local seamen coming on board to help stow cargo, food and some chickens. In conversation with him she also ascertained that, whereas the crew of the visiting ships would almost certainly be permitted to go ashore and find some local girls, once the local sailors found out that there were women on board the British ships, at least a few of them would be finding an excuse to get to the *Prince of Wales* to try their luck.

* * *

There were big sighs of relief from both the prisoners and the crew when they had their first glimpse of the Canary Islands. Judy's emotions were entirely different – she was becoming more excited by the day. Although to the convicts and more than a few of the crew, it had seemed a long journey from Portsmouth, the American girl had many thoughts and plans to keep her occupied throughout the voyage. Each day she made it her business to spend some time with a Spanish girl who helped her improve her Spanish. She felt that, if she had difficulty finding the American consulate, she might need to talk the local language.

With the favourable winds they encountered, it had taken no longer than a couple of weeks for the fleet to reach Teneriffe. Captain Phillip was anxious not to stay in port longer than necessary, and he immediately set about replenishing his supplies of water, meat and vegetables. Everyone on board was looking forward to having some fresh bread too, but because of its exorbitant price, Captain Phillip resisted whatever temptation he might have had to buy some.

From Judy's point of view, the first couple of days in the harbour were more than satisfactory. Just as the sergeant had predicted, there were many local sailors on board the lighters and it was amazing how, soon after they had boarded the *Prince of Wales*, some of them "disappeared" below – and returned an hour or so later with smiles on their faces and a gold coin or two less in their pockets. Quick to grasp the opportunity, Mrs B, having decided that it would be sensible to bring her two young harlots into the conspiracy, persuaded Alisha to get one of her men to return the next day with a pair of breeches and, in the same way, Amy acquired a bandanna and some suitably sized boots. So ardent and conscientious were the two girls in obliging their sailors on three consecutive days, that they received the required clothing without paying.

As the day for leaving Teneriffe drew near, they learned when the lighter that had been servicing the *Prince of Wales* would be making its final trip. Almost all this information had been supplied by a handsome young local seaman who had been pestering Mrs B to make Judy available to him. He swore to her that he was in love with the beautiful American girl and that he wanted to marry her. Using this intelligence, the clever woman persuaded her protégée to go along with the idea and to use him as an accomplice to get to the shore – and to the American consular office – and then to confess that she could not marry him as she was already betrothed but would pay him well for his help. He, realising that if he was to win his bride it was absolutely vital to maintain total secrecy, swore on oath not to mention a word about the escape plan to anybody.

* * *

Major Augustus Fortescue was Captain Phillip's senior victualling officer. He had embarked at Portsmouth with the fleet. His task was to travel as far as Teneriffe to establish satisfactory supply arrangements not only for Captain Phillip's fleet but as an ongoing arrangement for subsequent convoys going to Botany Bay. The major was a good man and a fine soldier who had fought with distinction on the Iberian Peninsula during the siege of Gibraltar. He was the younger son of Lord Archibald Fortescue and, like so many younger sons of titled families, he had spent most of his life in the army. Unfortunately, his lack of understanding of the Spanish language and his limited experience as a negotiator put him at a distinct disadvantage in dealing with the locals in Teneriffe.

Captain Phillip was aware that Midshipman Frank Scott spoke reasonably fluent Spanish and that he had been to the Canary Islands several times before when he was a member of the crew of the *Pont de Toulon*, a vessel belonging to his mother's French shipping company. For these reasons he ordered Frank to assist the major, who was greatly relieved. When it came to quality and price, the midshipman knew the names of the local merchants who could be trusted – and those who could not – and within a couple of days, a number of excellent contracts had been negotiated and both the fleet commander and Captain John Hunter – who was in command of the *Sirius* – were particularly impressed with the manner in which young Scott had handled this assignment.

They were even more pleased when it came to arranging Major Fortescue's return to England. Phillip sent for the young midshipman.

"Scott, you did well in assisting the victualling officer."

"Thank you, sir."

"Tell me, lad, as you spent a couple of years sailing between here and the Mediterranean, what do you think would be the quickest way to get the major back to England? As I think you are aware, he is to take my initial dispatch back to the Home Office and to report on the use of Teneriffe as a first port of call for subsequent fleets going to New South Wales."

"Sir, there are many ships sailing between here and Marseille. Some go by way of Madeira, some via Gibraltar and others go direct. Every week, at least two of The Bridge Company's ships sail from Marseille to London. They almost invariably call in to Gibraltar. The accommodation on the smaller ships is quite limited, but the bigger ones like the *Trentbridge* and the *Twinbridge* have excellent accommodation."

"If my memory serves me correctly, The Bridge Company is owned by your parents – is it not?"

"Yes, sir! I have written a number of letters to my family – both in Marseille and in London – so when I was on shore yesterday, I inquired about shipping movements and learned that the *Pont de Toulon* is due to arrive here any day. The agent informed me that she will unload some soap here and then leave for Funchal and Gibraltar."

"I shall pass on this information to Major Fortescue and I shall tell him to be ready to leave here on the *Pont de Toulon*. Will you please speak to the agent, this afternoon? I am anxious to take on whatever supplies we need and to continue on our way as quickly as possible."

"Aye, aye, sir."

On the morning before their departure, just after Captain Phillip had reboarded the *Sirius*, there was a commotion on the wharf, with people shouting and pointing out into the bay. It took him no more than a few seconds to see that, less than fifty yards from the wharf, a man had fallen overboard from one of the lighters taking stores and personnel from the wharf to one of his ships. He was soon to learn the details of the incident.

One of the marines, Corporal Sanchez – although a British subject, had a Spanish mother. He spoke Spanish well and, hardly had the fleet arrived in port when he had met one of the local ladies. Within a day or so he had decided to marry the girl and to obtain permission for her to accompany him to Botany Bay. The corporal and his bride were on the lighter on their way out to the *Prince of Wales*. Apparently one of the crew of the lighter had made disparaging remarks about the couple and an argument had ensued. During the mêlée that followed, Major Fortescue had tried to quieten things down and restore order. Somehow, he had become embroiled in the scuffle and was pushed – or fell – overboard.

There was a great amount of noise, both on the wharf and on the lighter – concern among the crew and laughter from the convicts. However, nobody appeared to be doing anything about rescuing the unfortunate officer who, unable to swim, was calling out for help each time his head came to the surface. Phillip was angry – not only because of the plight of the drowning man but also because the crowd of locals, who had gathered on the wharf, were regarding it all as a great joke.

"What in the hell is wrong with you all?" He shouted to several nearby officers and marines. "Can't any of you swim?"

That the captain's appeal had not been answered strongly suggested that, among the crew of HMS *Sirius*, swimmers were few and far between. However, just as he was about to shout out an order, he saw a splash as a young woman leapt over the side of the *Prince of Wales*. Although severely hampered by her clothing, she was swimming towards the man. Obviously in great difficulties, each time his head bobbed up he continued to feebly call for assistance.

The woman, who before she had jumped into the water had had the foresight to grab the end of a long rope, did not take long to reach the drowning man. By this time, a Royal Marine officer aboard the *Prince of Wales*, who had recognised the assistance the female lifesaver required, grasped the other end of the rope and, as soon as he could see that she had secured it around her shoulders and was holding the drowning man's head above the water, he slowly pulled the pair of them towards the ship.

Captain Phillip was annoyed that nobody from the *Sirius* had done anything to rescue the man and amazed that it had been one of the women on the *Prince of Wales* who, in spite of the difficulty of swimming when almost fully clothed, had probably saved the man's life. He turned to where Midshipman Frank Scott was standing, just behind him.

"Scott, go over to the *Prince of Wales* and bring that woman to me!"

A pinnace was already in the water and it did not take long for its crew to row the midshipman to the vessel from which the rescue had been made. He reported to Captain John Mason, the master, and announced himself.

"The fleet commander sends his compliments, sir. He wishes to speak with the woman who jumped into the water and saved the man's life."

The master turned away and barked out a few orders.

"It was no woman, Mr Scott, it was a mere girl of fifteen – a convict." He paused.

"At least she maintains that that is her age. She looks a lot older to me. You know, many of them lie about their age in the hope that the magistrate will have pity on them and give them a lighter sentence."

Scott, appreciating that the fleet commander would almost certainly want to see the convict's dossier, asked the master for it. In less than five minutes, it was produced. During the twenty minutes that followed, while he was waiting for the girl to appear, Frank Scott studied the file. When she appeared on deck he was quite taken aback. He had not really thought what she might look like; however, he certainly had not expected her to be such a stunning looking young lady – tall, attractive, athletic and with a truly beautiful face and a clear complexion. She was neatly dressed and her shoulder-length black hair was partially hidden by a blue bandanna that was tied – gypsy-style – behind her head. She looked nothing like any of the other convicts who were lolling about on the deck.

When she had been summoned by the captain, Judith Hyams had had a vague presentiment that her luck was changing. As she had been sent for by the governor of this new settlement, before going up on deck, she had put on her 'best' clothing, taken great care with her hair – and she thrust Mrs Earhart's letter into the inside pocket of her skirt.

"Mr Scott, this is convict Judith Hyams. Although I am thoroughly disgusted with the behaviour of most female 'passengers', I must admit that this young woman did well today. Please pass my compliments to the fleet commander and assure him that a full investigation is already taking place and that the appropriate action will be taken against all persons who have misbehaved – be they our men, locals or convicts."

"I shall do so, sir. Thank you."

* * *

An hour later, the young convict was standing before Captain Phillip in the chartroom of HMS *Sirius*. Scott announced her.

"Sir, this is Judith Hyams. It was she who rescued Major Fortescue. She is fifteen years old and is an American."

Amazed and shocked that it had been his senior victualling officer who had nearly drowned, the fleet commander was keen to ascertain the details from his midshipman. Scott, who had listened carefully to what the master of the *Prince of Wales* had told him, reported the incident in full. For a moment Captain Phillip looked at the young girl in silence. During the time the convicts had been in Portsmouth he had hardly had occasion to speak to any of them and, during the voyage, as there were no convicts on HMS *Sirius*, this was one of his first conversations with any of his consignment of Britain's unwanted criminals. In an austere but friendly way, and speaking slowly and in a quiet voice, he addressed her.

"So your name is Judith Hyams; you are an American and you are only fifteen years old?"

"Yes, sir, I am Judy Hyams."

"And you are very courageous."

"Thank you, sir."

"I cannot imagine how you could swim so well with all the clothing you women wear and, if I might say so, you look much older than fifteen."

"I am fifteen, sir. I turn sixteen on 12th July – and I removed my dress before I jumped into the water."

Arthur Phillip was a little stuck for words. This young woman – it was difficult to accept that she was merely a girl – spoke in an educated voice and had the confidence and maturity of an adult. There was something quite compelling about her that made him want to know more. He pointed to a chair.

"Sit down Hyams! After your tough swim you must be tired."

In a slightly hesitating way, she did so.

"I am all right, sir."

"Would you like a cup of warm milk or cocoa? We have just taken fresh supplies on board."

"Thank you, sir."

In a few minutes a sailor brought a jug of cocoa, two mugs and some biscuits on a tray and handed them to Midshipman Scott who placed the tray on a table that was at the young woman's elbow and filled one of the china mugs. The captain encouraged Judy to drink.

"You must indeed be both hungry and thirsty. The hot cocoa will make you feel better, I'm sure."

The meals on the *Prince of Wales* having been meagre, but for the young woman's good manners, she could easily have emptied the mug of cocoa and eaten several of the biscuits in no time.

For the next hour, in response to the many questions the Governor-Designate of New South Wales put to her, Judith Hyams told her story – from the time of her arrival in London. The only thing she omitted was that her instinctive – and impulsive – reaction at seeing the man drowning had temporarily dismissed from her mind her plans to jump ship and that, ever since she had taken the major safely back to the *Prince of Wales,* her only thought had been how to resurrect them.

She was still speaking when there was a knock. Captain Phillip, seeing the unfortunate Major Fortescue standing there, commanded him to enter and, having received his assurance that he had recovered from his unpleasant experience, asked him to report on his misadventure and on the loading of the stores. Seeing his rescuer sitting at the table, Fortescue asked Captain Phillip for permission to thank her for her bravery.

When he had done this, the fleet commander invited him to sit down as he felt that he would be interested to hear a little of his rescuer's background. At the same time he turned to the midshipman.

"Scott, would you give Captain Collins my compliments and ask him to join us?"

"Aye, aye, sir!"

Captain David Collins had been appointed judge advocate of New South Wales by the Home Office. Although still in his early thirties, he was an experienced army officer who before being recalled to take up this important appointment in the new colony, had retired to Kent. He was a cultured and handsome man of "cheerful and social disposition"[2].

By the time Major Fortescue had completed his account of what had happened, Captain Collins had entered the room and, at the fleet

---

[2] He was later to become lieutenant-governor of Hobart Town.

commander's invitation, had sat down at the table next to him. Phillip summed up in a few words the details of the major's rescue and the possible miscarriage of justice in the case of the young American girl.

"Collins, there are two quite important matters to be dealt with; firstly, the circumstances surrounding the…er "misadventure" of Major Fortescue; and secondly, the case of convict Hyams. Scott, we shall be a little time discussing the first situation and will not require you or Hyams to be present. I shall send for you when I am ready. In the meantime, you should take some notes concerning Hyams's background. The judge advocate could well need a written report."

After the departure of Scott and Hyams, the major explained the circumstances leading up to when he was pushed into the sea. He emphasised that, although the water was not particularly cold, the wind and the swell – and his cumbersome army uniform – had aggravated his already difficult situation. He was full of praise for the convict girl whose physical strength and reassuring personality had amazed him.

"Sir, by the time she had reached me, I was almost at the end of my tether. My lungs and stomach felt that they were full of water and I was having difficulty in maintaining consciousness. Even when I was back on the deck of the *Prince of Wales,* she did not let up; squeezing my lungs, helping me spew up water and getting me to breathe again. And Captain Mason told me that she was only fifteen years old."

Captain Collins asked a number of questions – all of them relating to the apprehension and punishment of the two men responsible. The problem was that they were local deckhands and, as such, they could only be dealt with by the local authorities. It was agreed that the judge advocate should talk to the British consul to ensure that justice would be meted out to them.

During the half hour or so that this matter was being dealt with, Frank Scott was learning as much as he could about Judy Hyams. Once he had been able to put her at her ease, she relaxed and gave him a full account of the circumstances leading up to her short but disgraceful trial and sentencing – and all that had subsequently happened to her. He was not only impressed with her frankness and her honesty; he was equally taken with her sense of humour and her intelligence. The way she spoke and her approach to everything they discussed made him feel that she was just like his mother would have been at that age – except that she was taller and, whereas his mother had a *retroussé* nose, Judy's was aquiline and, to his mind, particularly beautiful. He had not heard nearly enough of her story before the door opened and they were summoned back into the commander's room.

"Scott, pull up a chair for Hyams, at the end of the table – and you should stay here, too. It will be good experience for you."

From the top of the table Captain Phillip addressed the convict, starting his remarks by once again congratulating her on her bravery and repeating the major's gratitude. He explained the nature of the office of the judge advocate and the reason his presence during the discussion was important.

For the next ten minutes or so Captain Collins questioned Judy on her stay in the Cornishes' house and her trial. He asked her if she felt any of the domestic staff in the Bond Street house might have been able to be witnesses at her trial.

Having asked to be excused for what she was about to do, she stood up, turned away from the table and lifting her skirts in as modest a way as she could, she retrieved the letter she had had handed to her in Bow Street. When she returned to the table, she could see the disguised smiles on all the men's faces, especially Midshipman Scott's. She was no fool and she realised that her moment had arrived – and she was going to use it to her best advantage. In losing her chance to escape, she could well have found a better answer to her predicament.

"Sir, I hope I have not embarrassed you. I assure you that, although the behaviour of some of my fellow convicts, while they have been on board, has not been all that it should have been, I really do try to behave in a modest and comely fashion. This letter was handed to me as I was led out of the courtroom in Bow Street. It was written by Mrs Earhart, the housekeeper at the Cornish residence."

She looked towards Captain Phillip.

"With your permission, sir."

He nodded his assent and she handed the letter to Captain Collins. He read it and passed it to the commander who read it aloud –

Dear Miss Judith,

All of us here in Bond Street are quite shattered at what has happened to you. We are in a terrible predicament as we know we can do little to help you. I want to come and give evidence at your trial and, if I can pluck up courage, I still will. Ethel, the chambermaid has been in constant tears as, while she was in the dressing room adjoining madam's bedroom, she saw the major go into madam's room and take her bracelet from one of the drawers of her tallboy. After he had gone down the staircase, she peeped and, from the door of madam's bedroom, she saw him open one of your bags and put it inside. Hardly had you gone out of the front door and she came to me, weeping, and told me.

What is worse, we all know the magistrate, Judge Roberts. He sometimes comes here for dinner — whenever madam is away. He was here a few days ago, when Mrs Cornish had gone back to her mother's. (The poor old lady has taken a turn for the worse.) It was Mr Partridge's evening off and I was doing the dining room. In front of me and all, the major was telling Judge Roberts all sorts of dreadful things about you and the magistrate was promising to "give the little American upstart short shrift".

Even if you are well represented in court, we all think it would be a waste of time. Dear Miss Judith, before each meal, all of us in the servants' hall are praying for you. Truly we are.

Your obedient servant,

Doris Earhart (Housekeeper)

Judge Collins thought for a few minutes.

"Sir, even if the housekeeper woman had not written this letter, the lecherous, lying bastard, Cornish, must be raving mad to think that anyone other than a corrupt and evil magistrate would accept his cock and bull story. For a start, if this poor girl had stolen anything, would she tell her host where she was going? Of course not! The moment his guest left his house, would he rush upstairs to his wife's bedroom and search her tallboy to ensure that nothing had been stolen? Utter nonsense!"

The moment the name Cornish was mentioned, Major Fortescue almost stood up. He wanted badly to say something and, as soon as Captain Collins paused, he bounced to his feet.

"I know the Cornish family in Bond Street and I should like to add something else of importance. In '82, my regiment was engaged in the relief of Gibraltar. Major Bloody Cornish was also there and was charged with cowardice in the face of the enemy. He was placed under close arrest. As fate would have it, the three witnesses on whose testimony his conviction relied were all killed in action and the court martial had to be abandoned. He was given leave without pay early in the following year. As he is disgustingly rich, this did not worry him. The man was told in no uncertain terms that if he ever appeared in the mess again, he would not come out alive. The problem is that his wife is a most charming woman and is highly thought of. As soon as we can, we must get all of this material back to London. He is still an officer with the king's commission and he can still be court-martialled."

It was quite obvious that Captain Collins, too, was quite worked up. He seemed to have completely lost all the relaxed charm he had previously displayed[3].

"I shall write a letter to Lord Sydney. There is more than a fair chance that Miss Hyams can take out a civil action and claim substantial damages. The behaviour of Magistrate Roberts is another matter that calls for close scrutiny. I take both these matters seriously."

Captain Arthur Phillip looked at his watch.

"So do I, Judge Advocate; would you please explain to me the legal situation?"

"Sir, there are two immediate aspects of this case. Firstly, you have the executive authority to promulgate a pardon to any convict whose conduct warrants it. To quash a conviction, however, requires a judicial process and, as soon as we reach New South Wales and you are sworn in as governor – and a court of civil jurisdiction is proclaimed – you will have the power to do this."

"Thank you, Judge Advocate, for your advice."

He stood up and walked towards Judy. As he approached her, she rose to her feet. He asked her to resume her seat while he explained the difference between a pardon and a quashing of the conviction. Her

---

[3] As he grew older this ruthless and vengeful characteristic became much more evident. In fact, in Hobart Town he was quite renowned for the way he nonchalantly stood by and "took snuff by the handfuls" as he watched men being flogged.

understanding of the legal terms and their significance surprised them.

"Miss Hyams, it is my belief that you have been the victim of a grave miscarriage of justice and I can only express my regrets and my apologies for the many inconveniences, hardships – and the indignities with which you have had to contend. That you are an American citizen makes me all the more ashamed. All the necessary formalities to implement what Captain Collins has explained to us will be completed as soon as it is possible. You are to be moved from the *Prince of Wales* at once and, just so long as you are with us, you will be found suitable accommodation here on HMS *Sirius*. Captain Hunter is in command of this ship and he will ensure that you are made as comfortable as possible. Your impeccable behaviour during what must have been for you a particularly harrowing time has been remarkable and your spontaneous courage and skill in saving Major Fortescue has earned you the admiration and respect of each and every one of us. Judy, my dear girl, do you wish to be taken to England, to Boston or to Quebec? Wherever it is you wish to go, I shall ensure that your wishes are met."

Half laughing and half crying, Judy wiped her tears away with a handkerchief and took a deep breath. She was making a huge effort to ensure that her sense of humour was going to win over her other emotions –

"Sir, thank you for your kind remarks. The last few months have been a mixture of a hideous nightmare and an unbelievable experience. Apart from losing my father, whom I adored, all the other dreadful things that I have seen – and that have happened to me – I shall soon forget. Thank you, sir, for the offer to provide me with a passage to America or wherever I wish to go. For some strange reason, the idea of being one of the very first free settlers in New South Wales is a challenge I have no intention of missing. Many times since that morning in the rat-infested, Bow Street cell, when the pompous sergeant told us we were going to New Holland or New South Wales – he did not know which – I have thought to myself how exciting it would have been to be a pioneer in a new country, but never, never in a life time, as a condemned criminal. I have no family to go back to; I lost my mother three years ago and now that my father is dead, I have no ship in which to sail."

There was quite a long silence – broken by Governor-Designate

Phillip. Smiling warmly and patting the girl on the head, he praised her.

"You might be a sailor without a ship, Judy Hyams, but I know your father would be proud of you – really he would. I can just imagine what he would say if he were here today."

Judy, still overflowing with emotion, could not stop herself laughing.

"Excuse me, sir, for saying so but, not knowing that father of mine, I don't think you or anyone else could imagine what he would have said. In emotional situations, he was never one for serious words and, in circumstances like today's, he would think of something humorous to say…like…'My word, don't we all owe a lot to Major Fortescue! If he had not had the good manners to jump overboard, there would be no happy ending to our story'."

They all looked at each other and burst out laughing; Captain Phillip more than any of the others.

"Why on earth do you think that, Miss Hyams?"

"Well, sir, it is what I am thinking at the present time! And, please sir, everybody calls me Judy – except when they are angry with me."

There was more laughter and amazement at the girl's sang-froid. Before the merriment had fully subsided, the Captain took control.

"I may be angry with one or two people in London, but I am anything but angry with you, Judy. Scott, our guest must be given a meal as soon as possible. She is probably famished. This afternoon you are to take her back to the *Prince of Wales* to enable her to collect her belongings. For the present, all that the master need know is that there has been a dreadful mistake and that Miss Hyams will travel to New South Wales on HMS *Sirius,* as our guest. As we are sailing on tomorrow afternoon's tide, in the morning you are to escort her into the town to buy whatever clothing and necessities she might require. Major Fortescue, who is in charge of all the fleet's money, will provide you whatever funds you need. And please, Judy, buy a pretty dress for the dinner I am giving next week on 12th July – to celebrate the sixteenth birthday of a really fine daughter of the sea."

It was a happy and relaxed team of officers who shook the young American's hand and, as had been the case when Mrs B had shaken hands with Judy, they were all mildly shocked that a girl of not yet sixteen had such a remarkably firm handshake.

II

IN THE MIDDLE OF JUNE 1787 Major Fortescue disembarked from HMS *Sirius* and boarded the *Pont de Toulon*. He had with him a big bag of mail, including the reports for the Home Office of both Captain Phillip and the judge advocate and a number of letters Midshipman Scott and others had written. He also took with him a personal resolve to punish Major Cornish and his dishonest accomplice, Magistrate Roberts. He knew only too well how slowly and ineffectually the Home Office worked – even when Lord Sydney urged speed.

There was something romantically gallant in the major's nature and as this young woman had saved his life and had been the victim of two cowardly bullies, he had no intention of resting until the wrong they had done to her had been avenged. When, before leaving HMS *Sirius,* he had spoken of his intentions to his young assistant, Scott – and he had done so in an unequivocal way – Frank had told him that he had written to his father and his brother, Lieutenant Jean-Marc Scott-Quetteville of the Blues, and had told them the full story and that there was a score to be settled. So that everyone would avoid treading on each other's toes, Frank left his letters unsealed for the major to read.

Major Fortescue did not tell the midshipman that Captain Phillip had informed him that among the many dispatches and reports he was sending back to the Admiralty was notification that, before reaching Table Bay, he intended to promote Midshipman Scott to the rank of second lieutenant.

Before disembarking, Major Fortescue had a number of discussions with both Captain Phillip and Captain Collins, the judge advocate of the new colony. He wanted to make over a substantial annuity to Judy – to take effect as soon as they reached New South Wales. Knowing that mail to and from England would take years rather than months to arrive, he signed a Power of Attorney to enable the colony's senior executives to ensure that his wishes were fulfilled. He also gave Collins a copy of letters he intended to deliver to Barclay's Bank. He assured Collins –

"I shall be back in London months before you all arrive in Botany Bay and I shall have completed the formalities and the banking arrangements with the Home Office before you reach your destination."

In the dispatches Captain Phillip had sent back with Major Fortescue, he had stated that he had selected twelve midshipmen to take with him as part of the First Fleet, hoping that at least half of them would prove to be good officers. He knew that during the voyage to New South Wales there would be adequate opportunity for him to assess their knowledge, their attitude and their potential. He added that neither he nor the captain of HMS *Sirius*, Captain Hunter, were in the least surprised that Scott, who had been at sea for quite a few years, was in his competence and his maturity well ahead of the others. The lad had been trained by William Webster – the captain under whom, as a young officer, he himself had served – and learned the ropes. Although it was only a month since they had left England, during the extremely tense and difficult weeks in Portsmouth and equally in the port of Teneriffe, Scott had performed well – and the sooner he was given the responsibilities of a second lieutenant the better.

In his report he had also mentioned Midshipman Francis Hill, the master's mate. He was showing good potential and Phillip hoped to promote him in the near future. Although Phillip had made the decision to promote Scott, it was not his intention to inform him until shortly before they arrived in Table Bay, in mid-October.

* * *

While the First Fleet sailed towards Rio de Janeiro, Major Fortescue was returning to England. The weather he encountered was good and he reached Portsmouth by the middle of August. He had enjoyed his couple of days in Gibraltar where he had had to disembark from the *Pont de Toulon* and transfer to the *Trentbridge*.

As the three weeks at sea had given him ample time to complete his

• PART I – II •

reports, he stayed in Portsmouth for only a few days before going on to London, where his account of the first sector of the voyage to New South Wales and his recommendations concerning revictualling in Teneriffe were well received at the Home Office. From his point of view, he had two important matters that required his immediate attention: firstly, to see his solicitors about Judy Hyams's annuity and changing his will to make her the major beneficiary; and, secondly, to ensure that both Major Cornish and Magistrate Roberts were brought to justice.

Having read the letters, the soon to be promoted Frank Scott, or François Scott-Quetteville as he was known to his family, had written to his father and to his brother Jean-Marc, Fortescue called at Bridge House in the hope of seeing Sir John. He was disappointed to learn that Scott-Quetteville was in France working on the company's important steamboat project. However, when he was informed that Lady Scott-Quetteville was in the building, he was more than satisfied to have the opportunity of meeting her as he had heard much about her from François.

Lady Nicole had just received the letter from François, posted in Teneriffe, telling her all about the voyage from England and, after what he had to say about Judy Hyams, the major's visit was particularly welcome. Although most of what he had to tell her added little to what François had written, hearing everything first-hand meant so much more to her.

"Lady Scott-Quetteville, you probably think that as the young woman saved my life, I see her through rose-coloured spectacles. That well may be true; however, I can assure you that both Captain Phillip and Captain Collins share very much the same views about her as I have expressed to you."

Lady Nicole could not help smiling.

"And, reading at least three pages of the letter I have just received from my sailor son, I gather that he feels the same way about her, too!"

"I spent much time with young Frank and I must congratulate you on having such a competent and mature son. During the time we were together in Teneriffe working on the revictualling of the fleet, I would have been totally lost without him."

"That is good to know. Sir John will be gratified when I pass on your comments to him."

"As it will be gazetted in the very near future, I do not believe it would be out of order to inform you – in confidence – that Captain Phillip has promoted Frank to the rank of second lieutenant."

"That is indeed good news. I assure you that the news you have imparted to me will not go beyond the family until it has been announced."

The major cleared his throat and hesitated, before changing the subject.

"Madam, no doubt your son has informed you about the disgraceful and unforgivable conduct of a Major Cornish."

"Yes, that unfortunate incident covered nearly as many pages of François's letter as did the qualities, attributes and physical charms of his American lady love. He was quite emotional about it."

"And well he might be! I can tell you, Lady Scott-Quetteville, he was not nearly as emotional about the way she was treated as I was – and still am. If I catch up with the bounder, I shall horsewhip him to death."

"Please, Major Fortescue, don't do that! It would be most unwise. You may think I am being too flippant over a most serious crime. I promise you, I'm not. Cornish will get his comeuppance and neither you nor I need dirty our hands. As soon as I had read in François's letter what Judy Hyams had said she wanted to happen to the man, I said to myself – dear Major Cornish, you picked the wrong person when you behaved in such a criminally atrocious way towards your young American house guest, and you are going to pay dearly. You are a liar, a lecherous miscreant and an evil cad and, come what may, you are going to the new penal settlement in New South Wales – where you can rot to death."

Hearing Lady Scott-Quetteville's words, Major Fortescue was momentarily speechless. Although François had told him what a formidable woman she was in a crisis, he had not expected her to speak quite as unequivocally as she did.

"Truly, Lady Scott-Quetteville, you are just as your son described you – only more so! I had no idea that Judy Hyams had told Frank that she wanted him to suffer the same indignities and tribulations that he had inflicted on her."

"I make no apologies for saying that when I read this part of my son's letter, I experienced a warm feeling of empathy with her."

"I think that perhaps you are birds of a feather; and she has the same imaginative sense of humour that you obviously have. I shall never forget how well she conducted herself in Teneriffe. Within a couple of hours of the terrible ordeal in the sea with me, she was summoned to appear in front of Captain Phillip on HMS *Sirius* and I arrived there a little time later. She, a fifteen-year-old convict, was sitting at the big table with all the senior officers of the fleet. At no time was she overawed; in fact, in reply to a statement by the Captain that he knew how proud of her her father would be – and what he would say – she had everyone roaring with laughter."

The major then recounted, almost verbatim, the incident – and the reaction of Captains Phillip, Collins and Hunter, not only to her delightful sense of humour but equally to her composure and her sang-froid.

Although Nicole was impressed, she did not want to get too carried away or to permit her imagination to take charge of her thoughts.

"Major Fortescue, let neither of us spoil everything by having unrealistic expectations! François's feelings for the girl might not be reciprocated."

"I can assure you they are, Lady Nicole. She told me so, the day I left the ship in Teneriffe, when I said goodbye to her and thanked her again for what she had done for me. I informed her then that, as a measure of my appreciation I had made certain arrangements for her future and I handed her copies of letters I had written. I told her that they would explain everything. She protested that what she had done was very little and that she had already been more than adequately rewarded. When I asked her to explain she replied –

"Even if I had rescued half the Royal Navy, getting out of that hell hole, the *Prince of Wales,* and meeting the man I intend to marry, would have been a more than adequate reward..."

"You have no idea how much I should like to be there – just for a day – to see François and to meet Judy. I suppose it will be years before I see them again."

"Lady Scott-Quetteville, when the young lady expressed her affection for your son, she quickly added that I must not mention her remark to him, as she did not know how he felt."

"Major Fortescue, to be perfectly honest with you, I am more thrilled than I can possibly express myself in words. More than anything else in the world, I am living for my three sons to choose fine young women for their wives. Although in François's case it has apparently come much, much sooner than I ever believed it would, I am deliriously happy. You do not know how much I appreciate your visit."

"Thank you, my lady. I am learning quickly to understand why your son has said that you are the most perfect mother any son could dream for."

"That was kind of him. I am now impatiently waiting for François's next letter. I do not know from where it will be written or how long it will take to get here."

"The fleet will stop at Rio de Janeiro where there is an intermittent mail service operating. Letters usually come via Lisbon or Teneriffe. My father has friends in Brazil and he receives letters two or three times each year."

"Your father is alive still?"

"Yes, he will turn ninety in three months time. He lives near Goring."

"Then he must be Lord Augustus Fortescue."

"Yes. Do you know him?"

"No, Major, I have not had the pleasure; but I have met Archie, his son. He sometimes hunts with close friends of mine, Lord and Lady Bassett. Your brother has several beautiful horses."

"Being the elder son, my brother manages the family estate. However, when father dies, we will both share everything, equally."

"Then maybe we shall have the pleasure of seeing you at one of the Bassett hunts and perhaps you will return to Goring."

"I should be honoured to join you when you are hunting but I have no intention of becoming a country squire. I enjoy being in London and will continue to manage the family's interests here. I shall leave Archie to race his horses and raise his cattle."

There was another throat-clearing noise that heralded a change in the subject of the major's conversation.

"Lady Scott-Quetteville, you implied that it would not be difficult to have Cornish convicted and dispatched to the colonies. I willingly concede that the idea is probably more appropriate than what I had in mind; however, I can assure you that, until you advocated a slower but equally painful punishment, I was quite determined to take the law into my own hands. It is now my averred intention to let him suffer in the way he made Judy Hyams suffer. My best friend is a senior barrister in Lincoln's Inn. I shall lose no time in taking all the evidence I have to him."

"It will be interesting to watch the progress of events as they unfold. Filing a false complaint to the police, swearing an untrue affidavit, attempting to pervert the course of justice, and attempted rape – these are all serious charges. If all these things are thrown at your friend Cornish, it will not take his lawyer long to realise that there will be a trial full of filth and scandal that will, for months on end, fill the papers with lurid details of his murky and lecherous pastimes. And please do remember, sir, there are almost certainly many female servants whom, over the years, he has indecently assaulted or raped. It should not be difficult to track them down. I am sure that the helpful housekeeper could be useful. As among Cornish's crimes there are certainly some capital offences, it should not be difficult to arrange things in a legal way so that many of the charges could be dropped in return for a guilty plea on lesser charges, the sentence for which would be imprisonment. The man is probably so conceited that it would never enter his head that his sentence would be transportation. I have met his wife and I can assure you that she is a charming lady. I feel confident that for her children's sake – and her own – she would put pressure on him to do everything he could to ensure the trial and the embarrassing publicity associated with it was over as soon as possible. I believe that much of the money in the family is hers."

"You have been wonderful, Lady Scott-Quetteville. You have given me the outline of an excellent plan. I am going directly from here to Lord Sydney's office. I have several friends there who can help me. Is it asking too much of you to inform me how you would deal with the magistrate, Roberts? He should not be permitted to come out of this untarnished."

"Please do not think that I am being smug or conceited when I suggest that we should do one thing at a time. If I am not very much mistaken, once Mr Roberts sees that Cornish is about to get his comeuppance, he will take fright and perhaps flight, too. All you need do is to have him watched to ensure that he does not try to disappear."

* * *

When Major Fortescue left the offices of The Bridge Company on the Thames, he entertained high hopes of bringing the lying, lubricous Major Cornish to justice within a matter of weeks. However, he had not anticipated the difficulties of successfully prosecuting an offender in a criminal court without having witnesses actually present in court. He was not aware that affidavits and other sworn statements made by witnesses who are not able to be cross-examined by the counsel for the defence are often insufficient to obtain a conviction.

Eventually, after some months, the major was able to track down several young women who had worked in the Cornishes' Bond Street house. These proved to be valuable witnesses, as did Mrs Earhart, the housekeeper who had handed Judith Hyams the note as she left the courtroom.

Notwithstanding the advice of Lady Scott-Quetteville, Fortescue was worried that Magistrate Roberts could do something to enable Cornish to get off scot-free. When, in one of his many conferences with her, he mentioned his concern, she told him that she was as keen as he was to ensure that the magistrate was punished and that she, personally, had him well under control.

"I do not want to sound evasive, sir, but I have already set the wheels in motion to deal with him. Please assure your lawyer that you have my word that Roberts will not be in court when Cornish is in the dock. If the aim is for him to experience "penal servitude in the colony of New South Wales" it is most important that Cornish and his counsel think Roberts will be the magistrate trying the case."

The decisive way in which Nicole spoke convinced the major and, after much persuasion, he was able to unequivocally assure his legal adviser to do nothing more than have everybody concerned fully confident that Magistrate Roberts would be on the bench.

One of the Cornishes' kitchen maids who had experienced trouble from the major was twenty-year-old Enid Brown. On two occasions her tiny attic bedroom had been invaded by the master of the house and, each time, when his amorous advances were flatly rejected, he virtually raped the girl. Enid was by no means a virgin and it was not the first time in her life that she had been on the receiving end of the unwanted advances of men. However, after the second time she had handed in her notice to Mrs Earhart and had tearfully told her that "when it came to private things like having visitors in her bed, she was very choosy". Having been adequately pacified by the housekeeper, she collected a good reference from her and returned to Portsmouth where she lived with her Aunt Mary and Uncle Bill – a freelance sailor.

In the middle of October Enid received some good news from Mrs Earhart. The perverted major was to be charged and, if she could return to London to give evidence, money for her stage-coach fare would be sent to her. Furthermore, she could stay with the housekeeper's sister and she would be paid full wages for the time she would have to be in London. According to the barrister concerned – one of the top men in Lincoln's Inn – she might also be able to get some money in a civil action. The letter assured her that she would be asked to do no more than tell the truth and it warned her to keep the matter confidential. When she told her sailor uncle, Bill Brown, that she was thinking of going to London – and the reason for the visit – he was furious that he had not been told of the outrage sooner.

"You go, Enid! Get every penny out of the bastards you can. I 'ope they 'ang the geezer. If I get 'arf a chance to lay me 'ands on 'im, 'e'll be sorry 'e were ever born!"

Enid did go to London and had a truly great time there. Not only did she receive a full week's wages and have her coach fares paid but a really nice Major Fortescue, who seemed to be managing everything, drove her to the coach for her return to Portsmouth and gave her five sovereigns. In giving a detailed account of her London visit, Enid told her uncle that during the journey to the coach station, Major Fortescue had informed her about Cornish's assault on a young American girl who had been staying as a guest in the major's house and how he had planted jewellery in her bags.

"The poor girl was found guilty of theft and packed off as a convict to

New South Wales. Major Fortescue said that, if they do not hang Cornish – as they most probably would – that's where 'e'd be going, too. The major was real nice, 'e was. 'E gave me 'is address an' said that if 'e could 'elp me at any time I must write to 'im."

The first reaction of Bill Brown was to ask if this Major Fortescue had behaved himself.

"Wot was 'e like? 'E didn't try any 'anky-panky on yer, did 'e?"

"No, uncle, 'e's not like that at all. 'E treated me like a lady and carried me bag. 'E was a real gentleman."

Sailor Brown took note of the major's address and changed the subject. However, the next week, he decided to go to London for a couple of days. On his way back to Portsmouth in the stage-coach, as he thought about his meeting with the major, he could not help but agree with Enid that he certainly was 'a real gentleman' – and a generous one, too.

* * *

In the middle of 1789 Major Albert Cornish was arrested and charged with many offences, including rape, and attempted rape and perjury. His solicitor was warned that it would be a long and damaging trial and that much of the evidence to be brought out could easily cause the accused and his family distress, shame, acute embarrassment and humiliation. If he was prepared to plead guilty to several of the lesser charges, the trial could be kept quite short and the sentence, if found guilty, would be commensurately lighter. Cornish, confident that his friend Andrew Roberts would come to his aid, agreed.

On Thursday 13 October, the morning of the trial, without any prior announcement or notice, Magistrate Andrew Roberts was suspended from his duties and charged with corruption and perverting the course of justice. Less than an hour before the case was to be heard, Judge Andrew MacIntosh was appointed to sit in his place. This came as a terrible shock to both the accused and his counsel – but there was nothing they could do about it.

As anticipated, the plea of guilty on three of the lesser charges resulted in a short trial and, apart from the initial publicity, the

Londoners who relished reading, week after week, the lurid details of the sexual iniquities of prominent socialites, were denied one of their favourite, simple pleasures. What did raise eyebrows in Piccadilly and Mayfair was a short paragraph that appeared in the London papers on the following day. It was a list of names of convicted persons who had been sentenced to penal servitude in His Majesty's colonies that included Albert Cecil Cornish of Bond Street, London. And, on the same day, the papers reported "the suicide in his home of the suspended magistrate, Andrew Roberts".

As the weeks had gone by, Bill Brown had been watching the papers carefully, hoping to find Albert Cornish's name among those to take a one-way trip to the Tyburn gallows. When he read that he was to be transported to the colonies, he remembered his talk with Enid's friend, the nice major – and, living in Portsmouth, he knew that there was soon to be another fleet of ships, laden with convicts, sailing for New South Wales.

* * *

Albert Cornish spent only three days in the dingy, evil-smelling cells in London. With half a dozen other prisoners he was transported in a dirty old wagon to Portsmouth, where they were rowed out to one of the hulks. While he was clumsily scrambling up to the deck, his big bag of personal items dropped into the sea and, although a sailor rescued it for him, everything he owned became saturated. When he offered the sailor a gold coin for his trouble, the recipient, seeing that the hand Cornish had withdrawn from his pocket had three other similar coins in it, roughly demanded these, too. When the convict hesitated, he was even more roughly told that failure to promptly deliver would result in the heavy bag being dumped back into the sea. The sailor was handed the four sovereigns and the ex-major recovered his rather sodden bag.

For nearly two months, until early in December, Cornish experienced discomfort, hunger and humiliation such as he did not think existed. It was by far the worst experience he had ever had in his life. Hundreds of convicts were packed like sardines into every corner of the hulk and there was hardly room to walk anywhere without tripping over sprawling bodies. For washing, there was only salt water, the food was vile and it was impossible to escape the stench of urine and raw sewage. Many of the prisoners lacked clothing – and what they did have was often in tatters. Diarrhoea – and even dysentery – was commonplace and many people were so weak they could not drag themselves to the sides of the ship to vomit or excrete. Once each week there was a distribution of mail and some lucky convicts received letters from home and even luckier ones received bank notes, with which they could buy favours. Delighted when his name was called out to step forward to be handed a letter, Cornish actually wept when he opened it. It was an unsigned letter from a "well-wisher", written to remind him of the misery and suffering he had caused to the young American girl who had been a guest in his house. There was a postscript informing him that life on board the ship that was to take him to New South Wales would provide him with some useful lessons.

At last, after what had appeared to all the convicts to have been years of waiting, the prisoners were transferred to the ships that would take them to Botany Bay. They boarded the *Surprize,* the *Neptune* and the *Scarborough,* the ships of the Second Fleet – by far the worst transportation of convicts ever recorded in history.

* * *

The story of the Second Fleet is shameful and tragic. Whereas the First Fleet had been administered by the Royal Navy, the ships that followed two years later were all merchantmen under contract to naval agents. The inhumane treatment of the convicts, the cruelty of the guards and the generally quite uninhabitable state of all the vessels resulted in massive sickness and death. Of the 1017 convicts who embarked at Portsmouth, nearly 300 died during the journey. Of the 700 who answered the roll call when the fleet landed at Port Jackson, 500 were either seriously ill or dying. The colony, scarcely two years old, was expecting healthy tradesmen and labourers to assist them in their mammoth task of establishing a settlement. Instead, Captain Phillip's men had to set up dozens of tents in front of the hospital to accommodate the poor wretches, many of whom could only crawl from their ships, lousy, dirty and almost naked, to the hospital. Apart from their intestinal diseases, they were suffering from scurvy, malnutrition and infected wounds, mainly resulting from having been chained up each night with manacles so tight as to bite right through the flesh to the bone[4].

* * *

Albert Cornish was not one of those who answered that first roll call in Port Jackson. The *Neptune* had hardly left the English Channel behind, when the disgraced major was grabbed by a lusty great sailor and pushed into a small closet in which there was nothing but a big stack of canvas. Bill Brown, the seaman, knew everybody in Portsmouth and it had not taken him long to find out the name of the ship to which convict Albert Cornish had been assigned – and for him to sign on as an able seaman.

With a glint in his slightly inebriated eye, he stood in silence, looking his prisoner up and down. The giant man was smoking a pipe and there was a moist yellow nicotine stain on one side of his bearded chin, where saliva had been oozing out of the corner of his mouth. Although Cornish was not standing particularly close to the sailor, he was assailed by the overpowering – and nauseating – stench of a mixture of stale tobacco, liquor and human sweat.

"So you is Major Cornish of Bond Street and you raped my niece Enid – an' yer 'ad a go at the American girl, too. Didn't yer?"

The convict was trembling so much that he could not utter a word.

"Answer me, you ugly turd!" roared the sailor, as he landed a hearty slap across Cornish's face. "Answer me or I'll belt the livin' daylights out o' yer!"

The reply came in almost a whisper. "I think Enid did work for my wife."

"Fuck yer wife and fuck you, too. Yer know wot yer done an' yer goin' to pay for it. There's nothin' for nothin', is there? Now get your clothes orf quick smart, before I bash yer ugly face in."

---

[4] Following an inquiry into the brutality and neglect of the master of the *Neptune* and his officers, they were arrested and appeared in the Old Bailey to answer multiple charges – including murder.

Shaking, weeping and utterly confused, Cornish just stood there. A solid blow to the solar plexus sent him sprawling to the floor.

The sailor sat on top of the big pile of canvas stacked in the corner of the closet and, relighting his pipe, he looked down on the terrified convict. Filling the small space with smoke as he puffed away, he spoke in a quieter voice.

"Now look 'ere yer greasy lump o' shit, I got all night to spare, so I'm in no 'urry, am I? But you're goin' to get your clobber off or else I'm goin' to bash the livin' daylights out o' yer, d'yer understand?"

In almost a whisper, Cornish muttered that he had money and perhaps…

"Perhaps nothing!" roared the giant. "If yer 'ain't done wot I said within a minit, I'll knee yer in the balls so 'ard yer'll scream for a week."

It was only a few moments before the pathetic man was standing naked – trembling like a leaf. His eyes were closed in the vain hope that this hideous nightmare would disappear.

Suddenly, he felt a vice-like grip on his shoulders as he was thrust forward over the bale of canvas. Nothing happened for what appeared to him to be an eternity and then – a red hot thrust from behind that made him scream in agony. Again, again and again – the thrusts seemed to penetrate right through his bowels. As he screamed for mercy, he thought the torture would never stop.

At some stage during the rape, he had apparently lost consciousness, as the next thing he knew was that he was lying on the floor and his vile-smelling tormentor had left the closet. Through the partly opened door he could vaguely hear talking outside; and then there was silence. His face and jaw were throbbing with the first blow he had received, his abdomen ached and the excruciating pain coming from where he had been outraged was unbearable. More than any of his injuries, the degrading humiliation of being sodomised by the ugly brute was more than he could bear.

As he lay there, virtually paralysed, he could hear the waves and the creaking of the ship. He could not stop sobbing and his only wish was that he could close his eyes and die. About ten minutes later, just as the involuntary shaking of his body was subsiding, he heard heavy footsteps, as the big sailor re-entered the closet, holding a half empty bottle of whisky to his mouth. As he stood over his victim, he took a gulp and wiped his heavy lips with a hairy, tattooed arm.

Because he was lying on his side, Cornish could hardly see his tormentor's face – only his huge boots. Terrified of what was going to happen next, he did not have to wait long to find out. Brown spoke in a slurred voice.

"If yer reckon I've finished with yer, yer bit o' slime, yer 'ave another think comin'. Aven't yer? Remember, it was twice yer knocked off my little Enid – so I still owe yer one. Don't I?"

In case what he said had not caused Cornish enough anguish and discomfort, he jabbed his boot into the naked man's ribs. This was too much for the disgraced major – it was the final straw. His aching rib-cage, the red hot pain in his anus and the contemplation of more pain – and more humiliation – were too much for him to bear any longer. He suddenly jerked himself into action. Screaming hysterically, he leapt to his feet and, in a flash, he had pushed past the bearded seaman and within a split second he was on the deck, rushing towards the ship's side, blabbering incoherently. He scrambled on to a packing case and leapt into the sea.

The sailor stood, motionless, in the doorway of the closet and watched Cornish go. He nonchalantly struck a match on his coarse trousers and drew on his pipe. He spat noisily on to the deck, turned and leisurely re-entered the closet. Slowly and methodically, he searched every piece of the recently departed convict's clothing – pockets, linings – and the insoles of his fine leather shoes. Having stuffed banknotes, sovereigns and even some small pieces of jewellery into the pockets of his pants, he contemplated the bundle of expensive menswear that lay on the canvas and on the floor – yes, they were far too good to throw overboard.

* * *

Seaman Brown did not go to New South Wales. The morning following the departure from this world of Albert Cornish, when the convicts were all on deck having their roll call, he went below to where the convicts slept and searched the belongings of the late major and found many more bank notes and sovereigns – and a gold watch.

The day before the ship arrived in Teneriffe, he had a confidential chat to William Waters, the ship's doctor. In return for the watch, some gold cufflinks and a pair of almost new shoes – the finest Italian leather – he received a medical certificate from Dr Waters, stating that he was too sick to continue on the voyage to New South Wales. This entitled him to an honourable discharge from the *Neptune*.

A month later he was back in Portsmouth; quite a rich man. It had been his intention to give Enid fifty pounds as compensation for what had been done to her – not that she had been particularly fussed. However, it was some time before he could give her the money, as she had returned to London where Mrs Earhart had found her a good job, in service.

* * *

Major Fortescue was quite surprised when Seaman Brown appeared at his home in London so soon after their earlier meeting and he was momentarily extremely disappointed to learn that, unfortunately, Major Cornish would not be serving his sentence in New South Wales. However, when Brown explained in some detail the reason, the unhappy look on the major's face disappeared completely as he extended his hand to congratulate his visitor.

"Well done, Brown! You kept your promise and I shall keep mine."

As he sat in the stage-coach on his way back to Portsmouth, Bill Brown felt quite pleased with himself. Thanks to the big heap of money – and valuables – that Cornish left behind on the *Neptune,* when he suddenly decided that this world was no longer for him – and to the generosity of Major Fortescue – he would never again be poor.

III

THE LAST TWENTY-FOUR HOURS that the First Fleet was in Teneriffe were hectic for Captain Collins, Major Fortescue and Midshipman Scott. They were busy from dawn to dusk, dealing with the local authorities about the incident that had resulted in Major Fortescue being pushed overboard, loading the last of the stores, trans-shipping the major's belongings and the big bag of mail to the *Pont de Toulon*, and Judy Hyams's visit to the American consul. In making this call, the gallant major insisted on accompanying her.

After leaving Teneriffe, it only took a few days at sea before everything was quite normal again and a very happy Judy Hyams was enjoying life on HMS *Sirius*. In a totally strange environment, Midshipman Frank Scott's relaxed and friendly personality did much to help her feel at home on the warship and it was obvious to everyone that they enjoyed each other's company. The wives of the officers of the Royal Marines were quite shocked when their husbands told them of the ordeal the young American had had to endure and they made her especially welcome, particularly the younger ones.

The skipper of HMS *Sirius*, Captain Hunter, took an immediate liking to Judy and it did not take him long to realise that he had an exceptionally useful and experienced young person on his ship. Whether it was entering into the ship's ledger the details of the stores they had taken on board, making entries in the ship's log or recording crew sickness, Judy knew how to go about it. Her father had been trained in the Royal Navy before emigrating to America and, on the ship of which he was the captain, all the administration and operational records had been maintained in the same way as those of HMS *Sirius*. It was not surprising, therefore, that Judy, having lived much of her life at sea with her father, was at least as competent – and as useful – as most of the ship's petty officers.

At Captain Phillip's suggestion, during the day she wore the uniform of a midshipman, without any of the insignia of rank. When Captain Hunter first saw this fine looking, five foot ten inches young person standing erect and looking so businesslike, he half jokingly nicknamed her Petty Officer – a sobriquet that would have stuck with her – that is, if all and sundry had not changed the name to Pretty Officer. Immediately the word reached Captain Hunter, he realised his mistake and insisted that she be known as CPO[5].

Judy accepted all the banter with a good grace and, although she was almost always shy and reserved, from time to time she would come out with a brief comment or remark that left no one in any doubt that she had a keen, if irreverent, sense of humour.

From her first encounter with Midshipman Scott, when he boarded the *Prince of Wales* to escort her to Captain Phillip, she was as attracted to him as he was to her and a warm but – at first – quite formal friendship developed between them. As the weeks passed they spent more of their limited leisure hours together and it was not long before theirs was an intimate but – due to the geography of the ship and the exigencies of the service – platonic friendship.

While at sea, there was continual contact and exchange of letters between the ships of the fleet, especially when the seas were calm and there was little or no wind. As would be expected, it did not take long for Mrs B and her girls to learn about their friend Prettypuss's good fortune. In fact, even before they had sailed from Teneriffe, Judy had written them each a letter, thanking them for being such good friends to her and "for putting up with her" – as she had modestly put it.

Seven weeks after leaving the Canary Islands the fleet landed in Brazil. Although both François and Judy had visited many countries, this was their first visit to South America. During the two weeks the fleet was anchored in Rio de Janeiro, they went ashore several times together. Before doing so, Judy went aboard the *Prince of Wales* and visited Mrs B,

---

[5] Chief Petty Officer.

Alisha and Amy. They were overjoyed to see her, although a little over-awed — even Mrs B.

"Miss Prettypuss, dear, yer don't know 'ow 'appy I am to see yer. You've got no idea the rumours that 'ave been goin' about. They even said you'd been taken to the *Sirius* as a girl friend for the Cap'n."

Amy, laughing, added her own three-penny worth —

"An' d'yer know wot Mrs B said — 'Don't yer believe it — wot Prettypuss 'as got 'as a padlock on it — an' Cap'n Phillip or nobody else in the fleet 'as got the key. She's keepin' it fer after.' — that wot's she said."

Judy laughed — and so did they all. Mrs B, hoping their friend might be going ashore, asked —

"Miss Prettypuss, if yer get a chance woodyer please be able to buy me some pepper and some mustard and a coupl'a sheets of parchment?"

"That is a strange request Mrs B."

"Yer don't know 'ow useful a 'andful of the mix can be to throw in the face of an attackin' male. Men with their eyes full of pepper and mustard lose their urge quite quickly."

"Do you think you will be attacked Mrs B? Is there really a danger?"

"Not fer me but fer me girls there is. I want them to keep some in a parchment bag that won't get wet. There 'ave been a few nasty scenes on this boat since yer left."

"Of course I shall do as you've asked Mrs B."

The others also wanted chocolate and Mrs B wanted a bottle of brandy. Quite unabashed, she reached up her skirt and produced from apparently nowhere a small draw-cord bag, from which she plucked five sovereigns.

"If it's more, don't worry. I'll let yer 'ave it."

Pointing to a place quite high up on the front of her skirt, she assured Judy —

"There's plenty more where that came from."

Amy, as usual the clown of the party, having seen where Mrs B was pointing, laughed.

"She means more sovereigns — we all know she's got plenty more of the other thing up there."

A good-hearted clout from Mrs B silenced the would-be humorist.

There were some good shops in Rio de Janeiro and Judy, realising she was going to a totally uncivilised country, purchased fabrics and many haberdashery items, not to mention some new clothes and underwear. She regarded most of these purchases as being essential because all the convicts who boarded the *Prince of Wales* had been strictly limited in the amount of personal baggage they could take with them.

She did not forget the pepper and mustard, and the chocolate and brandy – and she delivered these to her friends, together with three dresses she had bought for them. Having had these wrapped together, she gave the package to Mrs B to open a little later. The letters she received from them afterwards not only expressed their appreciation for their presents but also for the chocolate and the brandy, all of which had been consumed within a week.

François was fascinated with everything he saw in Rio de Janeiro. He was especially interested in some of the horses that people were riding and that were in harness. On enquiring, he ascertained that all the best animals came from Argentina, where they not only bred excellent mounts but also trained them particularly well. He mentioned this to Captain Phillip who was impressed, and said that he would take note of what the midshipman reported.

"This time we shall purchase our livestock when we reach the Cape of Good Hope but on future voyages it might be sensible to call in to Buenos Aires."

As had been the case in the Canary Islands, Phillip had his worries in Rio de Janeiro – almost as much with the crews of the various ships of his fleet as with the convicts. For the local young men comprising the loading parties who manned the lighters, the female convicts were a diversion of which they did not wish to be deprived. In fact, they were much more interested in "fraternising" with them than they were in loading the ships. Once again, the captain of the fleet was relieved when they weighed anchor and set out for Table Bay.

* * *

Having experienced more than his share of problems while the eight ships were in Teneriffe and Rio de Janeiro, Phillip was aware that there needed to be some changes in the way his staff went about the major task of reprovisioning in Table Bay. It was all very fine that the two victualling officers he had brought with him had excellent records as naval officers; the problem was that they really knew nothing about livestock and the amounts of grain and other fodder they required for the long voyage to Botany Bay. Furthermore, they were not particularly skilful when it came to bargaining, especially when the merchants with whom they were trading spoke little or no English. He was, therefore, pleased that Midshipman Frank Scott was on board as he knew much more about animals and their needs than Major Fortescue had done and he was competent in the way he handled the vendors and merchants and was able to talk to them in their own language.

It was for this reason that, when they were a couple of weeks out of Table Bay, Phillip decided to announce Scott's promotion. He was confident that, for the purchasing and loading of the livestock, fodder, plants and seeds, Captain William Webster's protégé would make an excellent procurement officer.

In his terms of reference Phillip had been instructed to consider the advantages of setting up a small unit in the port at Table Bay so that, until the New South Wales settlement became reasonably self-supporting, revictualling and refurbishment could be done from there. If Second Lieutenant Scott-Quetteville could handle his current task competently, it was the captain's intention to send him back from Botany Bay to command this unit.

On 12 October 1787 the midshipman was paraded before Captain Phillip. The young man saluted smartly.

"I wish to inform you, Scott, that in the dispatch I sent back to the Admiralty from Teneriffe, with Major Fortescue, I reported that I was impressed with your knowledge and your bearing and that I was promoting you. I congratulate you, young man, you are now a second lieutenant, RN – and the time has come for you to resume your correct name."

"Thank you, sir."

The captain smiled broadly.

"When I tell you the nature of your first task you might not be as grateful."

He then explained what he wanted François to do in Table Bay and he mentioned in general terms the possibility of establishing a small presence there at some time in the future. He also told the newly promoted lieutenant that, while the fleet was in Table Bay, he should have his new uniforms tailored. Before dismissing him, he made a short speech such as is usually made by senior officers when promotions are announced.

"Young man, both the Scott family and the Quettevilles d'Anjou have built up a fine tradition as sailors and I am confident that you, in your turn, will bring honour to the uniform you wear. When we were in Teneriffe, I wrote to your patron, Captain Webster, and informed him of both your progress and my decision."

"Thank you, sir, I shall do my level best to justify the confidence you have in me."

"I am sure you will."

As François was saluting and turning to go, with a hardly discernible smile, the captain added –

"Are you aware that an officer is required to obtain the permission of his commander before he enters into a marriage contract?"

"Yes, sir!"

Arthur Phillip could not fail to notice how flushed with embarrassment the young officer's face had become. He endeavoured to defuse the situation.

"As I suppose you are aware this ordinance is an application of an old naval precept that forbids an officer from deserting his commander in order to go in search of plunder!"

There was silence. The unexpected promotion, the knowledge of his new responsibilities and his personal embarrassment seemed to momentarily cloud François's brain. The captain came to the rescue and explained that it was an old naval custom that, when officers are about to marry, at the dinner their shipmates hold to celebrate the occasion, a mock trial is sometimes conducted. The officer who is about to be a bridegroom is charged with "deserting his commander in order to go in search of plunder". Having been found guilty of the charge, the penalty is usually to perform some outlandish prank.

Phillip apologised for talking over the boy's head and told him that he thought his conduct towards Judy Hyams had been exemplary and he added that, since the day when she boarded HMS *Sirius*, both he and Captain Hunter had been more than impressed with her. Although still standing at attention, François relaxed a little.

"Sir! May I ask you a question, please?"

"Certainly, lad!"

"You do not know my father, but you do know Captain Webster. Do you believe he would think me a silly young fool if I proposed marriage to Judy Hyams?"

"I assure you, Scott-Quetteville, he would think you were a blazing idiot if you didn't – and so would I."

"I hope to be in a position to parade myself before you in the near future, sir."

"I look forward to that."

* * *

Long before even reaching Table Bay, Mrs B and her two girls had become quite wealthy – and they had become close friends, too. Both Alisha and Amy had the good sense to realise how lucky they had been to have had Mrs B to protect them and teach them. She safeguarded their money and, having eyes like a hawk, she told them which of the convicts – such as the leering Joe Mulligan – and which members of the crew, needed to be kept at arm's length. She warned them – as she had done when they left Teneriffe and Rio de Janeiro – that it was probable that, while in Table Bay, many of the men would get themselves infected and that, to be on the safe side, they must not do any "entertaining" for at least a week after leaving port. Once again, they heeded her advice and when a few of the other girls became sick, they guessed what the problem was.

* * *

During the four weeks that Captain Phillip's armada spent in Table Bay, Second Lieutenant Scott-Quetteville was busier than he had ever been in his life. He had to inspect the livestock before purchasing them and then to ensure that each of the eight ships was loaded with the maximum amount of cargo and animals that it could safely carry. He was also responsible for checking that there were trained naval and Royal Marine personnel whose task during the long journey it would be to look after the livestock and to provide fresh water for the plants and seedlings that had been taken on board. On each of the first two sectors of the journey there had been many losses due to pilfering – both by the convicts and members of the crews. To prevent a recurrence, he had to liaise with the masters of each of the ships to ensure there would be round-the-clock supervision over everything. Captain Phillip had ordered that all guards be armed and that any person caught in the vicinity of the livestock and stores be shot on sight.

Once again, before going ashore in Table Bay, Judy made it her business to visit the *Prince of Wales* and talk to her three friends. She was quite surprised when Mrs B handed her a canvas bag containing £200.

"Please Miss Prettypuss would yer look after this for me and me girls. It will be much safer with yer than with me. I've 'arf as much agen in with me things."

"Of course I shall, Mrs B. I'm sure that between here and New South Wales we can work out a good way to explain it."

"You don't need nothin' to explain anything. Yer can tell 'em I bort it with me from London."

As well as carrying out his purchasing duties, François managed to find time to be measured and fitted by Table Bay's leading "bespoke tailor" for his officer's uniforms. Judy Hyams accompanied him when he went for one of his fittings and she purchased several lengths of good material and some more haberdashery items from the tailor. When his height was measured François was surprised to learn that he had grown nearly four inches since he joined the navy. This explained why the sleeves and the trousers of his midshipman's uniform were inches short. The garrulous tailor made a point of inviting attention to this and mentioned that he would be "generous" in the cutting room so that, at a later date, it would be possible to do some "letting down". When François said he was on his way to Botany Bay – and explained where that place was, the tailor realised why the young lady who accompanied the young naval officer had purchased such a large order of seamstress's needs. He made them both laugh when he insisted on showing Judy how best to make any alterations at a later date. François felt that it would be inappropriate — at this juncture — for anyone to presume that Judy would be doing his sewing for him in Botany Bay.

"If, on her arrival in New South Wales, Miss Hyams decides to go into the tailoring business, I should certainly patronise her establishment. However, from the pictures that were painted by members of the last expedition to New South Wales, I do not think that tailoring or, for that matter, any clothing business that opened there would be particularly profitable."

The tailor did not see the joke; however, Judy Hyams laughed — and her laughter concealed that she had also blushed.

* * *

In Table Bay, of all the livestock that François had to purchase, the horses were of more interest to him than anything else. As in Rio de Janeiro, the Argentinian horses he inspected in Table Bay were the best. In addition to buying what he had to procure for the marines and the army unit, he obtained permission to acquire for himself two thoroughbred mares and an in-calf heifer. Of the mares one was already in foal and he had the second one covered before the fleet weighed anchor. Judy enjoyed going with him on his "horse" expeditions, as she had always been fond of horses and had learnt to ride as soon as she could walk. However, because she had been continually at sea since her mother's death, she had not ridden for more than three years.

The First Fleet, having remained for a full month in Table Bay, weighed anchor on 12 November and as the ships' sails were unfurled, the officers and crews, convicts and their guards, all knew that this was their last glimpse of the western world — and civilisation — perhaps for years; perhaps forever. It would not have been possible for anyone to fail to see the significance of the stores and livestock that had been loaded — stallions and mares, bulls and heifers, pigs, goats, sheep and poultry. A few comics among the convicts hid their apprehension by making animal noises and declaring that they were all on board a Noah's Ark. As well as the more than 500 animals, they had taken on seeds and seedlings, and trees and shrubs of many kinds. From Captain Cook's report they knew that the climate of New South Wales was similar to that of the south of

Africa and that for quite some time after their arrival, virtually the only things they would have to eat would be what they had taken with them.

Judy Hyams, without telling anyone, stocked up with many skeins of wool, reels of cotton and even leather to repair footwear – and some furnishings for a nursery. It was a difficult time for her, a virgin who had not yet received a marriage proposal. She was embarking on a journey to a destination where it would be quite impossible to purchase a single item for a trousseau or a layette. She laughed to herself as she thought of one of her mother's pet sayings – "If one does not think ahead, dear, one will be caught with one's pants down". In the present context, the expression had something amusingly contradictory about it.

* * *

For the first week at sea there was an eerie cloud of quietness that seemed to descend over the entire fleet. The compulsory – usually noisy and unruly – "Sunday Prayer Service" was subdued and many more people than usual listened to the Reverend Johnson's long – and boring – sermon. They were sailing into the unknown, to a destination where neither houses nor schools awaited them, no theatres nor hotels. In fact, there would be no buildings of any kind and no roads, coaches or carriages. On all the ships, countless stories were passed from mouth to mouth, about the black savages, cannibals and wild animals they would encounter – and these tales lost nothing in the telling!

During the second week at sea, things started to return to normal.

* * *

In November François proposed marriage to Judy Hyams. The chaplain of the fleet, the Reverend Richard Johnson and his wife, Mary, were travelling on the *Golden Grove*. But from time to time they visited HMS *Sirius*. They were both very interested in the young couple and offered them counselling. Much to their disappointment François and Judy declined the offer as graciously as they could and, when the Johnsons had returned to their ship – to pray for them, as they said they would – the young couple had a good laugh. The unworldly Richard Johnson had been a protégé of William Wilberforce and a staunch member of the Society for the Propagation of the Gospel. It was not surprising, therefore, that even before the announcement of a wedding date, he and his wife were making all sorts of plans for a special Nuptial Eucharist.

François, being a conscientious officer, always attended Sunday services – although both captains knew that neither he nor his family made any claim to be Christians. For Judy it was quite different. She was a Jewess and she was now a free settler. That she quietly and unobtrusively chose not to attend Sunday prayers was accepted without comment – although it did not go unnoticed – especially by the Reverend Johnson and his wife.

Life on board HMS *Sirius* was so humdrum that, not only Judy and François, but almost everyone else, were determined that the wedding should take place at sea. When Captain Phillip announced his approval, the excitement began. The bride, being a strict Jewess and a young woman with definite ideas of her own, created a few problems, the most serious of which related to the marriage service and to the selection of her attendants. Judy was adamant that she could not be married according to the rites of the Church of England – or by a Christian priest. Her mother would turn in her grave and, if her father had not been buried at sea, he would have done likewise. The Reverend Johnson was miffed and it was not until weeks after the wedding that he was pacified. Captain Phillip, who had almost adopted the girl as a daughter, ruled that the captain of HMS *Sirius* should officiate and that the service would be basically in accordance with the *Book of Common Prayer* – eliminating or substituting any words that Judy found unacceptable.

When it came to choosing her bridesmaids, Judy was uncompromisingly resolute that Mrs B, Amy and Alisha should be her attendants. If permission could not be granted for this, she would have nobody at all. When François told her that he had been informed that her choice was quite unacceptable to the captain, she wanted to know why.

"It was the corrupt British legal system that thrust me with these three women. From the time I was wrongly convicted in London, they gave me comfort, friendship and loyalty – during the worst period of my life. They are entitled – and will get – my total loyalty in return. It is not a matter concerning which there can be any compromise."

When she made this statement, all François could reply was —

"I do not believe it! It is not you speaking, my darling, it is my mother!"

As François had always been well received by the captain of HMS *Sirius*, Captain Hunter, he requested to be paraded to him "concerning a personal matter". As deferentially as he could he explained Judy's attitude and her reasons for finding what had been ruled so much in conflict with her conscience. The captain had enormous respect for the young American who, in her quiet and unassuming way, had become a really valuable member of his crew. When François had fully explained her attitude, he remained silent for more than a minute, as he waited for the captain to speak.

"I think you had better parade yourself to the judge advocate. I know that he has already demonstrated his feelings for Miss Hyams in that he has asked Captain Phillip for the privilege of giving her away. Better still, suggest to your fiancée that she should explain the reason for her request, to him."

François took this advice and Judy who, like most other women on the ship, regarded Captain Collins as one of the most handsome and charming men she had ever met, had no hesitation in approaching him.

"You have put your case well, Miss Hyams. I shall think about the matter and I shall talk to Captain Phillip and to Captain Hunter. Do I have your undertaking to accept, with a good grace, whatever solution to the problem the fleet commander and Captain Hunter reach? None of us can expect to get our own way all the time."

"Yes, sir, I shall."

The final outcome was that there was a formal wedding ceremony on HMS *Sirius* at which Judith's three friends, dressed in the clothes Judith had bought for them in Rio de Janeiro, were permitted to be present as her attendants. At the end of the service, they were returned to the *Prince of Wales* where the women convicts were given a special "party". The bridal pair were present for a short time, after which they returned to the *Sirius*, where Captain Collins hosted as near to a wedding reception as circumstances permitted — and what a great party it was.

IV

THE FIRST FEW WEEKS OF Judy and François's married life was quite a revelation. They were both virgins and as far as Judy was concerned she was almost totally ignorant of anything to do with sex. As her mother had died when she was only twelve years old – and not yet menstruating – it fell to a post-menopausal spinster whom she had always addressed as Aunt Fanny to enlighten her on the "facts of life". Aunt Fanny was not actually a blood relation but a close friend of Judy's parents who lived in the Hyams household to keep Mrs Hyams company when her husband was at sea. Being a somewhat unworldly single lady, Fanny was not really the ideal person to carry out such a delicate task. In fact, she did not know how to begin.

"My dear, I am sure your late mother, God rest her soul in peace, informed you about the changes a woman's body undergoes in her early teens…?"

Judy, whose twelve-year-old mentality was as prudish and easily embarrassed as the Jewish spinster's, muttered, "Y…Yes Aunt Fanny…"

However, even if Judy was going to qualify her affirmative response in some way – and she wasn't – these three words were all the prim lady needed to regard her *locum in parentis* responsibilities in so far as they related to imparting knowledge on such taboo subjects as puberty, menstruation and sex were concerned, as being well and truly discharged.

On one occasion Judy had stayed overnight with a girlfriend who had been quite helpful; however, apart from this extremely brief – and not all that illuminating – interlude, it was not until she reached the revolting hulk in Portsmouth that she received her first sex education. There, cheek by jowl next to Amy and Alisha, she was told all she needed to know — and much more — about the delights of — and the potential income from many and varied forms of sexual activity. She also learnt that it could be bliss or hell and that men who immediately afterwards rolled over and snored, leaving their lovers longing for more, were to be avoided at all costs. All this seemingly strange — and rather scary — information remained in her subconscious until François frightened all the bogey-men away as together they explored the mysteries of courting and physical love.

François was much better prepared than his fiancée. For a start, the conversation at home had always been open and enlightening, and between his parents and Johann and Enika, all of whom were quite uninhibited in the way they discussed all things and in the way they answered all of his — and his brothers — questions. Furthermore, when he was on leave, just before departing for New South Wales, Jean-Marc had started having an affair with Rachelle Bassett and he had passed on much valuable information. This, when added to the never-ending — but mostly apocryphal — accounts of the amorous conquests of his fellow midshipmen at the Portsmouth naval college and on HMS *Sirius*, had made François a particularly well informed, virgin sailor.

In their early courting days — and evenings — François found Judy extraordinarily shy — and even prudish when it came to discussing anything with a sexual connotation. However, once he had explained how, throughout his childhood, he had been brought up in an atmosphere of total candour, and that the family they intended to raise together would be reared in a similar environment, her inherent reticence gradually thawed and her impish sense of humour did the rest.

From this rather clumsy initiation into the world of Eros, the newly-weds quickly progressed with imagination and enthusiasm and it was not long before they became a near perfect pair of lovers.

* * *

The two-month journey from the Cape of Good Hope to Botany Bay was made in excellent time, notwithstanding the unfavourable winds and big seas the fleet encountered when they set out from Table Bay and which dogged them as they rounded Van Diemen's Land[6] on Christmas Day.

There was much excitement and many sighs of relief when, on 19 January, they sighted the entrance to Botany Bay and, on the following day they cast anchor. It had taken them eight months and one week to travel more than fifteen thousand miles.

Arthur Phillip was neither excited nor relieved; in fact, he could not imagine how Captain Cook could have described the place as being suitable for the establishment of a settlement. As he looked out on endless sand and the absence of the fertile land about which Cook had written such glowing accounts, he could not believe his eyes. That the "fine meadows" so enthusiastically referred to by Cook were nowhere to be seen disappointed him gravely. Being convinced that this was no place for a settlement, he was determined to find somewhere better.

Leaving the fleet at anchor, he started doing some exploring of his own and, much to his delight, on 21 January, he discovered what he described in his report as "the finest harbour in the world". He spent two days examining its bays and coves and finally settled on the place with the best natural springs – which he named Sydney – after the secretary of the Home Office. The fleet moved from Botany Bay on 25 January and they landed in Sydney on the following day. The union Jack was hoisted, the marines fired a *feu de joie*, many toasts were drunk and the wife of James Whittle, a Royal Marines drummer, gave birth to a son.

* * *

During the last two weeks on board, Captain Phillip concentrated on preparing his officers and men – and their wives – for the task that lay ahead.

"Some of the convicts we have on board will probably never see the error of their ways and repent. It is my intention to ensure we get a good day's work out of them – whether they like it or not. On the other hand, there are many who, I firmly believe, will genuinely try to become valu-

---

[6] Later Tasmania.

able citizens. For those who demonstrate their worthiness there will be pardons, land grants and the wherewithal to make a success of their lives.

"To many of you there will be allocated one or more convicts. I want you to do your best to train them and help them to become good citizens. The sooner we are able to sort out 'the wheat from the tares' the better – and the sooner those wishing to reform are separated from those who are nothing but a damn nuisance, the happier I shall be. In this regard, immediately proper accommodation is available, those performing domestic duties can, if you so desire, live with you."

Judy Scott-Quetteville listened attentively to what the Governor-Designate had to say and discussed the matter with her husband.

"I do not believe that Amy or Alisha are criminals. To me they were – and always will be – good friends. I should like to have them allocated to us. They can do domestic work and I can keep them busy sewing and mending. The officers and their wives will need this kind of service and so will the army and the marines."

"But what about your friend Mrs B? She would die of a broken heart if you took her two off-siders and left her to rot."

"Of course I am having dear Mrs B. She has told me that she is a midwife, a child's nurse and a cook..."

"And a madam and a pimp and probably a hundred other things as well."

"Do you mean that we should not have her?"

"Of course not, darling! Mrs B is a survivor. But may I make one condition?"

"Whatever conditions you like."

"That you teach the three of them to speak decent English. Mother would die if we returned to England with our children dropping their Hs and their Gs all around St James's Square."

Judy stood to attention and pronounced solemnly –

"And I should not blame her if she did, sir. Yes Second Lieutenant Scott-Quetteville, the servants will speak good English – and your children will talk good French as well."

He put his arms around her and gave her a big kiss.

"Formidable, ma charmante créature. Je t'adore!"

François talked to Henry Hacking, the quartermaster who was in charge of the employment of the convicts and as Judy had also mentioned a young man whom Mrs B had pointed out to her as being hardworking and honest, he included his name, too. This young convict had been working for his father who was a farmer near Henley. He had been convicted for fishing in their neighbour's part of the river. As so many of the officers' wives had expressed their concern about employing convicts, Mr Hacking was more than pleased that the young second lieutenant and his wife were prepared to have four of them. As unusual as the request was, he approved.

Judy took Mrs B aside and explained to her that this was a chance of a lifetime for her and her two protégées. It would mean that they would have to be smartly dressed and work hard and that they must immediately retire from prostitution for all time. She pointed out that, well dressed and well spoken, Amy and Alisha would soon find a really nice soldier or marine to marry, they would get a land grant and they would have a wonderful future.

Mrs B was quite beside herself with happiness and gratitude. Her only concern was her fear that the girls' past – and hers – would stick to them and that dozens of the men knew them as nothing more than whores.

"Mrs B, perhaps some of the people on the *Prince of Wales* might think that; but there were seven other ships in the fleet and nobody on any of those vessels knows anything about Amy, Alisha – or you."

"Miss Prettypuss, dear – beg pardon M'Lady – I'll tell yer one thing – me girls didn't go for the riff raff on the *Prince*. They cood 'ave 'ad any of 'em but I woodn't let 'em. They stuck to the sailors and the marines. They 'ad the money and they were a cut or two above the convicts."

"That is even better. And what about you Mrs B? I think you would be happy as a servant and supervisor."

"Me? I can turn me 'and to most things: midwife, waitress, 'ousework – yer know."

"What I want to do is to teach the three of you to sew. I want to set you up in a sewing and mending business. In Rio de Janeiro and in Table Bay I bought everything we are going to need."

"It is a wonderful opportunity Miss Pretty— I am sorry, I mustn't call you that any more. Can I call you Mrs SQ, please; I coodn't get me tongue around Scott-Kwettaville?"

"When we are alone that will be fine. When others are about it is better to say 'madam' or 'ma'am', don't you think?"

"I thought 'madam' was wot yer call the woman who runs a brothel."

Judy did her best not to laugh as she explained the various meanings of the word.

"Good! For the present let us stick to Mrs SQ. More important than what you call me is that you three really do behave yourselves – and that you do not get drunk, either. And please remember, I have a very large sum of money of yours. The money will come in very handy when you start to set up house. I am going to open bank accounts for you and the girls and I shall tell Mr Hacking that I have given you the money to start a new life when you get your ticket."

"Mrs SQ, nobody in my life 'as been anything like as good to me as you 'ave. I swear to yer on me mother's grave, I will never let yer down – and the girls won't neether. They worship yer."

"Well that is all settled. Please do not mention a word to anyone until your guards tell you to pack up your things."

"Yer know the money yer got of ours…well, between ourselves, Mrs SQ, I've got as much again in with me things."

"Keep it for the moment, Mrs B, we can sort things out later. You will probably be able to buy half of Botany Bay before you are finished.

* * *

Gregory Smythe, the farmer's son – the angler who poached in the Thames – was a shy young fellow who had hated every minute of the voyage more than he could express. His family were good Christians and for him to have been thrust headlong into a milieu of bad language, drunkenness and depravity was utter torture. When François spoke to him and told him what he had in mind, it was too much for Gregory – he burst into tears.

"Sir," he snivelled, "I would do anything in the world to get out of the hell I've been living in. If we had not reached New South Wales when we did, I think I would have jumped overboard."

Gregory was a big hefty young man of twenty-four. He had worked for his father who had a dairy herd and he had done some grooming for the local squire during the hunting season. He was quite useful with his fists and, after an encounter with a bully on the *Prince of Wales* in which the older man had come off much the worse, he had been treated with respect by the other convicts and the guards.

Amy thought he was especially handsome and, during the journey from Table Bay she had offered him "a treat for free" and in private – away from the others. He had blushed and said that it would not be right if they weren't married.

On the morning of 27 January, François found Gregory in a working party stacking stores on the grass. He explained to him that he had applied to Mr Hacking to have him assigned to him – and outlined what he would be required to do.

"My wife and I have two in-foal mares and a heifer that is in calf. The second mare is expecting her foal in September. We have a big plot of land on the river and we are going to build a house there. Your job will be to look after everything outside and to cut the wood for fires. We have seeds and seedlings and I understand we are to get some of the hens – and a cock – that came from the Cape of Good Hope."

Gregory's face lit up.

"God bless you, sir. I will work from dawn to dusk every day of the week, just as long as I can go to the Reverend Johnson's services on the Sabbath."

"Of course you shall. Mr Hacking will be talking to you later this morning. He will tell you everything else that you have to know."

"Once again, sir, thank you from the bottom of my heart. Have I permission, please, to say something?"

"Yes Smythe. What is it?"

"In all the ships there are tons of animal manure still – and straw. They are throwing it into the harbour. We must have it all for your garden. I promise to grow you the best crops of whatever seeds you have. The ground is poor here. With all that manure and straw, sir, you will have the best garden in Sydney Cove."

Gregory Smythe was as good as his word and, as soon as he had set up the tents in which the Scott-Quetteville pair would live until more permanent buildings could be erected, using a limber the second lieutenant was able to borrow from the marines, he collected every skerrick of horse and cow manure and straw he could lay his shovel on. He spent four days carting it to his master's allotment and then he went into the scrub and cut saplings from which he built palisade walls and a roof. As he had promised he would, he worked from dawn to dusk. For all of February and March, Amy and Alisha helped him by carrying the saplings from the forest into their clearing. Gregory Smythe was a true pioneer and his pardon and allotment of land – right next to his master's – was one of the first granted to a convict.

Unfortunately, the Scott-Quetteville's successful little farm and market garden were anything but typical of what happened during the first year of European habitation in New South Wales. Few of the colonists or convicts had any success in growing things. Because of this, during his first twelve months in Sydney Cove, Arthur Phillip was faced with rapidly disappearing stockpiles of food and fodder. This situation was exacerbated by the disappointingly low level of production of food from the small farms and market gardens the convict labour had been developing.

The failure of the English wheat to germinate, the poor quality of their axes, saws, spades and other tools, and the weevils that rendered useless the seeds they had brought with them, combined to make the governor's life a misery. Added to these worries was the pitifully slow and sullen attitude of many of the convicts and their guards, who really were not much better. Furthermore, he was in constant pain from a wound in his shoulder he sustained when one of the Aboriginals had attacked him with a spear.

Phillip dispatched ships to Batavia and the other South East Asian ports to replenish his depleted stocks, but as these missions only achieved limited success, he decided to send HMS *Sirius* all the way back to Table Bay, where he knew he could get adequate supplies of all essentials.

Second Lieutenant Scott-Quetteville, who had done so well co-ordinating the revictualling of the fleet in the south of Africa and who knew where good livestock could be obtained, was nominated to make this voyage. Although he was keen to obey his commander's orders, he was personally devastated that he would be thousands of miles away from his wife when she would be giving birth to their first child early in September. Being well aware that this would be the case, Captain Phillip gave the young second lieutenant the option of staying in Sydney until after his wife's confinement. Judy, however, was having none of it.

"François, it is your duty to go. My father was half way across the Atlantic when I was born and my mother said that it was just as well, as had he been mooching around the place, he would have been a proper nuisance."

Phillip, not at all surprised that she had adopted this attitude, assured the young couple that Dr John White, the colony's surgeon, would personally supervise the birth of their child.

**

Considering the conditions in which the settlers had to live and the obstacles they had to overcome, the progress made during the first eight months of the colony's occupation of Sydney was good. Many primitive storehouses were constructed as well as buildings to house the convicts. However, almost all the officers, including Captain Phillip, were still living under canvas. Thanks to the skill of Gregory, François and Judy had been able to combine their canvas home with a more permanent abode. Gregory split the trunks of small eucalyptus trees and by arranging them in a clever way, he had constructed weather-proof walls and a roof. Their abode, although quite primitive, was certainly much better than the tents in which the families of most of the other officers were living.

Until his departure from Sydney on HMS *Sirius*, François spent as much time as he could helping Judy and Gregory develop their allotment. All three – and Amy and Alisha, too – worked hard to overcome difficulties and obstacles and were rewarded with the success their efforts deserved. It was no surprise to anyone that the seeds that Judy had purchased in Rio de Janeiro and Table Bay germinated and matured much better than those that had been brought from England, and had been planted and cared for by the lazy uninterested convicts who were working on the government farms.

Like everyone else, the Scott-Quettevilles were constantly being assured that better building materials would arrive from England and, like the others, they also knew that unless Captain Phillip sent a ship to Table Bay to buy what they needed from there, it would be years before they had proper implements and tools – and housing.

After he had been in Sydney for a year and having listened to the many knowledgeable people who had come with the First Fleet – and those who had arrived subsequently – François wrote a number of letters to his mother and his brother Jean-Marc suggesting that The Bridge Company might send a ship to Sydney, laden with all the things that a pioneering community needed. He assured her that there would be back-loading and that the governor would be prepared to pay a price that would make the journey a profitable one.

One of the many letters François received from England was from his patron and mentor, Captain Webster. His purpose in writing had been to congratulate him on his promotion and the excellent reports on his performance that Captain Phillip had sent back to England. Webster informed François that The Bridge Company was building two new ships in England: both of more than one thousand tons. This letter François received in Table Bay when he returned there in HMS *Sirius* with Captain Hunter. Before his ship returned to New South Wales again, François replied to Captain Webster, suggesting that one of the new vessels might be given a name associated with the new British settlement in New South Wales. In this letter, too, he again listed all the things they needed in the new colony to enable them to construct permanent buildings. He expressed confidence that the voyage could be successful from a business point of view, as Captain Phillip had more than adequate funds to purchase all that was necessary "to ensure the grandeur of this the furthest outpost of His Majesty's empire".

* * *

The purchasing mission to the Cape of Good Hope was a resounding success but for François, the weeks he spent in the Cape of Good Hope were quite the unhappiest of his life. Having taken delivery of the mail from England and France, he read the letters from his mother and his two brothers, informing him of his father's death. He found it hard coming to terms with the idea that his hero and mentor was no longer there to guide him. Of course he adored his mother – she was kind and thoughtful, extraordinarily beautiful and excitingly youthful and interesting. But his father was the great tower of strength in the family and nobody could ever replace him. Added to this great sadness, François missed Judy and worried about her and her approaching confinement. At this time the great saving grace was Captain Hunter. He did his best to restore his second lieutenant's spirits.

"Son, I know exactly how you feel – I was about your age and at sea when my own father died. However, it was probably much worse for me. You see, we had had a really ugly argument at home just before I reboarded my ship and I never had an opportunity to apologise to him before he died. From our first port of call I wrote a long letter to him asking him to forgive me but unfortunately, by the time the letter reached England he had died. His death meant that I was left not only with sadness that only time could melt away but also with remorse that took years to leave me."

"Sir, my father was almost like a god in our house. He always said that he never knew his own father and he was going to make sure that his sons knew him. He used to attribute everything that was good in our lives to our mother and, in his slightly austere way he used to apologise for his ineptitude. He always made it easy for us to ask him questions but complained that, until he had studied the writings of mother's grandfather, the Count of Anjou, he knew nothing of life at all. I do not think this was true and that he only told us this so that we would all study the great man's philosophy of life."

"And did you?"

"Oh yes, we all did. It is our bible."

"Did you bring your bible with you? I should like to read it."

"It is in two big volumes and I have only brought the first one. The second one is at home with Judy. She wanted to read it when I was away. She studied the first volume on the ship, going to Sydney."

"I am intrigued, Scott, and I should really appreciate being permitted to borrow the book you have."

Having read *Les Memoires et les Écrits de Jean-Marc Quetteville, le Comte d'Anjou* — the English version — Captain John Hunter, soon to be governor of New South Wales, became yet another disciple of Anjouism.

* * *

Before François left Sydney in HMS *Sirius*, he and Judy talked endlessly about their expected child and, as the two mares François had bought in Table Bay were both in foal, between the two young marrieds, all three pregnancies were usually discussed at the same time. Teneriffe, the chestnut, was three months in foal when he had bought her and she had a beautiful chestnut colt at the end of July. Springbok, the bay mare, was not due until September. François complained bitterly that he was going to miss out on all the fun; however, he was there when the cow he had purchased in Table Bay — when it was well and truly in calf — produced a healthy heifer in April.

Because she was busy throughout the daylight hours, it only took Judy a few days to recover from her husband's departure and, as 3 September, the date on which she was expecting her baby to arrive, approached, she became more and more excited. Her first contractions commenced on time — in the middle of a rainstorm — and it continued to rain for the next two days. That she was living in a tent did not seem to worry her in the least — nor did it inconvenience Dr White who delivered her baby son who she immediately said would be called John — after François's father.

However, she was surprised — and thrilled — when, within a few minutes of handing over the little bundle to Mrs B who had insisted on being the midwife, the doctor announced —

"Well, well, what do you think?"

Judy, although a little exhausted, was blissfully happy to have a fine son to show her husband when he returned from the Cape of Good Hope, did not know what she was meant to think.

"What do I think? I think I am oh so lucky, Dr White, and thank you so much for being so patient with me."

"Well I'll tell you what to think — think how extra lucky you are — as there is another baby about to arrive."

Judy could not help bursting into tears. She did not know what had made the tears come – they just did. In less than twenty minutes Mrs B was holding the second baby boy.

"He will be Judah – after my father."

* * *

Several days later, Dr White called to see how Judy was managing and whether she had enough milk for the two babies. He was pleased when Mrs B assured him that both infants were sleeping soundly and were obviously well fed. Judy gave further assurances.

"We have Table Bay, our own cow, Doctor. François bought her when we were in the Cape of Good Hope. As soon as my boys need more than I have to give them, Table Bay will let me have some of hers."

"When this happens, you should water the cow's milk with about one third water – otherwise it will be too rich for them."

"Thank you, doctor. I shall remember that. Please tell me, have you ever done any circumcisions?"

"Yes, Mrs Scott-Quetteville, I have. Why do you ask?"

"Both my sons must be circumcised."

"But this is very rarely done in England – except by Jews – and with them, the rabbis do it."

"Well Captain Phillip, who thought of almost everything else, must have forgotten to bring one."

The doctor laughed.

"Knowing the high regard in which the governor holds you, I am sure, Mrs Scott-Quetteville, that if he had known before he left England that he was going to need a rabbi he would have brought one."

Judy, enjoying the levity that had been brought into the conversation, continued.

"Well as he has not done so, will you be able to be a temporary rabbi and do the job for me, please?"

"Of course I should be delighted. When would you like it done?"

"Next Monday, when John and Judah are ten days old. In some Jewish communities they say on the twelfth day but my father said it should be the tenth."

"Excuse me, but your father was Jewish?"

"Both my parents and me, too."
"But do you still follow the Jewish faith?"
"The faith yes – but the sacraments, no."

* * *

Captain Hunter, the skipper of the *Sirius,* was a remarkable man and an inspiring role model for the young second lieutenant Scott-Quetteville who sailed with him on several of his long journeys. A number of years before going to New South Wales, Hunter's ship had run ashore in the West Indies. His leg was nearly pulled off when it became caught in a cable and his right hand was severely wounded. To make matters worse, a blood vessel in his lungs burst. His unbelievable fortitude – and his survival – amazed everyone.

When sent by Arthur Phillip back to the Cape of Good Hope, in 1788, Hunter elected to go by way of Cape Horn and thus by the time his ship had returned to Sydney during the following May, he had circumnavigated the globe. It was at the end of this long voyage that the captain shook François's hand and, looking him straight in the eye, declared –

"As far as I am concerned, young man, your basic education is at last complete. You are now a proper sailor – congratulations!"

* * *

When François returned from Table Bay he, not knowing that Judy had bought many things for a baby when she had been there, brought back everything a baby could ever need. He learned – fifteen seconds after his arrival – that he was the father of twins and was overjoyed. He could not have been more thrilled and more proud of Judy and, when he produced all the things he had bought, she hugged him and told him how clever he was.

"You see darling François, when I was in Table Bay I only bought enough things for one baby. You have solved all my problems and have bought almost the same again. Thank you!"

"Tell me, you little hussy, do you not think that you were running a risk buying baby things before I had even asked you to marry me?"

"Of course not. If you had not asked me, I should have proposed to you!"

At a time he thought appropriate, François imparted to Judy the news of his father's death. She, orphaned at an early age could – and did – both sympathise and empathise with him. She was as sad that she had never had the opportunity of knowing the man about whom she had heard so much, as François was that he could not show his father the beautiful young woman whose fine twins would carry on the Scott-Quetteville name.

* * *

The next months were the happiest François and Judy had ever experienced. They played with their babies, they worked in their fields and they planned their future. The *Sirius* brought with it quite a bundle of mail for Judy: a helpful letter from the American consul in Teneriffe; a detailed statement of the assets of her father's estate and a letter from a Boston solicitor who was the trustee of his will. There were a number of other letters, including a letter of condolence from the owner of the ship of which Judah Hyams had been captain; and three letters from Major Fortescue. They all contained good news and collectively the correspondence made it abundantly clear to Judy that, in her own right, she was a wealthy young woman with property in both Boston and Quebec, a pension from the Canadian shipping company, a generous annuity from a grateful major and substantial credits in banks in three countries. She confessed to François that she really had no head for figures and that she felt that he should take care of everything for them both.

"François darling, I am so pleased to be able to tell you that thanks to my parents and the dear, sweet major, you and I shall never want. But please understand that I know nothing of finance or investment. Both the governor and Captain Hunter have told me that I am lucky that I married an excellent businessman who, as their procurement officer, has already saved them many hundreds of pounds. I want you to do what you think best with all the money and property that I appear to have inherited."

"Judy, although I know you are aware that my family is quite well off, I have not told you before – but I must confess that we are hideously rich. We own a third of The Bridge Company, one of England's most successful shipping and export companies and mother is one of the richest women in France. However, the Quettevilles of Anjou have always regarded wealth and privilege as being responsibilities rather than as a licence to indulge in ease, luxury and excess. We know that, more than anything else, people need education and training and that it is our responsibility to bring these things within the grasp of the under-privileged.

"Hand in hand with education is the necessity to provide medical care for them. Judy dear, I do not believe in these things just because my parents and forebears did. I fervently believe that, if we want to keep what we have, this is the only way to live. In France the situation is disgusting – more than two thirds of the people are virtually slaves. It amazes me that they do not revolt. I did not ask you to marry me because you were the most beautiful creature I had ever set eyes on – although I must admit that you were – and are. I married you because I believed that you would be a most wonderful life partner who could – and would want to – help me achieve all the things I have been talking about."

Judy laughed – and clasped François's hand.

"What a mouthful! But I get embarrassed when you talk like that. You are really gorgeous – but blind – to think I am pretty; but please go on thinking it. The only reason I do not tell you how handsome I think you are, is because I do not like seeing you blush! However, I did not fall in love with you because of your looks. It was your attitude to life that inspired me to think the same way as you do. On the *Sirius* I used to listen when you spoke to the sailors about their future and how they must improve their knowledge and skills. It was obvious to me, then, that you really cared about your subordinates and, after reading your grandfather's book for the first time, it just confirmed my first impressions that your family really do live up to their *noblesse oblige* motto. My father used to say that the verbal expression of people's feelings for each other does not reflect what is in their hearts nearly as well as the way they treat each other – and, in any case I get a little embarrassed with serious conversations on ethics. I know I am the luckiest girl in the world and I am determined to stay that way."

* * *

Shortly after their return from Table Bay, the old salt, Captain Hunter and the young one, sailed in HMS *Sirius* to Norfolk Island where disaster struck. The ship was wrecked on one of the offshore reefs. There it languished for nearly a year before it could be refloated, repaired and returned to Sydney. François had been ordered to return on an earlier ship and was allocated duties in and near the main settlement at Sydney Cove.

Apart from the months during which HMS *Sirius* was shipwrecked on the coast of Norfolk Island, Captain Hunter's ship was constantly on the move: to Batavia and other ports in the East Indies and to Table Bay to replenish stocks of stores – and animals. On most of these voyages the captain took Second Lieutenant Scott-Quetteville with him and because of these frequent and usually long absences, Judy was called on to manage the Scott-Quetteville household, its staff of convicts and its small farm.

The farm was, in fact, so successful that it was able to provide some fresh vegetables and eggs for the hospital. Each day Amy and Alisha, who had started their sewing and mending "shop" quite near the hospital, used to deliver the produce on their way there each morning. Both girls had kept their promise to Judy and had steered clear of the hotels and the social venues where the behaviour of the patrons left much to be desired. Not only were these places where prostitutes peddled their wares, but drunken orgies were the norm and there were frequent fights among the men and even instances when soldiers and convicts gang-raped some of the females.

Alisha and Amy, having heard about these attacks on women, seldom left the farm except when in the company of Gregory Smythe. During the first year in Sydney he and Amy became close friends and at the end of 1790 they became engaged. Three months later they – and Alisha, too, were given their tickets.

Mrs B who worked in the house for Judy – also earned some extra money by helping out as a barmaid in one of the hotels. Soon after their arrival in Sydney, she became friendly with a corporal from the New South Wales regiment. By 1791 this relationship had blossomed to a point where they were about to set a wedding date, when a disastrous smallpox epidemic broke out. This claimed the lives of nearly one hundred Aboriginals and many of the whites – including Mrs B. For Alisha and Amy – and Judy, too, this was a great sadness. From the moment she set had foot on what was soon to be called "Australian" soil, her conduct had been exemplary. She had mothered the two girls, advised Judy concerning the convicts who could be trusted; she had supervised all the convict labour – with a rod of iron – and had even cooked. More than anything else, she had worshipped the ground on which François and Judy trod – and had regarded the twins as her own personal property.

It was only after she had died that they all learned that her real name was Bessy Jones and that there had never been a Mr B. Her estate was worth over a thousand pounds – including the money she had accumulated on the *Prince of Wales*. This she left to her corporal and her two friends – to be divided equally between them.

* * *

Gregory worked from dawn to dusk for six days of the week. On Sundays he limited his toil to a few essential duties, he went to church and he read his bible. On weekdays, when the weather was very hot and humid or if it was raining, he would sometimes harness one of the horses and set out to bring Amy and Alisha back from their work.

One evening, seeing that the sky looked exceptionally heavy, he decided to meet the girls on their way home. It was in the early autumn and the weather was sultry and unpleasant. As was quite often the case, by the time the two girls had closed their A & A tailoring and mending shop it was already quite dark. They had set out on their walk home, hoping to reach the farm before it started to rain. They had not gone more than half a mile when a man who had been walking behind them grabbed them both by the arm and spun them around so that they were facing him. He was hefty, tall, unshaven and ugly – and they recognised him immediately. They remembered him well from the *Prince of Wales* – Joe Mulligan – one of the convicts of whom Mrs B had warned them to steer clear. On the ship he had kept pestering Amy to sleep with him until Mrs B had threatened to report him to the guards.

Almost at the same instant as he had swung them round, he punched Alisha hard in the stomach. She fell to the ground, winded or in a dead faint – or both. Seeing her motionless, he pushed Amy to the ground and, crouching over her, he almost shouted at her –

"Remember me, Joe Mulligan? When yer were nothin' more than a sneaky whore on the ship, yer were too choosy to 'ave me – weren't yer? Well, yer 'aven't got Mrs Bloody B to proteck yer now, 'ave yer? Well yer goin' to 'ave me now, wetha yer like it or not – an' ya ain't goin' to get no money, neetha."

Amy was terrified. She tried to shout out in the hope that a passer by would hear her but, as the man had one hand clamped tightly over her mouth, she was unable to make a sound. She tried to bite his hand but this also was impossible. His tirade continued –

"If yer go quietly an' b'aive yerself, yer won't get 'urt but one word out a ya an I'll slap yer pritty face that blinkin' 'ard, you'll wish yer were dead."

Feeling her face relax a little, Joe Mulligan took his hand away from Amy's mouth and began dragging her skirts up and reaching for her under garments. Amy started kicking at him violently and screamed at the top of her voice – "Help! Hel—…"

With one hand he slapped her face and with the other he stifled her screams – and before she could move, he grasped her hand in a grip of steel. "Yer bloody little fool, I told yer to go quiet. If yer make one more sound, wot I just gave yer will be nothing to wot yule get. If yer understan', nod yer pritty little 'ed an' I'll be nice to yer."

Amy was too frightened to do a thing. The weight of his legs made it impossible for her to kick him. She could see that his belt was already undone and that he had a sheath knife on it. She was terrified that he might use it to kill her.

"I'm gettin' impatient, Amy. If yer don't nod yer 'ed quick, you'll get a couple more slaps – 'arder than the last time."

Just as Amy was nodding her head, Alisha, who had regained consciousness called to him.

"Joe dear, wouldn't you rather have me?"

Hearing her voice surprised Mulligan and he turned around and faced her.

"You bloody bastard!" she shouted at him, as she threw a mixture of pepper and mustard in his eyes.

The pain was excruciating and he grasped his face with both hands to protect himself as both girls leapt to their feet and started kicking him as violently as they could. He was literally blinded with the pain and, as his eyes started to water and the mustard dissolved, it became even worse.

Amy, seeing that his trousers were completely undone, emptied the contents of her mustard bag into his groin, and, while he was writhing on the ground and holding his face – and swearing at them – she rubbed a handful of wet grass into his crotch to make quite sure that the mixture was irritating his penis and his scrotum. Within seconds he was literally howling with pain.

At that moment Gregory Smythe appeared and, quickly summing up the situation, he was at Amy's side in an instant. She almost collapsed into his arms, weeping. When Alisha gave him a brief account of what had happened, he almost went berserk. He grabbed Mulligan by the hair and half lifted him from the ground. He flattened his fists into his eyes, he kicked him in the groin as hard as he could and, as the man lay there on the ground, almost unconscious, he jumped on his knees. While he was meting out Mulligan's punishment, Gregory shouted at him –

"You evil monster! How dare you lay hands on my Amy! You will pay for this with your life; you do not deserve to live and until you die you will suffer."

Amy tried to pacify him.

"Gregory darling, he really did not do much to me. Alisha was absolutely wonderful, she saved me. It was a trick that dear old Mrs B taught us on the way out from England."

Although Gregory cooled down a little, his face was still flushed with anger.

"I have no intention of taking him back to the guards; he can stay here and rot until morning, when, with Mrs Scott-Quetteville's permission, I shall report the assault."

It was more than two months before Mulligan was well enough to stand trial. He was given one hundred lashes, an extra seven years gaol and was promptly dispatched to Norfolk Island where many re-offenders had been sent. He died there before he had finished his sentence.

PART II

The French Revolution

Liberté, Egalité, Fraternité

SEBASTIAN CHAMFORT *

1789 – 1799

---

* Sebastian Chamfort, a satirist, wit and poet, was an ardent revolutionist. He took part in the storming of the Bastille – and was a victim of the *Terreur* in 1794.

I

FOLLOWING THE PLANNED ASSASSINATION attempt in the Paris tavern in 1789, Comtesse Nicole d'Anjou had been rushed to the surgical section of the Medical School of the Sorbonne, where she lay in a critical condition – unconscious, with a scarcely discernible heartbeat. On either side of her bed were two of Europe's foremost doctors; Jean-Marie Lassonne, Comte d'Archiâtres, surgeon to King Louis XVI and his queen, Marie-Antoinette – and John Hunter, one of the greatest surgeons of the eighteenth century. Dr Hunter was held in the highest esteem on both sides of the English Channel; in fact, in 1783 he had been honoured by being made a member of the Royal Society of Medicine and Royal Academy of Surgery of France.

When the countess had been brought to the Sorbonne with her life hanging by a slender thread, although, at first, neither man thought that they could save her life, they did everything they could to restore a regular heartbeat and to introduce air into her lungs. However, Nicole had a number of deep gunshot wounds to her neck and back and severe damage to the side of her head. Apart from doing everything possible to clean up and dress these wounds, the doctors were waiting until they had a reasonably favourable prognosis for the countess's recovery before seriously tackling these other injuries.

From the moment she had been brought into the Sorbonne clinic, at least one of these doctors had been at her side and, for much of the time, they had both been there. Dr Lassonne, who had just returned to the room from snatching a few hours sleep, asked his English colleague if, in his absence, there had been any change in the patient's condition.

"I am pleased to say that, although her breathing is laboured and her heart beat is still irregular, she is better than she was yesterday. Right now, I am more worried about the blow to her temple as she crashed to the stone floor and the damage caused by that blunderbuss – or whatever it was that fired at her."

"You know much more about gunshot wounds than I do. I know that, during the past few years, you have had much experience in treating battle casualties and I am looking forward to learning from you."

"In treating these cases, infection is always our worst enemy. That and where the metal is embedded in the back and neck a penetration of the spinal cord is always on the cards. One has to be very careful. In Nicole's case, she was wearing a heavy coat and that gave her some protection. What is equally important is that she arrived here within an hour of the attack and we were able to clean her open wounds and thus reduce the risk of infection."

"Do you propose to start on her back or her head wound first?"

"I want to leave that firm bandage on her head as long as possible. With her still in a coma, it is impossible to know the extent of any brain damage. We must wait."

The following day John Hunter removed six small pieces of lead from the countess's neck and the upper part of her back. Although some of the fragments were deeply embedded in the flesh, none appeared to have damaged her spine. He douched the bleeding tissue with spirit and as he did so he thanked the Lord that his patient was unconscious. Lassonne was impressed with the English surgeon's skill.

"You have a great gift, Dr Hunter – and you must have studied anatomy for many years."

"Thank you for the compliment. I was very fortunate to have been taught by my elder brother William. He was not only a clever physician but also a great surgeon – and a remarkable teacher."

"He was indeed – and I was fortunate enough to have been one of his pupils, too. He was much older than you, was he not?"

"Eight years older – and it was a great loss to the profession when he died. He taught me most of what I know."

John Hunter, who had not only earned an enviable reputation at the

• PART II – I •

Surgeons Hall in London but also for his surgery on the field of battle, carefully studied one of the deep wounds. While he was carefully parting the tissues, he continued to talk quietly – almost as if he were talking to himself.

"We shall not know for some time whether there has been any nerve damage. Small pieces of bone on the wings of two of the cervical vertebrae appear to have been broken. One can only hope that Lady Nicole will retain the use of her limbs and that she will not suffer severe back pain for the rest of her life."

It was a great relief to both men when the wounds were dressed and their surgical work was finished. Leaving their patient under the care of one of the other doctors, they walked to the refectory to have their morning tea. Outside the building they could hear shouting and screaming in the street – and now and then the noise of gunfire. They were living in terrifying times and the Paris that they both knew and loved so well seemed to have lost its senses and its charm. They feared reading the papers as, almost every day, there were reports of murders, pillage and riots.

One of the victims of the outbreak of street violence that occurred outside the clinic had been the countess's uncle, the seventy-nine-year-old Comte Pierre de Quetteville, the former dean of the law faculty at the Sorbonne. He had been struck down by a gang of rioters, as he was alighting from his carriage. Dr Lassonne, a friend of the count, believed that he had actually died of a heart attack – a condition for which the French doctor had been treating him for some years. Knowing how close the countess was to the professor, both he and John Hunter agreed that, if she regained consciousness, it would be better to keep the news from her until she was stronger.

On the morning after the removal of the gunshot from the countess's neck and back, when John Hunter was carrying out his routine check of her pulse and heartbeat, he heard a scarcely audible murmur. He looked at his patient carefully and noticed that the completely bland expression on her face had changed, in that there was now evidence of discomfort or pain; her closed eyes were slightly screwed up and she was frowning. He quietly addressed her.

"Lady Nicole, can you hear me?...I do not wish to disturb you but, if you can hear me, perhaps you could move your face a little."

When there was no reaction, he repeated his request. This time Nicole opened her eyes slightly and seemed to try to smile – an obviously rather painful smile.

"That is wonderful, Lady Nicole! But please try and relax. You are doing very well indeed."

Nicole's eyes opened fully. She looked directly at the surgeon.

"That is nonsense! I am not doing at all well."

Dr Hunter tried hard to hide his amazement and his happiness. Not only had this extraordinary woman cheated death, even the few words she had uttered indicated that her brain was intact. He did not want her to exert herself or to have to concentrate. All he wanted was for her to rest.

He addressed her in a soft but confident voice.

"You really are doing very well – I mean it. But I want you to sleep for a little while longer. You have some nasty wounds on your head and back that must feel very painful. Please do not make any effort to understand why or how – just relax and sleep. Tomorrow we can talk – there is plenty of time."

"Yes, I will try. But no more tubes – please, no more tubes."

"Of course, Lady Nicole, no more tubes."

She closed her eyes and her facial expression seemed to relax. Without hurrying or alarming her, he felt her pulse and was delighted to find it a little stronger and more regular. While he was doing this, he kept his eyes on his patient. He turned to his assistant.

"From now on, Lady Scott-Quetteville must not be fed with a tube. We must use a spoon and we must be careful to listen to what she says."

"For what are we listening, doctor?"

"For her instructions. This woman is the daughter of the great French surgeon, François Quetteville, in whose memory our research clinic was named. She was his assistant and I have a strong feeling that she will know better than any of us what she needs. She is also the niece of Comte Pierre de Quetteville, whom we all know so well. They are a remarkable family."

• PART II – I •

The young doctor was both surprised and impressed.

* * *

From the traumatic night when he had taken Lady Nicole to the Sorbonne, not a day had passed without there being a personal visit to the clinic from Lord Dorset, the British Ambassador. After a couple of days it was quite obvious to John Hunter that the ambassador's interest was as much personal as it was official. Each day he would ask if the patient had regained consciousness, if any assistance was needed or if he could have anything sent urgently from London. He could not conceal his delight when, on the day following the operation, Dr Hunter informed him that Lady Scott-Quetteville had come out of the coma. He had, however, cautioned that she was not yet, by any means, out of the woods – and that it would be at least another week before they would be able to accurately assess the long-term prognosis.

The duke made no response. He very much wanted to see his friend but thought better of asking permission. The surgeon, recognising that there was a closeness between the ambassador and his patient, surprised him –

"Your Excellency, I wonder if you would be prepared to help me – and Lady Scott-Quetteville, too?"

"There is nothing in the world I would not do to help her."

"Later today or perhaps tomorrow, that is if all continues to go well, I should like you to quietly and dispassionately talk to her and explain the events of the evening of 15 July, when she was attacked. If you could do this slowly and carefully, it would be of enormous value to her. I think she would be more relaxed with you than she would be with me.

"Perhaps you could start by suggesting to her to just lie there and not ask any questions until you have finished. If, at any time during your talk, you feel that what you are saying is getting too much for her then you should tell her that what you have already said is enough for the moment and that you will come back tomorrow and finish your story."

There was another long silence.

"I think I understand what you want me to do, Hunter. Would you be happy if I went away now and thought about how to phrase what I have to tell her and how I can express myself in a quiet, disarming way? I could come back tomorrow afternoon."

"That is an excellent idea. If by some chance anything happens to make Dr Lassonne and I feel we are jumping ahead of ourselves and should wait a few more days, we shall send a messenger to inform you. The embassy is quite close."

The meeting between the Duke of Dorset and Lady Scott-Quetteville was an unqualified success. Although Dr Hunter had informed her that the ambassador had been a frequent visitor to the clinic to inquire after her and that he was visiting her during the afternoon, the look on Nicole's face when Dorset entered her room was one of surprise and happiness. When John Hunter pulled up a chair for him, he sat close to the bed, with his hand on the counterpane. Within a few seconds Nicole's hand had spontaneously clasped it. It was the first time she had given any indication that she was able to make any movement of this kind. Smiling with justified satisfaction, the surgeon excused himself and left the room.

Having quietly told her how pleased he was to see her and what a brave woman she was, Dorset sat back in his chair and asked her if she had any idea how she had come to be in the Sorbonne Clinic. She almost whispered.

She tried to slowly turn her head from side to side as if to say "No" but found the movement too painful. She replied in an almost inaudible whisper.

"No Sacky, I have no idea."

"Nicole dear, please do not strain yourself to speak, it might be better if you just look at me and perhaps talk with your eyes."

She answered him by smiling and, as she did so, he felt the slight pressure of her hand in his.

"Do you have any recollection of the night you were brought here?"

She spoke, this time a little louder –

"We had dinner. You and I had a lovely dinner."

For the next twenty minutes Dorset quietly led her through the evening – step by step – it was quite obvious by the look on her face that she had no recollection of anything that had happened after her dinner with the duke.

• Part II – 1 •

When he felt he had said enough for one day he suggested he would return on the following morning when they could talk some more. She smiled and there was a slight nod of the head.

He stood up to take his leave and moved to gently kiss her forehead. He heard the murmured "Thank you, Sacky dear" that acknowledged the kiss.

It took four visits before Nicole had grasped the whole story and each time her friend visited her she became more responsive and more able to articulate what she wanted to say. Both doctors were delightedly surprised at the giant strides she was making. They encouraged the ambassador to keep coming each day and, just as long as the progress continued, to draw out Lady Scott-Quetteville and encourage her to move a little and to speak.

* * *

Only five weeks after she had been brought to the clinic at the Sorbonne Nicole was informed by Dr Hunter that she would soon be well enough to undertake the journey back to London. In explaining that the dangerous part of the move would be the bumpy ride from Paris to the coast, Nicole assured her doctor that she would manage it and that she would write to The Bridge Company at once so that her brother-in-law, Charles Scott, could arrange a ship.

"That is wonderful news, Dr Hunter. To which port should they send a ship?"

"I am not yet sure. I intend to speak to Lassonne about that. He will know the best roads to the northern ports."

"If avoiding bumpy roads is an important factor, why could I not go down the Seine to Le Havre? There are many barges – and other craft, too – on the river and, although I am not seeking luxury, I am sure we shall be able to find something satisfactory."

The surgeon smiled.

"I can see that all you have been through has not damaged your brain in any way. Going down the Seine is an excellent suggestion and, more to the point, if you are travelling by river and by sea for virtually the entire journey, you could leave here as soon as the necessary arrangements can be made. I am leaving for London within a few days and I shall be looking after you when you reach home."

"From the bottom of my heart, Dr Hunter, thank you. Both you and Dr Lassonne have been simply unbelievable."

"After all you have done for the clinics in London, Marseille and here in Paris, neither Lassonne nor I could ever repay you."

"Thank you for your kind words – and for the good news about my return home. Within an hour I shall have written a letter to Charles Scott and I am sure the ambassador will have the letter delivered to him in London within a week."

* * *

Nicole's journey to England was quick, comfortable and trouble free. The fresh air, the blue sky and the warm autumn days – not to mention the anticipation of being once again in her own home – made her feel that she was once more alive. Irene, her personal maid, was as pleased as her mistress was. She had been with Lady Nicole for over two weeks – having been sent over from London by Harvey, the family's butler, as soon as he had heard about Lady Nicole's catastrophe. Irene, a country girl, had been scared out of her life since the day she had arrived in Paris. In the servants' hall at the clinic she had heard constant reports of robberies, rapes and even murders and – night and day – there was the intermittent noise of gunfire. The faithful Irene could not get home to London soon enough.

Immediately on receipt of Nicole's letter, Charles Scott, a capable – and perhaps a little over-conscientious – administrator, personally supervised every detail; including a comfortable litter, two carriers, a well provisioned galley and an excellent chef.

On her arrival home, every member of her domestic staff was lined up to greet her and, although an outdoor welcome had been organised, autumn wind and rain had forced Harvey to change his plans. The spontaneous warmth and sincerity of their greeting prompted her to ask Harvey to arrange for champagne to be served.

They carefully carried her upstairs on her litter and moved her to her bed. Totally frustrated with being lifted everywhere, she announced –

"After Dr Hunter comes to see me, I intend to stand up and walk. He made me promise faithfully that I would not move from my bed without his permission. Irene, my patience is now exhausted. I am not a cripple and I have no intention of being treated like one."

"M'Lady, Dr Hunter is wonderful and he knows how much you want to get better. Please be patient!"

In the middle of the afternoon the doctor arrived. After a thorough examination, he was satisfied that, far be it from her suffering any after effects from the journey home, his patient's condition had improved quite dramatically.

"Lady Nicole, it is nearly three weeks since I last examined you. I can honestly say that I am extremely pleased with the phenomenal progress you have made and Irene has assured me that you have kept your promise."

"Did she tell you that my promise expires at midnight, tonight?"

Dr Hunter ignored the remark and smiled.

"Let us do a couple of experiments! For a start I should like you to put your feet on the ground and then, once you are comfortable, I shall help you to stand up. You could feel quite dizzy and it is possible that you will faint. I shall be on one side of you and Irene will be on the other."

When she stood up, Nicole did feel quite unsteady and dizzy. However, after a few minutes, they had a second attempt and she felt much steadier.

"Right! It is now up to you two. I have brought you a wheel-chair and I suggest you use it for a week or two during which time your balance will return and your muscles become stronger. Please do not be too impatient. You know, at least as well as I do, if you hurry things too much, you will be the loser. The promise I want from you now is 'no long road journeys and no horse-riding – until I say so'."

"I promise. You have been wonderful to me and I mean it when I tell you that I have as much confidence in you as I had in my father."

"That is the greatest compliment anyone could pay me. Thank you! Except in case of emergency I do not think you need to see me until November."

* * *

Nicole kept her word — at first willingly but after a month or so she wanted to start riding and she wanted to go on a long trip in her carriage. She begrudgingly resisted the temptation and, once again, she was rewarded. She had secretly made it her intention to be riding before Christmas and to attend the Bassetts' New Year's Hunt. For many years this had been their exciting and happy way to begin the new year. The ball took place on New Year's Eve and the hunt always started at midday on New Year's Day — and in the evening there was a formal dinner party. The annual event was a great challenge to the athleticism and endurance of all concerned. Those who over-slept missed the pre-hunt breakfast and then had to sheepishly catch up with the hunt, an hour — or more — late. Others, who had wined more well than wisely, missed the hunt altogether — and paid the penalty. The rigidly enforced rule was that only those who had attended the ball, the breakfast and the hunt were permitted to be present at the dinner. Nicole made up her mind that she would be there.

The morning after Hunter's visit she was sitting in her new wheelchair looking out over St James's Square. Some athletes were training there. Some were jumping and hurdling, others were skipping or doing their callisthenics. An older man was with them — obviously their coach. Over the years she had seen this man from time to time — training his charges. Impetuously, she made up her mind that he was going to coach her back to fitness so that she could surprise everyone at Woking Grange on New Year's Eve.

She told Harvey to go over into the square and ask the gentleman wearing the brown jerkin if, when he had finished his training session, it would be convenient for him to come to No. 22 and speak with Lady Scott-Quetteville.

Claude Bennett, coach, fitness trainer and masseur, was a remarkable man. A university graduate and retired cavalry officer, he was the youngest looking sixty-five-year-old Nicole had ever seen. Standing more than six feet tall, he was a rugged specimen of a man. With greying hair, pale blue eyes, long nose and a strong, determined chin, he was definitely the kind of man that appealed to her.

He was as pleased to make Lady Scott-Quetteville's acquaintance as she was to meet him. He was a friend of Richard Tattersall and he knew most of the people in the racing world. Before even entering No. 22, when Harvey had explained the reason his mistress wished to meet him, Bennett replied that although he was not in the business of coaching or training, to help restore to robust health the woman who rode the mighty Eclipse would be a great honour. He lived in Pall Mall and he enjoyed training his sons, his eight grandsons and some of their friends. He also had a horse stud on the Thames, near Pangbourne.

* * *

Although David and Hélène Bassett did not come back from Etreham until three weeks after Nicole had returned to St James's Square, their two eldest daughters, Rachelle and Nathalie, visited her frequently. On all their visits, from the moment of their arrival, they filled the room with merriment and laughter. Much of their conversation was centred around accounts of the parties and the balls they had attended and the gauche advances of the young men whose carnal intentions had been so thinly disguised as to be laughable.

From their early childhood they had adored Nicole and had always called her "Cuzz" – because they thought she was much too young to be called aunt, and cousin was too formal. Some of their favourite memories were the times when their mother and Cuzz had taken them away on a "ladies only" holiday. For the Bassett daughters the uninhibited conversation, the laughs and the wisdom that seemed to constantly flow during these vacations made them unforgettable experiences.

When Hélène did return from France, before she even went to her home in Berkeley Square, she stopped to see her friend – and was more than agreeably surprised to see how well she looked.

"My darling, from what I read in the papers and from what Jean-Marc told us, I expected to see you lying flat on your back with bandages everywhere and one leg in plaster. You look wonderful."

"I am well on the way to recovery – but I certainly could not have survived if it had not been for Dr Hunter and a wonderful Frenchman, Dr Lassonne. And, more than anyone else, I owe my life to Sacky."

"My God! I cannot believe it. I remember him well; he used to come to The Cloisters."

"And at those cricket matches in Hambledon, too, he was quite a persistent pursuer! But honestly, Hélène, he has been wonderful, thoughtful, patient and understanding – and I gather he did all sorts of amazing things to bring me back to life. Dr Hunter assured me that Sacky worked a miracle on me."

Hélène laughed. "I am sure that if he had his way, it would not have been the only miracle he wanted to work on you."

"Hélène, dearest! The only man I have ever had was John – although he was so full of English complexes that lovemaking was something he really never understood, he was a wonderful, wonderful man and he gave me three equally wonderful sons. Nobody will ever replace him. My father used to say that the brain and the body of a woman living in celibacy cannot help but to atrophy – and eighteen months of it is enough for me."

"You have taken John Sackville as a lover?"

"No! But you would not believe how close I came, when I was in Paris."

"Why do you not rekindle the flame? I am sure it would not need much blowing."

"Alas! As usual, I have been too slow or too circumspect. I am not sure which. He already has two new flames: Heather McBride from Edinburgh and Christine Black – Viscount Black's daughter."

* * *

Not many weeks after Hélène's return from France Nicole read in the papers that the king had accepted the resignation of the British Ambassador in Paris, John Sackville, Duke of Dorset. He returned to London at once and one of the first things he did on his arrival there, was to write a brief note and have it delivered to 22 St James's Square to ascertain if it would be convenient for him to visit the Lady Scott-Quetteville. It was.

A few days later, on a warm, sunny autumn afternoon the duke's carriage drove though the gates of the Scott-Quetteville home – and Nicole could not have been happier. She was sitting in her wheel-chair, looking out over the square, when he arrived. She had asked Enika, her assistant, to pull back the curtains further than usual so that she could better view the passing scene. From the time she opened his letter until his visit, she had been looking forward to seeing him again. It was a happy reunion for them both as, although it had only been a matter of weeks since they had seen each other in Paris, it seemed much longer.

Having completed the initial greetings that were normal for close friends to exchange, the first thing Nicole wanted to hear from the duke was the details of her uncle's death – and his funeral. It was not that her sons and Dr Lassonne had failed to inform her already but rather that she wanted to hear it all again as they had all been rather vague in what they had told her.

"He died of a heart attack, a few days after you were admitted to the clinic, Nicole. Dr Lassonne, who knew your uncle and was one of his friends, told me that it was all very sudden and that death was immediate. He felt no pain."

"But I read in the *London Chronicle* that he was attacked by an unruly mob."

Dorset was well aware that, because of Nicole's critical condition at the time, both doctors had stressed to him – and to Jean-Marc and William – that she must be spared the details.

"Nicole, my dear friend, I give you my word that what you were told in Paris is the truth. I know Dr Lassonne well and he gave me an unqualified assurance that the count was living on borrowed time. Only two weeks before his death, Lassonne had visited him in his home and told him that he had suffered a minor heart attack and that he had to be very careful. At that time, Count Pierre had made it quite clear to the doctor that he did not want you or anyone else to know."

"Thank you, Sacky, you have – as ever – been a true friend to me. Jean-Marc told me that you had attended the funeral with him and William and that, after the service, you had taken them and the two doctors back to the embassy to lunch. Thank you for that, too. I know that you, like most kind and generous people, find it embarrassing when you are thanked; however, in case I have not adequately expressed my thanks to you for saving my life – Dr Hunter says it was nothing less than a miracle – I have something for you."

Nicole reached out to a table and handed a small package to her guest. Dorset opened the wrapping and the enclosed blue velvet box. It was a magnificent gold watch. It was inscribed – *To dearest Sacky, a miracle worker – and a wonderful man. With Nicole's love.* He just sat there staring at its beauty.

"Dear Sacky, that watch was made by John Jefferys, a master clockmaker. He was the man who helped John Harrison develop his famous 'longitude' watch. He gave it to John's father in recognition for the support he and The Bridge Company had given to solving the 'longitude problem'. You, who did more than anyone else to solve the 'keeping Nicole alive' problem, deserve it."

The duke was quite overwhelmed and found it difficult to make a coherent response.

He rose to his feet, kissed Nicole on the forehead and resumed his seat.

"Thank you, Nicole, it is – and will remain – my most treasured possession." He paused, "And you are the most unbelievable – and the most unbelievably beautiful woman I have ever met."

The remainder of his visit was subdued and strange. The gift Nicole had given him hardly left his hands. He could not refrain from looking at it, reading and re-reading the inscription and fondling it. Nicole could see that it had affected him emotionally. After about thirty minutes, she feigned fatigue and suggested that he should return the following day for lunch, when she knew she would be better company.

Enika saw him to his carriage and said that she looked forward to seeing him the following day.

* * *

When the duke arrived on the following day, he apologised for becoming somewhat emotional the previous day and excused his behaviour on the grounds that he had never previously been given a present that he treasured as much or that made him feel so spoiled. Nicole laughed off the remark by saying that perhaps that was because he had never before saved a woman's life.

Nicole had invited Enika to join them for lunch and she found what the recently resigned ambassador had to say about France intensely interesting. After the meal she wheeled Lady Nicole into the library and, having ascertained from her that she did not need anything from Piccadilly, she excused herself to go shopping.

On Nicole's desk was a silver picture frame containing portraits of two of her sons; a recent one of Jean-Marc that had been painted just after his promotion to the rank of captain, and William on horseback.

"You must be very proud of those two sons of yours – so well spoken and articulate in about four languages, such impeccable manners – and so damned handsome! When I met them both in Marseille, after John's death, I was really impressed – but truly, Nicole, the way they have developed in the last twelve months is remarkable. They have the composure and the maturity of young men in their mid-twenties. Do please tell me, have you had any word from your sailor son, François?"

"Yes, Sacky, I have had several letters from him from Teneriffe, from Table Bay and one from Sydney, the place where they have established the settlement in New South Wales – and one addressed to John from Captain Phillip, the governor. You would not believe it – François has been promoted to second lieutenant – and he is married. Not only is he married but, in a letter I received last week from his wife Judy, she informed me that I am about to be a grandmother. I am so excited that I am finding it difficult to think of anything else!"

"Congratulations Nicole, it is hard to imagine that you are old enough to be a grandmother. Please tell me, François is younger than Jean-Marc, is he not?"

"Yes! The girl he has married is eighteen and he nearly is, too. I was shocked beyond belief when I read the letter he wrote from Table Bay, informing me that he was about to propose marriage to a Jewish orphan whose father had been a sea captain. It was only after reading a beautiful letter from Captain Phillip, who considers the girl to be 'mature, courageous, strong and exceedingly beautiful', that I felt more comfortable with the situation. The captain had added that he would be proud if any son of his married such a fine young woman."

The duke repeated his congratulations and suggested that François had undoubtedly married a person very much the same as his mother.

"It would take me hours to narrate the whole story of how they met. It is as dramatic as it is long. Jean-Marc has also had several letters from François and I have had a visit from a Major Fortescue, who was the Royal Navy's victualling officer accompanying Captain Phillip's fleet as far as Teneriffe. The major spent nearly half an hour telling me all about this girl, Judith Hyams. She apparently saved his life and he has virtually adopted her and has made her the sole beneficiary of his will!"

"You don't say! That is incredible."

"Sacky dear, when you admit the girl into the International Lifesaver's Club – of which I am sure you should be president – you should ask her what she did that you did not do. The man she saved was far more generous than the miserly woman into whom you breathed life."

The duke, still a little embarrassed at being a reluctant hero, and whose repartee could in no way compare with the irreverent Nicole's, laughed – but neither loudly nor long. He asked to hear more about François's betrothal. Nicole obliged.

"What an amazing story! The name Fortescue sounds familiar to me. In our cricket team in Hambledon, we have an Archie Fortescue – a first-class batsman. I wonder if they are related."

"Quite possibly. The home of the major's family is not far from Hambledon – in Henley. He talked about a farm he had there and several properties in Kensington. I am sure he was not trying to impress me but, from the way he spoke, I should think he is quite wealthy."

"If he is Archie's brother, he most certainly is. They are Lord Archibald Fortescue's sons. Apart from their Hambledon property, the family own several streets of houses in Kensington. And there was an aunt, too, who left the boys a big chunk of Manchester."

* * *

Until he departed for Scotland, the duke was a frequent visitor to St James's Square and, after he left, Nicole felt a little more lonely than she was prepared to admit. This, however, did not impede her convalescence, which surprised everyone and which she attributed to her impatience to be able to once more ride and hunt.

As Nicole became more mobile, Claude Bennett was able to intensify her physical rehabilitation routine. At first the exercises were simple, with most of them being carried out while Nicole was seated. However, as the weeks progressed she began to do more walking and some elementary callisthenics. By the middle of September she was even walking briskly around St James's Square, as well as climbing up and down the stairs of her home. As the last week of October approached, she contacted Dr Hunter's rooms and made her appointment for 1 November. The two friends, who had not seen each other for a couple of months, enjoyed the interlude immensely, and John Hunter was pleased – but not surprised – with the phenomenal improvement his patient had made.

"When we were last together I warned you against horse riding and vigorous physical exercise, that is until I said that it was safe for you to do things of this nature. If you promise me to take it quietly at first, I think that it would not hurt you to ride and trot, although I do not want you to get on your horse without a mounting stool, at least not for another month. The real danger is that you should take a toss. This could have serious consequences. I think it will be another twelve months before your cervical vertebrae have settled down properly and the damage to your cranium is completely repaired."

Nicole almost jumped for glee. "I will make it to the Christmas hunt at Woking after all!" she said. When Dr Hunter did not quite understand what she had meant by this remark, she explained it to him and added –

"I have a wonderful person who is supervising my physical training. His name is Claude Bennett and he is as fastidious about not doing too much too quickly as you are. He trains his grandsons in St James's Square and is good enough to let me work with them."

"Well, just as long as he is keeping you in order, I do not think there is any reason for me to see you again. That is, professionally. It goes without saying that I hope, before too long, you will be once again continuing with your interest in the François Quetteville Medical Research Institute."

Within weeks, the work being done by the three clinics of the research foundation became Lady Scott-Quetteville's main interest.

* * *

By the end of November Nicole was once again riding in Hyde Park and during a weekend at Woking Grange, with her friend Hélène, she enjoyed taking several fences. In fact, spurred on by her success, she remained in Woking until the middle of the following week, riding for a couple of hours each day. As she did so, the one thought that continually excited her was that, as soon as François's tour of duty in New South Wales was finished, he and his family would return to England and then she would enjoy riding at Woking so much more, having her two young grandsons with her.

As always, the annual Christmas Ball, the breakfast and the hunt at Woking Grange were a great success and to the delight of the Bassett family and all her close friends, Nicole, having fully participated in these three annual fixtures, sat down to the formal New Year's Day dinner with the rest of them.

II

DURING THE WEEKS BEFORE HER being assaulted in the Paris tavern, in her capacity as one of the two Marseille delegates to the May 1789 Estates General meetings, Comtesse Nicole came across many interesting people from every part of France. Among them was a surprisingly large number of nobles who, like herself, had been nominated as representatives of *Le Tiers État* – The Third Estate. They were people who realised that the obscenely unfair distribution of wealth and opportunity – and the oppression of the poor – must cease, and that the tax burden must be shared by all. There was more than a sprinkling of radicals, university professors and bureaucrats who had their own personal agenda; and all the professions were well represented, too.

This disparate group of delegates representing The Third Estate held many meetings to work out their plan of action and also at these sessions were advisers and the members of the delegates' staff, some of whom Nicole recognised as being quite brilliant. She enjoyed meeting them and she found their ideas stimulating and their attitude to life inspiring. One of them, a cleric by the name of Joseph Fouché, impressed her more than any of the others – and it was not because he was a particularly attractive or charming man. This was certainly not the case; in fact, more often than not he was cold, direct and impersonal.

Fouché was a lecturer who taught Latin, mathematics and physics in a number of universities. He seldom opened his mouth during the many discussion sessions but those who wished to speak at the plenary meetings of the Estates General frequently sought his advice as to what they should say and, more importantly, what they should not say. Although he did not waste words, his answers to their questions, the depth – and the breadth – of his understanding of the matters being addressed amazed her. Little did she – or anyone else – have the slightest idea that this small, insignificant man would be one of the very few of those who started the French Revolution to be still alive and in power when Napoléon led the French troops into the Battle of Waterloo in 1815. The red-haired Fouché was neither handsome nor athletic; in fact, he looked rather frail. Nevertheless, there was something about his appearance that commanded attention: his pale blue, piercing eyes and his strong – almost cruel – thin-lipped mouth.

At an informal party on the evening of Sunday 31 May 1789 Nicole had the first of many long discussions with Joseph Fouché. It was his thirtieth birthday and Count Honoré Mirabeau had arranged a party in his honour. The count had invited Nicole to the gathering; however, preferring to spend the evening with the Duke of Dorset, she had declined the invitation.

"Comte Honoré, you know that I am not really a very social person. I do not think I would be able to make a contribution to the success of the evening."

"Comtesse, apart from asking your permission to disagree with your statement, please believe me to be quite sincere when I say that it is really important that you should know Fouché much better than you do. He is one of the most extraordinary men in France and he is important to our cause. When I informed him that I wished to arrange a birthday party in his honour, his first reaction was to ask me if it would be possible for you to be present."

"If you honestly believe that, as a delegate from Marseille, it is essential that I should be there, I shall be there."

"It is not only because you are one of Marseille's two delegates to the Estates General that he wants to meet you, it is because he is a great admirer of you and your family. You might be surprised to know that he has a copy of both volumes of your grandfather's memoirs and he quotes the old count to his students. Furthermore, he is a protégé of your uncle, Professor le Comte de Quetteville."

Nicole accepted Mirabeau's advice and attended the party. Quite late in the evening she returned to Rue du St Ésprit feeling that meeting

Fouché had been more than worthwhile and she fully understood why so many of the delegates continually used him as a sounding board.

Her meeting with this rather strange man took place about an hour after her arrival when the young cleric had approached her.

"Comtesse, it was indeed good of you to come here this evening to drink the health of a young man you scarcely know."

"Not at all, Monsieur Fouché. It is my pleasure to be here. May I wish you *bon anniversaire* – and may the forthcoming year be a great one for our common cause! Le Comte de Mirabeau has informed me that we have two things in common: a mutual belief in the philosophy of my grandfather and a great respect for my Uncle Pierre."

"That is indeed the truth, Madame. Would you think it impertinent of me to ask that we sit down for a few minutes?"

"I should find that most agreeable. I think I have many more questions to ask you than you have to put to me."

At the end of half an hour Nicole reluctantly suggested that she had monopolised the guest of honour for far too long and that it behoved her to let him return to the other guests. When he replied that he very much wanted to continue the discussion at a time convenient to the countess, she suggested that he might visit her in Rue du St Ésprit on the following morning. As they moved to rejoin the others he thanked her for the invitation and said how delighted he was to have met her.

Nicole had much to write in her diary that evening. The thirty-year-old cleric was quite the most unusual young man she had ever met. Early in their conversation she had asked him why he had taken Holy Orders and, almost immediately after he had finished his studies, he had forsaken the Church to be a teacher.

"Comtesse, my father always insisted that we were poor working-class people and that the only opportunity for me to study was to pledge myself to the Church. Having satisfied the examiners as to my intellect and my ability to speak, I was selected from many candidates. In truth, I have never accepted Roman Catholicism or even Christianity. My views on religion are very much those so eloquently expressed by your late grandfather, but I had no intention of telling that to the Monsignor presiding over the selection board!"

"Were you, in fact, a family of modest means?"

"We certainly were not. My father was a ship's captain and he owned plantations in San Domingo, as well as a large property in Pellerin. He probably made the decision to send me to the Oratorian Brothers because he spent much of his time away from home and he thought I should be safer with them than at home and going to the local school. I was a timid, spindly child and did not mix well."

"At what age was this?"

"When I was ten years old."

* * *

Their interlude on the following day turned out to be a series of exchanges of ideas on what France needed most, the extent to which the Estates General could achieve anything worthwhile and the future of the monarchy. After more than an hour of discussion, Nicole asked Joseph Fouché –

"What role do you wish to play in reshaping the way the people of France will live their lives?"

"That is indeed a direct question, Madame – and it deserves an equally direct answer. I do not see myself as a leader and neither do I consider myself to be a great orator. My skills lie more in understanding what men think rather than what they say – and the extent to which, if given the authority, they will put into effect their promises. I also believe that I am better than most people in anticipating what the future will reveal. In order to make the best possible use of my talents, I must, at some time soon, have myself elected to what you and your colleagues are advocating so eloquently – an *Assemblée nationale*. However, my sole reason for considering this to be essential is so that, having listened, learned and evaluated, I can help implement the agreed policy."

"But what if the radicals win control of the Assembly? They would murder every aristocrat in France!"

"If a fully representative, properly constituted *Assemblée nationale* legislated that all the nobles should be exterminated, and if I were ordered to have them killed, I should have no qualms in doing so. To save France we must have a democratically elected government that will govern and an executive that will not hesitate to implement the laws of the land with single-mindedness. For example, I do not personally believe that any good purpose can be served by beheading the king; however, if the majority of the General Assembly were to vote in favour of this, I should ensure that their decision was carried out without delay."

"I really appreciate your honesty, but your ruthlessness sends shivers down my spine."

"I hope you will forgive me, Madame, for saying so, but your inconsistency surprises me. Many years ago you were in conflict with a man you believed to have committed a number of crimes. Because you feared that he was sufficiently powerful to be above the law, you enticed him into your bedroom and murdered him in cold blood. You believed that you, personally, had the right to take it on yourself to be prosecutor, judge, jury and executioner. Nevertheless, you totally reject the idea that, if an *Assemblée nationale* of the people of France finds the king guilty of treason and I am called on to implement the sentence – and I carry out their orders – I am being ruthless and send shivers down your spine."

La Comtesse d'Anjou blushed and for nearly thirty seconds one could have heard a pin drop. Before responding to this extraordinary man's admonition, she extended her hand to him, not in the manner that a woman would but rather as a man might do to acknowledge defeat.

"Monsieur Fouché, your reasoning is logical and your criticism of my attitude is fully justified."

For the first time since she had met him, he smiled – a warm, sincere smile. He shook her hand firmly and, in a formal way, he kissed it.

"The reason I wanted to meet you, Madame, and get to know you, is that I admire you and I need your support. France is on the brink of a total collapse. In your grandfather's writings he continually warned that the persecuted poor would rise up and kill their oppressors. His words 'driven to desperation, we oft in mad directions turn' have haunted me, ever since I read them. It is my belief that the present revolt of the middle classes – is merely a stepping stone towards a revolt of the labourers and the unemployed – and I am sure that this second revolution will be a horrifying and bloody holocaust."

When he made this prediction, Joseph Fouché did not raise his voice, nor could Comtesse Nicole discern any vestige of revolutionary zeal in either his words or his facial expression. He sounded more like a competent physician informing members of the family of one of his clients the precise nature of the patient's malady, the course of the disease – and the ultimate outcome. She had no idea what help the man expected of her.

"Monsieur Fouché, I fully agree with what you have said. I think you are a remarkably astute man and if I can help you with money I certainly shall."

"Thank you, Madame, I do not need money; I have come to seek your help because, as well as being clever, like all the members of your family, you are one of the very few delegates to the Estates General who are quite selfless and without personal ambition. Furthermore, you are trustworthy and you are courageous. Although it would be utter folly to say so in public, there is hardly a single delegate to the Convention[7] whom I trust. There is not one to whom I believe I could turn for an honest opinion and, probably, there is not one who would not betray me if he thought it would further his own cause. I would stake my life on the belief that, in respect of these three things, you are an exception."

"Monsieur, I thank you for what you have said. Before giving you an answer I need some time to think and I should like to ask you two questions: would it be convenient for you to meet me here at the same time tomorrow? And would you think I was betraying your trust if I reported our conversation and your request to my Uncle Pierre?"

"Indeed not! It was he who sent me to you."

Joseph Fouché noted the surprised look on the countess's face as he reached inside his jacket and produced an envelope. He handed it to her.

"Le Comte de Quetteville told me that he will be in Versailles for the next two days for talks with the king, Breteuil and Necker. I met him this morning before they left Paris."

"If it were he who said I should give you my wholehearted support, I certainly shall – and if that is the case, a meeting tomorrow is probably not necessary."

Before Nicole could finish what she had to say, Fouché interrupted her.

---

[7] *La Convention* was soon to become *l'Assemblée nationale*.

"Nevertheless, Madame, I should still like to continue our discussion tomorrow."

As she showed her visitor out, Nicole was again struck with the confidence and uniqueness of the strange little man and she wondered how many other clever, unknown Frenchmen she would meet during the Estates General meetings.

When her visitor had departed, Nicole read what her uncle had written. He obviously had an immensely high opinion of the cleric-teacher:

"The man is close to being a genius and he is a survivor. There is nothing in the world about him to love – or even like – but there is much to admire and respect. For some people, there is certainly much to fear – but not, I think, for you. It is my belief that he would find your counsel valuable. I also believe he will not betray you and, if you think deeply about his attitude, I believe you will agree that he is right. As my dear father said many times, there will be bloodshed on an unbelievable scale – and this will happen whoever is in power."

Nicole did meet Fouché the next day. Their meeting was a long one – and, for the second time in two days, they shook hands.

* * *

Towards the end of 1789, when Nicole had fully recovered from the injuries she sustained in Paris, aided by reading – and re-reading – her diaries, she was able to clearly recall the discussions she had had with Joseph Fouché, and she frequently thought about him. In spite of considering that she was not quite ready to re-enter the political scene, she kept reasonably up to date by reading the Paris and London newspapers which were full of news and scandal about the recently established French Republic – and its leaders. However, Joseph Fouché's name seldom appeared. This did not surprise her in the least, as he was not a person who sought either the limelight or publicity. He preferred to influence the centre stage from the wings.

Not many weeks after her return to London she received a long letter – the first of many – from Fouché. It was obviously a well thought-out letter, his style was simple and he expressed himself succinctly and in an unequivocal way. The warmth of his words surprised Nicole, as did the anger and disgust he expressed concerning the attack in the tavern.

"That we have lost one of our very best reformers before the fight has hardly begun infuriates me beyond belief. I pray that you will fully recover and live to see what your grandfather so much desired – a France in which all people have freedom and hope. I assure you, Madame, I was devastated when I was told that the *salauds*[8] had murdered you and then, when they said that you had been maimed for life – although I was greatly relieved to know that you were still alive – I still felt that I had lost the one ally whom I knew I could trust."

Not until several years later – when Fouché referred to the letter – did he confess that the reason he had expressed himself in such strong terms had been as much to stir up Nicole's sense of duty and to provoke her to return to the battlefield, as it had been to express his concern for her health.

"The frequent letters I wrote to you, as well as expressing my sympathy, were written in the hope that, if there was a slender chance of you becoming strong and active again, a full knowledge of what we in Paris were doing might inspire you back to health."

After each of her meetings with Fouché, Nicole became more certain that locked away inside that puny, insignificant body was an astute, analytical brain, tireless energy, unapologetic zeal for the Republican cause and a self-confessed ruthless agenda for the *Assemblée nationale* that The Third Estate had fought so hard to establish. She appreciated his letters all the more as so many of the press reports were inaccurate and it was valuable for her to receive the latest information about the lobbying, plotting and intrigue that had been going on behind the scenes in Paris.

As was almost invariably the case, Fouché's plan was successful. His letters certainly did inspire Nicole to get well and strong as quickly as she could, and it was not long before she was champing at the bit to return to Mirabeau, Bailly and the others. Although she definitely felt pledged to support Fouché, she realised that it was important to keep this relationship strictly between their two selves. In her opinion – and it proved

---

[8] Scoundrels.

to be a correct assessment – the less their closeness was known to others, the better.

During a period of more than twenty-five years, from the meeting of the Estates General in 1789 until the Battle of Waterloo, although Nicole and Fouché had several disagreements, they remained staunch allies – each respecting the other's determination, ability, judgement and courage. Even so, it could not be said that there had been anything like an intimate friendship between them. In an ambience in which everybody was meant to *tutoyer*[9] their fellow citizens, and although Nicole addressed Joseph as *citoyen* when others were present, when they were alone they unconsciously maintained the formalities of *l'ancien régime* and, as the teacher-cleric was such a "cold fish", this formal mode of address came quite naturally to him.

Even before the outbreak of the Revolution, one of the dangers of corresponding between England and France was the risk of having letters fall into the wrong hands. After the storming of the Bastille on 14 July 1789 the situation became quite scandalous. Not only were envelopes opened and their delivery delayed, those who intercepted the mails were often bold enough to take copies of the contents. These could be handed to new Republican authorities or, better still, used for the purposes of blackmail.

For Nicole this did not present any great danger as she had access to excellent trans-Channel postal arrangements. The diplomatic bag could always be used to take mail as far as the British embassy in Rue Jacob. From there it was not difficult for one of Nicole's trusted couriers to hand-deliver letters to Paris and Versailles. For mail going to Marseille, Aix and Avignon, hardly a day went by without there being a Bridge Company vessel leaving for the Mediterranean. In England the situation was quite different: the Royal Mail was sacrosanct and delivery was prompt and secure. It never ceased to amaze Nicole how letters from Fouché always arrived within days of having been written and the postage stamp on the envelope was always an English one. Notwithstanding their confidence in their respective couriers, from time to time they had them followed.

---

[9] To speak to each other as equals.

Over all the years Nicole worked with Fouché, their relationship with one another was strained only once. This was early in 1793 when Louis XVI — or, as the members of the Convention insisted that he be called — Louis Capet — was on trial. Louis was arraigned before the Convention, charged with treason. Apart from the fact that the verdict of "guilty" was a foregone conclusion, there were many people who had been adamant that there should be no *peine de mort* — death penalty. One of these was Joseph Fouché and he, like many other delegates, had taken it for granted that there would be a secret ballot. When the radicals of the Jacobins — the strongest party in the country — vetoed this option, all the members of the Convention were required to mount the rostrum in turn and pronounce, in a loud voice, their vote. When it came to Fouché's turn, there was a hush as he was about to speak and a sigh when they heard his verdict — a not very loud "Mort".

The king's execution took place within one or two days. The following week Nicole and Fouché were together in a quiet café in Rue Saint Benoit — quite near the tavern where the attempt had been made on her life. During the meeting he suddenly interrupted the discussion they were having concerning Marie-Antoinette and said there was an important question he would like to ask her.

"Why are you so quiet today? Since we met an hour ago you have not smiled once. You have not asked after my wife — a thing you always do and you are not your usual relaxed self."

"Thank you for being so observant. I admit that, since last week, I have found it difficult to see you in the same light as I had until you voted for the king's death."

"And thank you for raising the matter. Personally, if I had had my own way, Louis Capet and his wretched family would have been banished to America — as Jefferson recommended when he was in Paris. The Girondins[10] strongly supported this suggestion. I moved among all the members of the Convention and, by listening and noting, it was not difficult to ascertain precisely how every member of the Convention intended to vote. Quite early in my investigation it became patently

---

[10] The second biggest party — the Moderates.

obvious that a majority of the delegates were adamant that the ex-king should die and that my vote would not make the slightest difference."

"So you changed your mind?"

"No, Madame, I changed my vote. Had I not done so, I would be seen as being quite out of step with Danton, Robespierre and the others and that would inevitably mean they – and with them the rest of the Convention – would have no further use for me. I believe in destiny – my destiny – and that is to be one of the major forces in establishing France as a powerful Republic where Liberty, Equality and Fraternity are the right of all citizens."

Nicole was silent as she thought about what this plain, frail-looking, red-headed man had said. She was still thinking when he asked her if he might continue. She smiled as she replied.

"Please do! I am intrigued with your logic."

"Madame, nobody in the world knows better than I do that you sincerely and fervently want the same things for the French people as I do and you, yourself, have told me that you believe that what the Convention votes for must be the law of the land. And yet I am well aware that you have been to France on a number of occasions and have assisted nobles and their families to leave the country."

Nicole blushed.

"You know a lot, Monsieur Fouché."

"Be that as it may, I only mentioned the point to make it easier for you to see that we have very much the same beliefs. You know that if the laws of a democratic country are not obeyed there will be anarchy but you also believe that if you, personally, can do a little good for innocent individuals who have unwittingly been caught in the crossfire, it is not going to frustrate the government in any way and it helps you to live with your conscience."

Nicole's laughter defused the debate.

"Touché! Monsieur Fouché."

For the first – and only – occasion in their many years of friendship, Joseph Fouché laughed out loud.

"And do not be too concerned about the spies who watch your every move. There are other spies watching them! Just as long as your actions are not a danger to the Republic, it is my responsibility to ensure that you are protected."

"I did not know that you were my self-appointed guardian angel."

"I am not self-appointed. When the Professor le Comte Pierre de Quetteville gave me permission to seek you as a close ally, he made me promise on oath that I would protect you – if necessary with my life. I have no intention of betraying that trust."

Nicole looked at her watch. She stood up to leave.

"Your loyalty, sir, will be reciprocated and I give you my word that my conduct will not make it unnecessarily difficult for you – only innocent people who have been caught in the crossfire."

When she walked around the other side of the table and politely kissed him on both cheeks, he just stood there like a statue.

III

When Nicole had first met Marie-Antoinette in 1773 the seventeen-year-old Dauphine was miserable, sexually frustrated and lonely. Nevertheless, she was highly intelligent and was making a big effort to fulfil the difficult role she had been unfairly called on to play. But in the unhappy years that had followed the ascension to the throne of Louis XVI, the queen had slowly descended to the level of the other idle, over-indulged nobility who inhabited the enormous palace at Versailles. There were hundreds of them – princesses, baronesses and countesses with apparently limitless money and nothing to do other than amuse themselves partying, gambling and having affairs with each other's husbands. Whereas the people of Paris seemed to accept superficiality, indolence and promiscuity as the norm for their own nobility, they were not slow to express disgust and horror when *l'Autriche* – the Austrian – behaved in the same way.

Neither did they have to look far to find another stick with which to beat the poor young Viennese puppy. She had failed to produce an heir to the French throne – an unforgivable sin. That her lazy, over-weight – and under-sexed – husband had, throughout the first seven years of their married life, failed to consummate their marriage, in no way mitigated the seriousness of her alleged crime.

During those difficult years Nicole had done her best to help the unhappy young queen but she had neither the time – nor the inclination – to persevere with her spoilt friend when her behaviour became as bad as the rest of the insincere parasites who lived in the palace. Like the many peacocks that were there, too, they did little more than strut around its beautiful parks and gardens.

In 1789, after the attempt on her life, when Nicole had arrived back in London, among the dozens of letters that soon arrived at St James's Square for her was one from Marie-Antoinette. This had been written several weeks after the incident and had been prompted by a vague newspaper account that had played down the seriousness of the attack. It had appeared under a headline – "A brief account of the assault on several of the delegates to the Convocation of the Estates General". The queen had later been given a more accurate account by the British ambassador, whom she frequently met at formal diplomatic receptions – and, if there was any truth in the constant rumours that spread around the palace, on a number of other much less formal occasions, too.

Her letter, as well as wishing Nicole well, was full of praise for King Louis and how good he had been to convene the Estates General.

Nicole had answered the letter in the most positive way she could. However, as the queen was completely out of touch with reality, she felt that she could not be anything like as helpful to her as she had been in the early years of their friendship.

The final break with Marie-Antoinette came in 1791 when Nicole received a hand delivered letter in which the French queen had pleaded for advice. Her problem was that life under the new regime was intolerable and – what was worse – she and Louis feared for their safety. The queen was determined to flee from Paris and seek refuge elsewhere in Europe and she implored Nicole to assist her and the king to escape.

Nicole wrote back at once and told Marie-Antoinette that to try to escape was the worst thing she could do.

"You have asked me for my advice. It is this – stay where you are and maintain your dignity. To try to flee from France would be fatal. Any plan to escape would be doomed to failure. The many enemies you have around you are just waiting for you to do something foolish. The moment you left Versailles they would pounce on you and drag you back in chains and put you on trial for treason."

Marie-Antoinette ignored Nicole's advice and, with the king and a large entourage, she fled the capital. By the time the royal entourage reached Varenne, they were surrounded by troops of the new National Guard and forced to return to Paris, disgraced and humiliated.

Nicole felt sorry for Marie-Antoinette but now that she and Louis had so badly compromised their situation, there was nothing that could be done to help them.

It was less than a month later that a second long and plaintive letter arrived, full of the queen's woes and the unfair manner in which the king and she were being treated. On this occasion Nicole waited several weeks before answering the letter and her reply was even more circumspect than her first letter had been.

In the envelope with the queen's letter had been a short note from Henriette Campan who expressed regret that the political crisis had thrown them apart and she hoped that the present problems would soon be something of the past.

For the next two years Marie-Antoinette's letters kept arriving, although by 1792 they were taking a month to reach London. The letter the queen wrote after the king's trial and execution was so pitiful that Nicole's reply was a sincere effort to express her utter horror at the callous barbarianism of the Paris mob who had taken leave of their senses.

Whereas Nicole knew full well that the people of Paris were far more determined to send Marie-Antoinette to the scaffold than they had been to rid themselves of their king, she expressed her hopes that, having made Louis the scapegoat for the sins of generations of his forebears, they would spare her to look after her children.

Nicole, who knew that it was quite impossible to do anything to save Marie-Antoinette, did not open the subsequent letters that arrived. When, a couple of days after the queen's death, on 16 October 1793, she read a newspaper account of her disgraceful trial and execution, she wept with sorrow and despair. The trumped-up charges against the queen ranged from theft and high treason to sexual perversion and incest. More than forty suborned witnesses gave false evidence to a court that was determined to have the queen publicly disgraced and vilified, and to a courtroom packed with hundreds of Parisians – and Parisiennes – who wanted to hear the worst and who cheered and applauded when the death sentence was pronounced. When she was guillotined they were even more jubilant – there were fireworks and singing and dancing in the streets. The world had gone completely mad.

IV

THE UNPRECEDENTED VIOLENCE AND wholesale bloodshed that the leaders of the French Revolution had instigated in France was totally deplored by the rest of Europe and by the middle of 1792, the rulers of many nations had become fearful that their own under-privileged might follow the example of their French brethren and rise up against them and throw their country into chaos. And when Louis XVI had been tried and found guilty of treason, the provocation was too much for Prussia, Spain, Holland, the Austrian Empire and Britain, all of which declared war.

The reply of the French revolutionary leader, Georges Danton, to what he described as "a Kings' Alliance" was to warn them that he would "hurl the King of France's head at their feet". In fact, he took the first step in this direction at the beginning of the following year, when he had the sovereign guillotined and his head stuck on a pike and displayed before thousands of cheering Parisians.

The Allied armies responded by invading France and advancing towards Paris. Danton met force with force and his large and inspired Republican army not only repelled the invaders but pushed on and, for a short time, the red, white and blue *tricoleur* of the fledgling Republic flew over Frankfurt, parts of Flanders and Antwerp.

An important part of the Allied army that forced the French to retreat back to Paris was a British expeditionary force including cavalry squadrons from the Inniskilling Dragoon Guards, the Blues[11] and the

---
[11] The Royal Horseguards.

Royals. For the recently promoted, twenty-three-year-old Captain Sir Jean-Marc Scott-Quetteville, this was his first period of active service and nobody was in the least surprised that he acquitted himself well during both the great cavalry exploits – Beaumont and Willems.

At the time when the Blues were about to return to England, Major David Black, who was in charge of Special Operations, selected Jean-Marc and several other officers to join him in a covert operation to rescue certain important nobles from France. On his subsequent return to England, he was granted some well-earned leave.

Lady Nicole was overjoyed at the totally unexpected return of her soldier son and insisted on having a celebration that same evening. It was an impromptu and relaxed home-coming dinner party, attended by Rachelle and Nathalie Bassett and a few other friends. The conversation and the wine flowed until the early hours of the morning, after which Jean-Marc, completely exhausted from his toils over the past weeks and his long journey from France, slept soundly for several days.

Before Jean-Marc's return to duty, Lord Bassett who, since Sir John had been killed, treated Jean-Marc as an adopted son, said he wanted to have a dinner for him at which he intended to invite Colonel Tuffnell, a former colonel of the Blues. These arrangements were subsequently changed as, before the arrival home of Jean-Marc, Nicole had arranged a dinner party to return the hospitality of the Prime Minister William Pitt, who had, on two separate occasions, entertained her at private functions in his home. After some discussion, Nicole and David decided to combine their guest lists and have the dinner at 22 St James's Square. Because his mother had not met Major Black, his commanding officer, Jean-Marc suggested that she add his name to the list and, knowing that he would not be back in London for quite some time, the young baronet had no intention of omitting Rachelle Bassett's name, either.

The dinner party was a great success and, in the politically and socially safe ambience of the Scott-Quetteville home, the young prime minister relaxed and was – as he had been on several previous occasions – quite the life of the party.

After the guests had left and before going upstairs to his bedroom, Jean Marc said goodnight to his mother and thanked her for arranging such a pleasant evening for him. While the two of them were alone, Nicole took the opportunity to mention to him that, earlier that day, she had received a letter from Joseph Fouché. She passed him the letter to read and waited a little time for him to make some comment. After a few moments silence, he asked her –

"You are not going to Lyon to see him – are you?"

"I most certainly am going – and for three reasons. Firstly, it will most probably be an extremely lucrative contract; secondly, it will keep the evil Republicans from throwing their weight around and compulsorily acquiring our properties in Marseille; and finally, if we do not become involved, someone else will."

"I am a little out of touch and I do not want to express an opinion on a topic I know very little about – but please Mother, be careful."

Nicole smiled in a happy but slightly accommodating way.

"In fact, Jean-Marc, I was not asking your permission to go, nor is it my business to ask – nor yours to tell me – anything about what you, Major Back and your friends do in France. On the other hand, I thought you might like to know where I shall be for the next month or so."

Jean-Marc took a breath in preparation to say something – but thought better of it. He kissed his mother good night – in silence.

* * *

The following morning, on the way to their country estate near Woking, Lord and Lady Bassett paid Nicole a short visit. Being particularly close friends, they spent quite a time discussing the conversation of the previous evening. David Bassett said he had been impressed with Jean-Marc's commander, the young Major David Black.

"It gave me a great sense of security to know Jean-Marc is serving under such a fine young man and it gave me even more happiness to meet up again with my old friend, Colonel Tuffnell, a fine soldier, if ever there was one – and sadly missed since his retirement."

Nicole, who had not previously met Tuffnell, thanked David for being the catalyst that brought the former colonel of the Blues to her home.

"He is charming, handsome and amusing. What more can a hostess ask of her male guests?"

"And he was one of the army's best regimental commanders, too. The good thing is that he left behind many competent young officers like Black who teach as much by example as they do by precept. For a man of only thirty-three, Black has seen more years of active service than most of his contemporaries. The prime minister informed me that he had seen Black several times in connection with secret missions in France and before that there had been excellent reports about him when he had been on secondment to our embassy in Paris. Pitt told me he was most impressed with the courageous and skilful manner in which he had masterminded a really tricky and dangerous mission in Paris."

Lady Hélène who, the previous evening, had seen the way Jean-Marc's eyes had lit up when the prime minister praised the daring of the major and his small team of officers in accomplishing their task, and being unaware that Jean-Marc had been part of the team, remarked –

"I am certain that had Jean-Marc been one of his officers in France he would have acquitted himself admirably, too."

Nicole smiled. "Within the four walls of this house, I can tell you that he was – and he did. As he is bilingual, he was given the task of doing most of the talking. However, because their work is by no means finished, the less the matter is discussed the better. I thought it was significant that while he was speaking about the sortie, the prime minister deliberately did not look in Jean-Marc's direction."

Retired Colonel, Lord Bassett, who apparently knew more about the current Paris scene than most, underlined the necessity for secrecy.

"And there are far too many wagging socialite tongues that do not realise that England – and especially London – is inundated with French spies."

Both women indicated that they fully agreed – and Nicole was quite outspoken about the iniquities of the French Revolution.

"I am quite disgusted. During the past two years, the savage cruelty of these new rulers of France is at least as evil as the king and *l'ancien régime* who murdered Hélène's father. Far too many members of the *Directoire* and the *Assemblée nationale* have completely lost their senses. They seem to have an insatiable thirst for blood and are torturing and murdering innocent people for no reason at all. I am sure they are spying on us — and anyone else here in London with property or business interests in France."

"Although we trust our servants," said Hélène, "the only time we even mention France is when we are quite by ourselves or are out riding. It really is hard for Jennings who is truly loyal and would give his life for us. As he is such a compulsive gossip, we really do have to be careful."

The Bassetts, having fulfilled the purpose of their visit — to thank Nicole for the excellent party and to ask her to join their Woking Grange hunt for the weekend — took their leave. They were heading towards Epsom, where one of their three-year-old fillies was having its first race. Rachelle, who had stayed overnight with Jean-Marc, looked more beautiful than ever. Her broad-brimmed, pale blue and white hat, with flowing ribbons — the Bassett racing colours — matched her charming dress. She always loved to wear these colours when her father's horses were running. Seeing her radiant, slightly flushed complexion, Nicole and Hélène exchanged glances and concealed their amusement; but not hidden well enough for the ever alert Rachelle. She bade her hostess goodbye.

"Thank you, Cuzz darling, for a wonderful dinner party and for having me to stay."

As she kissed Nicole she quietly added —

"But I hate both you and my simpering mother. You are very mean — and envious."

The three females laughed — and the two males had no idea why.

Major Black had stayed overnight at his club and, ten minutes after the departure of the Bassett family, he arrived in a regimental carriage to collect Jean-Marc for their return to Northampton.

* * *

When the plans for the Blues' first sortie into Paris had been worked out, knowing what an ideal overnight stopover Etreham would be for the escaped nobles on their way to the coast, the young captain had suggested it to Major Black. The idea was discussed with Lord and Lady Bassett and, at the appropriate time, three of the major's team — all reasonably fluent in French — had become live-in "farm workers" at the château – complete with well-forged "until after the harvest" exemptions from military service. They set about studying every small byway and track between Etreham and the coast and they became familiar with almost every house and property they would have to pass. This reconnaissance had taken them five weeks to complete and the care they had taken learning the routes was reflected in the total success of the second part of the "evacuation" plan – getting the nobles from Etreham to the coast.

On their way back to their barracks, the major imparted to his protégé a broad outline of the special mission that he had been given by the prime minister, two days previously. He began his explanation of what was going to happen in a rather strange way.

"Scott, when you are away from home, how often do you write letters – and to whom do you write?"

Jean-Marc did his best to conceal his surprise that such a question should be put to him.

"When we are apart, my mother and I exchange letters at least once each week; I write to my younger brother in Frankfurt quite often – and I write frequently to one of Lord Bassett's daughters. And, as one never knows when ships are going to New South Wales, I write to my other brother, François, about once each month."

"I presume that he is not there during the king's pleasure," quipped the major, smiling.

"No, sir! He is on Captain Arthur Phillip's staff. He is the victualling officer and he spends some of his time in Table Bay, procuring livestock and stores."

"An interesting job for a young man."

The major paused for a few moments and then surprised Jean-Marc a second time.

"Good! You and three other officers are being given leave and you are all going fishing in Scotland. Over the next few days I want you to write enough letters to your mother, your brothers and Miss Bassett, to cover you for six weeks. The letters should be consecutive and be about your happy times fishing. Captain Kinross of B Squadron comes from Nairne and he will tell you everything you can possibly want to know about that part of Scotland. These letters will be carefully dated and the envelopes left open. You will be briefed about the castle in which you will be staying, your hosts and the friends you meet there. If there are any answers to your letters, you will eventually receive them."

"Yes, sir! I understand completely. This is to be the cover plan for our return to France."

"Correct! However, we might come back to England by way of Nairne and stay there for some days. The two men we are to bring back with us will go on to Inverness, where they will remain for about a month."

"Do I have your permission to ask questions, sir?"

"As many as you wish."

"How many people will you take with you, sir?"

"The same five as last time – but with this task, I do not think I shall have to call on you, as before, to be a rough-speaking guard at the Paris barricade, a dissatisfied coach driver from Strasbourg and a drunken sailor in Le Havre."

"It was good fun – and it worked out well."

"Yes, but we must be even more careful than we were before. Although the loyalty of all the staff and workers at the Château Etreham is not doubted, the local representative of the Committee for Public Safety knows the place is owned by an English lord."

"Sir, we know that only too well. Completely without any notice at all, they suddenly send people to search through all the châteaux in the area and we know how painstakingly thorough they are. Monsieur Lambert regularly goes through every room and every cupboard with the proverbial fine tooth comb and there is not a single item in the place that could suggest that everyone in the Etreham château – proprietors, staff and workers – are not completely wedded to the ideals of the new Republic. Lady Hélène is French and the daughter of a martyr to the cause and everyone knows it. The Committee also knows that all the young men of military age who worked at the château will be sent off to join the army as soon as the harvest has been brought in; that is, if they have not already gone."

"But could not this erode the loyalty of their families?"

"No sir! Their families are still permitted to remain on the property without paying rent and they are being given the same foodstuffs as before. The Bassetts anticipated the call-up and acted quickly. They also provide food for the families of the local troops. Lambert, who was Lady Hélène's father's quartermaster, is very clever."

Neither of the two men spoke for several minutes and, although he wanted to know more about their next operation, Jean-Marc thought it would be more prudent if he waited for the major to speak. He did not have to wait long.

"Although the last report we received from Paris, four weeks ago, stated that the two men we have been ordered to bring to England are still free, by the time we get to Paris, they could well be in one of the prisons. If they are not, our task will be less complicated. To be on the safe side, I am working on the basis that we must either rescue them from prison or, more difficult still, waylay a tumbrel or two, on their way to *la Place de Greve,* where they have just erected one of these new decapitating scaffolds that the people call the Guillotine."

"I have read something about it in the newspapers."

"The new *Assemblée nationale* has voted almost unanimously to adopt this new way to execute people. The rationale behind the legislation is quite remarkable — until now it has always been customary for poor people to die a horrendously painful and lingering death, whereas the nobility have had the privilege of being given a quick and painless dispatch — usually with a sword or an axe. Well, things have changed! In France there is now equality in all things — even in the way they put to death their condemned citizens!"

"God! Haven't they more urgent things to consider? Who in the hell raised this ghoulish subject?"

"It was one of the Deputies from Paris — Dr Joseph Guillotin. He spoke at great length about the cruelty of some executioners and the lack of skill of others. He quoted statistics to demonstrate that, even when they are trying to be quick and merciful, as there are now so many victims to be liquidated, so tired do the headsmen become that, for the last executions, they are so exhausted that they have to wield their sword — or axe — three or four times before the poor prisoner is dead."

"You are not being serious, are you?"

"Quite serious! The newspapers have applauded the doctor and all the delegates who spoke in favour of his motion. In the French newspapers there have even been drawings of the model scaffold he produced to the Assembly. It was a Dr Antoine Louis, the secretary of the Academy of Surgeons who invented the machine and, according to all the journalists who witnessed the trials with animals – and even the dead bodies of humans – the sharp, heavily weighted blade can sever a head instantly. In the Assembly the doctor kept referring to it as the *Louisette* but the newspapers simply called it the decapitation machine. Almost immediately the Parisians started euphemising the death penalty as "paying a visit to Doctor Guillotin" – and now the word *guillotine* has stuck.

"We have already started building up a phantom escape route via Strasbourg. At places along the way strange things are happening – we have peasants driving carts that look like they could be carrying fugitives. We have had a big wine cask made with another barrel inside it. The idea is that if border guards spike a hole in the barrel, wine will pour out but anyone concealed in the inner barrel would be safe."

"Are we going to use it on our mission, sir?"

"Heavens no! We are going to ensure that it accidentally falls off a cart. The finder will rush with it to the Committee for Public Safety to get a reward and, from then on, they will empty every wine barrel that is heading to Germany. Nearly all the wine exported goes through Strasbourg."

"That appears to be a terrible waste of good wine, sir. My family has a big vineyard not far from Strasbourg and we export a large quantity of wine to Germany. I cannot bear to think of losing most of our wine."

The major, whose razor sharp brain had immediate solutions for almost every problem anyone might raise – and on any subject – did not disappoint his protégé.

"The answer to the problem is simple – put export wine in special barrels with removable tops so that the barricade guards can test each one without wasting the wine and ruining the cask – or bottle it all before it leaves the winery. Even so it is important to have a few bottles of the wine handy to give to the guards."

"We always do that, sir."

"As we want to keep the Channel route open, the escapees will be rehearsed so that, having reached the safety of England, they will tell people that they escaped by way of Strasbourg. Taking them to Scotland first is a further safety measure. The French have spies in Portsmouth and London – and the other ports in the south of England, too."

The major was looking out of the window of the carriage as he continued his briefing.

"Scott-Quetteville, I am giving you this early notice as I want you to go to Paris well before the rest of us – in fact, as soon as possible – and I want you to have a full understanding of our plan before you go. Unless we are forced to change everything, two people will remain in Etreham and the rest of us will be in Paris."

"Is it appropriate that the team members – other than you – should know anything about the two men we intend to bring back to England?"

"No reason at all. You have probably read that when they execute a noble or a wealthy landowner, they confiscate all his wealth. Already they have seized millions of francs worth of art treasures and paintings – and as much in gold coin. The proceeds from international sales and the money they have confiscated are paying for their new Republican army and its weapons. The many nobles who are still at large and the enormously wealthy people who fear for their lives are hiding their valuables in safe places and intend to leave them there until sanity and justice once more return to France and law and order is restored. Our two men, are, in fact, astute nobles – father and son – and are among the wealthiest people in France. They apparently have an extraordinarily well concealed hiding place for their own wealth and they have at least twice as much again of treasures belonging to their friends who have either been executed already or else who have fled the country."

"Sir, from what you have said, am I to take it that we are really talking about tens of millions of pounds of treasure?"

"Yes we are; but our aim is not to bring all the '*bonnes choses*[12]' back to England – at least, not at this stage. We are charged with rescuing the two

---

[12] Goodies.

nobles. If we are successful, the British will be entitled to one half of what we can salvage."

"Phew! But what about the treasures of the nobles who have already been executed?"

"This has yet to be negotiated; however, the father – we are to call him 'Paul' – is confident that the deal will be the same. He states he has a *Procuration* – Power of Attorney – over all the assets of many other French nobles; but this has yet to be verified. He has told our people that, when some of his friends, who are now dead, were arrested, they were offered immunity against prosecution for them and their families and a permit to leave the country, in return for their worldly possessions. You would not believe it but, as soon as their captors had laid their greedy, greasy hands on their captives' artworks and gold, they murdered them and their families in cold blood."

"The filthy bastards! How revolting!"

"Some of those who remain – or who are now safely out of the country – still have a fortune in gold, jewellery and works of art hidden in the count's special underground Midas cave, the whereabouts of which is known only to him and his son."

"This is a great challenge for us – save the two nobles and then go back for the loot. I cannot imagine anything I'd like better to do."

"Amusing, yes – but we are playing for big stakes – our lives."

"Sir, I am not suggesting it is going to be easy – but it will be fun, I am sure. Tracking down where King Midas has his cave and bringing the '*bonnes choses*' – as you call them – back to England will be even more exciting."

"The gold coin and the other cumbersome items will have to remain in France until goodness knows when – but the paintings and the jewellery we hope to bring back to England, little by little."

It was more than a minute before Jean-Marc broke the silence.

"Will the English government make a fortune out of all this?"

"Truly, Scott-Quetteville, I do not care one iota. Our job is to bring the two men back to Britain and then, some of the *bonbons* – as 'Paul' keeps calling them. Someone else can work out the arithmetic. However, I do know that the prime minister would like to use some of the money to enable him to ransom some more of the innocent people who are being murdered in their hundreds. Those blood-thirsty monsters, Robespierre and Danton — and their henchmen — have gone much too far. However, they might slow down a little after the lesson we taught them when we sent their expeditionary forces in Antwerp and Brussels packing."

"I shall always remember Flanders. Although it was probably just another battle for you, sir, for me it was anything but. It was my first time in action."

"And you did well, Scott. Although the Blues fought bravely and effectively, the whole operation was a bugger's muddle from start to finish. It was not until Colonel Vyse of the King's Dragoon Guards took over the command of our troops that we defeated the French at Beaumont and Willems."

* * *

As they drove into the regimental headquarters in Northampton — where they had just completed building the British army's first riding school — the major, seeing all the equitation activity, changed the subject.

"At last we have a proper place to teach young men how to ride. I can only hope that now we shall see an improvement in the standard of horsemanship in the regiment. Half the recruits and more than half the young officers could not ride to save themselves. They would fall off a hobby horse."

When their carriage came to a halt, the major who usually lost no time in alighting, did not move.

"When will you be ready to leave for France?"

"I shall leave tomorrow. It is not at all difficult for me to leave the country unseen — on one of The Bridge Company's vessels. I should like your permission, sir, to enter France through Marseille."

The request surprised the major.

"Do you have a special reason for wanting to go in such a roundabout way?"

"Yes sir! According to Lord Bassett, the direct route from Paris to the coast is now crawling with spies and informers. Hundreds of *émigrés*[13]

---

[13] The nobles who successfully escaped from France.

have flooded the north of France on their way to England and the National Guard – and nearly as many spies – are making it a particularly dangerous route. Before I report to you in Paris, I should like to look at Marseille as a possible port from which to evacuate them."

"Being aware that Marseille is your bailiwick and that your local knowledge and contacts there are excellent, I think your suggestion is sound. When you are in the south of France I think you should have a look at Avignon, too. Since they have voted by plebiscite to cut themselves off from the Vatican and become part of the French Republic, we are giving the city a wide berth."

"In your last briefing, sir, you told us all that, unless you are particularly confident, once you snatch our men from their prisons – or wherever – you prefer to hide them in France until things settle down and the coast is clear – or, at least, clearer. Is that still the plan?"

"Definitely so! The authorities are after literally thousands of nobles. Provided they have plenty of them to arraign before the people's tribunal and, from there to their new decapitation machine, they seem to be happy. After a couple of weeks of intense searching for those we have rescued from their clutches, they seem to forget about them.

"As soon as you reach Paris I want you to look carefully and thoroughly at our hiding places – the routes leading to them and the nearby houses from whose windows people entering and leaving can be watched."

"Yes, sir."

"Since every day counts, I hope to be in Paris before you get there. They are arresting nobles at such a rate that most of them have to rot in one or other of the Paris prisons for months awaiting trial. If our two men are still at large, we shall hide them away at once. If they are in prison awaiting trial – or worse – it is my intention to get hold of them without delay. If it takes another few weeks to get them out of France, it will certainly not be the end of the world. Any questions?"

"No sir!"

"I shall bring the rest of the team to Paris within five weeks – the sooner the better – and you know the rendezvous?"

"Yes sir!"

The two men alighted from the carriage, exchanged salutes and went their separate ways.

*　*　*

After the departure of Captain Scott-Quetteville for Marseille, Major Black and his young officers worked on a number of possible operational plans to bring the two French nobles to London. As well as being fully cognisant of all the facets of the royalist movement, each of these men had extensive knowledge of the organisation of the new Republican government in France and its National Guard. They had reliable sources of information and they were in touch with their spies whom they had planted in a number of the Jacobin clubs[14].

As the wharves of the ports in southern England were under the constant surveillance of French spies, the "special" force always travelled unobtrusively as deckhands and did nothing to attract attention. The small ships in which they made the Channel crossing had little difficulty in landing them in Abbeville in the middle of the night.

After their arrival in France, it did not take the major long to learn that all the streets of Etreham, Bayeux and Le Havre were infested with dozens of soldiers of the new National Guard and almost as many spies and informers. The Committee for Public Safety had publicly stated that it was fed up with the inefficient manner in which the checkpoints were being managed and the apparent freedom with which almost anyone could come and go as they pleased. An edict had been issued that if any of the guards permitted a noble or a royalist through his checkpoint or road block, the penalty would be death.

As soon as he landed in France, the major met his senior – and most trusted – informant and asked him about Lord Bassett's château.

"Sir, the news is not good. Although the local branch of the Committee for Public Safety have had the château where you stayed last time searched and have found nothing at all suspicious, a National Guard officer and three men have moved in and are actually sleeping there. The

---

[14] These Jacobin "clubs" were in all the cities and many of the larger towns in each Département (region) of France. They had a headquarters which assumed the authority to arrest, to charge and try – and to execute people.

route through Amiens to Flanders is as full of National Guard troops as Normandy is."

"Well, you have lived here all your life. Tell me, please, if you wished to get people to England, which route would you take?"

"If my life were at stake, I should take the long road south and head towards the Mediterranean, sir."

"Why – and how?"

"Why? Because there is much more royal support in places like Beaune, Lyon, Toulon and Marseille. From what we hear, there are far fewer troops and police in the south. To raise money, Robespierre has grabbed everything he can lay his hands on, pillaged the Catholic Church and compelled the clergy to take oaths of allegiance to the Republic. Flexing their Republican muscles, they have passed new laws covering each and every aspect of the people's daily lives. There are new laws that give women greater rights with regard to divorce; and Fouché – himself an ex-cleric – has come down like a ton of bricks on the clergy. They have all had to swear allegiance to the Republic – ahead of their duty to the Vatican, and those refusing to take the oath have been defrocked. There has even been an edict issued to end the celibacy of the priesthood and they are forbidden to wear clerical robes when they are not actually conducting a service."

The major laughed.

"From what I know about the Catholic clergy in France – and, for that matter, the English priests, too – celibacy is as rare as rocking-horse manure."

"And the confession box is where much of it goes on," added Lieutenant Palmer – one of the major's officers who was sitting with the pair of them.

The laughter that followed was terminated by Major Black who was keen for his agent to continue.

"The French people born and bred in the south are a law unto themselves and newcomers are always made unwelcome, be they Bourbons or Jacobins. They like neither the new Republic nor the people who are trying to force it on everyone."

"It is certainly a long and roundabout way to get from Paris to the British Isles but I think your appreciation of the situation is realistic."

The major, having thanked his informer and having seen him ride off, called his small team together.

"That settles it. We are not only wasting our time here, we are exposing ourselves and our friends at the château to unnecessary danger. We are moving at once to Paris. You all know the rendezvous and you all know the drill – keep just close enough to each other to be mutually supporting."

* * *

Captain Scott-Quetteville did not reach Paris until a week after the others. At first Major Black was annoyed that he had been kept waiting. Nevertheless, as Jean-Marc finished giving him a detailed report on where he had been and what he had done, he realised that the time the captain had spent in reconnaissance had certainly not been wasted. He asked Jean-Marc a number of questions and then went off to his room to formulate his plan. Fifteen minutes later he called his officers together.

"We now have as much information as we are likely to obtain and every day we wait could make our task more difficult. Please listen carefully! Our operation will unfold in three phases. The first phase will be meeting up with – or capturing – the two nobles we are to take out of this country. The second part of our operation will involve hiding them and then getting them to Marseille; and the final phase will be to get them on a ship and back to England. By far the most difficult part of the operation will possibly be the first."

When one of the team asked why this was so, he replied –

"They may have already been arrested and be in the Les Carmes prison, awaiting trial. It is the prison they are now using. In spite of all the executions, the other ones are full."

"Les Carmes!" exploded Scott-Quetteville. "Sir, it is as hard to get into or out of that hell hole as it is to get past the pearly gates of Heaven."

"Tell me, Scott-Quetteville, what you know about it."

"It has the reputation of being the worst prison in Paris. It is situated on Rue Vaugirard and, of the more than forty gaols in Paris, although it has only been used as a prison since August when France was bracing itself for a foreign invasion, it has already gained notoriety as a vile den of torture and murder. After the recent September massacres nearly a hundred priests – who would not swear allegiance to the Republic – were mercilessly hacked to death there. A noble who escaped gave me a graphic picture. The walls, stone steps, ceilings and the cobbles are splashed with blood and the pungent smell of unwashed bodies, human dung and urine makes many of the inmates vomit – rendering the place even more revolting. There are rooms they call dormitories and up to fifteen people are crammed into each of them. They are filthy vermin-infested cesspits where the privations and miseries of the prisoners are supplemented with painful infections that develop from rat bites."

"How nice! Were you able to collect any information about the routine of the place?"

"Yes sir. The only positive things I learnt were that there is always plenty of bread and that all the inmates are given half a bottle of wine, daily. Each morning, all the prisoners – male and female – are herded together into the forecourt. The names of those who are to appear before the revolutionary tribunal are announced. There is a cart there waiting and, with a minimum of fuss, the batch of victims disappears. They are tried and go straight from the tribunal to their place of execution."

"Thank you, Scott-Quetteville! You have painted a vivid – but not pretty – picture. How did your informer escape?"

He bribed a prison guard – promised him a fortune – five thousand livres in gold – and when, the same night as the count was spirited out of the place, he handed the money over to the guard, the fellow who had another cab waiting, gathered up his gold, leapt into the cab and drove off. Apparently he has never been heard of since. He told the count that he and his family would flee from Paris that same night."

"You say there are both men and women in the prison. Are they all nobles?"

"I think not, sir. The Comte de Chevrey, my informant, said he had never seen such a *mélange* of humanity in all his life. Nobles, senior army officers whose campaigns had failed, lawyers, teachers, artisans, deputies – and even laundresses."

Major Black could not help smiling.

"In France, they certainly give their generals a great incentive to win their battles. Just as a matter of interest, did the count tell you if the males are separated from the females?"

"He said that they were meant to be apart but, like almost all the other prisons in France, the place is a hotbed of rampant concupiscence. Apparently, the whole atmosphere is one of amorous frenzy in which all privacy has, by circumstance, been thrown to the winds. De Chevrey told me that, all through the night one can hear 'love talk, kisses and involuntary gasps of ecstasy'. The almost certain death that awaits them all seems to arouse in them insatiable sexual passion."

"Thank you, Scott-Quetteville, you will certainly have some good stories to recount in the officers' mess when we get back to Northampton."

The major studied his little map of Paris and asked Jean-Marc a number of questions concerning the route taken by the carts on the way to the revolutionary tribunal — and that of the tumbrels going to the Place de Carousel, in front of the Tuileries Palace where the scaffold of the decapitation machine had been erected.

"When I was here several months ago, the *machine* was in la Place de Greve. Apparently, sir, they moved it about a month ago. The route offers a number of opportunities for an ambush, particularly when there are two or three tumbrels going one after the other."

The following day they learned that as Major Black had feared, both 'Paul' and son had been arrested several weeks before he had arrived in Paris and, as was expected, they were incarcerated in Les Carmes. He immediately sent Scott-Quetteville to le Comte de Chevrey's contact to explore ways and means of getting his two nobles out of the prison. Having located the go-between who had arranged the Chevrey escape, Jean-Marc reported back the progress that had been made and the probability of having everything finalised quite soon.

* * *

In Rue Vaugirard, outside one of the pedestrian gates of the already notorious Les Carmes prison, a pathetically clad, unshaven workman was going through the motions of sweeping the pavement. He had been doing this in an unobtrusive way for more than an hour. A slovenly dressed corporal emerged from the gaol and as he passed the street-sweeper he was addressed.

"*Citoyen* Corporal Vernier! Can we meet somewhere and talk business."

The corporal did not turn his head to see who was addressing him – and he knew only too well the business the sweeper wanted to discuss. He did not even alter his stride.

"Same place – one hour."

He went on his way and the street-sweeper continued to clear away a few of the heaps of rubbish that littered the street.

An hour later, two men – the same two men – sat on a park seat, each absorbed in reading *La Réforme,* one of the left-wing newspapers. The spruced up street-sweeper came straight to the point.

"There are two more for you – both with good pockets."

"Assignats[15] are not acceptable – it's gold or nothing."

"Gold – I've told my people already."

"What have they been charged with? You know if it's treason it's five thousands livres."

"How much will it be if it's not treason? They have not yet been charged with anything."

"Two thousand each – and that's not dear. You know it has to be split four ways – the gaoler, *le charretier-de-merde*[16], the coalman and me."

"Is the *charretier* the same man as usual?"

"Yes."

"Same time?"

"Yes – and Wednesday – and 10 per cent tomorrow evening, here at eight."

"Too soon. I can't get the money before Sunday."

"Good! Sunday, at eight."

A few seconds later the now plain-clothed corporal departed and several minutes afterwards, the second man folded his paper and strolled off in the opposite direction.

---

[15] The currency introduced by the Revolutionary Government.
[16] Night cart driver.

• Part II – IV •

* * *

The sanitation arrangements in Les Carmes were in keeping with everything else there. The accommodation and facilities for the guards and gaolers were reasonably satisfactory but for the prisoners everything was disgusting. A cart arrived every second day to take away the sewage from the staff quarters, but the prisoners were not nearly as well served. The method of disposal was for the full latrine buckets to be tipped into some big barrels that sat on top of a big horse-drawn cart. The smell was vile and, as the four draught-horses that pulled the cart trotted along, sewage was liberally splashed on the cobbles.

The resourceful driver's imaginative brother, who was a *tonnelier* – a cooper – had made several big casks into which a person could be placed and sealed, so that the top of the open barrel would look the same as the other containers. A carefully concealed pipe was fitted to the lower compartment of the barrel so that the occupant could breathe. Even with this air tube, the smell was revolting; however, it seldom took more than an hour to reach a sufficiently safe place for the escaped prisoner to be unloaded. One of the agreed conditions was that, before the cart arrived at the prison, the driver had to ensure that the money had been placed in the casks the prisoners would be occupying; so that, if something went wrong – and it sometimes did – the gaoler and the guard would not miss out on their money. The sponsors of these escape attempts had to take all the risks.

The deposit for Major Black's people's escape was paid on the Sunday – as promised – and everything was prepared in the "safe house" where they were to be hidden. The only guard post that had to be passed was at the gate of the prison so that, once the *charrete* was heading along Rue Vaugirard, the main danger was over.

On the Wednesday the cart arrived on time and the prisoners were loaded into their barrels and "sealed" in. When nearly an hour had passed and they were still in the same place, they became apprehensive. They were later to learn that the gaoler and the corporal had held up their departure until they had checked the amount of money in the gold bags. The gate check, however, was quite cursory as the guards there did not want the revolting smell of the *charrete de merde* to remain near their guardhouse longer than absolutely necessary.

It was not more than two miles to the charbonnier's[17] yard and, a few minutes after their arrival there, greatly relieved, the escapees were able to breathe some fresh air and stretch their cramped legs. As soon as they had recovered, they were stitched into two sooty bags and loaded with other coal bags on to the wagon that was to deliver them to Rue des Fleurs. As it was evening, it was not at all difficult to carefully unload the two sacks into the street coal hole of their "safe house" without attracting attention.

Lieutenant Palmer was there waiting for them and not many minutes later, the major and another member of his team, who had been following at a safe distance in case of trouble, also arrived. The two freed men were overjoyed at being able to have a bath, put on some clean clothes, have their sores treated with disinfectant ointment – and sit down to a meal. Not much more than an hour later they were safely in bed and sound asleep.

The following morning the count and his son explored their surroundings and were amazed at what they saw. They were two levels below the ground floor of the building and they were in one of three big rooms that contained everything from a row of National Guard uniforms and a printing machine to a make-up table and mirror and racks of small arms. At a desk with a bright lamp on either side of it, a bespectacled Frenchman was busy forging Robespierre's signature on a *laissez-passer*[18]. Immediately in front of him were two genuine passes that he was copying. There were books in which names and addresses – all in code – were written and on the wall was a huge street plan of Paris. There were several open wardrobes, containing a wide variety of clothing, and boot racks on which there were dozens of pairs of boots and shoes.

The entry to this floor – the inner sanctum of the British Special Operations unit – was by way of a series of remarkably well concealed doors. As they were later to find out, part of the building had been sealed off by bricking up all the doorways but one. This led to another coal

---

[17] Coal merchant.
[18] A permit to travel.

storage cellar and the part of the house that was accessed from Rue des Fleurs. The small entrance from the cellar to the inner sanctum was well hidden and the door itself so solid that its existence was virtually impossible to detect – all the more so as the amount of daylight admitted when the hatch of the coal hole was raised, was negligible.

There were many houses in Paris that had access from the bedrooms of the upper floors to the back of the bedrooms of houses in the next street, the doorway between the two buildings being reached from the back of a big wardrobe! This not uncommon feature was popular as it made it possible for a lover to buy a house in the next street and thus have a safe way of reaching his *amante* unseen. It made *liaisons* much less *dangereuses* than they otherwise would have been. In the work that Major Black and his officers were doing, it gave them additional security.

The major advised his guests that it could be several weeks or longer before they left Paris and that, until they departed for the coast, suitable accommodation would be found for them. He asked the father for details of the "material" he had managed to hide away and he compared this with the inventory he had been given in Whitehall. Black was surprised – and pleased – to learn that the count's list was almost as long again as the one he had been given before leaving London.

"Monsieur, where on earth is all of this hidden?"

"There are two depositories – one is not far from Paris, in Chantilly; the other is in the mountains, in Provence."

"I apologise, Monsieur for having to be so direct – and appearing so untrusting. My instructions are that, before we leave Paris, I must inspect the cache of gold and chattels. The British government appreciates your position and I have here a document that gives you – and the people whose assets you are guarding – as much security as, under the circumstances, is possible."

The count studied the dossier the major handed him.

"I really have no option, but there is one thing of which I am quite certain – anything is better than that hell hole of a prison. Major Black, until my son and I were thrown into the dreadful place, I did not think that it would be possible for human beings to survive in such indescribably vile-smelling and filthy surroundings."

***

The next day they drove out of Paris to Chantilly to the vast Condé Palace. The Prince de Condé had fled from France in 1789 and the place was deserted except for the few peasant farmers who had moved into some of the many outbuildings. About one hundred metres beyond the walls of the palace was an old, stone barn, the roof and part of the walls of which had collapsed.

Leaving their carriage in the Chantilly woods, the count and his son directed David Black towards the dilapidated barn. Quite near it was a disused well, hidden from view by the barn and a sprawling rose briar and a couple of hawthorn bushes. With so many other empty buildings near the palace, it was no wonder that this virtually inaccessible place had been completely overlooked.

'Paul' entered the barn and after some noisy rummaging, he returned with a rope ladder and a big bag. Signalling to Major Black to follow him, he descended into the well and, twelve feet below the surface, he started removing old bricks, which he placed in the bag. Behind this masonry was a wooden hatch – a little over two feet square. He pushed it open and, without much difficulty he entered a big underground room. Black followed him. Looking inside the room he could see that there was a ladder – quite a strong one – against the wall and, by the time he had negotiated it and was standing in the room, 'Paul' had lit two lanterns. There, before the major's eyes, was the most amazing sight he had ever seen. Scattered everywhere were ornaments of gold and silver, many small paintings, sculptures, and boxes and bags full of jewellery, gold coins and trinkets. Against one wall were dozens of ornate, gilded picture frames – all of them empty. The count showed the major stack after stack of carefully rolled canvases, works of the old masters of France, Italy and Holland. Covered in cloth were heaps of old books – a manuscript of Martin Luther and first editions of Gutenberg and Caxton. David Black, before whose eyes there were treasures worth tens of millions of pounds, was speechless.

"And what is the value of all these magnificent things to us if we are not alive to enjoy them?" the count asked rhetorically.

The major was trying to focus on how he could safely deliver this treasure to his prime minister. His mind flashed back to the *Madre de Deus,* the Portuguese galleon the British captured at the end of the sixteenth century.

"Monsieur, surely you did not bring all these things into this room by way of the well?"

"Heavens no! There is an entrance through the barn, but to have removed the rubble, today, and to rearrange it afterwards would have taken more than an hour. My son and I come here as rarely as possible and always at night. We now remove paintings from their frames and prepare them for storage before we bring them here."

"I can well understand that."

Observing the count's slightly worried expression, he reassured him.

"You can rest assured that everything removed by us and taken to England will be properly accounted for."

"Thank you sir. I have been most impressed with the thoroughness with which you and your officers go about everything you do and, I can assure you, I have full confidence in your competence and integrity."

They reached Paris as it was getting dark and they alighted from the carriage a little way from the checkpoint at the big gates. They approached the barricade on foot and, with many people returning home from their work, their identity papers – the same as everybody else's – were hardly looked at. The carriage met them half an hour later and they went back to Rue de Chêne – the next street to Rue des Fleurs – where they entered their house in the same way as the major and his officers usually did – through the back of a wardrobe, on the first floor.

Later, after 'Paul' and his son were taken to where they would be staying until they left Paris, Black and Jean-Marc went out to have some dinner. David had a number of friends in Paris, all of whom knew where to find him when he was in France. When they had settled down and were enjoying a glass of wine, the major gave his colleague an account of his visit to Chantilly – describing everything in as much detail as possible. While Jean-Marc was sitting spellbound, taking it all in, a young man approached their table and quietly asked him if he would be as good as to follow him as a gentleman wished to speak with him.

"Monsieur, my friend, *citoyen,* I have just ordered my dinner. If you would care to come back here in thirty minutes, I should be very happy to meet this mysterious gentleman."

"But he is very important, sir."

"And so is my dinner!"

The man slunk away and David Black continued with his story.

Apparently the so-called very important man was prepared to wait, as the message-bearer returned as suggested. Having left David Black at the restaurant, Jean-Marc was led by the message-bearer along Boulevard Saint-Germain and, having reached an imposing property with a high stone wall and heavy wooden gates, the guide pulled the bell-cord. An old man in livery opened the pedestrian gate. As Jean-Marc entered the forecourt it suddenly came back to him that this was the home of Monsieur Bernard Creuse, the owner of the big *diligence*[19] and carriage company that had always provided carriages for his Uncle Pierre.

Monsieur Creuse was a charming man who, during Jean-Marc's boyhood, had taught him to drive all kinds of horse-drawn vehicles – some of them with as many as six in hand. He had one of the most successful transport businesses in France.

The entrance hall was beautifully lit and there were several large paintings on the walls. As Jean-Marc was shown into one of the reception rooms, Monsieur Creuse came towards him and gave him a warm welcome.

"How do you do, Jean-Marc? I am truly delighted to see you. I was walking past the *Café de ma Tante* and I could not believe my eyes when I saw you there sitting on the other side of the big window. I have not seen you since you were here at *l'École Militaire,* six or seven years ago. I thought you had left the French army and had gone to England."

"How really nice to see you, sir. Thank you for bothering to send your messenger to fetch me. How have you been keeping? I should expect that the way things are now in Paris, it is not easy to do business."

"You are right, life is terrible here in France and the world has gone quite crazy. Nevertheless, in spite of inflation and the cost of everything, business has never been better. Confidentially, I have to confess that I am

---

[19] Stage-coach.

making a fortune. Almost daily, nobles come to me and offer me the world to get them out of the country."

"Are you successful?"

"To date, very successful. All I need to do is to give them a month's training and well-forged identity papers."

"What training do you give them?"

"I teach them to drive a coach and four. Then they can work for me as drivers of my stage-coaches to places like Strasbourg and Wissembourg. The guards at the many checkpoints and the National Guard turn our passengers upside down and shake them to establish their identity and the reason they are travelling. When it comes to our drivers, all they want are copies of Paris newspapers, which, once one gets out into the country, are hard to come by and are expensive. We have no trouble at all getting good drivers in eastern France, to do the return trip to Paris."

"Very interesting, Monsieur Creuse, perhaps we may be able to do some business."

"When I saw you Jean-Marc, it did occur to me that you might be here to help some of your family's friends escape."

Jean-Marc had known this man since he was a small boy and he trusted him. In fact, ever since Uncle Pierre had introduced M. Creuse to the Quetteville family, the Creuse company had made all their carriages for them. Nevertheless, Jean-Marc felt that it was unnecessary to tell him about the work he was doing in Paris.

"What you say, sir, is indeed interesting. As a matter of fact, I have two very suitable men who would like to do one of your intensive courses in coach driving."

"Tell me about them!"

"One is what might be described as being past military age and the other, a corporal, has papers confirming that he is on 'harvest' leave from a National Guard unit in Marseille."

"Our coaches do not go to Marseille, but we have a daily trip to Lyon. It takes nearly four days to get there."

"My friends would both be happy to go to Lyon – and I can assure you, sir, that by tomorrow, the corporal will know more about the garrison there and the names of the officers than most of the soldiers in the regiment do."

"It is good to know you are so thorough in selecting people who wish to become *diligence* drivers. We insist that our trainees live at our depot, as we do not like them to be wandering about at night. It is so dangerous, you know. They are much safer here. Incidentally, how good are their papers?"

"They are excellent, nothing other than the best. I am sure that you would be impressed. Please could you tell me, sir, how much do you charge for the training course?"

"Unfortunately it is expensive – two thousand livres, in gold – but that includes the cost of their board and keep."

"Money is not a major problem, sir."

"It seldom is with these nobles – and they are more than willing to part with it if it can be used to buy them a safe passage to freedom."

After this interesting conversation, Jean-Marc excused himself and returned to his unit's house in Rue des Fleurs, where he gave Major Black a detailed account of his meeting.

"Very interesting, Scott! I should like to meet your friend Creuse as soon as possible, as we could easily have quite a few people who might find a course in *diligence* driving extremely valuable."

Sir, bearing in mind that my mother might well be in Lyon, I think I should go there in one of M. Creuse's coaches. I could be back within two weeks.

Having introduced Major Black to *citoyen* Creuse, Jean-Marc, well disguised as an attorney – and with a permit to travel – set out on his journey south.

V

ABOUT THREE HUNDRED MILES SOUTH EAST of Paris is Lyon. Dating back beyond the days of the Roman occupation, it has always been regarded as one of France's most important cities. Historically, the people of Lyon have had the reputation of being enterprising, industrious and with a mind of their own. In all countries it is almost inevitable that the confluence of two rivers attracts human habitation and development and, in this regard, Lyon is no exception. It is situated where the river Saône joins the Rhône; furthermore, since the days of Agrippa, Lyon has been the hub of the country's road system.

The dynamic and entrepreneurial nature of the people of Lyon dates as far back as the first century A.D., when its pottery industry became famous throughout Europe and, having been for centuries a crossroads for travellers, its trade exhibitions have attracted manufacturers and buyers from all over the world. During one of the cyclic economic slumps in the fifteenth century, with the active support of Louis XI, the Lyonnaise commenced a silk-weaving industry which, because of political and bureaucratic bungling, was painfully slow in developing. However, in less than a decade the mulberry trees were sufficiently mature to produce a substantial quantity of food for the growing population of silkworms. From then on the amount of high-grade silk increased annually and the industry flourished. In the same way as the enterprise of the Marseillaises made their city the centre of the old world's soap trade, so did Lyon become the silk capital of Europe.

* * *

The success of the many industrial applications of James Watt's steam engine in the second half of the eighteenth century brought great prosperity to England and, rather than causing the widespread unemployment so confidently predicted by its opponents, Watt's invention brought work for thousands more people than had been thought possible.

The next step in the forward march of steam power technology was to adapt it for maritime use and The Bridge Company, appreciating the impact that this would have on the shipping industry, embarked on an ambitious "steamship development" program. So important did the company's directors consider this project that Sir John Scott-Quetteville devoted all his time and energy to it. Wanting to work with a clever French engineer, the Marquis de Jouffroy, Sir John established a small research unit on the Saône, adjacent to where the marquis was developing a steam engine to power the big boats that serviced the industries on the Rhône and the Saône. Sir John brought with him his dynamic optimism, the technical expertise of his engineers and the capital the marquis's financially flagging development so urgently needed.

After many failures, the July 1783 trials on the Saône of de Jouffroy's *Pyroscaphe* were a great success; so much so that the barons of the *batellerie* – river craft industry – felt threatened and the hundreds of *bateliers* – boatmen – regarded the prospect of having steamboats on the river as the death knell of their employment. Protest meetings were held, followed by disruption, physical violence and sabotage. Rather than throwing down the gauntlet to this opposition, Sir John moved his operation to Paris, on the river Seine. There, with the patronage of Baron Louis August Breteuil, a senior minister in the French government who had invested in the project, he hoped to succeed where Jouffroy had failed. Unfortunately, the French minister and the British shipping magnate had both under-estimated the strength and the determination of the *batellierie* – and due to the lack of vigilance of the guards the minister placed on the site, the trials held in May 1788 were sabotaged in an attack that claimed Sir John's life.

However, several years before his death, during one of his many visits to Lyon, Sir John had been introduced to a brilliant young Frenchman, Joseph-Marie Jacquard. This twenty-eight-year-old Lyonnais had been brought up in the silk-weaving business. His father owned a spinning mill and his mother was a clever silk-weaver. When Joseph-Marie was only twenty, his parents died, leaving him their silk mill. With the financial support of Sir John and having studied the brilliant work of Vaucanson – the Inspector of Silk Factories – and James Hargreave's Spinning Jenny, the young Frenchman developed the Jacquard silk-weaving machine – that was destined to revolutionise the silk industry throughout the world.

The greater Jacquard's success, the less popular he became and, as had been the case in England with the Spinning Jenny, among the silk-workers in Lyon there was violent resistance to the mechanisation of their industry, resulting in physical attacks on the inventor and his technicians and in the destruction of many of his magnificent silk-weaving machines. However, with Sir John's continued support, Joseph-Marie persevered and, by 1788, there were more than fifteen thousand Jacquard looms in France.

Silk is a unique fabric – soft, warm and delicate; its shimmering beauty inspires a sense of feminine elegance and luxury and, no sooner had the new Jacquard looms started to weave their magic than the fame of the silks and brocades of Lyon spread throughout the world, so that, during the last two decades of the eighteenth century, the demand in Europe – and on the other side of the Atlantic – was virtually insatiable. Years ahead of his contemporaries, the far-sighted Scott-Quetteville anticipated the expansion of the industry and, at the suggestion of his wife, la Comtesse Nicole d'Anjou, a major investment was made through her Messageries Maritime de Marseille company. In the same way as The Bridge Company handled the export from Marseille of the Cheaulier Frères soap, so did Nicole's Marseille shipping company manage the export of many tons of silk from Lyon. As this was a French company – using French ships – the intermittent delivery disruptions, caused by the sporadic wars between England and France, were avoided.

* * *

The storming of the Bastille in July 1789, the spark that ignited the Parisians' powder keg of fury, was an explosion that, in no time, spread throughout France and, in the rioting and carnage that followed, Lyon had more than its share of violence and bloodshed. The Lyonnaises were well represented at the meeting of the Estates General in 1789 and, like many of the other communities in the provinces, the citizens of Lyon were quite emphatic about the way they expected their delegates to vote on major issues. While strongly advocating political, social and economic reform, they wanted these things in the framework of a monarchy – along the same lines as the British system.

They watched the course of events in Paris and the establishment of the *Assemblée nationale* and the more they learned about the failure of the new Republican government to curb the anarchy and mob violence in Paris, the more anxious they became. They did not like the constitution drawn up by the National Convention and they were confident that the promised national referendum would reject it. When the controlling party, the Jacobins, made it known there would be no referendum, the citizens of Lyon rose up in anger. The outcome was a ghastly civil war, with unthinkable violence and cruelty on both sides. The fighting continued until the middle of October 1793, by which time the Republicans had completely crushed the Monarchists and had embarked on a campaign of bloody retribution – the reign of terror.

Within weeks a punitive expedition was sent from Paris to make an example of Lyon such as would deter other cities from championing the monarchist cause. The unmitigated violence, torture and murder that followed the arrival of this "mission" was unparalleled in the history of France. As a measure of the brutality of those who carried out the orders of the Committee for Public Safety, within a few months, Lyon's population was reduced – by slaughter and by flight – from about 140,000 to 80,000. Hundreds of beautiful buildings were destroyed or vandalised and the homes of all those found guilty of treason were burnt down and their wealth confiscated. During one day, nearly one thousand Lyonnaise were put to death. Without labour and with many of the factories destroyed, the manufacturing, business and commerce of Lyon were at a complete standstill and unemployment and starvation were at the highest level they had ever been in the long history of the city.

* * *

When the overseas export of Lyon's silk – almost all of which was shipped from Toulon and Marseille — came to a halt, the effect on the nation's already crippled economy was disastrous. So much so that the government in Paris ordered a stop to the wanton murder and destruction in Lyon; and Joseph Fouché, the clever organiser and ruthless administrator, was ordered back there — to get the Jacquard looms weaving. Knowing the important role his trusted friend, *citoyenne* Nicole Quetteville, was playing with her export business based in Marseille, Fouché wrote to her, addressing letters to both Marseille and London, asking her to meet him in Lyon to discuss "an economic matter of the utmost importance to the prosperity and welfare of the Republic".

As was always the case, Nicole read the Frenchman's letter carefully and, having given much thought to its contents, she came to the conclusion that, as he had stated the business he wanted to discuss was very important, it was almost certainly because he had been given a difficult task by the Jacobin leaders — who now called themselves *La Directoire*[20]. It would certainly be an urgent assignment, the success of which was vital to the government — and to his own future.

None of the directors of *La Directoire* liked Fouché but they knew that of all the Jacobin hierarchy he was by far the most effective operator. Just so long as he could deliver them what they required, he was vital to their cause — but the first time he slipped up, like the generals who were defeated in battle and the other leaders who failed in their missions, he — and his life — would become redundant and he would have an appointment with that dreaded newcomer to Paris, Madame Guillotine. The urgency and importance of the matter was further underlined by the fact that the letter, having been written in Paris, had taken only four days to be delivered in London; furthermore, in the letter Fouché had given her the name of a hotel in London where she could safely deliver her answer — to a guest who had registered under the name of Robert Martin. She was most impressed by the thoroughness of the insignificant-looking but painstakingly careful little Frenchman.

Nicole answered the letter at once, agreeing to be in Lyon within

---

[20] *La Directoire* was not legitimised until 1795, but Robespierre's small group of confidants were often collectively referred to in this way.

three weeks but had added that she required a *laissez-passer* signed under seal by him personally. She informed Fouché that she would be entering France through Marseille and that a letter delivered to her château would be quite secure. She did not think it was appropriate to inform her fellow *citoyen* that she already had two passes – one signed by Robespierre and one signed by Paul Barras. She knew only too well that the authority and power of the Revolution's leaders were a day-to-day affair. In fact, she once made William Pitt laugh at dinner when she said that a French *laissez-passer* was very much like the entrance tickets to the big exhibitions in London that were marked "good for day of issue only"!

* * *

Having sailed from England, Nicole drove from Marseille to Lyon and, even before going to a hotel she drove straight to *citoyen* Fouché's offices. It was a long but interesting meeting, during which he brought her up to date with all that had been going on in Paris – the problem of dealing with half a dozen of the Jacobin leaders, all with their own agenda and all not very secretly jealous of each another. He explained that for him it had been an exhausting year during which he had been given a number of difficult assignments. There had been the problem of the priests. It had been his responsibility to bring them back into line and make them answerable to the Committee for Public Safety rather than to Rome. Fouché also spoke at length about the trial of Louis XVI and the voting on the death penalty.

When Nicole questioned him on his own feelings about the difficult tasks that had been given to him to accomplish, he did not prevaricate.

"As you well know, Madame, what I think or feel does not matter. We have a government elected with a big majority. If we are to be successful, we must not squabble among ourselves. I am dedicated to the French Republic and I will implement its policies – whether or not I personally agree with them. We all have our own skills – mine are not in leading or in laying down policy. I am better at ensuring that the laws and resolutions of the government are implemented with vigour and alacrity."

"Does it not worry your conscience when you are called on to do things you believe to be wrong – or cruel?"

"For anyone in France who intends to survive, a conscience is a luxury one cannot afford. Those who are ruled by their conscience will leave this world painlessly on our new machine."

"I am confident that you will not lose your head. You are much too careful and much too vigilant."

"But you deplore many of the things I do?"

"Not at all. I have no licence to pass judgement on you, Robespierre or any of the other leaders of the Revolution. It takes me all my time to do what I believe is my duty."

"And that is...?"

"*Noblesse oblige*! I do not have any trouble accepting that 'the gifted must give', and I have been given more than most people in the world, but..."

"But what?"

"To me, a woman, the wanton destruction of the lives and property of innocent people is abhorrent."

"Your grandfather warned us all that there would be a bloody Revolution. What is happening now is just as he predicted. It was inevitable."

"But, Monsieur Fouché, when will it stop?"

"Soon! When the pent-up hatred and humiliation of centuries of oppression and slavery have been bled out of the people. Soon! I can already see that the people's longing for revenge and their passion for blood is becoming assuaged."

"And the sooner the better."

There was quite a long silence before either of them spoke. Fouché smiled – one of his rare, thin-lipped, impersonal smiles.

"Madame, as I am sure you know, I did not entreat you to come all the way to Lyon to merely philosophise on the transition of France from being an almost heartless, feudal monarchy to being a democratic citizen's republic. The reason it is important that we talk is a matter of business – export business. Until recently, your Messageries Maritimes company, based in Marseille, handled the export of millions of livres of France's export business – but this is no longer the case."

"Monsieur, I think we still do handle more export business than any other company in the south of France. The problem is that France's exports have reduced to almost zero."

"I regret to have to agree with what you say."

Although all the deferential modes of address of the *ancien régime* were now definitely a thing of the past, Fouché's respect for the countess was such that he found it difficult to address her as *citoyenne*.

"Madame, I am well informed and I am able to report to you that the loyalty of your family's staff and employees in Marseille and their steadfastness to the Republican cause has been exemplary. Even in England, where we have many enemies and but few friends, the reports are all the same. Equally important to me is that your discretion when my name or my activities are being discussed has been unquestioned. Yes, Madame, you have been a true friend to me and I shall never abuse that friendship."

"Thank you, sir. Please permit me to make one point. Before the recent…problems…in Lyon, when our shipping company was handling some of the marketing for several Lyonnaise merchants – the last two shipments of silk we endeavoured to export for them were either waylaid by bandits or wantonly stabbed by the bayonets of malicious checkpoint guards who claimed that my men were hiding nobles inside the packages."

"On behalf of the Republic I apologise. If a report and a complaint are filed, your company will be compensated."

"A report has been filed, sir, and the – much delayed – answer was curt and negative."

"A copy of the correspondence will be all I need to correct the situation. In these difficult times we need friends; we already have more than our share of enemies."

The representative of the Committee for Public Safety looked across the desk as if to say that the matter needed no further discussion. Two errors had been made and, without further ado, they would be corrected. He continued –

"The property of the people of Lyon, who have acted treasonably against the State, has been confiscated. This includes hundreds of tons of silks of all kinds. The Committee has instructed me to judiciously dispose of it. That is to say, quietly, without causing the world price of silk to slump. Furthermore, the government wants the proceeds to be paid in a number of currencies."

He lowered his voice almost to a whisper.

"Some of it in English pounds."

"With the assignat constantly falling, I can well understand your request."

After a further silence the countess indicated that she knew precisely in what ways Fouché hoped she could assist him in carrying out his task. Having summarised them, she added –

"When I read your letter – and your request that I should come to see you in Lyon, I was reasonably confident that you wanted my company to assist in rebuilding Lyon's export business in silk. With this in mind, because *citoyen* Gerbier, my Marseille Manager, had to visit our family vineyard in Alsace, I have arranged for him to come here first."

"This is indeed wonderful news, Madame. When do you expect him to reach Lyon?"

"Tomorrow, I think. It depends on how soon he could leave Marseille. However, please be assured, Monsieur, we can help and we will help. Within a couple of days we shall have a detailed proposition to place before you. The only point I must make is that our Jacobin friends in Lyon, in their thirst for blood, have ruined France's export market in silk and it will take time – and money – to rebuild it."

"Even if others do not wish to acknowledge the truth of what you say, I do."

Realising that no good purpose could be served by remaining in the Frenchman's office any longer, Nicole suggested that she should go to her hotel and await the arrival of Robert Gerbier.

As she drove away from the government office, looking through the windows of her carriage, she became quite despondent at what she could see. The streets of Lyon were as dirty as they were deserted. There were heaps of debris everywhere, the remains of destroyed buildings and the dozens of burnt-out homes told part of the ugly story. Everywhere there were burial grounds in which both women and men dressed in black stood in small groups over the primitive graves of their slain loved ones. Even the flowers they had brought with them looked pathetic. She was relieved when the carriage pulled up at her hotel – the same one at which she usually stayed when she visited Lyon. It had always been a busy, bright, freshly painted building, with smartly dressed people – and big bowls of flowers – in the foyer and spruce young porters with smiling faces to carry the new arrivals' bags. It depressed Nicole to see that all that had gone and in its place was a nearly empty reception area, unlit lamps with smoke-stained lamp-glasses and one or two oldish, bearded men in drab uniforms, who did not look strong enough to carry themselves up the staircases, let alone the valises of the hotel's guests.

Nicole made her way to the second floor where, as she opened the door of her room, there was an envelope that, in her absence, had been pushed under the door. She recognised the writing instantly and the cheap piece of paper inside the envelope bore one word – DENNIS. She knew at once that Jean-Marc was in Lyon and that he had seen her carriage, she said to herself –

"He must have seen my carriage arrive. He would not have failed to recognise Dennis, the grey – my favourite harness horse."

(Nicole had so named the gelding as, like her old friend Dennis O'Kelly, he was a genial rogue but without any malice!)

* * *

As Nicole walked down the stairs she realised that the mission in France in which Major Black and his team of what she called "Daring Young Blues" were involved, had brought Jean-Marc to Lyon. Although she had some thoughts of her own as to the nature of their operation, she had no intention of asking him any questions. From her point of view, knowing the dangers of the work in which he and his friends were involved, to see him alive and well was a great joy – she asked for nothing more.

For more than half an hour Nicole remained in the stables at the back of the hotel. She was talking to her four horses as she so often did. Although they had been pushed a little to reach Lyon in good time, they were all in fine form and even though they had come with spare sets of horseshoes, she had ensured that the hotel's farrier had checked their feet carefully. The *valet d'écurie* – hotel ostler – was an old man of at least seventy years. He apologised for not being much help and explained that all the young men had been conscripted into the army and that he was doing his best in their absence. Nicole thrust some bank notes into his hand and asked him to go and buy some olive oil — for the horse's hoofs.

As soon as he had gone, her two coachmen, who had been employed at the Marseille château since they were boys, posted themselves as sentries to enable Nicole and a bearded old man with a big hat — whom the coachmen recognised as Jean-Marc in disguise — to talk to each other.

The conversation was brief and to the point and ended with Jean-Marc finding a hand trolley which he loaded with dirty straw bedding and manure and pulled it off to the dung heap, some forty yards away — and then he disappeared.

Intrigued with what her soldier son had told her, Nicole returned upstairs to her room, had a hot bath, an early supper and retired to bed.

The following morning Robert Gerbier and her accountant arrived from Marseille. After a short discussion with them, Nicole sent a messenger to Fouché's office to inform him that, if it would be convenient for him, she and her manager would be able to come to his office at any time. Having received a positive answer, a meeting was set up for early in the afternoon.

Fouché opened the meeting by inviting the countess to outline a proposition for the government to consider. The Frenchman was surprised and pleased with the simplicity of the proposal and stated that, on the basis of what she had put forward, there was no reason why a contract could not be drawn up straight away. Nicole's offer was based on the world price of silk in 1792 and, for all types of fabric Messageries Maritimes would pay 70 per cent of the going wholesale rate, they would guarantee to take an agreed minimum each month and also to prevent the bottom falling out of the market. The only stipulations were that all payments in currencies other than the assignat would be paid through Mayer Rothschild and Sons in Frankfurt and that for each convoy a regular military unit would provide an armed guard of at least two soldiers per *chariot* — wagon; that having been loaded and sealed in Lyon, none of the packages of silk would be touched by anyone until they were loaded on to one of the company's ships and that the company's staff would remain with the merchandise from the time it was delivered to them. Her final conditions were that, until the company had taken delivery of the whole stockpile of the fabric, it would have full control of the marketing and pricing of Lyon's total output and that all discussions in connection with the contract would be through *citoyen* Joseph Fouché or in his absence a person acceptable to the company.

Being a shrewd businessman, it did not take Fouché long to appreciate that each of the clauses Nicole had required to be in the contract was reasonable and necessary.

"Does the fact that we are possibly dealing with millions of livres concern you, Madame?"

"No! The only thing that can make the contract impossible would be the flooding of the market with cheap fabric. Although it would be too complex to include price increases in the contract, I am hoping to be able to restore the market and even improve demand. Our American and Canadian contacts are good."

"Madame, please forgive me for appearing impatient but when do you think you will be ready to move the first consignment?"

"Within one week of signing the contract. It is my intention to set out for Frankfurt first thing in the morning. I need to make certain banking arrangements with Herr Rothschild, and I shall be back in less than two weeks. *Citoyen* Gerbier will remain here to work with your lawyers – and ours – to draw up the formal agreement."

"Although our government agents do much banking business in Frankfurt, I do not know the name Rothschild. I assume they are reliable?"

Nicole smiled.

"They are relatives of my family."

Fouché nodded his approval and assured *citoyenne* Scott-Quetteville that he appreciated her positive response to his request and that he would make whatever arrangements were necessary to ensure her safety and comfort.

"There will be an escort at your hotel first thing in the morning. If you rest your horses at the border until you return from Frankfurt, they will be fitter for the journey back to Marseille. The escort will wait with your horses until you return from Frankfurt."

"Thank you! In today's troubled world, most people promise much – but fall short of their word. Your word, *citoyen* Fouché, is good, but your performance is always better. *Merci, infiniment!*"

VI

During the four weeks that the count – 'Paul' – and his son, Joseph, were learning their new trade, Major Black returned with his art expert to Chantilly to carefully pack a dozen small canvases – worth more than a million pounds – and some valuable jewellery – that M. Creuse said could be carefully put inside the upholstery of the driver's seat.

A week before the two escapees were to travel to Lyon, M. Creuse, who was particularly impressed with Jean-Marc's knowledge and efficiency, asked him if he knew how to get quite a large sum of money from France to Frankfurt.

"I have a dangerously large amount of gold here in Paris. I have no difficulty moving it about the country but my coaches and carriages may not leave France. I would pay 50 per cent of its value to have it safely in a bank in Frankfurt or London."

"Do you remember my mother?"

"Why, of course – la Comtesse d'Anjou, my dear old professor's niece. One of the most beautiful women I have ever met. I was indeed sad to read in the newspapers that she had been killed during the meetings of *les États Generaux*."

"Thank goodness, sir, that is not correct. She survived – she is once again very much alive. I mentioned her name as she sometimes goes to Frankfurt and she might be able to help you."

M. Creuse pricked up his ears at the word "sometimes" and when Jean-Marc said that she was helping the government re-establish the silk industry in Lyon, they rapidly concluded a mutually satisfactory deal.

After each of his meetings with M. Creuse, immediately on returning to Rue des Fleurs, Jean-Marc informed Major Black concerning the progress that was being made. In his report on this latest visit he mentioned the carriage maker's wish to remove some of his wealth beyond the borders of France.

"But will your mother have reason to go to Frankfurt?"

"She will have to go there quite often as she will be using my brother and two other bankers there to handle all the foreign exchange aspects of the contract with the French authorities."

"All very interesting, Scott-Quetteville; however, you and I are only interested in assisting nobles to escape and we must not become sidetracked. I think the work your mother is doing could be quite helpful to us in achieving our goal."

"Yes! The more I think about it the more I tend to agree with you."

Within a month, as promised by M. Creuse, the training of the two coachmen was complete and they – and the new coach – were ready to depart. However, back at Les Carmes, the disappearance of the noble and his son did not present the corporal and the gaoler with a very serious problem. As deaths from illness and, more particularly, suicide, were almost daily occurrences at the prison, their untimely departure from this life had been easily explained.

* * *

Leaving Captain Sir Jean-Marc Scott-Quetteville to travel to Lyon in the special new carriage that M. Creuse had arranged to be built, Major Black and the other three officers made their way back to Abbeville – the least guarded of the Channel ports – and several days later they were happily telling their – carefully censored – stories to the other officers of the Blues. The identity being used by Jean-Marc was that of lawyer for the Committee for Public Safety.

The two drivers of the carriage – a gift from M. Creuse to la Comtesse d'Anjou – looked smart in their uniforms. The younger one was returning to his Regiment in Avignon and his papers were in order. On leaving Paris, when they were stopped at the barricade, not only were all his documents carefully checked, but his baggage also. His uniform, army boots and hat were all well packed and he had a letter to another corporal in his regiment that his fiancée had asked him to deliver.

The zealous guard took it into the small office so that it could be read by his sergeant. The *cachet* – seal – with which his papers were stamped and dated – would hold him in good stead until he reached his destination.

The guard seemed much less interested in the older driver as he thought he had "seen that face before" when he had been driving another carriage. The guard had one look at the passenger's papers and turned a little pale. He saluted and apologised most abjectly to the lawyer from the Committee for Public Safety who was going to Lyon on business. The guard stammered that, had he checked the *citoyen's* papers first he would not have had to waste his time by carefully checking the drivers' *véritabilité*. The passenger made light of the situation.

"Not at all, *citoyen,* you are quite right to be thorough. None of us can be too careful, these days."

Three days later the carriage drove into Nicole's hotel in Lyon. The lawyer had left the carriage a few miles out of the city.

By this time, not only had the silk contract been signed but the first export consignment was ready for dispatch. La Comtesse d'Anjou, who was in Lyon, arrived back from a meeting with *citoyen* Fouché about two hours later, by which time the new carriage had been washed and polished. She was delighted with the gift, all the more so as her son who had appeared from nowhere, explained the deal he had done with M. Creuse. She informed him that as soon as the first silk convoy had been loaded and was on its way, it was her intention to travel to Frankfurt to personally handle the banking transactions relating to the sale of the merchandise.

There were three big wagons of silk and, in accordance with the terms of the written agreement, they were to have a mounted escort in the front and at the rear of the convoy. *Citoyen* Gerbier and his accountant were to ride in the carriage that was returning to Marseille. The two drivers from Paris would drive this equipage while the countess's two drivers would take her to Frankfurt – as they were well known by the border guards.

Two days later, just as the convoy was about to leave Lyon, *citoyen* Fouché appeared at the countess's establishment. He had a worried look on his face as he entered her office.

"*Citoyenne* – Madame, I am very embarrassed to have to come here. I have just received word from Paris that, whether you are aware of it or not, there are money, jewellery, valuable works of art and two fugitive noblemen hidden in your convoy. Knowing you and trusting you, I emphatically denied the allegations. However, as they reached me from the president of the Committee for Public Safety himself, I have come here personally to supervise the searching of your company's convoy."

"*Citoyen* Fouché, I sincerely appreciate your trust in me. Please have your people start their search at once."

Fouché's men knew precisely the weight and size of each of the twelve hundred packages of silk as they had been checked, weighed, sealed and recorded at the government warehouse. The three wagons were carefully examined as was the personal baggage of all the drivers – and even Robert Gerbier's. The three men could not have been more thorough in their search. They handed Fouché their detailed written report. Everything was completely in order and there was neither gold nor other valuables in any part of the convoy – and there were certainly no stowaways. The only discrepancy was that one bale of brocaded silk weighed more than was recorded in the documentation. This was quickly replaced by a similar bale[21].

The escorted convoy moved off on its way to Marseille, where the silk was loaded on to one of the company's ships which sailed on the following day for America. Two of the crew who signed on in Marseille just happened to be the drivers of M. Gerbier's carriage and when the ship reached Gibraltar they were transferred with half of the cargo of silk to the *Twinbridge*, the destination of which was London.

Somehow, unheralded, Captain Sir Jean-Marc Scott-Quetteville happened to be on board the French ship. He, too, transferred to the *Twinbridge* and was greeted like a long-lost friend by the captain.

* * *

Back in Lyon, *citoyen* Fouché insisted that the mounted guards who

---

[21] It was subsequently found that it contained five pieces of fabric more than it should have had. (Silk was always sold by the piece rather than by the yard.)

usually escorted his friend *la citoyenne* went with her to the border. In Frankfurt[22] she was met by her son William and she stayed with him for more than a week in the fine old house he had recently bought. Nicole, who was most impressed with his purchase, casually mentioned that, even if he had a wife and three or four children, there would be plenty of room for them all. With an impish smile, William replied –

"Well Mother, that is the reason I bought this place. I am soon to become a married man."

"How absolutely wonderful, William darling! It is indeed thrilling news. Have you informed Jean-Marc and François?"

"No, Mother, you are the first to know."

"Heavens above, there are so many questions I want to ask you I do not know where to begin."

"Let me save you the bother – her name is Gerda Hoffmann, she is just nineteen years old, tall, beautiful and quite gorgeous."

"Tell me darling about her family!"

"I shall do so, Mother, as soon as I have finished telling you about Gerda. She is an artist and she paints in oils. Her father is a well-known Hanoverian painter. Her mother died several years ago and last year her father who, incidentally is nearly sixty years old, remarried – a French marquise who is only two years older than Gerda."

"How is it that she is a marquise? Is that not strange?"

"I do not know if strange is the right word. When she was only sixteen, she was married off to a marquis, who was killed by the border guards as he was trying to escape to Germany. They both set out on horseback from Strasbourg, dressed as peasants. Nanette – that is her name – was riding about fifty yards ahead of her husband. The guards did not stop her but, seeing a peasant on a beautiful, well-groomed horse, they apprehended the marquis who, in trying to gallop off, was shot dead."

"Poor girl!"

"It certainly was a dreadful thing to happen to her; however, Mother, she is a really impossible creature. When she is not doting on her new

---

[22] In the eighteenth century Frankfurt did not belong to any country. It was one of 51 self-governing cities of the Holy Roman Empire – that boasted no less than 94 kings and princes and more than 40 church prelates.

husband, she is either crying or else in a violent rage. The slightest hitch to any of her plans triggers an outburst of almost hysterical fury. That Herr Hoffmann is very fond of his daughter makes Nannette insanely jealous. He only has to kiss Gerda or put his arm around her for the spoilt little brat to rush out of the room and slam the door. According to Gerda, the noises that emanate from her father's bedroom for hours after they both retire, have to be heard to be believed – and it is just as bad in the early morning!"

Nicole could not help laughing.

"Poor Gerda! It cannot be much fun for her. But please, William, enough about Nanette's nocturnal antics – I must know more about your fiancée. When will I be able to meet her?"

"Strange as it may seem, Mother dear, I thought you might ask that question. Gerda is coming to dinner tomorrow evening."

"That is really exciting. I am longing to meet her."

"I am sure that she will be thrilled to meet you. It will be a big surprise for her, as she has no idea that you are here in Frankfurt."

For the next half an hour William continued to answer his mother's questions, firstly about Gerda and then about his various business trips around Europe. When she was satisfied that she was well and truly in the picture, he ventured to change the subject.

"Now Mother dear that I have told you all my news, before we go to bed I must hear all about why you are here – that is, other than to see me; and naturally I want to have the latest news about Jean-Marc, François, Judy and the twins."

It was quite late that night before Nicole and William went to bed.

* * *

The following morning, as well as talking further about the family, they discussed the finances relating to the sales of silk with Herr Rothschild and Herr Eisen and she mentioned in passing that she and her two drivers needed a safe place to do some major repairs on her carriage. William had a large coach house at the rear of his house and he accompanied his mother and the drivers as they set about their task.

Monsieur Creuse had had the equipage specially made and when it was carefully and totally pulled to pieces, more than one hundred thousand pounds of gold and jewellery were found in its upholstery, hollow shafts, wheel hubs, harness and the rest of the woodwork. This was taken to Judengasse and handed over to Mayer Rothschild. Half the value was credited to a new client, Monsieur Bernard Creuse of Paris, the rest to Rothschild's distant cousin la Comtesse d'Anjou – who said to her son –

"Please have this carriage reassembled and discreetly disposed of. I do not want to take it back to France. It would be better to buy another one, don't you think? I understand from Monsieur Creuse that next time I come to Frankfurt, he would like me to travel in a similarly constructed equipage."

All that the amazed William managed to do was to give his mother a big hug and say "Mother darling, you are incorrigible!"

* * *

The evening with Gerda was a great success. Herr Eisen and his wife were also present. It had been they who had introduced William to his fiancée, some six months previously. When Nicole asked the couple when they intended to get married, Gerda explained that, as her father had to go to Austria to paint the emperor's portrait and expected to be in Vienna for quite some time, they had to choose either an early date or else wait until the following year.

"I prefer to be married as soon as possible...since I am among friends, I must confess that living with my new stepmother leaves much to be desired."

Herr Eisen, who had been handling the business affairs relating to the dead Marquis' estate, not knowing the extent to which the countess was in the picture, interjected –

"Comtesse, unfortunately, the young lady whom Herr Hoffmann recently married is both volatile and highly strung. At the bank, even a half hour with her leaves me with a headache – and in a bad mood."

Nicole turned to her future daughter-in-law.

"You poor girl! Please arrange the marriage soon and leave your father to cope alone with the tantrums of your young stepmother."

VII

NICOLE'S RETURN TO THE FRENCH border was quick and uneventful and her escort and her own horses, well and truly refreshed, were waiting for her in Strasbourg as had been arranged. As it had been a long time since she had visited her vineyard in Colmar, *Château de la Table,* she called there on her way back to Lyon. Karl Knopff, her competent and dedicated manager, had just finished crushing the year's *vendange* – his only comment being "a satisfactory vintage". His wife, whose friendly attitude and outgoing personality more than made up for her husband's taciturnity, was genuinely thrilled to see her. She assured the countess that the quality of the wine they had just made was the best for many years.

"Madame la Comtesse, you do not know how happy my husband and I are to see you looking so healthy and well. We heard from Monsieur Gerbier about those wicked people who tried to kill you. It was too horrible to be true. Karl said that, without you as head of the family, the vineyard would be sold to one of the new rulers of France and, if that happened, we would both go back to Munich. Didn't you Karl?"

"I did – and we would."

"Dear, if you are worried about the winepress, why do you not talk about it to la Comtesse?"

Nicole encouraged the man to relax and feel free to discuss anything and everything about the vineyard with her. Although reluctant to speak up, he eventually announced that he needed a new winepress and two *chariots* to convey the export wine to Strasbourg. As they were now bottling their wine, it took up so much more space to transport it. The countess, who wanted to demonstrate her support for her conscientious vineyard manager, was also aware that, because inflation was quite out of control and taxes had more than trebled in the last three years, it was difficult to find the cash to replace capital equipment.

"Herr Knopff, I shall not bore you by telling you about the difficulties we are all having these days. You know as much about them as I do – as you have your own problems, too. With the wretched assignat worth less almost every day and the people from whom we buy things wanting golden livres, poor Monsieur Gerbier is at his wits' end. Nevertheless, because you manage this vineyard so carefully and so successfully, I shall arrange for 5 per cent of all the money that comes in from your wine sales to be retained in a local bank account that you can operate. This will enable you to purchase whatever capital equipment you need, without having to wait for approval from Marseille."

"I have a big safe here where I keep my own money. If I am allowed to retain the real money – the gold livres – we receive from local sales in my safe, too, I could buy the winepress much cheaper."

"That is an excellent idea, Herr Knopff. I shall write this down before I leave here and take a copy to Monsieur Gerbier. I know he will be pleased to learn that together we have overcome the difficulty."

Frau Knopff could not control her delight and, knowing that her husband was quite incapable of expressing appreciation of any kind, moved towards the countess and clasped her hand.

"Madame, you do not know how happy this is going to make Karl. Not only will he be able to get the things he feels are essential for the vineyard, but also he will have the feeling that you have so much confidence in him that you trust him to run this place as if it was his own. Thank you, Madame, thank you!"

For probably the first time in his life, Karl Knopff looked happy. He addressed his wife.

"I told you that if the countess knew the problems I was having she would give me a new winepress and two *chariots*."

* * *

The following morning, having loaded some wine into the back of her carriage, the countess set out for Lyon where she found *citoyen* Fouché as busy as ever but in good spirits.

"It is good to know that you have moved the first consignment of silk, Madame. If it is not being either rude or impatient, may I ask you when you will be able to move some more — and when the government can expect some money."

The money will come as soon as the silk reaches America. I am quite confident that it can all be sold for cash at once. It is my intention to go to Toulon on my way back to Marseille. As soon as I can arrange shipping from there, we shall certainly take the second tranche. If Paris is pestering you for money, this could be arranged. It would cost 10 per cent to discount the payment for the silk already shipped."

"Of course they are pestering me! If, when each convoy of silk is delivered to your ships, you can arrange payment in gold I have the authority to reduce the sale price by even more than 10 per cent. You have no idea how complicated things are now, since they introduced the assignat. As its value is falling every day, bringing in gold from abroad is worth so much more to our government. Incidentally, you should be careful going near Toulon. Your friends, the British, have landed there and are occupying the city and our fleet has surrendered to them. The monarchists are almost as bad there — and in Marseille — as they were here in Ville Affranchie[23]."

"I am sure I shall manage to survive. As soon as I reach Marseille, I shall arrange for extra staff to come here and start checking and documenting the second shipment of silk. Provided you can ensure that they will be safe and free from harassment, they can remain here."

"Thank you, Madame! I promise you that your people will be completely safe. You do not know how important the success of this silk operation is to France — and it is also very important to me, personally. I assure you that, as soon as you have disposed of all the material owned by the government, I shall have you appointed managing agent for all the big silk mills. As you will have been involved in enormous expense in

---

[23] For a short time the name of Lyon was changed by the Jacobin rulers of France to *Ville Affranchie* — the "Emancipated City".

setting up a distributing network and a number of new markets, you are entitled to get something in return."

"Thank you, indeed, sir! I appreciate both your offer and the thoughtfulness that prompted it. However, if what we are now doing for France is as successful as I think it will be, we shall be in a position to provide the manufacturers of silk in Lyon greater scope for the export of their product than they have ever had. It would cost any competitor a fortune to get on equal terms with us."

"The real problem we face is that, in trying to set an example of Lyon, we have seriously compromised one of the most important sources of wealth in France. If your grandfather were alive, he would, no doubt, remind us that 'punitive expeditions seldom succeed'."

As the folly of destroying Lyon and killing the leaders of its industries was quite obvious from the outset, Nicole thought it better to switch the subject under discussion to something more positive.

"May I suggest that it would be a great help to the economic recovery of Lyon if you gave permission for us to take some of the current production of silk with each consignment of your stockpile. This would create employment here and enable the silk manufacturers to get on their feet again. For the first few months, we would be prepared to pay them cash on delivery."

"Provided it will not interfere with the disposal of our stockpile."

"I assure you, Monsieur, it will not."

"Then I shall issue the orders at once and I am confident that the news that the silk-weaving business is alive and well again will help bring back to Lyon many who left here in fright. It is with impatience that I await your return to this city."

* * *

La Comtesse d'Anjou was well satisfied when she set out from Lyon early the following morning. It never ceased to amaze her how desperate most business people are for cash. In the formal contract signed in Lyon, the new Republic was willing to sacrifice the silk from Lyon at a discounted price. It then was prepared to concede a further – substantial – rebate in order to be paid cash on delivery. It was quite unbelievable! The Messageries Maritimes Compagnie de Marseille was not only about to make more than a million livres out of the sale of Lyon's unsold silk but, if it handled the task well, it would become the world's biggest shipper and marketer of this much sought after product. Would not her grandfather, le Comte d'Anjou be pleased!

As she neared Toulon the signs of the armed conflict that Fouché had mentioned became evident. The roads were blocked and everywhere tented camps of soldiery had sprung up. When, about three miles from the port, the congestion on the roadway had brought her carriage to a halt, she alighted to stretch her legs. A military *équipage* had also been held up and there was much shouting of orders, as apparently the general whose vehicle it was, insisted that a path should be cleared so that he could proceed. He, too, was standing by the roadside. As he had his back to her, she could not see his face. She approached him and, as soon as he turned around, she recognised him – Général Paul-François, Viscount de Barras.

Nicole had met Barras many times, as he was one of the delegates to the Convention from the Département of the Var – very close to Marseille, both geographically and philosophically. His family went back centuries; in fact, one had even been canonised – a beatification that would certainly not be the lot of this disreputable member of the family. Fabulously wealthy, corrupt, greedy, totally libertine and thought by many to be bisexual, Paul Barras appealed equally to both loose-moralled women and innocent virgins. As well, his political colleagues constantly complained about his lifestyle and the number of eager young men in whose company he spent too much of his time.

At an early age, the general had served in India and, having been suspended from duty a number of times and cashiered at least once, phoenix-like, he had managed to rise – and to fly again. Nicole had to admit that he was extremely clever and that, in his dealings with her, he had been helpful and well-mannered. To her mind he was another Prince Cardinal de Rohan – not in looks but certainly in many other ways.

The general and the countess saw – and recognised – each other simultaneously. Walking towards her and completely ignoring the new protocol of equality, he bowed.

"La Comtesse d'Anjou! What a delightful surprise to meet you! Please tell me if I can help you in any way?"

"I am trying, not very successfully to get to my offices on the wharf and…"

He cut her off.

"At the moment, that is quite impossible, the British have occupied Toulon and we have laid siege to the town. I am trying to sort out the command of this place. Général Cartaux, the commander of our army here, is not in control of the situation. Before being a general he was a painter and I feel that he was better at his previous occupation! I have been sent here with *citoyen* Fréron as representatives of the people to make recommendations as to what we need to do to recapture the city."

At this moment, Fréron and several army officers appeared on the scene. Barras introduced the countess to them. She immediately recognised one of them: a twenty-four-year-old captain. He stood out from the others, not only because he was shorter, but more particularly because he was so untidily dressed. Before Barras could make the introduction, Nicole stepped forward.

"Napoléon Buonaparte! It is so nice to meet you again and to see that you are now a captain. We have not seen each other since you stayed with us in Etreham when you were at *l'École Militaire*."

"I am honoured to meet you again, Madame. I read about the cowardly attack on you, several years ago. It is good to know that you have recovered. Please tell me, how is my friend Jean-Marc? He was foolish to resign from the French army as he would have done well."

"He did not resign, Captain Buonaparte. The French army peremptorily discharged him!"

"Well, if I might be excused for saying so, Madame, more fool them. He was the best horseman at the school and had the best brain, too. Where is he now, *citoyenne*?"

Nicole avoided giving the captain a direct answer.

"We have a company in Marseille and Toulon, shipping merchandise out of France to earn some foreign exchange."

"Please tell your son that I am here. I should very much like to see him. He would be invaluable here, as all our guns are wrongly placed and I am sure that with him, together we could drive out the English."

Général Barras looked slightly annoyed. He terminated the conversation by suggesting that the countess should have a meal with them, after which they would look at the defences, whose dispositions the young captain had complained of.

They were all seated at a table in the private banqueting room of a restaurant, when Captain Buonaparte – who had been told that he was expected to be present – arrived. As he stood at the doorway, once again Nicole could not help noticing how unsoldierly he looked. He had a shabby hat pulled over his forehead and his ill-powdered hair was hanging untidily over the collar of his grey greatcoat. Unlike the other officers, his boots were badly made and unpolished and several buttons of his tunic were unfastened. He removed his hat and greatcoat and sat down with the others. As was becoming of a junior officer, he took little or no part in the table conversation.

* * *

After their meal, Général Cartaux showed Barras one of his 24-pounder gun positions. Looking at Buonaparte as he spoke, he waxed eloquent about the gun's capabilities. Général Barras asked the young captain what he thought was wrong with the artillery piece or its position.

"Sir, the gun is one of the finest pieces of ordnance in the world, but in its present position it is utterly useless. May I have permission to fire four shots at maximum range?"

"Go ahead, Buonaparte!"

Four rounds were fired and each time the ball landed harmlessly; well short of the coast. There was a stony silence – finally broken by Barras.

"What is your role here, Buonaparte?"

"Sir, I am on my way back from Avignon where I have been purchasing powder."

Barras turned to Cartaux.

"I am recommending that Captain Buonaparte be appointed as Commandant in charge of artillery here and that he be solely responsible for the redeployment of all the guns. I also recommend that until any further orders reach you from Paris, that you employ him in this capacity[24]."

---

[24] Général Cartaux was almost immediately replaced by Général Dugommier.

Cartaux, a most unsoldierly individual, whose uniform appeared to be covered from head to foot with gold lace, had to agree.

"Sir, I fully concur."

Barras, genuinely pleased that the countess was present, addressed Cartaux.

"Général, would you please have one of your officers find suitable accommodation for *citoyenne* Scott-Quetteville and her entourage – near my own. As she is a member of *l'Assemblée nationale*, representing Marseille, it will be good for her to see at first hand the British driven out of Toulon."

"Yes, sir. It will be done at once."

Captain Buonaparte made the point that, if he was to be in charge of the artillery, it would take at least a month to assemble a sufficiently powerful force to drive Admiral Hood and his minions from Toulon. Barras was impatient.

"Can you not be ready sooner?"

"No, sir! The admiral is no fool. He will not afford us the luxury of having two attempts to win this battle. Our attack on the English must be decisive. In just over a month I can have a concentration here of over two hundred of our 24-pounder artillery pieces – as well as howitzers and mortars. At the moment these are spread all along the coast – many of them sited badly. They must be brought here, dug in, and supplies of ammunition must be stockpiled. Furthermore, proper arrangements must be made for the heating of the balls. At the present time there is one central location where they are all being heated and it is taking many hours to transport them to the guns. The time wasted, the danger and the inconvenience of moving almost red-hot cannon balls long distances is totally unacceptable. We must have many fire units, all sited close to the artillery lines. As I have much to organise, would you please excuse me, sir – and Captain Murat, my aide? We have work to do."

"I accept your explanation, Buonaparte and I approve of your plan."

The newly appointed artillery commandant saluted – and departed in haste.

* * *

Early the following morning Buonaparte appeared at the hotel where the countess had been staying the night. They conversed for some time and she listened while he told her of his various postings since graduating from *l'École Militaire* and the people he had met. Although he was not a particularly articulate young man, he expressed his sympathy that Sir John had been murdered and he asked about Jean-Marc and his brothers. He then introduced a subject which Nicole afterwards came to the conclusion was the main purpose of the visit – Rachelle Bassett. He hesitatingly spoke in short sentences.

"Could you please give me the address of Rachelle, the delightful daughter of Lord Bassett? I wish to write to her. They are a fine family and I really did enjoy the holiday we all had in Etreham together. Rachelle and her sisters made me feel part of the family. I can never forget how openly they talked about everything. At first I was quite shocked and embarrassed; however, the way you and Lady Bassett joined in the conversation made me realise that it would be much better for everyone if they could bring their thoughts out into the open."

His hesitancy when he spoke and the slightly clumsy way in which he put his words together, suggested to Nicole that he was finding it difficult to express himself. She gave him the Bassetts' London address. He carefully noted it in a small black book he produced from his pocket.

"Do you think she would be pleased to receive a letter from me?"

"I do not know Napoléon. But I am sure she would not be offended."

"Madame, it is good to see you. I feel more comfortable talking to you than I do to most people. Although people are beginning to accept me as a soldier, as a person they treat me as a gauche, uneducated Corsican. They laugh at my bad accent and despise me because I am not rich like they are. But they will have to change their attitude soon. I am taking lessons in speaking French without an accent."

"I think you are exaggerating the situation, Napoléon, and you are imagining things that do not exist. Perhaps if you forgot about yourself and your perception of how people regard you, you might feel more comfortable, socially."

"Other than by marrying into a wealthy family, please tell me how I can become more acceptable, socially."

"If I did not think you were a brilliant young man with a great future, I should not bother to speak about such matters to you; however, as I believe that one day you might become a great general, I shall be frank with you."

"Thank you, Countess Nicole! Whatever you tell me to do, I will do. I promise."

"For a start, please stop imagining that people are looking down on you. I assure you, Napoléon, most people are so busy thinking about themselves that they hardly give you – or me or anyone else – a second thought. Once you believe this, most of your problems will disappear. Having said that, the other thing that is most obvious is your appearance! When I met you, yesterday, in the field and again at the luncheon, your hair was not done, you had shaved carelessly, you were not wearing gloves, your long boots were grubby and your dress was untidy and, most importantly, you have not smiled once since we met yesterday afternoon. You must concentrate on looking smart and attractive. Perhaps your soldiers do not mind, but I can assure you all women notice these things and hostesses only invite well-dressed, attractive men to their salons, receptions and dinners."

"Your sons are all tall and handsome. Even when we were all in our teens, they towered over me and made me feel insignificant. I am short and, even now, people tease me that my head is too big for my body."

"Once again, Napoléon, you are talking nonsense. You asked me to help you and I am trying to do so. Please write down each of the things I have said; attending to them will do more for your success and your happiness than you believe."

The black notebook came out again.

* * *

Six weeks later Buonaparte's guns opened fire and after an almost constant artillery barrage, during which more than seven thousand rounds were fired and, in spite of flooding rains, Toulon was retaken and Admiral Hood and his British invaders were driven off. During the battle, Commandant of Artillery Buonaparte suffered a slight wound – which he made light of. He was hailed as a brilliant artillery officer and tactician and, on the recommendation of Général Barras, he was promoted to the rank of Brigadier-Général of Artillery and almost immediately afterwards he was posted, in this capacity, to the army of Italy, whose headquarters was in Nice.

The countess spent the next few weeks in Marseille, working out with Robert Gerbier a satisfactory routine for accepting and exporting the consignments of silk from both the government stockpile and the merchants in Lyon, and the mechanics for the movement of funds. The original contract, signed in Lyon, was an excellent one, but the subsequent discounting deal and the additional arrangements with the individual silk-weaving companies transformed this "great contribution to the restoration of France's economy" into one of the most lucrative business arrangements in which the Anjous of Marseille had ever been involved.

* * *

Over a period of more than twelve months, in conjunction with Major Black, Jean-Marc worked with Monsieur Creuse in Paris, to take nobles to Lyon and then to Marseille, disguised as drivers. From there it was not difficult to conduct them safely to England.

Halfway through 1794 Nicole made another visit to Frankfurt in a second new *équipage* – well laden with gold, jewellery and art treasures. As she drove into Frankfurt she was not aware that her friend, *citoyen* Creuse, had been arrested and thrown into prison, charged with having secretly exported gold and works of art from France. It was fortunate that Major Black was in Paris at the time. He was able to get a message through to Creuse to deny all knowledge of the charge and challenge his accusers to prove that he had ever been in possession of such treasures or the means of exporting them.

Although, at this time, Jean-Marc was back with the Blues in Northampton, Black was fully aware that the redoubtable Lady Scott-Quetteville had taken the carefully modified carriage to Frankfurt; he acted at once. Dressed as an officer of the Republican army of the Rhine, he took the first *diligence* to Strasbourg, crossed the river and hastened to Frankfurt where he introduced himself to William Scott-Quetteville.

Having spent two days with him, he unobtrusively made his way back to England.

Nicole's visit to Frankfurt was virtually a repetition of the one she had made the previous year. Both Herr Eisen and Mayer Rothschild could not have been more satisfied with the progress the silk contract was making and the Jewish coin dealer – banker – was extremely pleased to handle Monsieur Creuse's second consignment of gold and valuables. When her carriage was loaded, ready to return to Lyon, Nicole expressed concern that William had not given her an *équipage* that had had all the upholstery and door linings replaced.

"William, I do not trust the French and I have no intention of being executed by them. Do you not think I should be better advised to return in a different carriage?"

"Mother, both the modified carriages – the one you brought last year and that in which you arrived last Wednesday – are identical. If you arrived back in Lyon in a different carriage, your friend *citoyen* Fouché would have reason to be suspicious. Trust me, Mother dear, it is better that you return to Lyon in the same vehicle that brought you here."

Recognising the logic in what he had said, Nicole set out for France and, as he had done on the two previous occasions, Joseph Fouché had arranged for her escort to be waiting for her at the border. The journey to Lyon was quite uneventful until she reached the outskirts of the city, where she was stopped by the guards at the barricade. There she was asked to alight from her carriage, and was presented with an envelope containing a letter from Fouché which she found quite incomprehensible. It was short and to the point.

> "*Citoyen Scott-Quetteville, I am instructed to have you arrested and tried for treason. The charge is that you have used a specially constructed carriage to take from this country hundreds of thousands of livres in gold, jewellery and works of art. Proof of this lies in the fact that the carriage in which you travelled to Frankfurt, can be shown to have secret compartments and removable panels. Your accomplice, citoyen Creuse of Paris, has already been arrested and he is in prison awaiting trial which will be conducted when your carriage has been searched.*

I regret that you have chosen to act in a way contrary to the laws of our Republic."

Silently cursing herself for not having insisted on using another carriage, she was taken to the big prison in Lyon, where she was peremptorily locked up with half a dozen other citizens suspected of wrongdoing.

The following morning, she asked in vain to see *citoyen* Fouché. She was curtly informed that he was unavailable and that he had nothing to do with her case. The rest of the day was for her one of disgust and anger. Three people who had been found guilty of treason by the tribunal were taken out to the scaffold and executed. A fourth prisoner, also found guilty, had acquired a knife with which he had first stabbed one of the guards and then plunged the blade into his own heart.

In the evening she was settling down in the corner of the big cell-like room in which she and several other women had been placed when the commandant of the prison arrived with two guards and behind them was none other than *citoyen* Joseph Fouché. As soon as the grille had been noisily unbolted, he stepped forward.

"*Citoyen* Scott-Quetteville, would you please come with me? It is necessary that I explain a number of things to you."

One of the guards was instructed to carry Nicole's things for her as the commandant led the way back to his office. Fouché ordered him and the others from the room.

"Madame, I cannot tell you how distressed I am. Over the past three days a number of wicked calumnies have been uttered against you and I assure you that they will be avenged. Let us not remain here a minute longer than we need. I will take you to my office where a proper meal awaits us."

Fouché, having spoken to the commandant and signed his book, escorted Nicole to his carriage. Less than fifteen minutes later, they were walking down a broad, well lit passageway towards his office. Although it was now well after nine o'clock, she could hear much activity and there were people working in a number of the other offices.

As soon as they were both settled, he waved a document in the air and handed it to her.

"This, Madame, is the report of the two inspectors who were sent all the way from Paris to prove the treason of *citoyen* Creuse and, by association, your guilt, too. The report makes it unequivocally clear that your carriage, made by *citoyen* Creuse's company does not have — and never did have — any secret compartments, removable panels or upholstery that would facilitate the concealment of chattels or documents. It states that its paintwork has not been tampered with and that in no way could you or *citoyen* Creuse have used it for the purpose alleged."

"Monsieur, I could have saved the inspectors the trouble of coming to Lyon. Perhaps it is just an unfortunate misunderstanding."

"Misunderstanding nothing, Madame. Can you not see? Indirectly, this is as much an attack on me as it is an attack on you."

Although by this time Nicole had a perfectly clear understanding of the whole scenario, she continued to play out her charade.

"I cannot see how anything unlawful I did could in any way incriminate you, sir."

"For a start, there were objections when I asked you to handle the Lyonnaise silk. They all knew that yours is the only company capable of handling the export of silk to Europe, Canada and America, but they wanted the government to handle everything so that they would get the kudos. They wanted to demonstrate that the new French Republic can do anything better than the big companies can."

"Even if the French Republic does not have the capital, the contacts or the expertise to carry out the task?"

"Exactly! Then last year, they insisted that you were trying to deceive me and were about to smuggle nobles out of the country in the packages of silk and that the vehicles you brought from Marseille had secret compartments. I had my inspectors check every single parcel of silk minutely, and I sent my report to Paris. I later heard from one of my personal informants that it was feared that the inspections I had ordered had been cursory."

"Perhaps that is why, immediately the silk was loaded on to our ship, two representatives of the local Jacobin club insisted on examining our vehicles again."

"I was not aware of that; but it does not surprise me.

"The week before last, two days after you had departed for Frankfurt, the two inspectors from Paris arrived with a letter from *La Directoire*, informing me of the arrest of *citoyen* Creuse and of your involvement with him. Their informant had claimed that Creuse had constructed the carriage in his own coach workshop and that it was bristling with spacious hiding places which he had filled with his money and valuables. They also swore that you were implicated as the courier. The implication was that I was protecting you. The inspectors had instructions to remain here and apprehend you immediately you returned."

Nicole gave him her best "restrained umbrage" look.

"There are always people who will stop at nothing to besmirch one's good name."

"As I am sure you are now well aware, I was forbidden to contact you other than to ensure you were arrested – hence my terse note."

"It did cross my mind that you wanted me to read between the lines."

After they had dined, Fouché accompanied his colleague as she was driven to her hotel and, on the way there he apologised once again for the "shocking ordeal" that she had been forced to endure, adding –

"Madame, I assure you that the promise I gave you when we started working together five years ago is not forgotten – nor will it be. If circumstances are ever such that you are arrested and put on trial, I shall do whatever I can to facilitate your escape. I am telling you this now, as it is important that both your sons are aware of my promise. We live in dangerous times. Tomorrow I must return to Paris. Since the execution of Georges Danton and his fellow conspirators in April, many strange things have occurred. Robespierre has hardly appeared at the Convention and there is dissatisfaction everywhere. I can assure you, Madame, there is not a single member of the Convention who is not fearful of being the next to be guillotined."

"When will this bloody *Terreur* stop?"

Fouché leaned forward and, in almost a whisper, he replied.

"Unfortunately, it will continue just so long as Maximilien Robespierre is there."

"If that is true, we must get rid of him at once."

"I wholeheartedly agree; but, of all people, you, Madame, must not use that word 'we'. Your hands are clean and they must stay that way. Mine and those of Paul Barras are already well stained with blood."

* * *

Nicole did not sleep well that night. Her twenty-four hours in the filthy Lyon prison and the plight of its inmates haunted her – as did her still vivid picture of the faces of those who were about to be executed. As she lay in bed with her eyes wide open, what puzzled her more than anything else was how William knew that the carriage had to be rebuilt in such a way that even a minute examination of it would fail to detect that it had been used to smuggle large quantities of Monsieur Creuse's valuables out of France. And what did Fouché and Barras intend doing to Robespierre? What if Robespierre knew what they were about and had them killed first?

As she lay there, sleepless, she resolved to distance herself from this hideous holocaust. She had grown to hate everything about the new Republican regime in France. Throughout the country, the cruelty and the bloodshed of the *Terreur* sickened her and she felt that it was no longer possible for her to work in an atmosphere that was constantly polluted with brutality, intrigue and jealousy.

In 1789 she had wholeheartedly supported the Convention because she believed that the establishment of a national law-making body representing the people would improve the lot of the poor and the workers on the lower rungs of the economic and social ladders. Over the next five years, those who claimed they would transform France into a country where Liberty, Equality and Fraternity would be the right of every citizen, had beheaded their king and queen – and half the nobles – of France and, not content with this, they set about exterminating everybody whose politics were at variance with their own. And yet, the lot of the under-privileged was no better than it had been under the *ancien régime*. The country was not being governed by the Estates General, as they promised it would be but by a *Directoire* of five men elected by the left-wing, regional Jacobin clubs. Since coming to power, these radicals had set up tribunals of their own to charge, arraign and pass death sentences on whomever they wished – and then to summarily confiscate their entire estates.

It was with all these aggravating thoughts weighing heavily on her mind that she eventually dozed off into a restless sleep – and when she awoke at dawn, the same thoughts were still tormenting her. Setting out for Marseille as early as she could, she was determined that, for the next couple of years, Robert Gerbier would handle the silk contracts and the trips to Lyon and that William – dear William who had probably saved her life – was more than capable of managing all the banking aspects of the deal.

Although Joseph Fouché had virtually told her what was about to happen, it was quite a shock to Nicole when, less than two weeks later, she read of the arrest and execution of Robespierre and all his lieutenants. The effect of his death was electric. It was if the great pall of fear that had been hanging over the Convention had been lifted and everyone was now able to breathe a little more easily. Fouché, Barras and Tallien had triumphed and they would end the *Terreur* and the tribunal would be abolished.

They were as good as their word and this did in fact happen. Even so, Nicole made as few Channel crossings as possible each year and, when she did, she spent as much time as she could in Marseille and as few days as possible in Paris. She would have been far happier not going there at all but, because of the family's widespread interests in the country, she had to ensure that nothing fell into the clutches of the ruthless, greedy Jacobins.

VIII

ON ONE OF HER FEW VISITS to Paris, Nicole met Paul Barras at the theatre. They were both in the same party of *délégués* and, as was invariably the case, he was with an elegant, well-dressed young woman whom he introduced as Vicomtesse Rose Beauharnais, the widow of the patriot Général Alexandre de Beauharnais. During the long supper that usually followed evenings at the theatre, Nicole found herself sitting next to this strangely attractive lady and had an opportunity to learn a little of her past. Like most Parisians, she knew quite a lot about the Beauharnais family and the handsome but dilettante Alexandre who had been guillotined some eighteen months previously; but all she had known about his Créole wife was that she had been one of the first women to obtain a divorce under the new laws which gave women the same rights as their husbands had for generations enjoyed. In the early months of the *Terreur,* Rose's estranged husband had been suspected of having royalist sympathies and had been thrown into the revolting Les Carmes prison. In the witch hunt that followed his arrest, Rose, too, had been incarcerated in the same prison.

Nicole found Rose a charming and fascinating woman and as the evening progressed and the champagne flowed freely, the conversation between them became quite intimate. They talked about their children, their childhood and about life.

Rose Beauharnais asked Nicole –

"Do you believe in 'destiny'?"

"My grandfather, whom I adored, had a wonderful saying – *Hasard est le nom de Dieu quand il ne veut pas signer!*[25] Yes I do believe in destiny. Do you?"

---

[25] Destiny is God's name when He does not wish to sign!

"When I was a young girl in Martinique, my girl friend and I went to one of the famous fortune tellers for which our island is renowned. She told me that, one day, I should be empress of my country."

"I wish you luck, vicomtesse!"

"But she also said that it would bring me no happiness."

Little did either of them know that, within a very few years, one of the most remarkable metamorphoses of all time would occur, in that the beautiful, sensuous Créole, Rose Beauharnais, would emerge as Josephine, Empress of France.

Born in 1763, Rose Tascher de la Pagerie, the viscountess was a daughter of a well-known French Créole family who lived in Martinique. Like so many of the French who had settled in that part of the world, Rose's family had extensive sugar plantations. Worked by harshly treated slave labour, cane sugar – or, as it was so often called, white gold – was indeed a profitable business. The Créoles – the French who had emigrated to the colonies of the Windward Islands such as Martinique – were accepted by the European French, but with certain reservations; very much as, fifty years later, the English viewed the colonists of Australia – except, whereas the Antipodeans visiting London were all thought of as being the owners of vast acreages of land and thousands of sheep, the Créoles were perceived as being sugar millionaires. In all other respects the same perceptions and prejudices prevailed – and the same judgements were made. For a start, their vulgar accent was an insult to the ear, their conversation – if any – was banal and, as far as their social graces were concerned, they were conspicuous by their absence. Rose had arrived in Paris the epitome of all these attributes.

She had been brought up on a sugar plantation in Martinique, adored by her mother and coddled by her slave nurse. During her early childhood, the family plantation had been decimated by a horrendous hurricane, a disaster from which the Tascher de la Pageries never really recovered.

Like so many other daughters of Créole families, Rose was shipped off to Paris where her marriage to the nineteen-year-old Alexandre, son of the Marquis de Beauharnais, had been arranged. The marriage was for her family – and for her – a great joy and a particularly satisfactory solution to the problem of finding a suitably acceptable and adequately rich husband. For Alexandre, a handsome young officer whose libido was as overdeveloped as his ego, the idea of marriage was nothing more than an annoying impediment to his social and sexual extravagances. A few years before his marriage, a fellow army officer, Choderlos de Laclos, had written *Les Liaisons Dangereuses* in which he vividly portrayed the profligate lives of Paris's loose-living upper class. The publication of this book had caused an uproar and when it was known that the story was based on living people, the tongue wagging and finger pointing that went on in *le grand monde*[26] provided a field day for the scandal-loving Parisians. Alexandre Beauharnais's own life mirrored that which Laclos had so colourfully and accurately described in his novel.

Using his army duties as an excuse for long absences from his three years younger bride, Alexandre spent as much time away from her as he could and he hardly ever saw the two children she bore him. Socialising and womanising whenever and wherever he could, he found Rose dull, uninteresting – and a total social failure. This was rendered all the more unfortunate because she adored and worshipped him. The unhappy union was terminated when Alexandre made a series of scurrilous and totally unfounded allegations concerning his wife's sexual conduct. In spite of the strenuous efforts made by Rose's family and his, too, to persuade him to withdraw his fabrications, Alexandre remained as obdurate as he was vindictive and prurient. It was in this climate of domestic acrimony that Rose separated herself from him.

In Paris, the Church owned much of the real estate, including many convents where spinsters, widows and deserted wives could live in congenial surroundings. Not all these hospices were religious institutions abounding with prayer, meditation and virtuous living. In fact, of more than one hundred of these convents in Paris, a number of them were quite luxurious. Small suites and even apartments were available and, provided they attended prayers, the inmates could receive guests and come and go as they pleased.

The convent of Panthémont, within the walls of which Rose

---

[26] High society.

Beauharnais spent the next few years of her life, was as elegant as its surroundings. Situated in Rue de Grenelle in Faubourg Saint-Germain, its stately buildings were set in a park-like garden. It was here that the gauche young Créole was thrust into a cultured society of educated and accomplished women. They dressed impeccably, their *maquillage*[27] was exquisite, their manners were polished and their conversation was scintillating.

Rose was a quick learner. She listened to their conversation and she slavishly copied their accent and their turn of phrase. She noticed how they walked, how they sat down and how they held their tea cups – and she learned to do everything as they did. Above all, the young Créole paid attention when they talked about men, about their affairs – and about their lovemaking techniques, about which they talked quite freely. With each month that she lived in the convent of Panthémont she became more like the others, more like an elegant, polished young woman of *le grand monde*.

While she was serving her apprenticeship in the convent, having listened to the wise words – and the advice – of her fellow inmates, she realised that she had grounds for redress of the wrongs inflicted on her by her husband. Her friends at the convent knew people in high places and they assisted her in filing a formal complaint against Alexandre. They rehearsed her in what she should say to the *Maître* who investigated such cases and, although it took seemingly ages for the wheels of officialdom to turn, much to Alexandre's chagrin, a judgment was made against him. The court ordered him to apologise to Rose and to provide her and their two children with the wherewithal to live where she so desired, in surroundings appropriate to her station in life.

It had been thus that, after an unhappy and lonely four years of married life, at nearly twenty-one years of age, Rose Beauharnais emerged from the convent a captivating, sophisticated young Parisienne with the natural charm, seductiveness – and even voluptuousness – for which Martinique, her motherland, had always been famous.

In 1789, when Louis XVI called together the Estates General, the ambitious Alexandre Beauharnais had himself elected as one of the

---

[27] Make-up.

reformist nobles representing Blois. He played his hand brilliantly and was soon advancing in the ranks of the newly formed *l'Assemblée nationale*, and it was not long before he was made its president. His term of office completed, he returned to the army where, due to the incompetence and falling from favour of a succession of senior generals, he found himself chief of staff to the commander of the army of the Rhine. Within months he was a divisional commander and finally, in 1793, he was given command of the whole army.

Not a particularly capable tactician or administrator and far more interested in being in the arms of the wife of another officer or a prostitute – he cared little which – he was soon disgraced and discharged. The inquiry that followed and the allegations of dereliction of duty made against him by the Committee for Public Safety were much easier to prove than had been the groundless charges he had levelled at Rose in the early years of their marriage. In 1794 he was incarcerated in the dreaded Les Carmes prison, to await his trial.

That the unfortunate Rose was a vicomtesse and the wife of a disgraced general made it almost inevitable that she, too, was arrested and thrown into prison – the same gaol as was Alexandre. Not surprisingly, in the revolting conditions of Les Carmes there was *détente* and even warmth between them; in fact, they wrote joint letters to their children, but this was as intimate as their relationship became, because they were both too busy having affairs; Alexandre had fallen madly in love with Delphine, the beautiful widow of Général Custine, who had been guillotined shortly before Beauharnais had arrived at Les Carmes. This did not worry Rose in the least as she had become besotted with the brilliant and dashing Général Lazare Hoche, one of the finest soldiers in the new Republican army. Although he was a few years younger than Rose, his wisdom, his temperament and his good humour did much to make her life more bearable. There was the added benefit for Rose in that he, being a not yet convicted top army general, was entitled to his own room and to proper meals – which Rose shared – and appreciated at least as much as he did. The ardour of neither of them appeared to be dampened by the fact that, less than two weeks before he was arrested, Lazare Hoche was married to the delightful sixteen-year-old Adelaide Dechaux.

As was the case for all the other prisoners in Les Carmes, the four lovers were required to attend the assembly each morning, when the names of those who were to be taken to the tribunal for trial – and, from there to the guillotine for execution – were read out. Each day, it was a tense and terrifying time for all of them, hearing a name announced and then watching that person walk unemotionally through the door to the waiting tumbrels. This stoic exit was a ritual agreed to by all the prisoners and, to their credit, but for a few exceptions, it was honoured by them all.

On 21 July Alexandre's name was called out. Both Delphine and Rose, paralysed with shock, clung grimly to Hoche. Like hundreds of victims before him, Alexandre walked, his head unbowed, through the door. This was only a few days before Robespierre was arrested, tried and executed on the same scaffold.

Ten days later Rose Beauharnais was released into a Paris that was almost unrecognisable. Although she was greatly relieved to be once again united with her children, she found life intolerable. The filth, stray animals and gangs of marauding youths in the streets, shortages of all the necessities of life and spiralling inflation made life difficult, dangerous and unpleasant. With her possessions still held under lock and key by the authorities, being desperately short of money, resourceful and particularly attractive, Rose made it her business to survive – in the only way she knew how. She found a succession of wealthy men who considered her company as being so refreshing and beguiling that they were anxious to help her through this difficult period of her life. It was in this context that she decided to renew her acquaintance with Joseph Barras, one of the most powerful men in France and it was only a few months after the beginning of this liaison – not all that *dangereuse* – that Nicole first met Rose at the theatre in Paris.

* * *

To Nicole's mind, everything in Paris seemed to have gone berserk. Nobody seemed to be doing anything about hygiene and the police appeared to be powerless – or without the will – to curb the wave of violence and crime that had the city in its grip. Equally unacceptable were the new rulers of France who were behaving in exactly the same way as the royalty and nobility of the *ancien régime* had behaved. In some respects their conduct was even more reprehensible in that, whereas the nobles had almost invariably enjoyed their gastronomical and alcoholic excesses and their frequent sexual orgies in the privacy of their palaces and their châteaux, the new upper class were brazenly flaunting themselves and their debauchery. The women frequently appeared in public wearing little more than diaphanous togas and it became quite popular to have the bodices of their dresses fashioned in such a way as to fully expose one of their – usually ample – breasts.

Rose acted as hostess to most of Paul Barras's receptions and dinners, both in Paris and when he was in residence in his country estate. One of these dinners was enough to persuade Nicole that Paris was no longer a place for her to socialise.

Under the three sparkling, luminous chandeliers in the grand dining room – and led by the evening's host and Rose – the entire company of guests laughed and drank while they happily participated in almost every form of licentiousness from aphrodisiacal dances to blatant lovemaking.

Nicole, for nearly two years the assistant manager of The Cloisters, one of London's elite seraglios, was neither a prude nor a killjoy, but during her journey back to London, she resolved not to pay another visit to Paris until cleanliness, order, sanity and propriety had returned.

* * *

Not long after Lady Scott-Quetteville returned to London in 1795 Napoléon Buonaparte met Rose Beauharnais. The previous year, that had started so propitiously for him, turned sour when Maximilien Robespierre and his close associates were put to death. The young general, in charge of the artillery of the army that was about to invade Italy, was a close friend of Robespierre's brother, Augustin. He was suspected of being a Robespierre supporter and was suspended from duty. The ambitious and unscrupulous young Corsican had no qualms in unashamedly denouncing both the brothers Robespierre, and was reinstated. Nevertheless, he found it difficult to be accepted for any worthwhile military appointment. As all such postings were made in Paris, he moved into l'Hôtel de la Tranquillité and did his best to set up some contacts. After weeks of inactivity, with little more to do than wander the streets, he became depressed – as he so often did when things were not going the way he had planned.

Hoping to get some support, he went to see Paul Barras who, with Robespierre out of the way, had become more powerful than ever. Having been close to Buonaparte during the battle to recapture Toulon and having formed an extremely high opinion of him as a soldier and a leader, Barras had little difficulty in finding him a planning appointment with the Committee for Public Safety.

A couple of months later, in October, there was an uprising in Paris and an unruly mob marched towards the Tuileries Palace where the *Assemblée nationale* was meeting. Barras, now virtually the *generalissimo* of the armed forces, saw this revolt as being a dangerous threat to the government. He ordered Napoléon to immediately prepare to defend the Tuileries. With Joachim Murat[28], a dynamic young cavalry officer, he quickly moved several batteries of guns to the scene and positioned them to meet the mob if they continued to converge on the Convention – which they did. Thousands of Parisians – men and women – surrounded the palace, shouting abuse. One or two shots fired by over-excited protesters were enough to incite Buonaparte into action. He ordered his gunners to fire over open gun-sights at the mob. The result was as terrifying as it was decisive. Hundreds of Parisians were killed, hundreds more were wounded and the mob quickly dispersed. It was the end of the uprising and whereas, once again, the young general was hailed as a saviour, many members of the *Assemblée nationale* were horrified with the violent and ruthless manner in which he had carried out his orders. He brushed his critics aside, stating that it had been nothing more than a "whiff of gunshot" – a comment that was to go down in history.

Once again Barras was impressed with the young Corsican and invited him to his magnificent home in the Luxembourg Palace. He congratulated him on the manner in which he had carried out his orders and informed him that he would be shortly taking up the appointment of

---

[28] In 1800 he married Napoléon's youngest sister Caroline. He was later made King of Naples.

commander of the army that was poised to invade Italy to drive out the Austrians. He referred to Buonaparte's role in quelling the uprising.

"You certainly carried out my orders to break up the mob. For that you deserve my praise."

"Thank you, sir!"

"Between us, I think it would be fair to say that perhaps the task could have been done with less loss of life."

"Sir, it is always difficult to make decisions in situations like the one to which you refer. Uprisings of this kind can easily get out of hand and when that happens the loss of life can be much greater."

"What you say is correct, Buonaparte, and I can tell you something else, too; you acted in a way that your critics – and there are more than a few of them – can no longer say that you are not an unequivocal supporter of the Revolution."

"Thank you, sir!"

"Buonaparte, sit down, please!"

Barras, who was also standing, drew a chair close to where the young artillery commander was seated. He continued speaking.

"You are an excellent officer and I am sure you will go far, but you worry me in that, when you are not either in the field with your troops or in a headquarters studying your military plans, you seem lost. I think you would do better if you mixed more…er…socially – if you know what I mean."

"To be successful socially, one needs position, connections and money – all of which I lack. Sir, do you remember *citoyenne* Scott-Quetteville, whom we met before the relief of Toulon?"

"Of course I do; but I cannot for the life of me see what she has to do with your social life. Why do you ask the question?"

"I have known her and her family since I was a cadet in *l'École Militaire*. She was very good to me and I stayed with her family during our vacations. She is so unlike the people in the upper echelons of society – so different in every way. During our several meetings in Toulon, she gave me some advice concerning what I should do to be more accepted socially. It was more about my personal appearance than anything else."

"That is interesting, Buonaparte. I have noticed that, since you were in Toulon, the manner in which you wear your uniform has improved in a number of ways. I can assure you that a man's appearance will do more to get him a bride – or a mistress – than almost anything else."

"Sir, nobody in France has been more successful with women than you have. Even before you were as famous as you are today, women – married and single, young and old – would die for you."

"Why this flattery, Buonaparte?"

"Believe me, sir, what I have said is not flattery. Sincere appreciation, yes, but flattery, no! You have been a wonderful patron to me. The other senior generals either look at me as if I were a piece of social dung or they are jealous because I am dedicated to my profession and have studied military history and because my troops believe in me. You said that a man's appearance is 'almost' the most important attribute in capturing a woman. What is it that is more important than appearance?"

Paul Barras, the compulsive womaniser and seducer, laughed.

"There are two things that are more important: one is the thing between your legs; the other is the skill with which you use it."

"Very confidentially, sir, as far as my body is concerned, nature has not been at all kind to me. I am several inches shorter than any of my officers and, to address them, I have to look up…and what is between my legs is a disappointment not only to me but to every woman I have ever bedded. Some have even laughed at it. Over the years this has somehow sapped my sexual confidence and, in consequence my ability to satisfy my lovers. I must confess, sir, that at times it has made me so depressed that I have even contemplated suicide."

"What nonsense, Buonaparte, there is no finer general in the army of the French Republic. You must at all costs stay alive, but that the very thought of unleashing yourself with gusto inside a woman does not fill your mind and your loins with almost uncontrollable passion is a shocking state of affairs. I promise you, young man, I shall find someone who will cure you of your malaise."

"I have always had a passion for virgins because I believe they will not compare me unfavourably with their former lovers and, for this reason, when I find a woman who is not a virgin, I always give her a new name.

This allows me to fantasise and believe that, because she is being made love to with a new name, she is once again a virgin!

"We all have our fantasies, Buonaparte, and I shall do my best to help you turn some of yours into reality. I shall introduce you to one or two young women who could be helpful to you socially, too. In my opinion, a few more social graces and some nights of passion will not hurt your military career, either. I look forward to hearing from you how you fare with the beautiful, vivacious – and promiscuous – Thérésia Tallien[29], the young woman to whom I recently introduced you. If she fails to awaken some good old-fashioned lust in you, I still have another card up my sleeve – an ace."

As things turned out, his association with Thérésia Tallien was a disaster. She laughed at Buonaparte's proposal that they should become romantically involved with each other and declared that she had heard too many stories of his *tout petit bonhomme*.[30]

Her unkindness even extended to mentioning to her friends his reluctance to take a daily bath and that he had scabies – a chronic condition that was to remain with him throughout his life. This rejection was almost too much for the already morose and sullen young general. However, Paul Barras came to the rescue and was as good as his word. As one of France's wealthiest, most powerful leaders – and one of the most profligate – women were to him quite expendable. Within weeks he masterminded – and directed – a romantic and historic drama that would bring matrimonial success within Buonaparte's reach and, at the same time, solve one of his own small problems.

The heroine of his drama was to be his mistress, the Countess Beauharnais. There was no doubt that Rose was an accomplished lover: seductive, imaginative and sexually fulfilling, but he knew from past experience that it was time for her tenure of office as his *maîtresse déclarée* to be terminated. It was not that he was wearying of her or that she no longer aroused him; nothing could have been further from the truth. It was more because for him, the compulsive roué, the apophthegm – the

---

[29] Wife of Jean-Lambert Tallien, one of the post-Robespierre Jacobin leaders, the strength of whose libido was notorious.
[30] Tiny Tim.

chase is thrilling but the appetite not lasting – was so perfectly apt. The novelty of exploring fresh fields and the challenge of new sexual conquests were essential parts of the game he played.

He considered that to pass Rose over to the six years younger Napoléon had considerable merit. She had social credentials of the highest order and, if there was anyone in the world who could arouse him, it would most certainly be she. Furthermore, he had not overlooked the fact that, for quite a few years to come, the general would be leading France's armies, firstly in Italy and then goodness knows where else. While he was absent, Rose, who had always lived well beyond her means, would inevitably need extra financial support – and would know where to find her former lover.

The two young people's first social engagement, carefully orchestrated by Barras, could not have been held in more beautiful surroundings – his sumptuous residence, the Luxembourg Palace – now called *La Palais de Légalité*. The cream of Paris society were there, dressed in their finery. The wine was the best and, in spite of the acute shortage of food throughout the country, the dinner was extravagantly delicious.

Under the magnificent, sparkling chandeliers, Rose looked irresistible. As she walked across the dance floor, every head turned in her direction. Not only her beauty and her *décolletage* that accentuated her voluptuous body attracted their attention but, equally, the seductive movements of her hands and her languorous – almost mulatto – way of moving. Napoléon Buonaparte was completely smitten. Her olive skin, her beautiful eyes and her slightly husky voice with a nuance of Créole accent mesmerised him and banished the demons that had for so long haunted his mind: his impecuniosity, his lack of social graces, his shortness of stature and his phallic inadequacy. This was the most fabulous woman he had ever set eyes upon – and he was determined to claim her for his own.

In the harsh daylight of the morrow, there was no fading of his vision of this wonderful woman or a softening of his resolve. On the contrary, he realised there was a further reason why she should be his wife; no woman in Paris had better social and political connections than Rose and there was no man nor woman for whom so many doors were open. Then and there, even before he knew her well, he informed her that Josephine was a much more beautiful name for her and that, in the future, it would be the name by which he would address her.

At first Rose – now Josephine – was quite ambivalent about the attentions of Général Buonaparte. Over the past few years, she had met many generals – and had entertained more than a few of them. There were two factors, however, that influenced her in making a decision about this short young man whose head seemed a little too big for his body. Firstly, Paul Barras had assured her that his star was rising and that, in his opinion, it was indeed a bright star that could easily dominate the sky – and she knew what an astute judge and how influential Paul Barras was. Secondly, from her childhood, Rose had always nurtured a feeling that destiny was calling her. This feeling dated back to the incident that occurred well before she had arrived in France.

In Martinique, as in all the islands of the Caribbean, voodoo and the occult played a far bigger part in people's lives than was the case in France. It was not particularly surprising, therefore, that, at thirteen years of age, Rose Tascher de la Pagerie and two of her girl friends decided to visit old Euphémie, the local sorcerer, who had the reputation of being one of the most accomplished occultists on the island. Her potions had worked, she had cured people where doctors had failed and her predictions had come to pass. In the case of the three young girls, the word picture she painted of how each of their lives would unfold turned out to be precisely as she had said. For Rose she foresaw two marriages and she quite accurately described each of her future husbands-to-be. She predicted that the second husband would become famous and that she would become greater than a queen. In conclusion she warned young Rose that all this success would bring with it regret and much unhappiness.

Throughout Rose's life Euphémie's prophecies remained in the forefront of her mind and she often referred to them. Even when she was imprisoned in Les Carmes, her belief in her destiny never left her; in fact, this more than anything else made her feel confident that, while every day the people around her were being marched off to the guillotine, she would stay alive.

Rose considered the young general to be a lacklustre lover and he was anything but an Adonis to look at. There was another important consideration: he was nowhere near as wealthy as any of the other men with whom she had been romantically or sexually involved. As things turned out, it was as much her sense of destiny as it was the urging of Barras that eventually made her decide to accept Napoléon's proposal of marriage.

Several days after the engagement was announced, Nicole received a visit from Paul Barras, who was still the most powerful man in France. When they were talking about the forthcoming marriage of Napoléon Buonaparte to Rose Beauharnais, Barras suddenly changed the subject in a way that Nicole thought surprising.

"Madame la Comtesse, I believe you know Madame Genet-Campan?"

"I presume you are referring to Henriette Campan, who was Queen Marie-Antoinette's First Lady of the Bedchamber?"

"Yes, that is the lady to whom I refer."

"I certainly do know her and I hold her in the highest regard. I have not heard from her since the outbreak of the Revolution. As a matter of fact, I was fearful that she may have been a victim of the witch hunt that followed the overthrow of the monarchy."

"No, thank goodness, that is not the case. After several particularly difficult years, she is alive and well. By selling her jewellery — which incidentally included some valuable pieces given to her by the queen — she has scraped together enough money to buy the Hotel de Rohan in St Germain-en-Laye and she has converted it into a *pensionnat* — a private boarding school for girls. My friend, Rose Beauharnais, wishes to know if it would be a proper establishment in which to enrol her daughter Hortense."

"As a matter of interest, sir, who suggested to you that I might know Madame Campan?"

"As you are most probably aware, we have all the police files relating to the close contacts of Marie-Antoinette and there is evidence that, through the British Embassy, you were supplying Madame Campan with English newspapers."

"That is quite true. As she was a close friend of mine, I was doing that regularly. However, in answer to your question, my opinion of Madame Campan is such that I can assure you that if my own grand-daughter was at the appropriate age, I should have no hesitation in suggesting that she should attend any school under the direction of Madame Campan."

Rose's daughter, Hortense Beauharnais, did so well at this school that Napoléon arranged for his sisters, Caroline and Pauline, to be enrolled there too. Apart from the fact that Caroline, much to the annoyance of Madame Campan, received constant nocturnal visits from Joachim Murat, Napoléon's military protégé[31], she too benefited greatly from Madame Campan's influence. So impressed was Napoléon with Henriette that after he became First Consul, he appointed her to establish a school for the daughters of those Frenchmen who had been decorated with the newly created Legion of Honour.

The wedding of Josephine with Napoléon took place in an upstairs room of what had once been a grand hotel that had been requisitioned by the Republican government and let fall into disrepair. It was being used as the *Mairie* – town hall – of one of the municipalities of Paris. Admittedly the ceremony left much to be desired. To begin with, as both Rose's family and Napoléon's, too, had boycotted the wedding, there were only a handful of people present. The bridegroom was two hours late, the officiating celebrant was apparently not licensed to perform the ceremony and Napoléon's witness was under age – and therefore not legally eligible to sign. Furthermore, both the bride and groom had misstated their ages; Rose had reduced hers by three years and her groom had added a year to his. This was done to make it appear she was only twelve months older than he was!

Napoléon later – when writing his memoirs on St Helena – described his first night in wedlock as being "unsatisfactory", stating that they were both tired after a long day and that Josephine's dog, Fortuné, not only insisted on sharing the marriage bed, but added injury to insult by biting his leg.

The following day, Général Bonaparte[32] made the final plans for his army's invasion of Italy and then departed for the campaign that would cover him in glory and deliver him considerable personal wealth. He had badly wanted to take his Josephine with him; however, in its wisdom, the

---

[31] She married him shortly after leaving the *pensionnat*.

[32] After his marriage to Josephine, Napoléon made strenuous efforts to appear more "French" and less Corsican. He took speech lessons to improve his French accent and he dropped the letter "u" from the spelling of his family name.

supreme headquarters – under command of Général Barras – withheld her passport. This decision was made because it was considered that the young general, being besotted with his bride, might pay too much attention to her and neglect his military duties.

* * *

It was only a few weeks after Nicole's return to London that a date was set for William's marriage with Gerda. Although the engaged couple only gave their families and friends six weeks notice, it promised to be "one of the events of the season".

The plans for a big wedding had to be suddenly changed, however, owing to a heart attack suffered by Herr Hoffmann. This proved to be fatal and, in spite of his young widow's dramatically tearful insistence that there could be no wedding for at least six months, a quiet ceremony was held in Frankfurt. The entire Scott-Quetteville family arrived from London – including little Ettie – and Herr Eisen, one of the Hoffmann family's oldest friends, gave the bride away. Herr and Frau Rothschild were invited and although their religion precluded their presence in the church, they attended the reception that followed. Nicole, who introduced them to many of the guests as her cousins, made them feel proud to the point of embarrassment. For Mayer, who for years afterwards kept the invitation on the mantelpiece of his parlour, it was one of the proudest days of his life.

The wedding reception was a happy family affair that lasted well into the night and it was a rather exhausted and sleepy bunch of Scott-Quettevilles who set out for London the following morning. Seven-year-old John and Judah, who had been allowed to stay up until after eleven o'clock in the evening, slept all the way from Frankfurt to Mainz, where they boarded a large barge that took them down the Rhine to the coast and the ship that was waiting to take them back to London.

Being only three weeks before Christmas, the main social event they were all looking forward to was the annual Woking New Year's Eve ball, followed by the breakfast, the hunt and the formal dinner. For Lord David, who had celebrated his eighty-third birthday a few weeks previously, this hunting weekend was the main event of the year – all the more so now that his daughters and Nicole's sons had grown up and had spouses, fiancés and friends to be there, too.

The ball was as colourful as ever with what David described as "the finest bunch of the most beautiful of England's elegant young women and the cream of England's handsome young men", being present.

As had been expected there were quite a few empty seats at the pre-hunt breakfast; the absentees all being from the "young brigade" – who had danced into the early hours of the morning. However, that they had, by missing the breakfast, thereby forfeited their right to be present at the dinner that evening, was irrelevant because disaster struck when Lord Bassett fell at one of the jumps and was rolled on by his horse. It was not that he had lost any of his riding skills but rather that his mount shied when a riderless horse cut right across in front of him just as he had taken off. He never regained consciousness.

Although he died as he had always wanted to go, his death was a great shock to Hélène, his three daughters – and to Nicole. For a number of years David had made no secret of the fact that he wanted to die when he was out hunting or riding and he had, on a number of occasions, made it abundantly clear that, if this should happen at the New Year's hunt, there must be no cancellation of the planned dinner or any of the other festivities. The Scott-Quetteville menfolk mourned him as they had their own father and Judy had been equally sad.

Hélène, in honouring her husband's wish, decided that the dinner that evening would go ahead as planned and that all – even the breakfast absentees – should be present to drink to David and to "see him over the Styx."

Within a week of the funeral, Hélène and Nicole had left for Etreham, together with the three Bassett daughters and Judy. They spent three or four weeks there, quietly mourning a strong courageous soldier, a wonderful husband, an adoring father and a wise and loving friend.

IX

IN 1775 THE BRIDGE COMPANY board of directors resolved to research and develop an adaptation of James Watt's steam engine for propelling ocean-going ships. So important did the board regard this project that Sir John Scott-Quetteville, the managing director of the company, devoted almost all of his time to it. Meetings were held with James Watt and a facility was built on the Thames in London, on the Isle of Dogs.

The work progressed well for the first five years and, because similar work was being done on the river Saône, near Lyon, by the Marquis de Jouffroy, there was much sharing of technology between the two projects. When the French syndicate ran into financial difficulties, Sir John assisted them with an infusion of capital and loan funds and he sent a team of his engineers to work with them. Although success was achieved in 1783 and Jouffroy's *Pyroscaphe* became the world's first steamboat, there were two major difficulties: firstly, the boiler being used was not nearly big enough to provide steam for an ocean-going vessel; and secondly, the project was sabotaged by the *bataliers* – the companies who owned all the rowing boats that handled all the river trade. Sir John moved his operation to Paris where as soon as success was in sight, sabotage not only dealt the project a heavy blow, but claimed Sir John's life.

Regarding steam power as being of fundamental importance to the future of the shipping industry, The Bridge Company steadfastly persevered with the project. Until his death in America, in 1790, Senior Captain William Webster took over the management of the venture, which was incorporated as the British Steamship Company.

From the time he became Prime Minister, in 1783, William Pitt recognised the enormous significance of the work Scott-Quetteville and his team were doing and he was instrumental in arranging for the Royal Navy to become actively involved.

* * *

Thomas Coutts, for many years one of London's leading bankers, had been chairman of The Bridge Company since 1766 and, although he had retired from business, he maintained his interest in the company. On Webster's death, he advised the board to consider bringing back to England either François Scott-Quetteville from New South Wales or William from Frankfurt. Lady Nicole, also a member of the board, had her say.

"Firstly I agree wholeheartedly that the future of both this company, and the Messageries Maritimes de Marseille company, too, depends on our ability to lead the shipping industry into the age of steam. It is imperative, therefore, that we have a forceful, competent person leading our research team. As far as either of Sir John's sons are concerned, there are two things to be considered: which of the two – if either – is prepared to forsake his present career and become an executive member of the company and how long we are prepared to wait for the son concerned to acquire a thorough knowledge of steam."

Sir Jean-Marc, the oldest of the three Scott-Quetteville sons, whenever his military duties permitted him to be in London, was also present at some of the board meetings of the family's company, and was present at this one.

"Mr Chairman, whenever we three brothers have the opportunity, we discuss the affairs of our family company and when we are apart, which is for far too much of the time, we constantly exchange our ideas by letter. Although his passion for the maritime applications of steam claimed our father's life, all three of us recognise that unless at least one of us devotes his energies to the development of steam, the future of our family company will be either bleak or else it will have no future at all."

Since Jean-Marc had been appointed to the board, Thomas Coutts had formed a high opinion of him and, although he, like everyone else close to Jean-Marc, knew that he was determined to remain a soldier, he was also aware that he wanted to serve on the board and, subject to the exigencies of the service, play whatever role the board wanted him to. He thanked Jean-Marc for his informative comments.

"Your remarks are particularly helpful, Sir Jean-Marc. Do you have any idea which of your brothers is more likely to return to England – and to us?"

"Yes, Mr Chairman, François has informed me that he is willing to do so – and he has read every technical and policy report from the start of the project until six months ago. The more up-to-date papers are somewhere on the high seas, on the way to him."

Coutts and Charles Scott and Captain Richard Wilmott – who recently filled the vacancy caused by William Webster's death – all found it difficult to believe that these three brothers, the oldest of whom had just turned twenty-one – the heritors of the company – took their family business so seriously. Said Charles Scott –

"Jean-Marc, your father would be proud of you three boys, being so vitally interested in his company's future."

"Father often talked to us about The Bridge Company and it was he who told us to work out which of us should be the mastermind – as he called it – on steam. François jumped at the idea and William and I were pleased, although we would have been prepared to do the job if we had to."

Thomas Coutts, who had always been fascinated by the way John Scott's sons stuck together as a team, was relieved that what he thought might turn out to be a major problem was virtually a *fait accompli*.

"Sir Jean-Marc, where is François now? In the jungles of New South Wales?"

"Mr Chairman, I do not know if there are any jungles in or near Sydney. He is either in that town or in Table Bay. The trouble is that Captain Phillip, the governor of the colony, will be reluctant to lose him."

Captain Wilmott joined the discussion.

"I still have many friends in the Admiralty, both here and in Portsmouth. I can assure you that what Sir Jean-Marc says is true. In several of his reports, Phillip has made favourable mention of François's enthusiasm and his business sense and John Hunter, the captain of the HMS *Sirius*, who is one of my close friends, informed me in a letter that he has a bright future as a sailor."

Lady Scott-Quetteville was all smiles.

"Mr Chairman, I think we have discussed this long enough. My New South Welsh twins are nearly two years old and I am longing to see them. I should like to move that Captain Wilmott goes straight from this meeting to whomever he knows at the Admiralty and emphasises how important it is to me, a grandmother, to see my daughter-in-law and my grandsons and that they should be repatriated forthwith. As an afterthought, I do not mind if he mentions the steam project!"

Although there was laughter all round, the older men at the table could not help thinking that Lady Nicole looked more like a young mother than a grandmother. The chairman suggested that a motion, slightly differently framed, would reflect the decision of the board "to make representations to the appropriate authority to have Lieutenant François Scott-Quetteville returned to England, to be seconded to the British Steamship Company's important steamboat project". He added that by requesting a secondment, the door would be open for François to return to the navy at a later date.

Nothing else on this matter was minuted, as they all knew that Lord Grenville, who had taken over from Lord Sydney as secretary of the Home Office, was a client of Coutts Bank and also one of Thomas Coutts's personal friends.

* * *

From the time that representations were made to the Admiralty early in 1791 for François to return to England to take over the "steamboat" project, every ship going to or from New South Wales carried long letters from Lady Nicole and Jean-Marc in London and from François and Judy in Sydney, full of plans and suggestions for the future.

François's letters to London reflected his optimism concerning the success of the new colony. He wanted to erect several buildings in Sydney – as business propositions – and he also wanted the skilled tradesmen and materials needed for this project and to build a decent house for his family. Scott-Quetteville had been granted a tract of land right in the middle of Sydney Town and some broad acres on the Hawkesbury river. He and Judy had inspected the area and were very impressed. However, for the present, they had far too much work to do on their little farm in Sydney Town to think about anything else.

Nicole and Jean-Marc both wanted François back in London as soon as possible but they respected his enthusiasm for the wide open spaces and warm climate of New South Wales. Every letter they received from both him and Judy was full of the magnificence of Sydney harbour and the almost unlimited possibilities that lay ahead for those who were prepared to work. Their letters were so convincing that Nicole had second thoughts about trying to persuade him to return. In her heart she wanted to give him whatever he needed to make his dream come true. She shared her thoughts with Jean-Marc.

"Although I believe he is the right person to head the steamboat project, we must respect his wishes. He is no fool and it could well be that we are not listening intently enough to what he is trying to tell us."

"I agree, Mother; however, I can assure you that François is as committed to steam as the rest of us. His letters to me are full of the importance of steam power to the future of both the Royal Navy and our company. I believe that we can put a proposal to him that he will find attractive and that will not compromise his long-term plans for Sydney."

"What sort of proposition did you have in mind?"

"We shall have our new ship, the *Sydney Bridge*, fitted out, ready to sail, in about five or six months. We could load it with all the things he has said are necessary for his building project and his house and I am sure we could entice a number of families to migrate to New South Wales. If François would be prepared to spend four or five years here in England until we have solved the last remaining problems to enable us to build steamships, he could then return to New South Wales. Incidentally he has no idea that we have named our new 1100-ton ship in honour of his colony."

"I am sure he will be pleased about that, but if he is to be here for five years he will need to have a manager there and a competent person to run his farm, too. Do you think we could find anybody who is sufficiently reliable?"

"Major Templeton, who commands a squadron of the Blues, is about to retire. Every time I mention François's name, he tells me how he would love to retire to New South Wales and become a pioneer. He has only three months to go before he hangs up his riding boots."

"Does he know anything about farming?"

"No, he doesn't; but he is a very good administrator – and he is excellent in the way he handles his men. They all respect him."

"Jean-Marc, do you remember Anthony Buttrose?"

"Do you mean the son of old Buttrose, the head groom at Woking Grange?"

"Yes! Last month when I stayed the weekend in Woking with Hélène, I had a long talk with Anthony – a long listen would be a more accurate description of our interlude. Apparently, he has a cousin in the Royal Marines who is already in New South Wales. His wife and three children are with him. They have been given a hundred acres of land and are going to settle there. If Anthony and his family are prepared to travel to New South Wales, they, too, would qualify for free passages, a land grant and some stock."

* * *

The next day Jean-Marc wrote to François, passing on to him the thoughts and suggestions of the board and those of their mother. He outlined the discussions that had taken place in the board room and at home and their willingness to support his plans to invest in the new colony. He also mentioned Anthony Buttrose and Major Templeton. Having given his brother as clear a picture as possible of how everyone at home was thinking, he summed up by suggesting that, if he would be prepared to return to England for a time, in his absence, Major Templeton could live in his house and be his manager and that Anthony Buttrose could manage his farms. On the other hand, if François did not wish to return, there was no reason why both Templeton and Buttrose could not, with the family's support – if necessary – settle permanently in what François had described as the most exciting place in the world. His letter concluded with an assurance that both he and their mother wanted him – and Judy – to do whatever they felt would give them the most happiness.

Jean-Marc's plan was for the *Sydney Bridge* to take to New South Wales all the things François had requested, then sail to Batavia, where it would load cargo destined for Europe. The ship would then return to Sydney, by which time François and Judy would have made up their mind about their future.

After sending off his letter to François, Jean-Marc had placed an advertisement in the press. The results were extraordinary; he was inundated with replies. After conducting dozens of interviews he had no difficulty at all in finding many highly skilled tradesmen with impeccable references and a genuine desire to settle in the new colony of New South Wales.

After three exciting months of planning and preparation, the *Sydney Bridge* sailed down the Thames on 16 July 1791. On board, as well as the Templetons and the Buttrose family, were more than a dozen skilled tradesmen and their families, all looking forward to a new and better life in New South Wales. During the long voyage Major Templeton, who was in charge of the group, was able to establish an excellent rapport with the would-be migrants. In this he was more than ably assisted by his wife, Florence, who took a keen interest in the welfare — and the problems — of the women and children.

After a long but uneventful voyage the *Sydney Bridge* sailed into Sydney harbour, on 22 March 1792. François, who sighted the ship about an hour before she pulled into the wharf, could not restrain his feelings of elation. He galloped his horse back to his house to impart the exciting news to Judy.

As soon as the landing formalities had been completed, they hurried on board and were greeted by none other than Captain Richard Wilmott, the senior captain of The Bridge Company's fleet. It was one of the great moments of François's life. His family had named this fine, new vessel in honour of the town of which he and Judy were pioneers and had sent a shipload of all the things he had for four years longed for. When they inspected the bills of lading and the inventory of building materials, tools, furniture and household goods, they could not believe their good fortune. He expressed his appreciation to the ship's captain.

"Captain Wilmott, it would not be possible for you to understand the full significance to this settlement of the people and the cargo you have brought here in this beautiful ship. It is quite impossible for me to find the right words to tell you how wonderful it is going to be for us to have a proper house to live in; but it goes much further than that. Seeing what you have brought from England is going to inspire many other people to do precisely the same thing and, before long, there will be a growing number of free settlers coming to live in Sydney Town. Within a few years there will be hundreds of skilled artisans building houses, schools and warehouses here. Sydney is going to grow into a fine city with beautiful buildings, parks and houses. I am quite certain of it."

"Lieutenant François, I am charged to tell you that Lady Scott-Quetteville and other members of our company's board of directors have received many reports from the Admiralty and the Home Office, praising both you and Mrs Scott-Quetteville's achievements. Your work in Table Bay and the example you have both set in rehabilitating a number of the convicts has not gone unnoticed. Captain Hunter, too, in his reports, has praised your performance and has marked you down as a naval officer who will go far."

With a big smile, he added –

"And he was not just referring to the fact that, together with him, in HMS *Sirius*, you circumnavigated the world.

"It has been a most exciting and challenging time for everybody, sir, and my wife and I both feel that we are fortunate to be a part of it."

The captain then handed François a big parcel of mail.

"There are so many letters for you both that I think it is going to take you weeks to read them all."

* * *

Captain Wilmott sought an audience with Captain Phillip and explained to him that The Bridge Company was prepared to establish regular contact with the new colony and that he looked forward to working closely with him and his administration.

"It would appear, Wilmott, that young Scott-Quetteville has been trying to persuade his family that one day Sydney is going to be something more than a penal colony."

"Indeed he has — and quite successfully, too. His wife's letters have been equally full of optimism."

"A most remarkable young woman, Wilmott, and what extraordinary circumstances that resulted in her coming here. I can tell you, sir, her first interview with Collins and me on HMS *Sirius* was something I shall never forget. A mere girl at the time, not yet sixteen, with the sang-froid of a person twice her age."

Richard Wilmott laughed.

"As we all met Major Fortescue in London, your Excellency, we have had detailed accounts of the drama surrounding his rescue, the shocking way she had been convicted of a crime she had not committed, her charm and her *savoir faire*."

"To be fair, Wilmott, what you heard was probably much less of an exaggeration than you might think."

"If you wish to know what I think, your Excellency, it is that the Scott-Quetteville family is singularly fortunate in having her as a member of the clan."

"I have heard a lot about Lady Nicole and, although I am not personally acquainted with her, I look forward to meeting her when I return to England later this year."

"I was not aware that your tour of duty is nearly over."

"It certainly is; in fact Major Grose, who is lieutenant-governor, will be in my seat — in that capacity — when I leave. It is not yet known if he will be appointed as governor. Confidentially, I must admit that I had the temerity to strongly recommend John Hunter[33]."

"I have known him for years. He is a clever and courageous sailor. I have the highest regard for him and I agree with you he would be an ideal person."

"...And he knows as much — if not more — about this place than anyone else."

Major Francis Grose had arrived in the colony in February 1792 and, having expected to find a primitive and totally undeveloped colony, he was pleasantly surprised that, under the leadership and perseverance of

---

[33] After much debate in Whitehall, Hunter became governor in 1795.

Arthur Phillip, houses had been built, farms were beginning to flourish and ships were starting to call regularly.

When Phillip introduced Major Grose to Captain Wilmott, he was unimpressed and although the lieutenant-governor promised his full co-operation and support for The Bridge Company's plan to send ships to New South Wales, his attitude and general conversation appeared to be — and subsequently proved to be — quite superficial.

Captain Wilmott was surprised when an Aboriginal named Bennelong was ushered into the room. Phillip made the introduction. The man was dressed as a European and spoke reasonably good English.

From the outset Governor Phillip had been of the opinion that if he was to make peace with the natives it would be necessary to study their culture and learn their language. In spite of his best efforts, for the first eighteen months he had no success at all. He considered that, if he could "capture" a couple of Aboriginals and treat them well, he and his officers could get closer to them and learn about their customs and their language, and he had sent Lieutenant Bradley to kidnap some Aboriginals. He returned several days later and reported to the Governor.

"I captured two of them, sir."

"That is not what Lieutenant Scott Quetteville told me. He said there is only one of them."

"That is correct sir; the second captive gnawed through the rope we used to tie him up — and he escaped. We still have the other one. His name is Bennelong."

"Good! But use chains on him. It will take him a couple of years to bite through them."

As things turned out, Bennelong appeared to get on well with everyone and as the months went by he was given more freedom, but during the following May, he disappeared — much to the annoyance of Governor Phillip. Six weeks later there were reports that there was a stranded whale on the beach at a native village called Manly, and Bennelong and the other members of his tribe were feasting on it. There were in fact more than two hundred of them.

With a squad of soldiers, Phillip set out to recapture Bennelong. As the patrol neared the beach an Aboriginal warrior leapt at the governor and wounded him with a spear – quite badly. Bennelong, in an effort to prevent what might have developed into widespread bloodshed, agreed to return voluntarily to Sydney in return for an undertaking from the governor that there would be no retribution for the act of aggression against him. Although he became addicted to alcohol, Bennelong was valuable to Phillip both in the teaching of the language and culture of his tribe and in negotiating with them.

"Bennelong has helped me to understand the way Aboriginal people think and has taught me a little of his language. He is a very interesting person and, when I return to England, in December, I have promised to take him with me. You know, Wilmott, we all came here thinking the natives were wild savages. They are nothing of the sort. Like so many white people, they are happy with their way of life and do not want to change it. I believe that we have much to learn about their culture."

Phillip's remarks were in no way spoken in a patronising or condescending way and were appreciated by Bennelong who asked the sea captain many questions about life at sea and life in England[34].

* * *

The first few days after the arrival in New South Wales of the *Sydney Bridge* were hectic for both François and Judy; getting the Templetons and the Buttroses settled in; finding temporary accommodation for the families they had brought with them and building a secure warehouse in which to store the shipload of materials and equipment. There was also the important decision that they had to make – about their own future. As was so often the case when François had difficult problems to solve, he went to see Captain David Collins, the judge advocate. Their discussion was short and to the point."

"I do not know what you are worrying your head about, Scott-Quetteville. The Admiralty has issued an order that you are to be seconded – and that is final. You have no choice."

"Sir, had I been informed that such an order had been issued, I should not have wasted your time."

---

[34] Arthur Phillip took Bennelong and another Aboriginal back with him to England in the *Reliance*, in December 1792. He was presented at court to George III.

"I am surprised that you have not been informed. The order reached us last week, when the ship arrived from London. Having answered your question, I should like to add one important point; adapting steam power for maritime propulsion is by far the greatest challenge facing the Royal Navy. Heading the steamship research team in your family's company is an appointment of enormous importance. That you are considered, by those who should know, to be a person suitable to handle such a task, is a great compliment."

"I shall do what I am ordered to do, sir, and I shall certainly put all my energy into the task. Nevertheless, from a personal point of view, helping to establish New South Wales as a great colony – and Sydney as a great city – is something on which I have set my heart."

"My boy, I appreciate your point of view and I am sure that when you have finished your task in London, you and your family will return here and continue with your good work."

When François informed Captain Collins about Major Templeton, the Buttrose family and his plans to become involved in building and farming in New South Wales, the captain was most impressed.

"In putting your family's money into the development of New South Wales, I do not for one moment think that you are making a mistake. Today, of the three thousand people here in Sydney, all but six hundred are convicts – not counting the sixty-two free settlers who arrived on the *Sydney Bridge* last week. That is to say, your family has increased the number of genuine colonists by 10 per cent."

"…And, as four of the wives who came with our artisans group are pregnant, sir, that number will soon increase."

Hunter smiled.

"That does not surprise me in the least. They were on the high seas for nearly eight months and there was not much else to do. Was there?"

* * *

When François passed on to Judy the purport of Captain Collins's remarks, she was not altogether happy.

"Captain Collins is quite right. Once the Admiralty had issued the order, we had no choice. On the other hand, I am surprised that your brother or someone from your family's company, having asked the Admiralty for you to be seconded from Captain Phillip's staff to go to England, could then write and assure you that it is up to you to decide. In my opinion, they decided for you."

"You are right, dear, but I might have contributed in some way, in that for the past three years, I have been strongly advocating a more aggressive approach to the development of steam and even suggesting ways of speeding up our research. Had not the *Sydney Bridge* brought all those skilled people and the materials to build our house, I do not think I should have hesitated to jump at the opportunity of going back to London."

"I promise you, darling, I am so happy being with you and the children that I do not mind where I am. Perhaps it is a good idea to go back to London and meet your mother and your brothers. When I know them well, I shall better be able to understand the way they think. Of one thing I am sure – my next sojourn in London is going to be much happier than my last one."

"I promise you, Judy, I shall protect you from having unwelcome nocturnal visits from creepy, naked men who want to leap into bed next to you."

"You, my darling one, can do as much leaping as you want to do – clad or unclad."

* * *

Early in March 1793, the *Sydney Bridge* sailed up the Thames with the François Scott-Quetteville family on board. Although Nicole was not a particularly demonstrative person, never in her life had she shown as much excitement as she did during the month before the return of François with her two grandsons and Judy, her daughter-in-law. She could not think about anything else. François had been a lad of fifteen when he had sailed off to New South Wales in HMS *Sirius* with Captain Phillip and although he was an excellent correspondent, she felt that he was so far away that he had gone to another planet. She kept wondering what he would look like and whether, as a twenty-one-year-old young man he had lost his delightful spontaneity and boyish enthusiasm for everything. She had heard only good things about his young wife, Judy, and was longing to meet her, too. From the time of her engagement to François, she had written long interesting letters about her life in the new colony and the little farm that they had carved out of the wild bushland near Sydney.

When Nicole had discussed buying a house for François's family, Jean-Marc suggested that he should be given their father's house, 12 St James's Square – where he had lived before they moved into No. 22.

"But that is really yours, Jean-Marc," had been his mother's comment.

"Mother, I want François to have it. I shall be in the army for years and by that time I think I should like to go and settle in New South Wales."

From then on, Nicole was in her element. As soon as she had been able to terminate the lease of the short-term tenants, she had the whole place redecorated; everything from François's room at No. 22 was moved into his new home and all the furniture from both the day and the night nursery as well. There she stopped. Jean-Marc, who had been highly amused at his mother's wild enthusiasm, wondered why she would go no further.

"They tell me that my daughter-in-law is like me, with a mind of her own. I have no intention of even thinking about how she wants her own home furnished. It would be an unwarranted intrusion...Jean-Marc, you cannot even begin to understand how I am longing to meet François's Judy. Already she has given me two grandsons and, according to François, she has been quite wonderful in the way she has looked after him. I shall wait and see what she wants to do by herself and what she wants me to do with her. I am sure she will not have a horse, so that will be my first present to her."

"She will be thrilled, I'm sure."

"I am so worked up about their homecoming. I am frightened that I shall overdo everything. Please tell me one thing, dear – if I wait until a fortnight after they arrive, am I allowed to have a welcome home party for them? We have not had a real party since darling John was killed."

"Of course we must have a party and of course you can really let yourself go in arranging it. Recognising your perception of your two grandsons, I am sure Judy will not mind if you have little John and Judah dressed up for the occasion — one as the Christ child and the other as Moses in the bulrushes."

* * *

At seven o'clock in the morning, it was cold and it was wet underfoot. It had been raining overnight and the wharves on the banks of the Thames were slippery. As there was not even a vestige of a breeze, it would be halfway through the morning before everything dried out, but the sky had already cleared and there were a few stars to be seen. As usual, there were lamps burning in Bridge House, as the cleaners were still busy. Within the next half hour the first members of The Bridge Company's staff would arrive at work.

A horseman came cantering along the wharf and pulled up outside the building. The horse was a sure-footed animal and both he and his rider seemed oblivious of the wet brick paving. Having tethered his horse to a hitching post, the rider banged on the door with his fist. When there was no reply, he knocked sharply with the butt end of his riding crock. From inside came a voice.

"Alright, alright, I'm comin'. There's no need to be impatient, is there?"

It was not long before the visitor heard the inside latches and bolts being unfastened and an old man appeared. His name was Gubbins. Although he had the title "night manager" his job was a cross between a janitor and a night-watchman. He and his wife had lived in Bridge House for more than twenty-five years.

"Oh! It's you Barney, is it? 'Ow far away is she — and which one is it?"

"It's the *Sydney Bridge* and she is about five miles away — an' unless a breeze blows up, she'll not be here much before Easter."

"That's a bit of a 'zaggeration, isn't it? We are only just into Lent."

"Do you think I should ride on and tell Lady Nicole — or do you want me to go back to me spot on the river and wait until another of our ships appears?"

"If there's no wind there'll be no ships. So you might just as well ride to St James's Square an' tell her Ladyship."

Two hours later the welcoming party was assembled on the verandah of Bridge House. This was where seaman usually sat while they waited for interviews for employment. There were some chairs there and a table and, during the winter months, at each end of the verandah there was a brazier. On days when passenger ships were arriving or departing, the area was always roped off and reserved for the friends and families of the passengers. On this particular morning, Gubbins had lit the braziers early and they were giving out a good heat.

Having been waiting impatiently for more than an hour, Nicole leapt out of her chair when the *Sydney Bridge* rounded the bend in the river and came into view. She had not seen François for six years and, for the past week, she had been becoming more and more excited at the thought of seeing not only him but also – for the first time – her two grandsons and her daughter-in-law, about whom she had heard so much. Jean-Marc, who had been in constant touch with François by letter, had driven to Portsmouth and boarded the ship there. Knowing how busy everyone would be during the first week or so after François's arrival in London, he felt it would be a good idea for them to have a day together at sea, to catch up on all the important news and to talk about the steamship project.

Hélène Bassett and Rachelle, knowing that Nicole might be waiting on the wharf for a long time, were there to keep her company and, by the time the *Sydney Bridge* had tied up, they were almost as excited as she was. They thought it more appropriate to wait on the verandah and let Nicole go aboard alone.

Not having fully come to terms with her grandsons of four and a half years old, Nicole had expected to see quite small toddlers and she could not believe her eyes when she saw John and Judah – both really big for their age. Having been well rehearsed by Judy, the twins introduced themselves, first in English and then in French. They spoke at the same time.

"How do you do, Maman[35], we are John and Judah."

And then John added –

"Judah has darker hair than I have – and he runs faster."

Judah then produced a huge bunch of almost ripe bananas.

---

[35] The name the François Quettevilles had always used when referring to Nicole in front of their children.

"Maman, we have brought you some bananas from Teneriffe. We both ate too many and they made our tongues feel funny."

Longing to take them both in her arms and hug them, Nicole contented herself by bending over and kissing them on the head.

"I am so thrilled to meet you both; but you are so big. I expected to see two very small boys."

"We will soon be five, Maman."

"And so you will be, darling Judah."

Nicole could wait no longer. Her eyes had been darting backwards and forwards from the twins to Judy and back again. She wanted to talk to all three at once. She put her arms around her daughter-in-law and hugged her. Although Judy was wearing a top coat, it was quite obvious that she was pregnant.

"Welcome to England, Judy, and thank you, dear, for everything – for looking after François, for giving me such fine, strong, handsome grandsons and for all your beautiful letters. You have made me so happy – and how thrilling to learn that you are expecting a third child, soon. What a lovely surprise!"

"Maman, thank you – I hope you do not mind me addressing you in that way but all of us call you that."

"That is a lovely name for me to have. Who thought of it?"

"I did", said Judy. "It is the name I used in addressing my grandmother – who was very beautiful and loving."

"I hope you will always continue to call me that. You will have to excuse my behaviour. I can honestly say that, never in my entire life have I been as happy as I am today. There is so much I want to say to you, so much for which I want to thank you and so many questions I want to ask you, I am completely tongue-tied."

François, who had been highly amused at the twins' performance and his mother's uncharacteristic demonstration of her happiness, tried to bring Nicole down to earth.

"Judy dear, I can assure you that this is the first time ever that mother has been stuck for words and I cannot for the life of me guess why. I have written many letters to her to tell her how wonderful and beautiful you are and, in my own modest way, I have assured her that ours are the most handsome children in the world. The way she is carrying on, I think she was expecting me to arrive with a lubra and a couple of piccaninnies."

"I have no idea what a lubra is or piccaninnies are, François; but I think you might be being a little rude. You did not mention in any of your letters that Judy was pregnant."

"That is because, when I wrote my last letter to you, Mother, she wasn't. We have been at sea for more than six months."

Nicole, Judy and the boys went ashore and left Jean-Marc to discuss the unloading of the baggage and its transport to St James's Square. Hélène and Rachelle were almost as excited at meeting them all as Nicole was. Rachelle was especially happy to see François. She gave him a hug and kissed him.

"You look terribly handsome in your naval officer's uniform, François. I cannot get over how much taller you are. You must have grown four or five inches since you left England. You are now as tall as Jean-Marc; and trust you to have found a beautiful girl to marry. Truly, she is gorgeous – and so young looking."

For quite a few minutes they all stood in a huddle under the covered verandah and chatted. As soon as Jean-Marc joined them, he suggested they should leave for home. Hélène, who wanted them to have the day to themselves, invited them all to join her for tea on the following afternoon and left with Rachelle. The Scott-Quettevilles followed soon after and drove along the embankment towards St James's in the family carriage.

For young John and Judah, the huge London buildings were a revelation. This was really the first city they had seen as, during their journey from Sydney, they had only stopped for a day or two at each of their two ports of call. Furthermore, at both Rio de Janeiro and Teneriffe they had been forced to anchor in the bay rather than being moored to a wharf. This meant that the boys did not have an opportunity to go ashore and see the cities and the sights. They were fascinated with the dome on St Paul's, the bridges over the Thames, the big buildings and the rows of houses and gardens.

Several times during the long voyage from New South Wales, when Judy had thought about London, a few Major Cornish ghosts had sent one or two shivers down her spine. However, the warmth of the welcome she had received, first from Jean-Marc and then from Nicole and the Bassetts, had frightened most of them away. Seeing her two boys so thrilled to be in London and the manner in which her mother-in-law had welcomed her into the Scott-Quetteville family, had made her feel very happy.

As their carriages drove into No. 12 St James's Square, Nicole explained that the house was a belated wedding present from her and her other two sons. Judy gasped and, for nearly a minute she was quite speechless. When she regained her composure, she threw her arms around François's neck.

"Are we not the luckiest people in the world, François?" and to Lady Nicole –

"Maman, dearest, what a fantastic present! What a wonderful surprise with which to welcome us to London! Thank you! Thank you!"

For the first time in her life, Judy, an only child – and orphaned at an early age – felt that she belonged to a family. Until then she had seldom given much thought to the happiness and self-confidence that a family can give to each of its members. After that day she thought about it often and whenever she did, she realised how extremely fortunate she was.

The next few weeks were filled with continuous excitement and exploration for them all. From Nicole's point of view the rides in the parks were the greatest fun. From the day when she had heard that the Admiralty had fully supported the idea of François being seconded to the steamboat project, she had had visions of riding in the park with a toddler sitting in front of her, just as she had done with her own baby sons; but it did not turn out anything like that. François, on one of his trips from Sydney to Batavia for supplies, had bought two fine young Timor ponies. He and Judy had worked on these so that as soon as John and Judah could walk they were lifted on to them. Before they were three they had learned to hold the reins and by the time they reached London, the two boys could cope quite well. The ponies were both fillies and had been honoured with the names Nicole and Veronica – as Judah could not get his tongue around the word Véronique.

The boys, having been taught to swim in the Parramatta River, were almost amphibious. They had always wanted to swim in the harbour at Sydney Cove but, as several of the convicts and two of the soldiers of the New South Wales Corps had been taken by sharks, they were, with some difficulty, dissuaded from doing so.

Two months after her arrival in London, Judy had a daughter to whom she gave the name Nicole, in the hope that she would grow up to be as wonderful and beautiful as her grandmother.

Within weeks of the baby's birth it was decided that it would be confusing to have two Nicoles in the family. At first they called the new arrival Nicolette, soon abbreviated to Ettie. Her grandmother loved this name and, having reminded François and Judy that, when first she arrived in London more than twenty-five years previously she was always called "Ettie", they agreed that this was just the right choice for the name of their daughter.

Of course Judy wanted to know why people had called her mother-in-law by this name. Nicole then imparted to her the story of how she had fled from Marseille and, on her arrival in London, she had used a false name Henriette Martin and that the girls in The Cloisters where she worked had contracted this to Ettie. They both thought it was a wonderful story – and a wonderful name.

* * *

From the early months of her friendship with François, Judy knew how the Quetteville family planned the education and development of their children. She was determined that her children would be brought up in the same way and she called on Nicole to assist her in selecting two tutors. During the summer months they all went to Marseille – and spoke nothing but French – and once a year they visited Frankfurt and stayed with William.

In the winter, when it was difficult to spend much time out of doors, the children loved to play at Nicole's house in the big playroom which was really more like a gymnasium than a room. In one corner was the huge tumbling mat on which François and his brothers had practised their *Shao Lin* wrestling. When John and Judah asked what *Shao Lin* wrestling was, François tried to explain it to them and when they pestered him to teach them, he placed an advertisement for a teacher in the weekend newspaper.

From four answers he found an excellent seventeen-year-old Chinese girl, Chong Mei Lin, whose father was an attaché in the Chinese embassy. She was short and slight but she was a brilliant exponent of the art. Judy and François joined in the lessons too, and, at the age of nine, Ettie, who was already showing signs that she was going to be at least as tall as her mother, insisted on joining the classes. As the age gap – of five years – between the twins and their sister was too big for her to wrestle with her brothers, Mei Lin brought her younger brother and sister to St James's Square with her. This proved to be a great success and, by the time Ettie was fifteen years old, she was ready to take on her two hefty brothers and, although she could not claim to be better than they were, she could certainly hold her own.

Judah was the more aggressive of the twins. He always claimed that, as he was born nearly an hour after John, he was the younger brother and had to be the stronger. When John said he wanted to be a sailor like his father, Judah decided that he would follow in his Uncle Jean-Marc's footsteps and become a soldier. These decisions were made when the boys were hardly in their teens and, over the succeeding years, neither of them wavered; John went to Portsmouth and, in 1804, he became a midshipman – in time to be a small part of Nelson's historic victory at Trafalgar.

Judah went to a military school in Prussia and subsequently became an officer in the Blues. He fought with them in the Peninsular War, when they were brigaded with the First and Second Life Guards. Fighting as the "brigade of guards" they covered themselves with glory. Having had this valuable early experience in Europe, they both moved on to more distant shores – to Sydney.

Within a very few weeks after François returned to London he became totally immersed in the steamboat project and it was not long before he realised that the development of the paddle steamer needed to advance a long way further before it was sufficiently reliable to be regarded as a commercial proposition for The Bridge Company's ocean-going ships. In order to speed up this research, he organised three teams of engineers –

one working on the Isle of Dogs on the Thames, one in Scotland where William Symington and his partner were making good headway using a stern-wheeler paddle, and one in France where the American Robert Fulton was advancing. By the middle of 1796 each of these groups was well-established and doing good work. They were also experimenting with steel as being a better material than wood for the hulls of steam-propelled ships. Six months later a fourth team was dispatched to Wilmington in America where John Fitch was working on a smaller project.

One of the reasons François always enjoyed his visits to his Wilmington unit was that it reminded him so much of Sydney; particularly the warmth and the blue skies. Neither he nor Judy was unhappy to be living in England but neither of them had anticipated the extent to which they would miss their life in New South Wales. For a start, they found the constant cold weather and rain of London almost unbearable and, even in the summer, they found that there were few really warm days. Having frequently reminded themselves how much they missed their life in Sydney, it was not long before they began planning to return there – at least for a visit. The boys missed the wide open spaces even more than their parents did and they gleefully greeted the news that they were returning there for a holiday.

Major Templeton and Gregory Smythe had written regular letters informing them of the progress he and his convicts were making on their little farm in Sydney, and on their big property on the Hawkesbury river, and by the middle of 1796 – during one of the frequent bursts of cold weather – François decided that they would return to New South Wales and see for themselves how much the colony had developed. When he discussed his plans with Judy, he found her wildly enthusiastic.

"Truly, François, I don't think I can put up with rain and grey skies any longer! I just long for warmth and sunshine. I am sure that the boys will adore such an adventure! When do we plan to go?"

"The point is that I cannot be away from the steamboat project for much longer than two years. It has developed momentum and I am not going to let any other shipping company get ahead of us in establishing the first fleet of steam-powered ships."

"If we count on the voyage taking seven months in each direction, we will only have ten months in Sydney. Do you think that will be enough?"

"I am afraid it will have to be enough as I don't think I can stay away any longer. If we come back around Cape Horn, I could stop in Wilmington, Delaware, on the way home to have talks with our engineers there. If we do that, perhaps we could stay in Sydney a couple of months longer."

When Judy informed Nicole of their intention to go to New South Wales, she was surprised – and anxious to accompany them.

"Would you and François feel that I was intruding if I came with you?"

"Maman darling, we should be overjoyed; and I know the children would, too."

Until the day they boarded their ship, Nicole could talk – or think – of nothing else.

* * *

As things turned out, the trip to New South Wales was even more productive and enjoyable than they expected it would be. The Scott-Quettevilles were amazed at the progress that had been made in the five years since they returned to England. Not only had Major Templeton completed the building of their own home, but the other commercial buildings that François had planned as well. Good deposits of clay had been found and there were several brick kilns operating in the colony. Furthermore, some of the local stone proved to be excellent for building and many of the convicts had been trained as stonemasons.

Nicole enjoyed the voyage and the three ports at which they called on their way to Sydney. Nearly everything she saw in Sydney inspired her and, at least half a dozen times, she told them that she could fully understand it if they all decided to stay there. Captain Hunter, who had heard so much about Nicole from François, was a perfect host and he insisted that she accompany him on his many visits to the outposts and country settlements.

The three children, especially the two boys, loved the new house and all the exciting things that were happening every day; the swimming – both in the sea and the Parramatta river – and all the fresh fruit and vegetables that the farm was now producing. Amy Smythe had produced two babies and Alisha was now married to a Royal Marine Corps man. Although Amy and Alisha were too busy in their own homes to spend much time sewing and mending, the tailoring and sewing business had become quite big and very profitable.

François was surprised how many of the convicts from the First Fleet, who had completed their seven-year sentences, had established themselves as really valuable citizens. Nearly all of them had been granted tracts of land and they were making as much money as they could ever have made in England.

With the arrival of more free settlers from England, and the growing number of ex-convict settlers, Sydney was developing into an interesting and enterprising community. There were regular cricket matches, dances and concerts, and for a short time one of the main attractions was the theatre that had opened in Bell Row[36]. The Quettevilles were amused to see a sign at the entrance to the theatre "Entrance one shilling – or the equivalent in meat, flour or vegetables"[37]. They were surprised at the quality of the performance they witnessed and were disappointed when, several weeks later, they learned that the governor had closed the theatre, the reason being that, when the "patrons of the performing arts" were enjoying themselves watching anything from Shakespeare to a modern play, their unattended residences were being robbed! This and a plague of pick-pocketing in the theatre itself had become so out of control that it seemed a little too soon for a penal colony to have the luxury of a theatre!

For François, one of the highlights of the voyage to New South Wales was the amount of time he was able to spend with his former commanding officer – and mentor – Captain John Hunter, who had returned to Sydney in 1795 as governor. As a young midshipman – and second lieutenant – François had held Hunter in awe and, having circumnavigated the world twice as one of his officers, this feeling of reverence developed into something much deeper. The successor to Arthur Phillip was not only a great sea captain and an example to all those who were

---

[36] Bligh Street.

[37] At this time there was an acute shortage of silver and copper coins. This prompted people to pay in kind for some goods and services.

privileged to serve under him, he also became François's guide, philosopher and friend – his teacher and his patron. During the six years that Quetteville had served under him, Captain Hunter had showed him how to combine the secret ingredients of successful leadership – optimism, dynamic energy, confidence and humility.

Because of the special relationship that François had developed with his former skipper, he was completely unbalanced by a remark the governor made during one of their many meetings.

"Quetteville, now that you are back in New South Wales, I should very much like you to stay here and help me with my work. Together we can build Sydney into one of the great cities of the world."

"Your Excellency, for you to put such a proposal to me is the greatest compliment that anyone in the world could give me. In replying to such an enormously important proposition, if I did anything other than express my sincere thanks and ask for some time to consider the situation, my sea captain would be more than disappointed in me – he would be downright angry with me!"

"Well said, Quetteville. I am sure that I shall hear from you when you are ready to talk further."

That same evening, after Nicole had retired to her room, François and Judy discussed the governor's proposal late into the night – and again on the following morning. Having made up their minds concerning their future, an appointment was made for François to see Captain Hunter.

He was unequivocal in what he had to say.

"Your Excellency, no person has influenced the way I think and the way I see things as much as you have done. I can honestly say that I have never been happier than I was during the years as one of your junior subordinates on HMS *Sirius*, and the prospect of spending the next five years – perhaps more – as a member of your staff is both exciting and enticing.

"My brothers and I have grown up as a team and, whenever one of us has an important decision to make, we do our best to consult each other. Such was the case, in '92, before I made the decision – reluctantly – that my immediate future lay in the development of the maritime potential of steam power. At that stage we all believed that, apart from being vital to the future of our family's business, early success in this field was equally important to the Royal Navy. I do not believe that, during the last five years, anything has happened to persuade me to think otherwise. However, if you tell me that I should reconsider the matter, I should most definitely do so."

The governor was genuinely impressed.

"Quetteville, you are quite right. When the Admiralty informed me that you were to be seconded to pursue the development of steam, although I was reluctant to lose one of my best young officers, I fully agreed that you would put more dynamism into the project than anyone else I could think of. When you were here the other day, it was selfish and stupid of me to have made the suggestion that you should return to my staff. You are where you ought to be until the job is done. My sincere hope is that you will have succeeded in your work on the steamship project in sufficient time for you to return here one day as Governor."

Both François and Judy shared the same hopes.

* * *

On the way home, the visit to the shipping yards in Wilmington, on the river Delaware, was a great success and The Bridge Company's steamboat team were working in the shipyards of Crocker and Ficket. François was very pleased to be able to inspect the tug they had built using two paddle wheels. This was able to move at six or seven knots.

On his arrival back in England, too, he was more than satisfied with the progress being made on the company's other steamboat projects – in Scotland in partnership with William Symington and Patrick Miller and on the Isle of Dogs, in London.

* * *

The success of the voyage to New South Wales unsettled the Scott-Quetteville household far more than they had anticipated. From the time they returned to London at the beginning of 1799, hardly a week went by without at least one of the children asking their parents when they would next be going back to their lovely home in Sydney. Both John and Judah were determined to return there as soon as possible, and although they were not yet twelve years old, there was nothing they liked doing more than talking to their father about their plans. In these talks with his father, John made no secret of his ambition –

"I am going to Portsmouth to learn to be a naval officer as soon as I am old enough, Father, and then I am going to Sydney."

"I don't think that is in any way impossible. If you are good at mathematics and study astronomy, you should have no problems in passing your examinations. However, I think you should take an interest in steam power, too, as by the time you are the captain of a ship, I am sure that it will be fitted with steam paddles."

"May I please come with you when you next go to the works on the Isle of Dogs?"

"Of course. You may come with me as often as you like."

Judah was as equally determined as his brother to go to the colonies.

"I want to join the army and be an officer in the New South Wales Corps. It will be fun to be in Sydney with John in the navy and me in the army. I hope Uncle Jean-Marc will not be angry that I shan't be applying for a commission in the Blues."

In the years that followed the twins often raised the subject about their proposed emigration to New South Wales. François emphasised the need for them to study and to read everything they could about the progress that was being made in the new colony and he let them read all the newspapers and articles that came his way.

It gave both François and Judy much happiness to observe how, over the next decade, the twins never wavered from their original plans and, by the time they were nineteen, they had finished their training and were serving fifteen thousand miles away in a country that people had started to refer to as Australia[38].

---

[38] The date from which the word Australia was officially used was 1817, by Governor Macquarie. However, from 1814, Matthew Flinders, in his correspondence, referred to "Australia" by name. Even before this, the term *Terra Australis* was used from time to time.

X

IN JUNE 1796 – SEVERAL MONTHS before the François Scott-Quettevilles and Nicole set out for their holiday in New South Wales, Nicole was enjoying the summer sunshine that poured into her library through the two big bay windows. As she was reading the morning papers, a bold headline – Disaster in Frankfurt – in *The Times*, attracted her attention. This was followed by a report that the victorious French army, having defeated the Austrians at Lodi, had bombarded Frankfurt so heavily that nearly half the houses in the hopelessly overcrowded Jewish ghetto had been destroyed by fire.

At the time, her eldest son, Captain Sir Jean-Marc, was on leave and was sitting with her in the library. Shocked by the report, she passed the newspaper to him.

"I do hope that William and Gerda are safe and well."

"Their house is a long way from Judenstrasse. I am sure they will be safe."

Nicole continued reading.

"It is terrible, Jean-Marc. More than one hundred people killed and very few of the herring-gutted buildings have been left standing. I do hope Mayer and Gutele Rothschild and their children are alive and well."

"How long is it since you have seen them, Mother?"

"More than eighteen months. Gutele's little Henriette was three. However, Mayer and I still write to each other quite often and, for the past five years, Mayer has been handling all our German and Austrian business, including the silk contract with the French government."

"For heaven's sake, how many children has that poor woman had?"

"Twenty – but only ten have lived."

"My God! You are happy with the business he does for us?"

"I could not be happier. About ten years ago I deposited 50,000 livres with him and also gave him £5,000 to invest in coins. Last year he returned the £5,000 to me with a long letter – written in flowery language – thanking me for what he described as the first deposit for the Mayer Rothschild bank. He added that out of the profit he had for me, he was holding £25,000 worth of coins and he hoped I would pay him a visit soon to inspect them and to decide which ones I want to keep and which I want to sell. He also informed me of the amount of interest I have earned on the deposit. Having read the report of the bombing and the fire, I think I must go to Frankfurt and see the dear man."

"Is that safe with the French occupying the city?"

"I am still a French *citoyenne* and I am sure I shall be safe. I might even meet your friend Bonaparte."

"He has certainly come a long way. He now commands the French army in Italy. Somehow I do not think he would be pleased to see me. Do you?"

"The last time I saw him was in '93 in Toulon, just at the time when Vicomte Paul Barras appointed him to be general in charge of artillery. At that time he asked after you and told Barras that you and he could tactically deploy the French guns much more effectively than they were at that time. When he expressed annoyance that you had deserted the French army, I made a point of reminding him that this was certainly not the case and that it was the French army that had discharged you."

"That is true. They saved me the trouble of getting rid of them. What was his reply?"

"I think he said something like 'more is the pity'."

* * *

Only a week after reading about the Frankfurt bombing Nicole received a letter from William in which he informed her of the tragic news that the bombardment had destroyed his house. However, for him, something a hundred times worse had happened – his young wife Gerda, who had been at home at the time, had been killed in the enemy attack. William, who was devastated, explained in his letter that at the time of the French bombardment he had been in Hamburg and that he had not known of the disaster until he had returned to Frankfurt two days later. To make matters even worse, the nineteen-year-old Gerda was almost four months pregnant.

Within two days of receiving this information Nicole was on her way to Frankfurt to join William. She sailed to Amsterdam and travelled in a private carriage from there. Nicole remained with William for two weeks, during which time he decided that, rather than try to rebuild his house, he would move to another part of Frankfurt and start his life again. Having Nicole with him made his burden of sadness much lighter; all the more so when he heeded Nicole's advice to return to London for a couple of months to stay with her in St James's Square and to spend some time with Jean-Marc.

About a week after she arrived in Frankfurt Nicole visited the Rothschild family. Having inspected the damage caused by the French bombardment and the fires that it started, Nicole was much relieved to learn that, although many of the Jews had lost their homes and their possessions in the fire, the loss of life had been minimal. Apparently, as soon as the French artillery had begun their bombardment, the inhabitants of Judenstrasse had locked their houses and fled. Nevertheless, having lost everything they owned, the Jews were forced to start again from scratch. The stoic way in which they accepted this tragedy in their lives amazed Nicole. Within days of the end of the bombardment, they had started to clean up the whole area and had removed the debris and by the time she had reached Frankfurt, they had begun to erect new and better houses, schools and hospitals. Although the fire had been a major catastrophe for them all, it was by no means the first big fire they had had to endure. Being so hopelessly over-developed and crowded, it had been partially destroyed by fire on three previous occasions.

Not only in Frankfurt but throughout French-occupied Europe, Republican French soldiery, police, civil administrators and investigators were everywhere. Businessmen and bankers were being investigated and mail was being opened and read. For this reason it was much safer to do business personally and, because his interests were so scattered throughout Europe, William had to spend more time travelling from city to city than he did in Frankfurt. New laws and regulations were promulgated almost daily and this, too, made doing business during the French occupation fraught with difficulties.

The importation of any merchandise from England was prohibited and the handing over of securities to English bankers and agents was equally *verboten*. The penalties for breaches of these regulations were harsh – heavy fines together with the confiscation of the contraband merchandise or securities – but enormous quantities of textiles and other English goods were being continuously smuggled into Frankfurt.

About this time Mayer Rothschild was found guilty of smuggling into Frankfurt a huge consignment of high-quality English cloth: muslins, quiltings, dimities, velveteens, shawls, checks and jaconets. Every bolt of cloth and piece of silk was confiscated and publicly burned – except for that which the French officers and soldiers spirited away and which eventually found its way back to Paris. There were rumours that Mayer Rothschild had concluded a deal with the police to substitute a large quantity of local and French cloth for most of the beautiful imported fabrics. The police were said to have been paid a healthy share of the resultant profit when the material was sold on the black market.

* * *

In this difficult and disturbing climate Mayer and Gutele Rothschild were overjoyed to see the countess who spent many hours in their company, learning about the major changes that were going on in their lives. Nicole was particularly pleased to learn that Gutele, whose twentieth child had been born in 1792, and who had previously told Nicole that she had retired from motherhood, had kept her word.

As a result of the French bombardment and the fire that followed in its wake, the damage caused to the Jewish ghetto was catastrophic. So much so that, while Judenstrasse was being rebuilt, the Frankfurt authorities were forced to allow the Jews to temporarily rent both housing and business premises outside the ghetto.

As well as enjoying the social aspects of the visit, Nicole and William had many business discussions with both Mayer and Gutele and, in these, they were sometimes joined by the three eldest Rothschild sons. During one of these interludes, nineteen-year-old Nathan, who usually had much more to say for himself than did either Amschel and Salomon, announced that he wanted to go to England and to build up a business there. He asked the countess what she thought of the idea.

"Although the laws regarding the rights of Jews to do business are much more lenient in England than they are here in Frankfurt, there have been a few too many dishonest immigrants who have given the Jews a bad name, but I'm sure that, provided you move with care, the house of Rothschild could establish itself in England."

Mayer, in his usual modest way, sounded a note of caution.

"I am nervous of grand titles like 'the house of Rothschild'; we are simply Mayer Rothschild and Sons. It is more appropriate and less pretentious."

The shortish, solidly built Nathan was far more forthright.

"After I have been in London for a few years, things will be different. We work harder than most of the *goyim*[39], and we are prepared to work on smaller margins. I know we will be a success."

Nicole did not want to discourage the young man but suggested he needed to tread carefully.

"Nathan, your family is mainly involved in the sale and financing of textiles. Would it not be better to open a business in Manchester first and, as soon as you fully understand the market there, to move down to London?"

Amschel, who had been listening attentively to the conversation, had his say.

"Nathan, what the countess has said is exactly the same as father is insisting on. Knowing you, within five years, you will have either made a fortune and moved to London – or gone *meckoolah*[40]. In any case papa is adamant that you remain here until you turn twenty-two."

The countess laughed and said that she was confident that Nathan would be a success and that they would all be proud of him.

* * *

---

[39] People other than the Jews.

[40] A Yiddish word = broke (bankrupt).

Mayer Rothschild was, if nothing else, a very private person who kept his own counsel and who did not discuss his business with anyone. Nevertheless, he regarded his cousin, la Comtesse d'Anjou as being the exception. In fact he felt honoured that Gutele and he and their adult sons could sit down with the countess and William Scott-Quetteville and discuss with them some confidential aspects of their business and their plans — and aspirations — for the future. Even so, at times he was a little fearful that his exalted cousin might not approve of some of his business practices or that she might have heard rumours that he operated outside the law or that he and his sons were becoming "too big for their boots". Although both Nicole and William were sufficiently worldly to appreciate that jealous rivals and anti-Semites would say — and do — anything they could to discredit Mayer and his sons, the emerging Jewish banker felt he should raise the matter with them. One day during Nicole's visit, when they were by themselves, in his own somewhat flowery way, he addressed her.

"Cousin Countess, over many years, you have constantly demonstrated your confidence in my ability and integrity. I believe it is my duty to invite your attention to one or two matters in relation to the way we do business."

"I assure you I am well aware of how you go about your business and I do not feel that there is any reason for you to make any explanations. If the other bankers and businessmen with whom my sons and I do business were as honest and open as you are, I would be delighted."

Not to be deterred, Mayer continued.

"Madame, probably you will hear exaggerated accounts of our success. I hope you are not disappointed in me when I admit that more than a few of these stories have been started by us. Although I do not believe in boasting, I have found that it is good for business if people think we are clever and successful. Nevertheless, we make sure that it is someone other than us who spreads the rumours.

"You might also hear that we have bribed government officials in order to be selected to handle their business. I can assure you Cousin Comtesse, if we do not respond positively to their requests for low-interest loans or other financial concessions, government officials will not recommend our proposals."

"Cousin Mayer, please do not excuse yourself for doing what everybody else is doing. It is not necessary. Not a week goes by without at least one powerful businessman coming to one of our companies offering our managers an attractive incentive if we would be prepared to steer business in his direction. You would not be doing nearly as well as you are doing if you did not gain the confidence and goodwill of senior government officials."

"This is what I keep telling my sons. They must be known and respected by the governments and the rulers of many countries. Furthermore we must never be greedy. Our charges and our interest rates must be lower than those of our competitors and we must be quicker and more thorough than they are."

"I am sure you are all of these things Cousin Mayer."

"Oh dear, how I wish that what you say were true. Nathan is sharp and clever – but he is far too careless. He leaves too many i's undotted and too many t's uncrossed. He is a worry."

"I am sure he will improve when he is on his own and has nobody to turn to."

"I hope you are right. When I decide that he is ready to go to England, I hope you will not be offended if I ask you and your sons to keep an eye on him."

"As I said before, it will be a pleasure to do so; however, as you have reminded him, he needs to be patient and wait until he knows a little more about international finance."

* * *

As Nicole came away from Judenstrasse she marvelled at the success of the strange but brilliant man with the hard-working, well-trained sons. As was always the case after visiting Mayer Rothschild, she passed on to William the purport of her discussion with him concerning the necessity to give gifts and personal loans to clients.

"He has said much the same to me, Mother – in fact, several times. On each occasion I have assured him that in Europe and in Britain, bribes – so euphemistically called incentives – are normal and the more senior the official or minister the bigger the bribe."

"Some years ago when I was talking to Paul Barras — one of the most corrupt men I know — I asked him why the French government pays such a pittance to its civil servants. He replied that it was not necessary to pay them any more — as they all collected many times their salaries, in bribes. And he should know, William. Each year he receives a fortune in personal payments, 'gifts' and *honoraria*."

"I think the reason Herr Rothschild made his little speech to you was because his respect for you is almost awesome and he would be devastated if, as a result of people telling you he was boastful or dishonest, you thought ill of him."

"I think he is unique. The way in which he has established himself not just in Frankfurt but in the rest of Germany, in Denmark and Austria is quite remarkable."

"And the rigorous training he has put his sons through, too."

"Will you be able to cope with young Nathan?"

"He is still young — he'll learn. He will take short cuts and make mistakes, but Manchester is a tough school and I am confident he will succeed. He is imaginative in his thinking and incredibly energetic — and what is equally important he is determined to prove himself to his father."

* * *

Only a couple of years later events moved quickly for the Rothschilds. Indirectly through the Landgrave[41], Prince Wilhelm, who had been banished by Napoléon, they were entrusted with a number of the Danish government's loan contracts. Karl Buderus, the prince's banking manager, also brought other business to them. Having recognised Rothschild's brilliance, he had purchased a small interest in his firm.

By the beginning of the nineteenth century the Rothschilds had become established not only in the international textile trade but also in the field of finance and banking. In addition, the silk contracts with the weaving companies in Lyon, that followed the completion of the countess's dealings with the French government, kept the three Rothschilds busier than they had ever been.

---

[41] Title of a German ruler of several provinces.

All these factors combined to persuade Mayer to yield to Nathan's incessant pleadings that he be allowed to move to England, so in 1799 the young man went to Manchester to set up an export business. Where it was expedient for him to present himself as representing his better known father, he did so and, on those occasions when it was more advantageous to appear as an English firm, he was as British as the House of Commons.

Nathan was undoubtedly a brilliant young man with a natural flair for trading and banking. He had a lightning-quick brain and he was capable of working effectively for many more hours each day than most of his competitors. However, both Mayer and Amschel looked on him as being something of a loose cannon on the deck that could not only miss the target but could, at the same time, cause major damage to the Rothschild ship. Because he was quick to take offence — and at least as quick to give offence — Nathan sometimes lost business that he should have retained, and he failed to clinch deals that were there to be won, but he had many more successes than he did failures and his contribution to the Rothschilds' profits grew rapidly.

Nathan's move to England was at a difficult time. The French army was occupying almost half of Western Europe and, in an effort to cripple England's foreign trade, imports from England were totally banned. Nathan was undeterred by the threats of huge fines and the confiscation of the goods themselves. He, like dozens of other traders, smuggled textiles into Europe by every means he could and for the most part he was successful. Nevertheless, he was caught a few times and, on these occasions, his losses were high.

Within a surprisingly short period of time, Nathan Rothschild most certainly did fulfil Nicole's prophecy. During the first fifteen years of the nineteenth century the firm of M.A. Rothschild and Sons was destined to become one of the major banking houses of Europe.

With tireless energy, great entrepreneurial skill and tenacity of purpose, Nathan overcame the inevitable consequences of his carelessness and his brashness. Within ten years of arriving in England he had closed his Manchester office and had moved to London, where he opened an office in New Court, at which address the Rothschilds remained for nearly two hundred years.

* * *

While Nathan was fighting to establish himself in Manchester, back in Frankfurt, Mayer and his oldest son Amschel had their battles, too. The prohibitions and restrictions brought about by the French occupation and the equally thwarting anti-Semitic regulations made it almost impossible for them to survive – let alone prosper. In his own quiet but effective way, the old Jew would not give in. He battled against the odds – and won. Slowly he forced the local authorities to accept him – and the other inhabitants of Judenstrasse, too. He had himself appointed as a court agent of the Emperor of Austria and when Prince Wilhelm was banished and his financial empire was under siege, it was often to Mayer Rothschild he turned when he needed someone trustworthy to front for him.

In 1810, when Frankfurt was transformed into a duchy, the Archbishop of Mainz suddenly became Baron Karl Theodor Anton von Dalberg. Several years previously, anticipating that the archbishop was destined for greater things, Mayer Rothschild had raised a loan for him – and became close enough to him to be in a position to perform an unbelievable service to his compatriots in the Jewish ghetto.

Rothschild waited until Frankfurt's finances were in a desperate situation and loan funds were almost impossible to obtain. Then he approached von Dalberg.

"With the finances of Frankfurt having reached a crisis situation I believe that the Jews of Frankfurt could do a great service to our city."

"You already pay high taxes each year for the 'protection' the city gives you."

"Yes, your Highness, we do. We pay higher rates of taxation than the rest of the citizens of Frankfurt."

"Well, how do you think you can help our city? I do not understand."

"If we paid the State ten years of taxes in advance, would you grant us the same civil rights as all the other citizens of Frankfurt?"

"I would, Herr Rothschild, but the city fathers would not agree to such a concession."

"Your Excellency, would twenty years of taxes, paid in advance, influence their thinking?"

"Frankfurt is so desperately short of money they would be raving mad not to accept such an offer. But it is indeed a large sum of money. Do you think the Jews can raise nearly five hundred thousand gulden?"

"In return for their full emancipation – yes."

Thus, for nearly half a million gulden, Rothschild bought the Jews their freedom. He paid the money to Dalberg and he discounted thousands of pounds worth of his bonds and advanced him a personal loan of some eighty thousand gulden so that he could afford to go to Paris to baptise Napoléon's son. The millstone of oppression and humiliation had at last been removed from around his neck – and from around the necks of the other Frankfurt Jews, too.

To Baron von Dalberg, Mayer Rothschild was something more than a source of money. He had a genuine respect and admiration for the old man and this was evidenced by the appointment of Mayer to the prestigious electoral college of the newly formed Département and the announcement that he was its official banker.

Not many years after Nathan went to Manchester Mayer's youngest son, Jacob, started to get itchy feet. He was enthusiastically supported by Nathan, with whom he was in constant correspondence. Each time Jacob raised the subject with his father, he received the same answer –

"You are still too young, my son, you must first learn more about our business. Your time will come soon enough."

In 1811 the young man finally had his way.

One of the factors that influenced Mayer Rothschild to give his blessing to the move was the change in the status of the Jewish population there. When Nicole was in Frankfurt on one of her visits, he expressed his concerns to her.

"I am worried about Jacob going to France. Everybody we know who has visited Paris tells us that the authorities have always been as harsh on Jews as those here in Frankfurt are; but we have heard that since the Revolution things are better. Is this correct?"

"I am sure it is. When the Convention first sat, in 1789, Comte Honoré de Mirabeau and I were the delegates of the Midi. We were able to force through the *Assemblée nationale* a measure to completely emancipate the Jews, and this has now come into effect. In fact, the Jews now have the right to elect a member to the Convention."

"This is wonderful news, Cousin Countess."

"Under King Louis there were fewer than five hundred Jews in Paris – now there are nearly five thousand living there. Already they are flocking to the Republican colours and many have been promoted and are officers. My friend Joseph Fouché, the Minister of Police, tells me that he has more than one hundred Jews in the Police Force. I do not think that you need be at all apprehensive about Jacob being in Paris. I am confident that he will do well there."

"Would not a name like Jacob Rothschild be a disadvantage to him?"

"No, Rothschild is a good name. Perhaps James would sound better than Jacob."

* * *

During the first years of the eighteenth century, the amount of business they were undertaking for the deposed Landgrave Prince Wilhelm, contributed in no small measure to the success achieved by the Rothschilds. This was because Napoléon, having defeated in battle most of the armies of Europe, launched a vendetta against him. Not only had Wilhelm's Hessian troops fought against the French, but he had also financed the armies of the smaller powers that had taken up arms against the invading army of the French Republic. Prince Wilhelm had taken refuge in Prague and from there he found it virtually impossible to manage his investments and properties which were spread over Europe. He had palaces full of art treasures, safe deposit boxes in banks and dozens of wealthy clients who were required to make regular interest payments to him.

Bonaparte's ministers and senior officers exerted great pressure on these debtors to hand over their interest and their principal repayments to them, and the commanders of Napoléon's armies invaded Wilhelm's palaces and confiscated many of his works of art and much of his furniture. Faced with this predicament, the Landgrave appointed the Rothschilds to act as his agents to collect the money that was due to him and to hold it in safe keeping for him. Not only did Mayer and his sons manage to handle this task competently and unobtrusively; they were able to use Wilhelm's money to make substantial profits for themselves, and they were also able to derive a healthy income from the volatile foreign exchange market.

Wilhelm had much of his fortune invested in England, and no sooner had Nathan Rothschild moved from Manchester to London than he was able to play a major role in handling his affairs, but it was not only the business he transacted for Wilhelm that helped Nathan establish himself quickly in London. His first big coup was to arrange to move nearly £800,000 to Spain to enable Sir Arthur Wellesley to pay the British troops in the Peninsular War. To execute this lucrative – but risky – contract he worked closely with his brother James (Jacob), who had arrived in Paris in 1811.

The reason the British government sought a banking house to move such a large sum of money to Spain was because of the danger of enemy attack on a ship carrying so much gold. As was always the case when having to pay troops serving in overseas wars, payment had to be paid in gold and silver and the last thing the British government wanted was for a ship laden with gold to sink to the bottom of the ocean.

The *modus operandi* of the transaction was for the treasury in London to deliver the gold to the London banker who, for an agreed fee, would be responsible to hand the same amount of gold to Wellesley's paymaster in Madrid – less a considerable amount of commission.

In the few short years between the arrival of James in Paris and the Battle of Waterloo, the House of Rothschild almost catapulted itself from being relatively small time international financiers to becoming well established, international bankers. One of the most important reasons for this was that Great Britain had armies not only in Spain, Portugal and other countries of Europe, but also because the British government was substantially subsidising the armies of her less affluent allies.

At that time the normal way commanders of expeditionary forces paid their troops was to draw bills in the countries in which they were operating. These negotiable instruments enabled the purchaser to have the bills presented in London where they would receive gold.

In 1811 Sir Arthur Wellesley, the commander of the allied forces on the Peninsula, had drawn so much gold against the bills he had signed that the value of the English pound had dropped substantially due to the saturation of the local market for British bills. With his brother James's support, Nathan Rothschild was able to exploit this situation to the full. He moved gold into France and into other cities of Europe and he used hundreds of thousands of pounds of this gold to buy paper drawn on Madrid; that is to say, the bills he purchased could be cashed for gold in Spain and paid over to the British commander to pay his troops and those of his allies.

So well did the Rothschilds handle this business that they were given the responsibility to shift gold to nearly all those countries in Europe where British soldiers were fighting, and where Britain was being called upon to subsidise the armies of her allies.

This new form of international finance earned enormous profits for the Rothschilds. Added to these earnings were the fees they were being paid by Prince Wilhelm. Within less than five years they had emerged as one of Europe's wealthiest bankers.

PART III

Napoléon Bonaparte

Despotisme, Egöisme, Népotisme

La Comtesse Anjou

1799 – 1815

I

IN THE DECADE FOLLOWING THE overthrow of the French monarchy, all cross-Channel voyages to Britain by the French were viewed with suspicion by the vigilant Republican authorities. Before leaving France, all travellers were required to supply detailed information concerning the length of their stay in Britain, the reason for their visit, the people they planned to meet and the business they planned to discuss. Nothing was left to chance and there was a highly competent French intelligence network in England to shadow all French nationals and to check – and report – on their every move.

There were no exceptions from this security screening and even ministers like Joseph Fouché were closely watched. For this reason, whenever he wanted to talk to his close colleague, *citoyenne* Nicole Quetteville, she had agreed to cross the Channel to meet him – usually in Paris – or sometimes in a town nearer to one of the Channel ports.

In September 1799, only a few weeks after her return from New South Wales, Nicole received a hand-delivered letter from Joseph Fouché. As usual, it contained all the latest news from the Convention and *La Directoire* and it finished by mentioning that it was far too long since they had seen each other. He went on to suggest that, if it would be convenient for madame *la citoyenne* to come to Paris, he would be delighted to see her. As Nicole felt completely out of touch with events in Europe, she promptly accepted the invitation.

She arrived in Paris three weeks later. On reaching her hotel, a message from the minister was waiting for her, suggesting that she should meet him in his office. Fouché had only returned to Paris from The

Hague a few weeks previously where for some time he had been the French minister.

At the end of July *La Directoire* had made yet another cabinet shuffle, in which Fouché had once again been appointed as Minister of General Police. Aware that Nicole had just returned from the British penal colony in New South Wales, Fouché was looking forward to learning about the climate, the natives – and the health and rehabilitation of the convicts who had been sent there. She answered his questions and went on to inform him about the rapid development that had taken place in Sydney, the number of offenders who had been granted remissions and pardons and the system of land grants to the army personnel and even prisoners who had earned their freedom[42]. He was amazed – and impressed.

"In England, they are much more enlightened than we are here in France. We, too, transport our unwanted criminals overseas. However, ours are sent to terrible places like Guinea. We think we are being clever as we sell them to planters as slaves. Some of them either die or are killed by their sadistic guards on the ships that transport them. Most of the others die of yellow fever or smallpox – or else they are beaten to death by their masters. It is a national disgrace and, looking at it from a pragmatic standpoint, it is an inexcusable waste of our resources."

"As well as taking his wife and me, my sailor son François took our three grandchildren to New South Wales with us. They just adored the place and, since their return to cold, wet England, they have not stopped talking about Sydney and are champing at the bit to go back there. I must admit that I am nearly as enthusiastic to return as they are."

Before speaking about the economy of France, the *Assemblée nationale* and *La Directoire*, Fouché once again congratulated his visitor on the contribution she and her companies had made – and were still making – to the ailing French economy.

"The speed and competence with which your people were able to dispose of the stockpile of silk in Lyon was quite remarkable and the

---

[42] Tickets-of-leave were also granted to convicts whose conduct had been good and who had money of their own to buy property. The ticket-of-leave holders had freedom to work for wages in New South Wales but could not leave the settlement until they had either finished their sentence or had been granted a pardon.

• PART III — 1 •

amount of overseas currency that the proceeds earned for the treasury has been far in excess of our expectations. Furthermore, now that your Marseille company is handling almost all the exports from the silk merchants in Lyon, the flow of gold into France from this source is once again up at almost the same level as it was before the Revolution. I must also add that the success you achieved has done much to enhance my own reputation. You have been a true friend to me Madame. Please accept my sincere thanks."

The countess smiled broadly and reassured the minister.

"*Citoyen* Fouché, my dear friend, I am delighted that you have been considered the mastermind of the Lyon silk project. For our company in Marseille to have earned a handsome profit was for us a sufficient reward. However, to learn that you, personally, gained something too, pleases me more than you could believe."

"I am well aware of the profit that the Messageries Maritimes company made and I can assure you that they earned every livre of it. The Lyon silk industry is now contributing more to the economy of France than it ever did — and I might add that the management by your French shipping company of the export business of the Cheaulier Soap Company has been every bit as successful."

Once again Nicole tried to make light of Fouché's compliments.

"It only goes to show how your policy of Liberty, Equality and Fraternity benefits everybody, does it not?"

Joseph Fouché did his best to respond to her smile in kind but, as he seldom smiled, it was not a particularly successful effort. He changed the subject to the politics of the day.

"I am indeed sorry that you are no longer a member of the *Assemblée nationale*. Ever since the Convention first met, the various factions within both the Five Hundred and the Council of Elders[43] have been at each other's throats and there is neither trust nor leadership in either house. The people are becoming more and more restless because few, if any, of the aspirations they nurtured when we threw off the Bourbon yoke have

---

[43] After the *Terreur* the *Assemblée nationale* had become bicameral — the Council of the Five Hundred and the Council of *Les Anciens* — the elders.

237

materialised. So much so that the monarchists are once again attracting thousands of Frenchmen to their cause. They do not pause for a moment to think how totally useless – and hopeless – the man whom they would like to become King Louis XVIII really is. The people who are swinging to the right – towards the monarchy – are saying that a weak leader is better than no leader at all and therefore they see little future for the Republic as it is today."

"Surely there must be one or two dynamic young people in the *Assemblée nationale* who have the strength and the ability to lead?"

"*La Directoire* wants the impossible – a strong man with 'the hand and the head to lead'. However, they insist that this leader must be somebody whom they can manage. They chose young Général Joubert and made him general in charge of the Paris Army. A month or so ago, he was sent off to fight the Prussians at Novi and, before the battle was half over, he had been mortally wounded. Now the press and the people are clamouring for Général Bonaparte – but the members of *La Directoire* are frightened of him."

"To me it appears inevitable. From what I have read in all the papers – both here and in England – he was not only victorious in Italy but equally so in Egypt and there is not a man in the army who would not die for him."

"Although I dread to think about where he might lead us, he is very much to be preferred to having the Bourbons back again."

"Do you think he will want you in his government?"

"My informants tell me that he has no time for me and that he does not trust me. Be that as it may, he will have certainly heard that mine has been one of the few voices among the rulers of France that has demanded that he be recalled from Egypt to lead France back on the road to prosperity."

"What you have told me certainly gives me much to think about, but I'm sure that you did not 'suggest' that I come to Paris to be brought up to date with the current political and economic situation."

"I asked you to come here because I am well aware that, although Napoléon does not know you well, he has a great respect for all that your family has done for France and for the example your grandfather, your father and you, in your turn, have set the other nobles. It is my belief that he would listen to you and heed your advice more than he would that of any of the members of *La Directoire*."

"In reply to your last two comments, I should suggest that Bonaparte is more interested in efficiency and aggressive action than he is in affection or even trust. I have sufficient respect for his judgement to be confident that he knows that you are the most competent and thorough civilian 'general' in France and that he will want you to ensure that his commands are obeyed. I believe it would be appropriate for me to wait for quite a time yet before deciding if any good purpose would be served for me to become adviser to – or confidante of Général Bonaparte. From what I know about him, he will not want either an effective *Assemblée nationale*, *La Directoire,* or any advisers. He will demand total power. From the time when he had his first command in Toulon, he has asked for full control and they have let him have it. When he was in Italy it was the same story – and likewise in Egypt. When he is leader of France he will make that same demand – and it will be granted to him."

* * *

While Nicole was in Paris she witnessed some unforgettable scenes. Napoléon arrived back there on 15 October 1799 to a tumultuous welcome by the people. He was hailed as a saviour. The tens of thousands of Parisians who thronged the streets cheering him made his progress towards his home in Rue de la Victoire slow and difficult. In spite of the joy and merriment all around him, from a personal point of view, the last few hours before he reached his house were, for him, a period of great anguish and anxiety.

Almost everyone in Paris was aware that his wife, Josephine, had been blatantly unfaithful to him – continuing her affair with Hyppolyte Charles, the same young man with whom she had been sharing her bed within weeks of her marriage to Napoléon four years previously. Thanks to his brothers, who hated Josephine, Napoléon, who loved his wife truly – albeit possessively – had been made well aware of this relationship. In fact, he was determined that the first thing he intended to do on his return to Paris was to banish her from their home and sue for divorce. In his absence, the Buonaparte brothers made sure that Josephine was aware of what the future held for her, with the result that the moment she heard that her husband had landed in the south of France, she set out to meet him, before they could do so and poison his mind against her.

As Napoléon had approached Paris by an unusual route, Josephine missed him altogether and this resulted in him arriving home to find that she was not there. Thinking the worst, he immediately had all her belongings packed, ready for her final departure.

Two evenings later she returned, only to be denied entrance by the servants at the lodge. Turbulent, tearful scenes prevailed throughout the night – and all through the next day. However, when on the following morning, Napoléon's brother, Lucien, arrived at the house, he found his sister-in-law and his brother in bed together – sufficiently reconciled to be closely intertwined in a lovers' embrace!

For the next three weeks one political crisis was quickly followed by another. There were confrontations, firstly, within *La Directoire* and then with the Council of the Five Hundred; there were plots and counter-plots – and there were threats and counter-threats.

By 8 October it was all over – *La Directoire* was no longer; the Five Hundred was retired. Napoléon had won the day and he, together with Sieyès and Roger-Ducos were elected as the three consuls who were to rule France. One of the remarkable aspects of all the lobbying and in-fighting was the performance of Napoléon's wife, Josephine. The fact that she was *persona grata* with so many influential people, and that she was a charming and determined woman with great social skills, were important factors that influenced the outcome of the fight for power. Even her sternest critics had to concede that she had well earned her place as wife of the First Consul of the Republic.

*   *   *

Hardly had the ink on the documents appointing the three consuls dried, when Napoléon – with the almost unanimous support of the people of France – moved to rid himself of the other two members of the triumvirate. Before the end of the year he was officially appointed First Consul and he and Josephine moved – first, into the Luxembourg Palace and shortly afterwards into the Tuileries. It was at this time that the first signs of Napoléonic hubris made themselves manifest. One of these was that – in the fashion of all monarchs – he signed his name in its simple baptismal form, "Napoléon" – and he restored most of the protocols and formalities of the *ancien régime*.

Neither were the changes he initiated by any means all superficial or bad; and they did not stop at the palace gates. The streets were cleaned – and cleared of stray dogs and even pigs; years of ugly graffiti were scrubbed off buildings. In the theatres, those of the stage performances that were considered to be too lewd were banned and the *libellistes* were curbed. Much of the street prostitution was wiped out. At last, the French, who had become bewildered – and lost – in a morass of political, social and economic squalor, had a strong leader who was determined to restore their country to its former glory.

For the bohemian "Consulesse", this involved an exceedingly difficult change in lifestyle and, to her credit, she adapted quickly to the strictures of her new – exalted – situation. Her fast friends were banished from the court; no longer did she wear her revealing, diaphanous English muslins; in their place were opaque silks and brocades from Lyon. At a formal reception held shortly after the new court protocols came into force, a number of the female guests appeared in the decadent dress of the years of *La Directoire*. Napoléon showed his displeasure in an obvious way; he heaped several of the big fireplaces with huge logs of wood that roared into flames and made the rooms unbearably hot. He pointedly remarked that, with a number of the guests so sparsely attired he, as their host, had to ensure that they did not catch a chill! The point was well taken.

If any of Josephine's detractors – and, apart from the members of Napoléon's family, they were but few – were of the opinion that she, as consort to the First Consul, would be found wanting, they were in for a shock. Even in the traumatic weeks between Napoléon's return to Paris and the actual *coup d'état*, she more than proved her ability as a negotiator and a go-between. She was well known to all the people Napoléon wanted to know, she was loved by the masses and, on those occasions when her husband's rather blustering approach failed, she was usually able to charm people into acquiescence. Almost all the people in high places and the senior officials who walked in the corridors of Parisian power, regarded the Napoléon-Josephine consulship as an excellent combination.

From this time until their final parting, nearly a decade later, the Bonapartes' private life was both dramatic and traumatic. It consisted of an almost endless series of what can only be described as theatrical dramas, the scenarios of which followed a set pattern. *Act I*, presented a torrid affair between Napoléon and some young beauty; in *Act II*, Josephine berated her husband and became hysterical; in *Act III*, there was always shouting and screaming as Napoléon made lame efforts to justify his behaviour – and the final *Act* was invariably a bedroom scene in which a romantic reconciliation – and a physical fulfilment – took place!

First, it was a young girl friend of Josephine, who was living in the palace with her. His performance with his second mistress continued for much longer and was even more embarrassing, as the affair was talked about all over Paris. It was with Marguerite-Josephine Weimer, a beautiful, fifteen-year-old theatre star, whose stage name was Mademoiselle George. Many years after her affair with the First Consul, the scandal-mongering Parisians were treated to a feast of erotica when Mlle George published her memoirs containing a detailed account of their many intimate interludes. When Napoléon's affair with the actress had come to its inevitable conclusion, there was a succession of other beautiful women who, in their turn, took her place.

* * *

During the last week of May 1804, the Senate proclaimed the First Consul as "Emperor" of the French Republic and in December of the same year the coronation of Napoléon I and the Empress Josephine took place in Notre-Dame. It was a magnificent spectacle of pomp and pageantry – all the more so as Pope Pius VII had come from Rome to officiate. He arrived in state, supported by a huge retinue – nearly twenty cardinals and bishops and more than one hundred priests and officials from the Vatican. Arrangements had been made for them to be accommodated in the Tuileries Palace – where they occupied one entire wing.

As was so often the case when Napoléon had international celebrities to welcome and entertain, he delegated Josephine to welcome the pontiff. In her charming and captivating way, she proved to be an admirable hostess.

Ever since Napoléon's return from Egypt – and probably even earlier – Josephine had been worried that, because their union had not produced children and by virtue of the several irregular aspects of the civil marriage ceremony, Napoléon might, in one of his many outbursts of rage, want to annul their union. She chose the night before the coronation to safeguard her matrimonial situation. She sought – and was granted – a private audience with the pontiff. When she had confessed that her marriage had not taken place in a church, he was so disturbed that he insisted that this should be rectified before the coronation took place. Napoléon objected strongly – as he had to a number of other conditions laid down by the pope. Whereas Pius VII had reluctantly yielded to the emperor on all these other scores, he was adamant that there would be no coronation until the marriage had been sanctified by the church. As the coronation was to be on the following day, Napoléon had no alternative other than to agree – and within a matter of hours, a private marriage was solemnised by Cardinal Fesch, Napoléon's uncle who, after his nephew had been made First Consul, had first been appointed Archbishop of Lyon and then, in 1803, he was given his cardinal's cap.

The smallest detail of the almost bizarre coronation ceremony was not only reported in every newspaper in France – and across Europe – but also in the memoirs of at least a dozen notables who were witnesses to the historic event. Apart from the magnificent extravagance of the décor, the ecclesiastical robes, the military and diplomatic uniforms and the gowns – and the millions of livres of glittering diamonds and other jewels – the manner in which that memorable day unfolded was remarkable. The guests were ordered to be in their places at an early hour and a series of administrative delays resulted in the ceremony commencing many hours after the appointed time. It was more than six hours after the guests arrived when Napoléon and Josephine walked up the nave of the cathedral. Had there not been dozens of colporteurs surreptitiously selling sausage rolls to the hungry guests, some of them might have fainted from hunger! The pope was anything but happy to have been kept waiting for two hours for the emperor and the empress to arrive; and he was even less amused when, immediately he had blessed the two crowns and placed them on the altar, Napoléon virtually grabbed hold of his crown and ceremoniously placed it on his own head. There was a clearly audible, muffled gasp as he followed up this presumptuous gesture by placing Josephine's – much smaller – crown, firstly on his own head and then on the head of his consort.

From early evening until late that night, the Parisian sky was ablaze with fireworks and there were singing, dancing and revelry in the cafés and in the streets. However, the emperor and the empress remained alone in their private suite at the Tuileries Palace – they had both reached a station in life that, until a few years previously, was well beyond their wildest dreams.

* * *

Not long after Napoléon's coronation, determined to be master of Europe, he was heading for the battlefield at the head of his army. In 1805 he was victorious over the Austrians, the Russians and Prussians at Austerlitz. He exacted as much by way of reparations from his defeated enemies as he could and he rewarded his ally, the Elector of Bavaria, by accepting his beautiful daughter, Princess Augusta, as a suitable bride for his stepson, Prince Eugène Beauharnais. Eugène had distinguished himself as a leader in Italy and had been rewarded by being made viceroy, there. A few months later Napoléon had a further military success at the historic battle of Jena.

The following year he marched on into Poland where he fell in love with the beautiful sixteen-year-old Countess Marie Walewska. One of the most lovely young women in Europe, Marie had been orphaned at an early age and was married off to a seventy-one-year-old count. Napoléon, at thirty-six, was as magnetically drawn to the young countess as she was to him. Much to the Empress Josephine's chagrin, they both fell in love. The affair continued for several years and culminated when

• PART III — 1 •

Marie presented Napoléon with a son, who subsequently adopted French nationality and who in years to come, as Comte Alexandre Walewski, was to become an eminent French diplomat.

It was during Napoléon's affair with Marie Walewska, in October 1809, that Comtesse Nicole was invited to the Tuileries Palace to a formal reception. Although she was in Paris at the time, she was not particularly enthusiastic about accepting, but Henriette Campan suggested they might arrive together.

About an hour after their arrival at the palace, Joseph Fouché, who had been sitting with Napoléon, came over to where Nicole was standing with Madame Campan and, having greeted them both in a formal and impersonal way, he quietly indicated to her that the emperor would like to speak with her.

"There is an ante-room behind the double doors to the left of where he is standing now. Would it be convenient for you to be in the ante-room in fifteen minutes from now?"

"Sir, it would be an honour. It is quite some time since we have had an opportunity to talk *à deux*."

At the appointed time, Nicole left her friend and entered the ante-room. The two flunkies who stood at the doorway, who had been instructed to admit her, bowed ceremoniously, and having shown her to a chair, withdrew. Nicole, knowing how chronically unpunctual Napoléon always was, expected to wait at least half an hour for him to arrive. She was agreeably surprised when in less than two minutes the emperor arrived. She stood up and curtsied.

"Please Comtesse Nicole, do sit down! This is not in any way a formal meeting."

"As you wish, your Majesty."

The emperor pulled up a chair quite close to where she was sitting.

"Being a captive of my own making, behind a solid wall of deference and formality, I am quite isolated. Everybody tells me what they think I want to hear and, for this reason, I am loath to ask anyone for personal advice. Furthermore, every matter I discuss confidentially with the people close to me is, having been distorted and taken out of context, passed on to at least half a dozen wagging tongues."

Knowing how subjective Napoléon had always been, Nicole played along with the same theme.

"I knew Emperor Joseph of Austria quite well and, of course, Queen Marie-Antoinette. Both these monarchs have told me very much the same thing."

"Madame, from the time we first met in Toulon, I have had great respect for your integrity. At that time, you gave me stern but good advice. I smarted under your criticism; but I appreciated your frankness and your sincerity and, since nobody has thrown the words you spoke back into my face, I firmly believe that you have not spoken about our meeting."

"However, your Majesty, you yourself did raise the matter with the Marquis de Barras."

"It was in a spirit of appreciation of the good advice you offered me."

There was a silence before Napoléon continued speaking.

"I have come to you again, Comtesse, not as a sovereign, but simply as the leader of France – and, once again, I am seeking your advice."

"If I can help you to serve France I certainly shall. And you can be assured that whatever we discuss will remain between us and nobody else."

"Thank you! Firstly, may I ask you if you believe that, now we have liberated the people of France from the tyranny of *l'ancien régime*, it is better for our country to have a monarchy rather than to have to put up with a weak and leaderless *Assemblée nationale*?"

Nicole thought carefully before replying –

"In principle, yes, I do."

"In which case, I wish to put to you my dilemma. If a monarchy is to prevail in France, there must be a clear line of succession. To have fighting – and possibly civil war – when I die, could result in losing all we have fought for and for which countless Frenchmen have died."

"Perhaps I can help you by coming quickly to the point. What you want to know is – in order that you might have a son to follow you, should you divorce the Empress Josephine and marry the Arch-Duchess Marie-Louise of Austria."

"You are extraordinarily perceptive, madame."

Nicole did not consider it appropriate to advise the emperor that for months this possibility had been debated throughout France and Austria. Nor did she mention that she was well aware that Napoléon had already discussed the matter in detail with Marie-Louise's father, the Emperor Francis I. She was certain that he had made up his mind what he intended to do and was hoping that she, someone whose opinion he valued, agreed with him.

"Your Majesty – if it is certain that the empress cannot have further children, one cannot but be drawn to the conclusion that a divorce and a re-marriage is advisable. In this way there is every possibility that you will have a legitimate son and heir. However, there are two matters of paramount importance and these must be viewed objectively."

"If you would be so good as to enlighten me, I shall act accordingly – even if I do not agree with what you recommend."

There was another silence while Nicole thought carefully how she should phrase her next statement.

"The first of these matters is something that must not be taken into account, in fact, it must be completely forgotten. And the second matter must be given the fullest consideration in the way your divorce should be handled."

"Comtesse, I am intrigued. Please continue!"

"The matter to be totally forgotten is that both the empress and you are by nature promiscuous people. In any of the discussions leading up to a divorce settlement, no good purpose can be served for either of you to drag in any of the other's sexual peccadilloes."

Napoléon was about to make a comment but at the last second refrained from doing so "...and the other matter?"

"Furthermore, since the day when you were appointed First Consul, the empress, Josephine, has exercised extraordinary self-discipline; she has dramatically changed the way she has lived her life and the company she has kept. During the difficult weeks – and perhaps months – that lie ahead this must be in the forefront of your mind."

"Thank you for what you have said, I can assure you that I agree with every word you have spoken and that your advice and recommendation will be implemented."

"Those who are advising you and who are drawing up the necessary legal documents will do well to remember that the empress is held in high regard by the people of France. They not only respect her, they love her."

"Is there anything else that you think I should know?"

"Josephine is a highly emotional person. It is obvious to the world that she loves you passionately – only a woman who felt that way about you could have given you the support that she has given you. During the exceedingly difficult and emotional weeks that lie ahead, you must, even if you are provoked, remain gentle and understanding."

"I shall do my best and I shall ensure that the terms of the divorce are generous. I assure you, madame, the Austrian arch-duchess is to me little more than a 'walking womb'. France must have an heir to the throne and it will be her task to produce one."

"Your Majesty!"

"I made that remark to convince you that I am sincere. I shall always love my Josephine – and I shall always love Eugène and Hortense, too. No father or step-father could ever have finer, more worthy children."

* * *

Napoléon kept his word and did everything possible to ensure that Josephine was treated in the manner that a dowager empress should be treated, but her constant tears and tantrums made his task anything but easy.

* * *

The new empress was not well liked by the French, who had loved Josephine and who had already been forced to put up with one Austrian arch-duchess. Marie-Louise was jealous of Josephine and strongly resented every measure of respect and affection that Napoléon demonstrated towards his former wife. Her letters to her father, however, confirmed that she really did love her husband and she was as delighted as he was – or nearly so – when she became pregnant.

As had always been the case for a royal birth in France, the long list of officials whose duty it was to be present, were all there; and these included Eugène and Hortense, whose role turned out to be Napoléon's main pacifiers, during a long and difficult childbirth.

As the hours of the new empress's labour continued, the *accoucheur,* who had been, for some time, using instruments – without success – was of the opinion that both the mother and the child would die. Eventually, after the baby was born, the sole concern of the doctor was to save the life of the mother. The baby, thought to be dead, was left lying on the floor. One of the nursemaids grasped it by the feet, slapped its bottom and gave it a teaspoon of brandy. The baby gave a cry – and from then on it went from strength to strength!

During his wife's long and difficult labour Napoléon was despondent, agitated and alarmed and kept walking in and out of the room. Hortense was doing her best to placate him and to maintain his spirits. After fearing the worst, that he would lose both his wife and his child, when he was told that both the mother and the baby were well, he could not contain his relief and his joy.

Outside the palace the artillery was standing by, with orders that, if the child was a girl, there would be a twenty-one gun salute – and, for a boy, one hundred guns would be fired. The huge crowds in the streets cheered with excitement when the order to commence firing was given. To a man – and a woman – they counted out loud as one after the other the guns went off. When the twenty-first gun was fired, there was a prolonged and eerie hush. The seconds went by in total silence. Then came the roaring boom of the twenty-second gun – and the crowd became delirious with joy as, for nearly an hour and a half, the right royal salute continued. It was a triumph for the emperor who, remembering his promise to la Comtesse d'Anjou, wrote a letter to Josephine "without whose great personal sacrifice", this could not have happened.

*   *   *

Not long after the birth of his son Napoléon made the greatest mistake of his life. He commenced his ill-fated march on Moscow. From the start of the advance beyond the Vistula river, the invasion was a total disaster. The more extended his lines of communication became, the more exposed were his troops to the constant attacks of the Russian Cossacks and bands of peasants. The more he was forced to rely on local resources for food and fodder, the more thoroughly did the Russians implement their "scorched earth" policy, and no sooner had he entered Moscow than the Muscovites burned the city to the ground. If this was not enough to guarantee his defeat, he was constantly receiving dismal news from Spain, where Sir Arthur Wellesley's[44] British troops were inflicting one defeat after another on the French. The news from Paris was just as depressing, as the economy was close to bankruptcy and the news of well over a hundred thousand casualties from the Eastern front and from Spain had caused great discontent and unrest.

With the onset of the long, cold Russian winter, Napoléon and his defeated army had no option but to retreat. With their starving horses dropping dead, they were forced to trudge through the snow: exhausted, hungry and cold. Having lost their artillery and having used up all their ammunition, they were virtually defenceless against the marauding Cossacks and the local peasants.

* * *

By the end of 1813 Napoléon had lost the confidence of the people of France, his heretofore adoring, faithful army had had enough and the economy of France was in tatters. The rest of Europe was fed up with the emperor and were demanding a restoration of the monarchy.

Waiting in the wings since the beginning of the Revolution had been the brother of the guillotined King Louis XVI – Louis, Comte de Provence. He had fled from France, in 1791, at the same time as his brother had made his abortive attempt to leave the country, and he had wandered around Germany, proclaiming himself as King of France.

In April 1814, Napoléon's abdication was demanded. This precipitated a recurrence of his youthful determination to commit suicide. He chose a cocktail of belladonna, opium and white hellebore[45] which did little more harm than to give him ghastly pains that lasted for hours. Having recovered, he set about negotiating the best possible terms for his abdication.

---

[44] Sir Arthur Wellesley, soon to be created the Duke of Wellington.
[45] A plant, the powdered roots of which were used to kill lice and caterpillars.

• PART III — 1 •

The French people were exhausted by seemingly endless wars and economic hardship. Under the leadership of, in turn, Danton, Robespierre, *La Directoire* and Napoléon, they had failed to find the holy grail of *Liberté, Égalité et Fraternité* that each, in turn, had promised them. Before the end of May, Napoléon had been forced to abdicate and Louis, Comte de Provence, had entered Paris as Louis XVIII.

* * *

Within days, at the age of forty-four, Napoléon Bonaparte was transported in HMS *Undaunted* to Elba. As a measure of the power he still had, the terms agreed to in the Deed of Abdication signed by Britain and his other European adversaries — including the new French Bourbon monarchy — were staggering. The deed allowed him to be the virtual ruler of Elba, with a bodyguard of one thousand men — including cavalry and artillery. The signatories also undertook to pay him an annual pension of two million francs for life and, in addition, Britain agreed to give him — as his personal property — the frigate of his choice, HMS *Inconstant*.

When Napoléon had been forced to abdicate, almost everybody expected that, under the reinstated King Louis XVIII, things would settle down and France would start rebuilding its almost bankrupt economy, but this was not to be. Leading up to Bonaparte's departure for Elba, the rulers of the powerful countries of Europe signed treaties with each other — and then signed secret treaties with other countries. Each ruler had his own agenda — and, in most cases, a secret agenda as well.

Under the rule of the old, weak and incompetent Louis XVIII, France was once again in turmoil. As the *émigrés* returned from Britain and the other countries to which they had fled when the Revolution had broken out, they found Paris quite different from the city they had known. Their palaces and châteaux had become museums — or had been sold — and they demanded that the king should give orders for their property to be returned to them. This caused widespread dissatisfaction among the people who had bought and paid for these confiscated estates. Education became, once more, something that only the rich could afford and almost all the good reforms of the Republic were abolished and the rights and privileges of the *ancien régime* restored. By the end of 1814 the support for Louis had evaporated and there was more discontent throughout the country than there had been during the previous April.

Confident that this would be the case, from the day he landed on Elba, Napoléon set about preparing his escape. He still had dozens of fanatical supporters in almost every town and village of France. Within weeks of his banishment, a network of informants ensured that their deposed emperor was aware of the mood and feelings of the people, the locations of the various units of the army, the names of their commanders, and the location of their weapons and other armaments. The best of Napoléon's former officers were encouraged to swear allegiance to the royalist cause and to offer to enlist in the army that was being formed by Louis XVIII's government.

With his efficient and loyal band of informers, it did not take Napoléon long to learn that the political pendulum was quickly swinging back in his favour and, by the beginning of 1815 he was confident that the time was ripe for him to make a triumphant return to France. In order to make his escape, unnoticed, he had to wait until Colonel Campbell, the British officer who had been posted to Elba to ensure he did not leave the island, set out on one of his periodic trips to Italy. This happened during the last week of February. Hardly had he departed when Napoléon loaded his troops, his cavalrymen and his cannon on to HMS *Inconstant*, and, with two other ships, he sailed for France.

On 1 March he reached the French coast and landed near Marseille, between Golfe Juan and Fréjus, and immediately set out for Grenoble, gathering peasants and some of his former soldiers on the way. Word that he had returned to France spread like wildfire, not only all over France but throughout Europe. Within days, Louis XVIII had summoned his army chiefs and ordered them to march on Napoléon and shoot him on sight. Not satisfied that his royal command was sufficient to ensure that this threat to his throne was quickly and permanently removed, he insisted that the *Assemblée nationale* pass legislation not only to summarily execute Napoléon but all his followers as well. The leaders of the allied forces – Russia, Prussia, Austria, the Low Countries and England – were at that time meeting in Vienna. They were equally alarmed and agreed to form an alliance to destroy Napoléon and his followers.

By the time the former emperor had reached the gates of Grenoble, on 16 March, the local commander had deployed his troops to stop his advance. When the two opposing forces were within musket range of one another, Napoléon, dressed in the army uniform he had worn as Commander-in-Chief of the French army, slowly walked forward and presented himself as a target. Simultaneously, three things occurred: the local commander gave the order to fire; Napoléon prepared to make a speech; and the entire Grenoble army force cheered and yelled – "Long live the Emperor! Long live Napoléon." The gates of the city were opened and, within the next twenty-four hours, Napoléon's army trebled its size. He pushed on towards Paris.

As his triumphal march continued, the number of his supporters grew, almost hourly. A week later he was nearing Dijon and, as he entered a town called Clamecy, a fine looking gentleman, formally dressed, walked up the steps of the town hall and, in a loud voice, he began to address the people. Seeing this man, wearing a top hat and a long overcoat – and hearing his authoritative voice – a large crowd quickly gathered. From his pocket he withdrew his spectacles and put them on. He unrolled a formal address, announced himself as Général Allix and commenced to read Napoléon's proclamation, announcing that he was once more the Emperor of France. Within minutes, the mayor had called out the guard and almost immediately an officer and twelve men appeared with orders to arrest the general. As they were about to step forward to take hold of him, in a loud voice the general announced, "In the name of the Emperor of France, I am now assuming command of this town. The Bourbon colours will be pulled down from the twin spires of our church and the *tricolores* will be hoisted. I call on all good citizens to wear our national colours at once. Those who do not do so will be considered traitors."

Amid thunderous applause from what was now a huge crowd, the officers and the gendarmes who were about to arrest the general, removed the Bourbon emblems from their hats and, from nowhere *tricolores* and cockades appeared. A town had been captured for the emperor's cause by one intrepid man. Although perhaps not as dramatic as had been the case in Clamecy, city by city the people of France were forsaking the Bourbon Restoration and were returning to Napoléon.

Less than a week later, in the middle of the night, the king and his entourage fled the Tuileries Palace and headed toward Belgium. What followed was quite bizarre. As if nothing untoward had happened, the Royalist appointed ministers and departmental heads simply dissolved and the former Republican incumbents quietly went back to the offices they had vacated eleven months earlier. Among them was Joseph Fouché, the Minister of Police. It was not because Napoléon trusted him that he wanted him to fill this important portfolio; but rather because he recognised the brilliant little man's thoroughness and administrative ability. Whereas the French newspapers, usually so anxious to create crises out of nothing, reported the flight of the royal family and the return of Napoléon in quite a sober fashion, the foreign press proclaimed that Napoléon had overawed the people, who had succumbed in fear.

Napoléon had marched from the Mediterranean in less than three weeks and had reinstated himself as emperor without a single skirmish or any loss of life – and, once again, had proved that he was a genius.

As the reinstated emperor of France, one of the first things Napoléon did on reaching Paris was to write to the heads of all the European governments, offering an olive branch of peace and asking them to allow him to rebuild France as a peace-loving country. These letters were not well received; in fact, the foreign ministers of the alliance – Russia, Prussia, Austria, England and the Low Countries – met to establish the best way to rid themselves of this "Corsican plague". It was not only because they feared the threat of an attack from Bonaparte that they were in no mood to accept his regime; being monarchist states, they feared the spread of democratic republicanism.

* * *

Except for the first few months of her married life, whenever she had been in England, Lady Scott-Quetteville lived at No. 22 St James's Square. For her the spring was a great time to be in London. The ground was not yet too jarring for the horses' hooves, the roses and the tulips were in full bloom, most of the horse chestnut trees were still in flower and there were many sunny days in which to enjoy life to the full. And of all the rooms in the house from which to enjoy the scene that St James's offered, her library on the first floor was ideal. Its two big, bay windows afforded a grandstand view to see everything that was happening in the big square. If there had been any one thing that gave her cause for disappointment, it certainly was that, during the forty-five years that she had lived there, there had been so many new buildings erected and these had blocked out much of the view of the Mall and St James's Park. As she sat at her desk in the library – as she so often did – one of Nicole's favourite pastimes was watching the people walking on the footpath in the square and trying to guess where they were going.

During the morning of 10 May 1815 she recognised the tall lean figure of a man who, for more than twenty years had – from time to time – called at her house. Sometimes he wore spectacles and sometimes he had a moustache. On one occasion he had a beard. Although he was almost six feet tall, one would have to describe him as nondescript; a person whose appearance did not attract any special attention. In all the years that he had been coming to the house, Lady Nicole had never spoken to the man. He always came to the front door and he always had an envelope to deliver and he invariably asked for the butler. If it was another member of the domestic staff who answered the bell – and it usually was – he politely made a short statement.

"I have a letter that must be personally handed to the butler. If the butler is not in I am instructed to hand the envelope to Lady Scott-Quetteville's private secretary."

Although during the past decade he had not usually called more than once or twice each year, the senior staff members were aware that he was to be treated in a polite way. On some occasions, as he handed over the document, he would say –

"I shall return tomorrow, at this time, in case there is an answer."

It seemed remarkable to everyone – except Lady Nicole – that not once in all the years he had been coming to the house had he arrived when Lady Nicole was not in.

On his 10 May 1815 visit, his ritual changed in that his second sentence was different. Having handed the envelope to the butler, he added –

"I shall return this afternoon to ascertain if there is an answer."

When Norman Harvey, who had been John Scott's butler at the time he had married Nicole, turned seventy, he had retired and gone to Richmond to live with his daughter. Six months previously, his son, Alfred, who had been a senior member of Lord Grosvenor's domestic staff, had replaced his father and, among the many instructions passed on to him, were the details of these rather unusual visits and how to handle them. Although nothing had ever been said to either father or son Harvey, it was tacitly understood that Lady Nicole regarded the visits as important.

When Harvey had brought the envelope to her and she had passed on the message about a reply, she nodded her head and said –

"Harvey, would you please have the carriage ready as soon as comfortably possible? I shall only be out for an hour or so – and would you do several other things as well? First, please tell Annie that I shall be leaving for France very soon, probably tomorrow, and that I shall probably be away for less than two weeks – and to pack my things at once. Secondly, would you ask whoever is on duty to be ready to saddle up and take a letter down to The Bridge Company in ten minutes time? And finally, I should like to have a note delivered to Mrs François's house for me. It will be ready in a few minutes."

Quite used to receiving three or four orders at once, Harvey excused himself and went about his business.

Having written a short note to François's office and to her daughter-in-law, Judy, Nicole set out in her carriage but had returned in less than an hour. She had paid a visit to Berkeley Square to the Bassetts' house, where she had learned that Lady Hélène had left for Etreham several days previously and that she would not be back for a fortnight. This news pleased her.

A few minutes before noon Judy arrived at No. 22. Having greeted each other in their usual effusive way, Nicole surprised her daughter-in-law when she asked –

"Judy darling, you remember Joseph Fouché, do you not?"

"Yes, of course I do. I remember him as the Frenchman who, when all his enemies have been guillotined, has survived. Why do you ask?"

"I have to go to France, immediately, to see him. As I have no wish to go to Paris, I have asked him to meet me in Etreham. Hélène is there at the present time. I know it is short notice but would you like to come with me?"

"Maman, dearest, you have never interfered in my life and I have no right to be telling you what you should – and should not – do. However, you will be turning seventy-one in less than a month and I think that international diplomacy, planning and plotting is something that others should be doing."

"Darling, until this morning, I had not heard a word from Monsieur Fouché for almost a year. Reading between the lines of his letter, I believe I have no option other than to meet him and at least hear what he has to say. In any case, it is spring and a week with Hélène, making out we are forty years younger than we really are, will be fun. I know it is short notice but I thought it would be even more enjoyable if you came too. Incidentally, has Ettie returned from Marseille?"

"No – but we are expecting her any day."

"I should have loved it if she could have come too."

Thinking that Nicole wanted to make an immediate start, Judy was already on her feet and making towards the door. She laughed.

"You are quite impossible, Maman; but of course I shall come with you. François will not be back from New York for at least a fortnight. The trials of the American steamboat were due to take place last month. In any case, another – important – reason I want to come with you…" she laughed as she continued "…is because it has now been agreed between your three sons and me that I am to keep a close eye on you. With Napoléon back in Paris and every country in Europe determined to get rid of him, I am sure that the cunning Monsieur Fouché wants you to murder either that fat, old fool Louis or Bonaparte himself – or both of them. When do you propose to go?"

"Tomorrow morning, if possible – I sent a note to François's European manager at the office. I am expecting the messenger to return in less than an hour. Will you remain here and have lunch with me until he arrives? We shall then know when a ship can take us to Le Havre."

"I had better go now, dear. I have several appointments to cancel and a few other chores that need my attention."

***

As they were sailing down the Thames on their way to Le Havre, Nicole had plenty of time to tell her daughter-in-law about Fouché's letter. It was short and to the point –

> *"Certain circumstances have arisen that have important consequences for both you and me. It is my belief that you are in a unique position to be of inestimable value. Can we meet in France?"*

Although Nicole appreciated that Judy was at least as perceptive as she was, she felt she should add her own "between the lines" explanation to ascertain if Judy had interpreted the contents of the note in the same way as she had.

"I take the 'certain circumstances' as being either Napoléon's amazing – and bloodless – coup d'état or the aggressive way the other countries of Europe have reacted to it."

"I agree with you, Maman, that one of these two possibilities is the most likely – perhaps both."

"And, from many of the letters I have received over the years from this extraordinary little man, the 'both you and me' most certainly means 'England and France'. As Fouché is always considerate, I take his request to meet in France is only because his circumstances are such that he is unable to come to England."

"I would agree with that, too."

***

Lady Hélène Bassett was overjoyed to have Nicole and Judy staying with her. They had long rides together and caught up with the latest news about their children and grandchildren. Also staying in the château with them were two teenage daughters of Hélène's second daughter, Nathalie. They were as carefree, happy and vivacious as only sixteen- and seventeen-year-olds can be. Being at least as enlightened and open-minded as Nicole and Hélène had been when they were young – and had remained – they had the older women in peals of laughter as they described the balls and parties they had recently attended and the young men who were paying attention to them. Although Judy, whose teenage life had been entirely different, could only feel a little envious of them, the two old ladies, who had known the parents and grandparents of the young people of the social set to which the two girls belonged, had many comments to make. Such remarks as "I am sure he is not nearly as bad as his lecherous father was" or "her grandmother was a bolter too; she must have inherited it from her" were frequent.

As they sat by the fireside in the evenings, Hélène would relate stories about her childhood in the château and about her father, Colonel de Basseville, and how he had taught her about farming, dressage – and about life. They were intrigued to learn about her brothers and how they had been killed in the futile attack on Minorca and how her father – the girls' great-grandfather – had been virtually murdered by "that evil bastard, Louis XVI". As she relived the memories of the past, the teenagers thought it was hilarious that she and Nicole had both worked in a brothel. After they had consumed a few glasses of wine, the girls, their tongues happily unfettered, plied them both with questions about The Cloisters – who went there, what it was like and whether they had enjoyed what they were doing. Virginia, the older of the two girls, asked her grandmother –

"I think I should like to work in a nice seraglio. Grandmother, what do you think my father would say if I asked his permission?"

Before Hélène had a chance to answer the question, Elisabeth, the younger of the two girls, burst into laughter.

"Take no notice of her, Gran, she is worried that she's missing out on too much fun."

Hélène pretended to ignore the interjection.

"Virginia, dear, some girls choose to wait until they are married before they become sexually involved with men, others have sexual needs that require more immediate satisfaction. With regard to this second category, frankly, I can see little difference between a promiscuous girl who is leaping into bed with a series of eager, inept and insensitive young men and one who is working in a well run seraglio. What do you think Nicole?"

"As long as a woman does not feel cheap; as long as she feels that she is maintaining her dignity and as long as she is not running health and pregnancy risks, I think it is a case of *chaque une à son goût*. And I might add that a girl will learn much more about avoiding disease and becoming pregnant in a place like The Cloisters used to be than she will listening to her social friends."

There was a silence while her words sank in. This was followed by short speeches from Virginia and Elisabeth, acknowledging how lucky they were to have a grandmother like Hélène and an "aunt" like Nicole who knew how to mix fun, laughter and wisdom better than most people half their age.

Nicole and Judy had not been at the château more than two or three days when the spruce, black carriage – complete with footman and two outriders – arrived. Nicole welcomed the Minister of Police and introduced him to Lady Bassett and to her daughter-in-law. In doing so she was aware that Fouché probably knew almost as much about the de Basseville family as she did. Having made arrangements for his horses, and the *équipe* that he had brought with him, to be looked after, Hélène invited him inside to freshen up before having lunch.

After a pleasant meal, Nicole, taking Judy with her, led her guest into the conservatory where it was easy to discuss matters privately. She opened the discussion by stating that, because of her age, she had brought Judy, her alter ego, with her.

"Monsieur Fouché, I am fully aware how careful you have to be and, having said that, I assure you that there is no person, male or female, in whom I have more trust than I do in Judy."

"And I assure you Madame, that every report I have ever had, since Madame Scott-Quetteville arrived in London more than twenty years ago, has been such that would confirm your opinion."

He added, with a vague suggestion of a smile –

"But then, again, she is half French."

Judy, not at all embarrassed by this conversation, addressed the Frenchman.

"Monsieur, I am pleased to be here because my husband and my two brothers-in-law – and I, too – who almost worship the ground on which my mother-in-law treads, feel that it is time for her to retire from international affairs. In 1789, at the beginning of the Revolution, she was very nearly murdered. At that time she was forty-four years old – and everyone said she was too old to be involved in the things she was doing. Having miraculously recovered, she has continued to expose herself to personal danger for more than twenty years. Although I am aware that I do not have her skills, I am just over forty-four years old and fit. I can also state that I am as French as the Countess is and I fervently believe in the same things as she does."

Fouché was impressed – as much with the sincerity of Judy's remarks as he was with her words. He found it hard to believe she was over forty. She looked at least ten years younger and he said as much.

"I have always thought the countess had – and still has – an endless supply of the elixir of youth. I now believe that she has you imbibing the same tonic. Madame, I can assure both you and the three Scott-Quetteville sons that, at the time when the countess feels that she wishes to hand over to you, I shall be as willing and proud to accept you as my comrade in arms."

Nicole, who had been amusing herself in silence listening to them sparring with each other, decided that it was time to discuss the matter for which Fouché had asked her to come to France.

"Well now you have both apparently finished talking about me as if I were a painting on the wall, can we not get on to more pressing matters? The most relevant sentence in your discussion was that it will be I who decides what I do – and when."

Although she laughed as she made this statement, they both knew she meant what she had said.

As he so often had done when he was about to introduce a serious matter, Fouché rose to his feet.

"Mesdames, Napoléon is about to join battle with almost all of the strongest military powers in Europe. Although I am the first to acknowledge that he is a military genius, it is not possible for him to win this war he is about to start. The battles that will soon take place are going to be fought on many – widely separated – fronts. The Prussians and the Russians can move against us in large numbers from the east, the Austrians can invade France from Italy, and Britain, with its command of the seas, can invade France from anywhere it chooses – from Calais in the

Channel to Toulon in the Mediterranean Sea. There are only three generals whose leadership skills he really trusts – Murat, Grouchy and his former aide, Général Rapp. He has neither the command structure nor the means of communication to achieve victory. The longer the war continues, the greater will be the number of French casualties."

Nicole who was particularly interested in what was happening in the south of France and neighbouring Italy, was well aware of France's military problems in that part of the world.

"Monsieur, I do not think that the brilliant Joachim Murat or his fine army will be of much assistance to Général Bonaparte for quite some time. He has had a costly defeat at the hands of the Austrians and his army has suffered many casualties."

"I was about to lead up to that unfortunate situation. The emperor was badly affected by Murat's defeat. It was not just because he is his brother-in-law but equally because they have been close friends since the 'whiff of gunshot' incident in 1795. It was Murat who commandeered the guns that Napoléon used to defend the Convention."

"Many people have never forgiven Napoléon for that brutal attack on virtually unarmed civilians."

Fouché, wanting to proceed to the actual purpose of the meeting, continued.

"There is another serious matter that will inevitably compromise his chances of success – his health."

"Do you know what is wrong with him?"

"As he is so secretive about such matters, it has been difficult to find out anything from him; but I am on good terms with his personal surgeon, Baron Larrey, and, although he is intensely loyal to the emperor, he has asked me what I think he should do if Napoléon's health deteriorates to such a degree that he cannot effectively command his enormous army. It appears that he has two particularly tiresome complaints. He is suffering from a bladder infection that is constantly irritating him and causing him to have to pass water frequently. His other condition is even more inconvenient and embarrassing for him – for years he has been ignoring the advice of his surgeon who has been imploring him to have an operation to remove his haemorrhoids."

"Poor man!"

"His piles are now so bad that he finds it distractingly painful to ride his horse. Where he used to go from place to place mounted, now he travels in his carriage whenever he can. The cumulative effect of these two maladies has not only made him distressingly irritable with everyone but it has also affected his concentration. Several times lately I have seen him just sitting on a well cushioned chair, with his head in his hands."

"Baron Larrey is the most brilliant field surgeon in Europe. I used to know him well when I was working with him and Dr Lassonne, at the time I was establishing the research clinic in Paris. They were both close friends of Dr John Hunter, the man who, with Lassonne, saved my life. John Hunter, who in his time was recognised as the leader of the battle surgeons, used to tell me about the brilliance of Baron Larrey."

"I have not heard of Dr John Hunter for years. Is he still alive?"

"Unfortunately, no! He died more than ten years ago and I miss him sadly. He was one of my closest friends."

Realising that she had strayed from the *raison d'être* of their meeting, she steered the conversation back on course.

"Monsieur, I fully accept your reasons for being so convinced that it will be quite impossible to win a war against the combined armed forces of the rest of Europe, but I do not see where I can do anything to either prevent the war or influence its outcome."

"Madame, may I ask you if you are aware of the term 'Order of Battle'?"

"I have not heard the expression since I was a girl. I remember my grandfather showing my sister and me some old documents and one of them was the Order of Battle of the French army before a battle against the Austrians. It was a long list of the regiments involved, the names of the commanders, the numbers of horses and things like that – and attached to it was a map showing where all these regiments were."

"That is precisely what an Order of Battle is. I have here with me the Order of Battle of the French army, as it was at the beginning of this month. It is my belief that if the British had the document it could shorten the war by many weeks – or even months. It could save the lives of tens of thousands of fine young French soldiers. I should like this document to get into the hands of the British prime minister as soon as possible."

Having quickly recovered from the shock of what Fouché had just said, Nicole asked –

"Are there not ways of achieving this, other than by using me?"

"Madame, you do not know how much espionage is going on at the present time. There are so many people working for both sides. Take, for instance, England's foreign secretary, Lord Castlereagh[46] – a totally dishonest and unreliable man, who is loyal to neither England nor any other country. He is not a man of his word – and he is a liar."

"I think he has now been replaced or is about to be. I have only met the man on one or two occasions and I have to admit he did not impress me at all. If you believe that you do not have any other way of getting this document into the hands of the British prime minister, I shall certainly do as you have asked."

Nicole had known Joseph Fouché for many years. Personally, she found it hard to come to terms with the apparent ease with which he was able to abandon first his party and then his emperor. In looking at the situation, much of her dilemma was that she could see the logic and the good sense in what he was trying to do. When she had finished commenting on the foreign secretary, there was silence during which they were both waiting for the other to say something. It was the Frenchman who spoke.

"On behalf of the people of France, thank you, Madame! In my opinion it is extremely important that the British prime minister and the Duke of Wellington see it as soon as possible."

"They will, I assure you, sir."

"One further point, Madame! Every day the situation is changing in France – more units are being raised, divisions are moving from one side of the country to the other, leaders are being dispensed with and armaments are being changed. For this reason, I am required to deliver a more up-to-date Order of Battle to the emperor in Beaumont, where he will

---

[46] At this time the Earl of Liverpool, the prime minister, had little time for Castlereagh but found it impossible to sack him.

be at the end of the second week of next month. It would be valuable if you were somewhere near the Duke of Wellington's headquarters at that time. The Duke of Wellington will probably have been told that the emperor will have his headquarters elsewhere; however both he and his bodyguard formation, the 1st Grenadiers of the Guard will be where I have stated. Furthermore, it is important that the Duke of Wellington should know that there are several versions of our country's Order of Battle! In order to confound the traitors in our midst, I have had these carefully prepared and it would be quite impossible for anyone to know that they are forgeries designed to mislead. Already copies have found their way to Vienna, Moscow and Frankfurt. Perhaps the British have a copy, too."

"As you are aware, my son is on the duke's staff. Whatever you deliver to me will reach the allied Commander-in-Chief, without delay."

"Yes, but is it not possible that your son could be absent from the duke's headquarters? He often takes secret orders from the duke to the commanders of the armies of the other countries of the alliance."

"Whatever the circumstances, you can be fully confident that either my daughter-in-law or I will ensure that whatever you deliver to us will reach the duke promptly. Your courier should stay close to me until I am in a position to inform him that I have done what you asked me to do. In case you need to contact either of us, both Mrs Scott-Quetteville and I shall be in London until the end of the first week of June, at least."

"Thank you, Mesdames! It was indeed good of you both to come to France."

Having made this statement, the Minister of Police stood up. Nicole was well aware that he would want to hasten back to Paris.

"Knowing that you will not wish to delay your return to Paris, I have not invited you to stay the night; however, the captain riding with you by now will have been given two hampers for you to take with you. It might enable you to save a little time."

"Thank you, Madame la Comtesse. As I have probably said more than once previously, there is nobody in the world to whom I owe more or in whom I have more trust than I have in you. France is fortunate to be able to claim you as a daughter."

He paused and then, addressing Judy, he added –

"I am confident that the same can be said of you, Madame."

They all moved toward the front door of the château. Nicole extended her hand, as she had always done; however, Fouché surprised her by putting his arms around her in a warm embrace.

* * *

Early next morning, Nicole and Judy left Etreham and set out for Le Havre. Hélène insisted on driving with them to the coast. They had not gone more than a mile when the driver stopped the carriage, climbed down and came to the door.

"Madame, Lady Bassett, our carriage is being followed."

Hélène looked at Nicole, as if to ask her the reason. Nicole told the driver to signal to the horseman who had stopped about fifty yards down the road, to come forward. Seeing that he was a captain of the National Guard, she asked him the reason for his presence.

He saluted her.

"Madame, my orders are to escort you to your ship and to see you safely aboard. There are still marauders on the country roads."

He turned to Lady Bassett.

"I am also to provide you with protection on your way back to Etreham, Madame."

* * *

Not until they were out at sea did Nicole and Judy have a chance to discuss their meeting with Fouché. Nicole wanted to get some reaction from Judy.

"Well, Judy dear, what do you think of my friend, M. Fouché?"

"Strange – and deep! I should rather have him as a friend than as a foe."

"I apologise for not having brought you into the conversation more. Would you like to have said anything?"

Judy laughed.

"No, but it would have been fun to have asked him to pass on to Napoléon our best wishes for a speedy and painless removal of his piles and an equally rapid emancipation from the iniquitous irritation in his bladder."

Nicole, appreciating her daughter-in-law's typically "Quetteville" sense of humour, replied –

"Somehow I do not believe he would have passed on your thoughtful message to the emperor or even have informed him that he had had a meeting with us."

She changed the subject.

"As soon as we reach London, we must ensure that our fat little envelope is handed to Lord Liverpool as soon as possible."

"I am sure that Lady Liverpool would arrange a meeting with her husband if you asked her."

"Just for fun, why don't you contact her, Judy? You know her better than I do. You have sat with her at all of the 'steamship research' functions. I agree with you and the boys, the sooner an old woman like me hands over things of this nature to you the better."

"Maman darling, you are not an old woman. It is just that we all adore you so much and do not want to lose you."

"Good! Then you will come to Belgium with me and whatever has to be done we shall do it together?"

"I certainly shall."

"I must confess something else, Judy. In all modern land battles, more wounded soldiers die because they are just left to lie, untreated, on the battlefield for days after the military encounter is over. Quite often the only attention they get is from local women who not only treat their wounds but often take them to their homes and care for them until they have recovered. I believe that you and I can be quite useful in Belgium."

"From the time when you first mentioned about going to where the Duke of Wellington would be setting up his headquarters, I have suspected that you had something on your mind other than being a Fouché postman."

"One of the things that worries the life out of me is the almost absolute neglect with which the British army treats its wounded. The French are generations ahead of us. Baron Larrey, who has been so wonderful in the help he has given to the François Quetteville Research

Centre in Paris, has set up a highly sophisticated medical service to ensure that the wounded are treated promptly and evacuated quickly. We must try to do the same for our British soldiers."

Within an hour of reaching St James's, Judy had written a letter to Lady Liverpool. The messenger who delivered the letter to Downing Street asked if the prime minister's wife was at home and if she wished to send an answer. The reply was that Lady Liverpool would see Mrs Scott-Quetteville at eleven o'clock the following morning.

It was a short – but satisfactory – meeting. Judy explained that she and Lady Nicole had just returned from France with something of great importance to be handed personally to the prime minister, as soon as possible.

"Of course, my dear, I shall see that Robert receives your message as soon as the House rises this afternoon. I shall contact you immediately thereafter." She added, "It is amazing the way you and your husband are so brilliantly carrying on the work started by each of your parents."

"My husband's parents, actually, Lady Liverpool; although she is very much my own mother, too."

"Will it be you or Lady Nicole who comes to see Robert?"

Judy smiled.

"Whomever you think he would prefer to see."

"Knowing Robert, I am certain that he would hate to miss the opportunity of seeing you again. After the last dinner at which you and your husband were present, he spent at least fifteen minutes waxing lyrical about you."

* * *

It was mid-afternoon when a messenger arrived at the François Scott-Quetteville home with a note for Judy from the prime minister's secretary asking if nine o'clock the following morning would be convenient for her to call at No. 10 Downing Street.

Having arrived a few minutes before the appointed hour, Judy settled in the antechamber to Lord Liverpool's office, but hardly had she sat down when the door opened and the prime minister invited her in.

"Welcome Mrs Scott-Quetteville! Please sit down! Would you care for tea or coffee?"

"A cup of weak black tea would be very pleasant thank you, my Lord."
"And I shall join you."
He turned to a liveried servant and passed on the order.
"Please tell me all! I am quite intrigued to discover that you, still a young woman, are a diplomat and also the mother of three grown-up children."

Without wasting any more time on small talk, Judy briefly explained the reason she, rather than her mother-in-law, was present and Lady Nicole's long-standing relationship with the French Minister of Police. She then gave him an abbreviated account of the meeting with Fouché in Etreham. She handed over the envelope containing the Order of Battle of the French army. In silence, the British Prime Minister broke the seal and opened the envelope. He quickly scanned the document. Although his French was by no means fluent, he could easily recognise just how valuable the document would be in the hands of the Duke of Wellington[47].

"This is quite unbelievable. I do not know how many French lives it will save by us having this priceless information – but I am certain that it will save hundreds – perhaps thousands – of British lives. This document will leave this very day for Belgium so that the duke receives it as soon as possible. As a matter of interest, do you know why it is that the Minister of Police is given the task of supervising the collation of a document like the Order of Battle?"

"Apparently Napoléon does not trust more than a handful of his generals and they are much too busy with matters within their own command to be able to handle a task of this nature. Furthermore, Fouché knows more about who the traitors – and the possible traitors – are. He is almost certainly the only man in France with the resources and the ability to be able to deliver a document such as this to the emperor, unread. I should mention, sir, that a more up to date version of this Order of Battle will be handed to either Lady Nicole or to me on the fourteenth of next month."

---

[47] For many years after the end of the war, the passing over to the British of the complete Order of Battle of the French army by Fouché was widely publicised and hotly debated on both sides of the English Channel.

"I am dumbfounded! You amaze me, Mrs Scott-Quetteville. Tell me please, where this hand-over will take place?"

"Close to where the Duke of Wellington will be at that time."

"How in the deuce will Fouché know where that will be? I'm certain that even the duke himself does not know."

"Please accept my word that, if Joseph Fouché says he will do something, he will. Lady Nicole has asked me to assure you that, in more than twenty years of dealing with him, he has never failed to keep his word."

"That is indeed reassuring. We only know him as a devious schemer — slippery and perfidious. Your mother-in-law is an amazing woman."

"And I am a fortunate woman to be a member of her remarkable family. It is her intention to be in either Antwerp or Brussels by the twelfth. I am sure you are aware that dozens of people from England are already there. Cricket matches, receptions and balls have already been arranged. So many wives, particularly the younger ones, are so fed up that their husbands miss half the season because they are away from home on military duty that many of them have decided that this year they are going to be close at hand and join in whatever social activities might be offering — and they will ensure that there are many of them."

"I have already heard this. I hope they know what they are doing."

"As you are aware, sir, our family has ships going to the continent every day. The number of bookings on these vessels is higher than it has ever been."

The purpose of the meeting having been achieved, Judy excused herself and when Lord Liverpool learned from her that she intended to walk back to St James's Square, he offered her his carriage. In thanking him, she assured him that the walk through St James's Park on a lovely morning in spring was just what she needed.

Part IV

The Battle of Waterloo

Wellington's Triumph – Napoléon's Nemesis

15 – 18 June 1815

I

ON 12 JUNE LADY SCOTT-QUETTEVILLE and her daughter-in-law arrived in Brussels and moved into their two-bedroom suite in one of Brussels' best hotels. Within less than an hour, the forty-five-year-old Colonel Sir Jean-Marc, her elder son, appeared at the door of her suite, looking as tall and handsome as ever. The duke and his staff had several suites in another hotel, only a few hundred yards away. As was always the case, it was a warm and happy reunion – all the more so as Jean-Marc was particularly close to Judy, whom he regarded as "the sister he had been waiting for". Among many other reasons for being fond of her was that she was wonderful in the way she looked after his mother.

At the time of Jean-Marc's arrival, Judy had been in her bedroom adjoining the sitting room of the suite. Before asking her to join them Nicole wanted to have a few words in private with Jean-Marc. One of the few disappointments of her life had been that he had never married. For years he had always laughed off the inevitable inquiries as to why, with the glib comment that he was waiting to find the right woman or that no woman would ever want to marry him. On this occasion when his mother brought up the subject, she was a little more direct and persistent than usual.

"Jean-Marc, we have an unwritten rule in our family that forbids any one of us to pry into the life of another member of the family – and I do not believe that I should be given exemption from that restriction…"

Before she could complete the sentence her son interjected.

"Mother darling, you want to know why I have never married and for a long while I have had it in mind to tell you. When I do give you an explanation you will appreciate that I have no intention of embarrassing or hurting other members of the family."

"I am certain that whatever you told any of us about your private life, none of us would be embarrassed. All of us thought you would marry Rachelle Bassett and, when she eventually married a Canadian and went to live in Quebec, we were all a little sad."

"Not as sad as I was, I'm sure, but let me explain my feelings to you. In '93 François returned from New South Wales with Judy and the twins. She was such a beautiful young woman with all the qualities of the person I had always wanted to marry that it was difficult for me not to fall in love with her. She was more like you than I ever thought any woman could be. Within six months I made up my mind that the best thing for our family would be for François and her to follow on from you. It would be a totally untenable situation for whomever I married to be continually feeling inferior to Judy."

"Darling, I follow your reasoning but that doesn't mean that I agree with it. I'm sure you could have found a wonderful young woman whom we all, including Judy, would be more than happy to look up to. However, having said that — and meant it — from my own point of view, from my first meeting with her, Judy has been a really important part of my life. Jean-Marc, although within our family our feelings for each other remain largely unexpressed, I hope you know that I look up to you as a man who is as fine and wonderful as your father was — and much more emancipated."

Jean-Marc kissed his mother's forehead and changed the subject.

"Do you mind if I ask Judy to join us so that we can discuss her foray into international diplomacy and intrigue?"

"Please do! I hope you appreciate what a good obedient woman I am, heeding to the urging of my children to take a back seat and let the next generation do all the exciting jobs."

"Yes, Mother, you are being good, although coming to Belgium to be on the fringe of one of the biggest battles in history is not my idea of even semi-retirement."

"You will have to thank the Lord for small mercies, Jean-Marc. At least what I am doing is a start."

A few minutes later Judy joined them and, sitting around the larger of the two tables that were part of the furnishings of their suite, Nicole gave Jean-Marc the details of the letter she had received from Joseph Fouché and her decision to go to France to meet him.

Having introduced the subject, she asked Judy to continue. She did so and finished by describing her meeting with Lord Liverpool. Jean-Marc informed them of the Duke of Wellington's reaction to receiving the genuine Order of Battle.

"The duke was more excited about getting this document than I have ever seen him. Between ourselves, a number of Bourbon supporters have come to the duke armed with documents they say are the authentic Order of Battle, each of them differing widely from the others. That he now has something that is really up to date and authentic, is of great importance to him and his staff."

"Monsieur Fouché told me that his office had produced a number of misleading documents and had allowed them to be either stolen or copied by unauthorised people."

"The duke has said that he is particularly anxious to meet you both and has instructed me to extend to you an invitation to join him for dinner this evening. If you accept, his carriage will be here at five o'clock. This last week the weather has been shocking; it has hardly stopped raining, and the duke hopes you will make use of the carriage rather than risk a soaking. Right now, the clouds are getting darker than ever and we are expecting another deluge like we had yesterday."

The dinner with the duke was quite informal. Apart from several corps commanders and their wives, there was the crown prince, William of Orange. He was the rather unimpressive son of King William, who had only come to the throne in the post-Napoléonic reshuffle. As Belgium now came under Holland – and a big battle was about to be fought there – King William was of great significance to the allies.

Prince William was twenty-two years old and had for a time been one of the Duke of Wellington's aides-de-camp in Spain. He had shown himself to have great physical courage, but little else. The duke had invited him to dinner because there had been an almighty row between the duke and King William, who had insisted that he – and not Wellington – should be Commander-in-Chief of the allied armies.

Wellington had bluntly told the king that, if he – Wellington – was not the overall commander and the battle went the wrong way, the Belgians would have to defend Brussels themselves – as the British would pull out at once. Having been completely out-generalled – perhaps, blackmailed – by the duke, King William capitulated and appointed him as field marshal of all of the armies of the Netherlands. The price Wellington had to pay was to be burdened with the inexperienced, twenty-two-year-old Prince William as his second in command.

At the dinner, Colonel Sir Jean-Marc Scott-Quetteville and Wellington's chief of staff kept the conversation on a pleasant note and the duke made a conscious and quite successful effort to be gracious. However, when, shortly after the meal had finished, the prince asked to be excused, the duke was not slow to rise and see him to the door.

A few minutes later, a rather attractive young woman entered the drawing room. She was introduced as Lady Frances Webster. She apologised for not having been present at the dinner. She sat down in the chair next to Judy that had just been vacated by Prince William. As both Nicole and Judy well knew, she was the duke's current lady love. Judy later remarked to Nicole that it was very noticeable that, as soon as she entered the room, Wellington became a different person. He cheered up considerably and laughed and joked.

It was inevitable that before long the subject under discussion would be Napoléon Bonaparte. The duke said that the one thing about the man he found most difficult to come to terms with was his blatant nepotism.

"The nerve of the upstart – he made four of his family sovereigns and the rest, princes or duchesses. He even had his uncle – an almost unknown curé from Corsica – appointed first as Archbishop of Lyon and he then made him a cardinal."

Nicole agreed with the duke.

"I do not know what is worse: the Revolution that professed *Liberté, Égalité et Fraternité* and delivered poverty, fear and hatred or Bonaparte who also promised *Liberté, Égalité et Fraternité* and delivered *Despotisme, Egöisme et Népotisme*."

They all laughed. Said the duke –

"I really like that. I must remember to quote you."

• Part IV – 1 •

"But not until after the battle, please, sir!"

* * *

The following morning Nicole and Judy went for a walk around the park opposite their hotel. It had rained for most of the night and it looked like being a hot and humid day. Having walked for half an hour, they wandered through the stable area at the back of the hotel, where the carriage houses and horse stalls all seemed to be full. There was a hive of activity as horses were being groomed, stalls were being mucked out and carriages were being polished. Nicole's purpose for going there was to see if there was a suitable vehicle for her to hire. When she discussed her requirement with the stable master, he was quite negative and unhelpful. Just as they were leaving to return to the front of the building, a tall, red-headed ostler approached them. He addressed Nicole.

"Excuse me Madame, but am I correct in suggesting that you are la Comtesse d'Anjou?"

As the man had spoken in French and had used her French title, Nicole felt confident that he was one of Fouché's agents.

"Yes, you are correct."

"My instructions are to identify you so that, if I should have a package delivered to me to hand to you, I should know I was giving it to the right person. I understand that you wear a signet ring on the first finger of your right hand."

Nicole removed the glove she was wearing and extended her right hand to the man. He looked closely at the ring and was able to identify the shield engraved on the ring. The man apologised again and explained that he was obeying his orders and he hoped he had not given offence.

"Certainly not. This afternoon and tomorrow morning I shall be walking near here – and the day after tomorrow, too, if necessary."

"Thank you, that would be more convenient for me, as I am kept busy here all the time and it is difficult for me to absent myself from my duties and get suitably attired to enter the upper floors of the hotel."

The man was off before she could say anything else.

Whether it was walking through the foyer of the hotel or through the streets of Brussels, Nicole and Judy were surprised to see the number of people who had come from London. There were dozens of women they knew and there were even more they did not know. They had not been in the city twenty-four hours before invitations to social engagements arrived at their hotel. There was a cricket match arranged for 14 June and there was much talk about the Duke and Duchess of Richmond who had apparently sent out invitations for a grand ball for the fifteenth. The senior generals of the armies of the countries of the alliance would certainly be present and it was thought that the Duke of Wellington might also attend.

Remembering that Joseph Fouché had said that he hoped to have the French army's final Order of Battle delivered to them on 14 June, the two women did not want to move out of Brussels until they had received the document from his agent and had passed it over to Jean-Marc to hand to the duke. Just after nine o'clock, when Nicole and Judy were returning from their morning walk, as they strolled past the coach-house they noticed the red-headed ostler trying to catch their eye. Five minutes later they were walking up the stairs of the hotel to their suite, with a well-filled, sealed envelope in Judy's hand. About mid-morning, having received a message at the duke's headquarters, Jean-Marc went to the hotel and took delivery of it. He stayed for only a short time and then rode off on his big, black, seventeen-hand stallion. When they had returned to their suite, Judy could not help remarking how handsome both horse and rider looked.

"Truly, Maman, Jean-Marc is a magnificent looking man, is he not? And his horse matches him perfectly. You know, it would have been an inexcusable waste if he were anything but a soldier. When I saw him riding with the duke yesterday, I could not help but feel that Jean-Marc looked so much finer and so much more like the leader of an allied army."

"He certainly is a fine man – but so is your François. He may not be as tall, but he is at least as athletic as his brother."

"Nobody has to remind me about that. François is the most perfect man in the world. I could never try to compare him with anyone else – and he has given me three wonderful children, too – and without him, I should never have found you or your family. The day I married François I told him I was the luckiest girl in the world and, looking back over our twenty-eight years together, that good luck has never left me."

Nicole went to her jewel case and brought out her Cellini brooch. She passed it to Judy to hold.

"I am sure I have at some time told you the story of this brooch, have I not?"

"No, Maman dear, but on a number of occasions I have heard you say that it is your special talisman."

Nicole spent the next fifteen minutes telling her daughter-in-law the necklace's history.

"It was made by a famous, sixteenth-century goldsmith and sculptor, Benvenuto Cellini. He lived in both Florence and Rome, and among the many magnificent works of art he produced were this brooch, La Fortuna, and the earrings and bracelet I am holding. He presented these jewels to Pope Clemente VII who passed them down until they were owned by Pope Clemente XIII, who gave them to Cardinal Bandini who, in his turn, presented them to my father as an expression of gratitude for saving his life. On the very day that he was murdered he gave them to me. It would take me hours to tell you about the many times La Fortuna has brought me remarkably good fortune. I should like you to have the jewellery now and with it I give you my thanks for all the happiness you have brought our family – and, in particular, to me personally. I can only hope it brings you the same luck as it has brought me."

Judy stood up and walked over to Nicole and embraced her. As she did so, Nicole could see that there were tears trickling down her cheeks. Having expressed her thanks for the gift, Judy studied the stones and the workmanship of the beautiful brooch, its magnificent central emerald surrounded by concentric rings of sapphires, rubies and diamonds. She lifted it up to the daylight and was enchanted by the way it sparkled. At that moment, the bell on the door of their suite tinkled. Judy quickly hung the heavy gold chain from which the brooch was suspended around her neck and almost reverently tucked the brooch inside her dress.

Judy kissed her mother-in-law's forehead and went to answer the bell. She was confronted by an army officer wearing the full dress uniform of the Hussars. Standing stiffly to attention, he clicked his heels and saluted.

"Excuse me Madame, I am Captain William Verner of the 7th Hussars and I am seeking Lady Nicole Scott-Quetteville and Mrs François Scott-Quetteville."

As he spoke he opened his *sabretache*[48] and produced from it two large envelopes. Judy was well aware that he was bringing invitations to the Duchess of Richmond's ball.

"I am Mrs François Scott-Quetteville and Lady Nicole is here with me."

"Mrs Scott-Quetteville, Her Grace, the Duchess of Richmond sends her compliments and apologises that your invitations to her ball have not been delivered to you before now. It was only yesterday evening that she heard that Lady Nicole and you were in Brussels."

"Would you please come in, Captain Verner. We shan't keep you waiting many minutes. As it was only yesterday that we arrived from London, Her Grace is indeed kind to invite us."

Judy led the captain through the foyer of the suite into the sitting room, where Nicole was standing by the window, watching the crowds of people walking along the street below. Judy made the introduction.

"Mother, I should like to introduce Captain Verner, of the 7th Hussars. He has personally delivered these two invitations to the ball being given by the Duke and Duchess of Richmond, tomorrow evening."

Having made the appropriate remarks and having asked the captain to be seated for a few moments, both women opened the envelopes and read the invitations. They promptly wrote their acceptances and handed him their two envelopes. Within a few moments he had been accompanied to the door and, with a repeat dose of heel-clicking and saluting, he thrust the envelopes into his *sabretache* and was off down the staircase.

With a smile, Judy half-teased her mother-in-law.

"You see, Maman, hardly had I put my wonderful talisman around my neck when I received an invitation to a ball, so that I can proudly wear it in public."

"Judy, dear, you would be surprised how many times I have worn La Fortuna as you are wearing it now, inside my outer clothing. I have one other talisman that never leaves my body – my signet ring. It was given

---

[48] Document pouch carried by cavalrymen.

to me by my grandfather who told me that it had been passed down for several generations. There are, in fact four identical rings."

"When we were on HMS *Sirius*, François told me that he, his two brothers and you had one each – all the same."

Nicole nodded her head in confirmation and, as she did so, she removed her signet ring from her right hand and gave it to her daughter-in-law.

"I have always told myself that, when it is not appropriate to wear my brooch, my ring will take care of me – and when I wear both, I am doubly protected."

"But, Maman, now that you have given your beautiful brooch away, it is all the more important that you keep the ring."

"No…I have had more good luck than anyone in the world. It is now time for me to hand the ring to you."

Judy looked closely at the ring and studied the shield and the engraved motto *Noblesse Oblige*. She recited the words as she studied the ring.

"*Noblesse Oblige,* or as the old Count Jean-Marc paraphrased it – *The gifted must give.* Studying his memoirs I have learnt how abundantly he gave and it is not difficult to see where your father and you learned to live up to your family motto. It makes me realise that, having been given so much and having been so spoiled, I owe a lot more than most people."

"Since the day you arrived in England with François, you have always been a true giver, Judy, and I have never been more certain of anything than I am that you will never change. But, enough of this talk! If we do not stop at once, we shall both be in tears. Now that we have successfully passed over the document to the duke as we promised we would, we are free to do what I believe is almost equally important. Let us go out and buy some clothes like the local peasants wear. Then we can go where we please. If we are in the allied lines, we are the mother and the wife of a redcoat, and if we are anywhere near Napoléon's troops, *nous sommes deux françaises*."

"Maman darling, do you think this is a good idea? Please remember that I am responsible for you. If you have no regard for yourself, think how furious with me those three sons of yours would be if anything happened to you."

"Nothing will! But, as you will see before many days are out, there is going to be much work to be done. There are going to be wounded by the thousands and most of them will be left to die in the mud and slush. When the fighting stops, as it almost always does when the sun goes down, we can quietly go out into the field and save the lives of some of the soldiers."

"This is going to be something completely new for me. Quite a challenge!"

"I have no doubt at all that you will be more than equal to any challenge, but it is going to be more gruesome than you can possibly imagine and I must prepare you as my father prepared me."

"You have done this work before?"

"Yes, Judy! When I was sixteen years old, there was a battle with the Austrians and I implored my father to take me with him. I can still hear him warning me – Nicole, you may not come with me unless you can steel yourself to be quite tough and impersonal. We shall have no time to comfort people or to get upset at the horrific things we shall see. Those whom we are sure are about to die, we must try and relieve their suffering; those whom we can patch up, we do so – and those we can get back to a hospital, we tell whomever will transport them, how to care for them *en route*. It is probable that we shall not be able to treat even a fraction of the casualties, so we just go about it quietly and do our best. Remember, we do not have the luxury of getting churned up inside or stopping to weep, we have too much work to do. There will be mutilated bodies everywhere – men and horses, dead and alive. Not until it is all over do we pause to discuss the futility of it all."

"He then asked me if I still wanted to go with him. Of course I told him that I was more determined than ever. Before we reached the battlefield, my father repeated that speech to me, twice – and I was glad he did; although I must admit what I saw on that field of battle was even more ghastly than what he had described. It was only my stubborn determination not to let him see how horrified I was that pulled me through."

"Thank you, Maman! I know that I am much older than you were when you had your 'baptism of fire' – but I realise how important it is to have realistic expectations. Thank you for painting such a vivid picture."

• Part IV — I •

Nicole went to the corner of the room where there were the two big panniers that she had brought with her. On the top (removable) layer were cloths and bandages, some scalpels and knives, suture needles and waxed thread, forceps, biting blocks and many other medical instruments and supplies. In the lower layer were bottle after bottle of medicines: tincture of opium – and solid opium, too – mercury and antimony compounds, many bottles of overproof whisky and brandy, glycerine and magnesium sulphate. Everything was carefully packed in linen and woollen cloth. Underneath the lower shelf were two canvas haversacks. There was a carefully written inventory in the lid of the trunk. Judy was nonplussed.

"Where on earth did you get all these medical supplies in such a short time before we left London?"

"While you, Judy, were in conference with the prime minister discussing serious matters of State, I was at the Royal College of Surgeons, offering them a substantial donation if they could prepare and have delivered to our wharf two containers such as they would provide for an army hospital. I told them that two doctors were sailing for Antwerp on the following morning and that the staff at the college should beg, borrow or steal to ensure that all the necessities were included."

As Judy was going through the contents of the pannier, she saw two saws.

"My God, Maman, you are not going to cut off anyone's leg, are you?"

"I do not think so, but perhaps some of the surgeons will be able to save men's lives with them. That brilliant Baron Jean Larrey has written a number of papers on battlefield surgery and he contends that nine out of ten amputations that are carried out within the first twenty-four hours are successful."

In silence the younger woman held one of the surgical saws.

"I have often heard of the fortitude of soldiers and how they can withstand excruciating pain without complaining. I find it difficult to imagine what they must go through.

"You might be surprised, Maman, but a couple of years ago, when Ettie was nursing on one of the ships going back to England from the Peninsula laden with the Duke of Wellington's wounded, she assisted with several amputations."

"No! Did she? She is amazing – she was only seventeen when she was doing that work. You know, Judy, it means so much to me that she is working with the Research clinic in Marseille – and loving it."

"She was due back from the south of France last week. Before we left London, I left a letter for her at home, in case she returns while we are away."

"When I was a girl, my grandfather used to talk a lot about physical pain and how widely the pain threshold of one person differs from that of another. When I was working with my father at his clinic in Marseille, I was always astounded at how quickly people recovered after having limbs amputated. It is amazing how some people can learn to cope with intense pain."

Judy, who had been listening intently, replied –

"There is much about the subject in the count's big book and I found his theory quite fascinating. He contended that the rationale behind the merciless – and, to my mind, senseless – floggings meted out to the boys at schools like Eton are meant to teach them that they must learn to accommodate intense physical pain."

"My grandfather was adamant that there are far better ways of teaching this lesson and he deplored the idea of having to associate the suffering of pain with wrongdoing. He was so much against what he called the Etonian ethic that he did not want either of his sons to go to England to school. Véronique and I used to laugh when he told us that the English flog the brains out of their boys and teach them nothing other than how to accommodate pain and how to die bravely in battle. But I am afraid it is true."

As Judy fossicked through the open pannier, she thought to herself that, within the next week, there would probably be thousands of those same Englishmen having to die bravely. She stopped short when she discovered a wooden pistol case in the bottom of the pannier.

She looked suspiciously at her mother-in-law.

"Maman dear, one does not repair the ravages of battle with a pistol. Why, for heaven's sake, did you bring these?"

"They are really important, Judy – and there is one for each of us. We are going to see many horses maimed and wounded beyond all hope of recovery. The least we can do for them is to give them a quick and painless death."

For the rest of the day Judy was particularly quiet. Nicole appreciated that she was contemplating the challenge that lay ahead of them and, for the most part, she left her with her thoughts. In the afternoon, they hired an open cab and went southwest of the city as far as Nivelles where there were some beautiful farms, especially along the road that ran east to Quatre-Bras and on to Ligny. Several times, Nicole stopped the cab and surveyed the scene. There were grain crops almost ready to bring in, some cattle and one or two farm horses. She spoke to a farmer and learned from him that the wise landholders had already moved their animals far away, as there was about to be a big battle. Judy asked Nicole if she was looking for anything special.

"Having seen the incredible build-up of the allied army — and knowing from what the duke said last night about Napoléon's half a million men under arms — it is obvious that the French intend to capture Brussels. The Duke of Wellington swears that, within a few weeks, he will have destroyed the 'bloody Corsican' for all time. Whereas Napoléon has overstepped the mark before and has been defeated, the duke has been less flamboyant and has never lost a major battle. I am confident he will defeat Napoléon; even so, if you and I are to be of any use, we must be much closer to the battle than Brussels. What I am looking for here is a place to stay that is closer to where we shall be working."

"My darling, incorrigible Maman..." she paused. "Right, let's find a really nice farm that we can return to each night and wash all the blood and mud from our hands and faces."

It did not take them long to find a château that looked a possibility. They drove up the driveway to the main building. Before they could alight from their vehicle, a rather fine looking, middle-aged woman approached them. She was carrying a flower basket that was full of roses, peonies and tulips. As Nicole did not understand Dutch and only a few words of Flemish, she addressed the woman in French and, having introduced herself and Judy, she explained what she was seeking. She added that, although they were both half-French, they regarded themselves as being British. The châtelaine, Madame Dufeu, was charming and said she would be very happy to have them staying in her château.

She explained to her visitors that her husband was a colonel in the Belgium cavalry and, although he left at dawn each morning, he returned home in the evenings. One of her sons was a lieutenant in the same regiment and the other one was reading law in one of the Oxford colleges. When Nicole asked if she could rent one of the outbuildings, Madame Dufeu was quite adamant they should stay with her and her husband in the château, as her guests – and that they should have lunch with her before returning to Brussels.

Immediately after lunch they left Madame Dufeu and, at her suggestion, drove along the road to Quatre-Bras. The closer they came to the township, the greater was the military activity. There were troops and guns everywhere; the artillerymen were unloading ammunition; hay and fodder were being taken to the cavalry's horse-lines and there were dozens of soldiers pitching tents. A number of mounted officers were looking through their telescopes to the south, towards Charleroi. Listening to some of their conversations, it was evident that there were tens of thousands of French troops concentrating forward of that town and that it would not be long before the battle began.

At the Quatre-Bras *carrefour*[49] they headed north towards Brussels. The traffic on this road was even heavier and the going was slow. About halfway along the road towards Brussels, a colourful cavalcade of senior officers rode past them, travelling in the opposite direction. It was the Duke of Wellington and several members of his staff, including Jean-Marc. The duke, looking handsome and as impressive as ever in his smart blue uniform and white cape, was mounted on a magnificent chestnut horse. As the officers rode past their cab, Nicole commented –

"How beautiful!"

"I have never heard you speak about Jean-Marc in this way."

"I was not talking about my son; I was referring to Copenhagen – the Duke of Wellington's horse. He is really beautiful. Did you know that he is a grandson of Eclipse?"

---

[49] Crossroads.

"You mean your Eclipse, the outlaw?"

In feigned outrage, Nicole responded.

"He was no outlaw. There are only two words to describe him — utterly perfect."

"Hélène has shown me David's scrapbook. From all accounts, you were as magnificent as he was. In the various papers there were comments that were made by people like Sir Charles Bunbury and Richard Tattersall. Your skill and courage amazed them. Tell me, Maman, how old were you then?"

"That was in 1769, when I was twenty-four. It is a long time ago."

As they passed through Mont St Jean, they witnessed a hive of activity and thousands of soldiers, guns, limbers and carriages. It was obvious that there was a corps — or, perhaps, an army — headquarters being established there. Further along the road north to Brussels was the small town of Waterloo, where the Duke of Wellington had set up his headquarters in an inn.

There were hundreds of soldiers walking in all directions. Quite a proportion of them were billeted with private families and were walking to or from their billets. Because it was a multinational force and the troops from each country had their own distinctive uniforms, there were green, brown and scarlet uniforms, all mixed in together. Some of the Belgian soldiers who, when Napoléon overran the Low Countries, had been conscripted into the French army, were still wearing their blue army uniforms, with only the insignia and headgear changed.

At midday they returned to Nivelles and gave Madame Dufeu an account of their morning's reconnaissance. At lunch Madame Dufeu explained to her guests that there was hardly a home in this part of Belgium that did not have soldiers or officers billeted with them. She had commented that, in general, the British soldiers gave much less trouble than the Russians and Austrians; some of the British officers, however, had behaved badly. Apparently some of the larger homes had been requisitioned and, when the Belgian families had returned, not only had there been extensive damage and many breakages but their cellars had been broken into and much of their wine had disappeared. Hearing that British officers had behaved in this way had not given either Nicole or Judy any happiness.

After lunch they returned to Brussels. When they reached the outskirts of the city, Nicole asked the coach driver to take them to the yard of a really good horse and vehicle dealer. As they were making their way there, she explained that they needed their own transport and that they wanted to buy something small, mobile and stoutly built. The first place they visited was quite ordinary and with a poor selection of horses. However, there was an elderly man there who directed them to a much better establishment, near the centre of the city. There they found precisely what they needed – a small but solid *chariot*[50], a strong, older horse, full harness, enough quality fodder for four or five days, and a water bucket. The *carossier* – carriage-maker – wanted to sell them a younger, slightly bigger horse but Nicole explained that she would be driving the vehicle through the battle zone and that she must have a horse that was used to gunfire and would not become fractious on the field of battle[51].

"If that is the case, I have just the fellow for you."

He showed them a chestnut gelding that had been used by a Belgian officer to move all his belongings from place to place.

"This chap will not turn a whisker if a cannon ball whizzes past him or if there is musket fire right next door to him. He is a veteran of the wars. Incidentally I have for sale the *chariot* he used to pull, complete with all the harness."

As this was precisely what Nicole required, she purchased the horse, the harness and the *chariot* and she arranged to return for her purchase early on the following day. Feeling that they had had a particularly satisfactory day, they returned to their hotel.

* * *

Next morning Nicole really enjoyed driving their new *chariot* through the busy Brussels streets as she made her way back to the hotel to meet Judy who had been buying some gifts for Madame Dufeu and some good

---

[50] A small four-wheeled trolley, with a flat tray-top.

[51] It is astonishing how quickly horses can adapt to battle conditions. After only one or two days in the line, they can cope without difficulty with the noise of cannon and muskets.

French wine. Realising that they would have to feed and care for dozens of soldiers until they could be evacuated, she also bought a good supply of biscuits, tea, coffee, sugar and cheese. They then went to the hotel and, having collected all their baggage, except the clothes they would be wearing to the ball that evening, they set out for the Dufeu château. In spite of the traffic, they reached their destination in just over two hours.

On their arrival, the châtelaine showed them to their rooms and, although a little embarrassed at her guests' generosity, she graciously accepted the gifts and the wine they had brought with them. During the meal she explained that, when she had informed her husband that two English ladies were coming to look after the wounded and that they would be staying in the château, he was surprised – and very moved. He said that he thought that his wife and her sisters should immediately start setting up a hospital in two of the big barns and the carriage house so that they could care for the wounded that Nicole and Judy would be bringing in. Madame Dufeu fully concurred and informed her husband that they had already started converting the outbuildings. She also mentioned that both her sisters and one of her nieces would be arriving after lunch to prepare for the following day. Both Nicole and Judy were impressed and relieved.

Madame Dufeu also passed on to them the news that the fighting had already begun and that the road to Quatre-Bras had been cut. The Prussian cavalry had been forced to withdraw.

"Last night my husband told me of the tens of thousands of troops that are slowly converging on Brussels. The story going around the Belgian lines is that the Duke of Wellington is drawing Napoléon into a trap and that the French will be annihilated, but my husband feels that the allies might have been caught napping."

Nicole, who had often heard Jean-Marc talk about the Peninsular War, was philosophical.

"Whenever there are masses of cavalry fighting each other, the tide of battle seesaws backwards and forwards until one side collapses with exhaustion. From our point of view, it means that there will almost certainly be more casualties than we can possibly cope with. I am concerned that we are going to be terribly short of people to look after the wounded."

"That is precisely what my husband says; but we shall have quite a few helpers. As well as the château staff and servants, this afternoon my sister and some of the family servants are coming here to help."

The smiles on the faces of the two English women told their own story. Although Judy had, from time to time, helped the surgeon on her father's ship when there had been accidents and, on one occasion when one of the masts had snapped and had fallen on to the deck causing a number of casualties, she recognised her own limitations. More importantly, if Nicole and she were in the field, to her mind it was essential for there to be a surgeon back at the château.

"Madame Dufeu, this evening we are going to a big ball in Brussels. My brother-in-law – Lady Scott-Quetteville's son – is a colonel on the Duke of Wellington's staff. We shall be seeing him there and we are sure that he will assist us. When he knows what we all intend doing here, I am confident that he will ask the duke if we may have a surgeon detailed to come to your hospital, to supervise everything and carry out whatever operations that need to be done."

"That would be excellent. When I was speaking earlier, I meant to mention that we intend to turn one of our own *chariots* into what the French call an ambulance[52]! It will save you from having to come all the way back from the battle."

Madame Dufeu insisted that the family carriage should take her guests back to Brussels for the night and bring them back in the morning.

"It will be so much better if our coachman drives you to the big ball this evening, too. He will like that, as it will enable him to stay overnight at my father's house, where his brother is working."

* * *

The Duke and Duchess of Richmond had a magnificent mansion in Brussels, on one side of which the city's leading coach-maker had a vast carriage house. It was here that the duchess hosted what was to go down in history as the Waterloo Ball. Preparations for the much talked about function had been in progress for more than a week and, as the evening of Thursday 15 June, drew close, almost everything was in readiness. The

---

[52] The coining of the word was attributed to Baron Jean Larrey, the great French surgeon.

duchess had but one concern: the danger of having to cancel the ball due to the closeness of the enemy.

Because Brussels had been a hotbed of rumour and, to some extent foreboding, the duchess had asked her husband to consult with the Duke of Wellington to ascertain if, in going ahead with the ball, they were being foolhardy. She was thrilled – and relieved – to hear his comment. The duke was unequivocal –

"Richmond, you can tell your wife from me that it is quite safe for her to hold her ball, and that to show the nervous and pessimistic people of Brussels how safe their city is, I shall be present at the ball – and I hope to have the honour of dancing with her. Francis Drake finished his game of bowls and then sailed off and destroyed the Spanish armada. I shall dance with the Duchess of Richmond and ride off to destroy the French army!"

"Darling, that was positively sweet of him, the naughty man. I am quite certain that he would much prefer to be dancing with Frances Webster than with me."

With this encouragement from the Commander-in-Chief, the duchess went ahead, with renewed vigour, with the final preparations for the ball. The dancing would be to a full military band and there would be several ensembles to welcome the guests as they arrived.

Together with more than two hundred other guests, the two Scott-Quetteville women were received in one of the Richmonds' large reception rooms and from there they were conducted, via a covered way, to the huge ballroom. Although the ceiling of the carriage house was not very high, the dozens of crystal cluster lamps glittering along the walls and the big candelabra on the many tables around the dance floor, gave the large room the appearance of being much loftier than it was. The flower arrangements were superb and the duchess had even brought some paintings and Persian rugs from the villa to complete the metamorphosis from unadorned coach house to stately ballroom.

Many of the wives and lady friends of the officers had brought their ball gowns from London, not to mention their sparkling tiaras, necklaces and bracelets. Even so, it was the menfolk who stole the show. The British army officers in their regimental evening dress – of many different colours – looked outstanding; but the commanders of the armies of Prussia, Russia, Austria and the other allied countries were by no means upstaged. Adorned with the sashes and jewels of almost every known order of chivalry – and an even greater number of medals for bravery – they made an unforgettable spectacle. Almost – but not quite – as flamboyant as the military men were the diplomats, nobles and the French *émigrés*. The only man in the room whose *tenue* was at all out of step with the rest was Lieutenant-General Sir Thomas Picton, one of the finest soldiers in the British army and one of Wellington's divisional commanders. His baggage had gone astray and he appeared "regimentally naked". Even two days later, when the battle was in full swing, he was seen riding up and down in front of his troops, urging them on, wearing a civilian brown overcoat and a peculiar round hat. The following day, still out in front of his division, he was shot in the forehead and he fell from his horse, dead.

As Judy surveyed the extraordinary scene of grandeur, it would have been quite impossible for her to imagine that within less than seventy-two hours, dozens of the fine, handsome, gallant men who were at the ball – and thousands who were not – would be lying dead on the battlefield.

With a glass of wine in her hand, she watched the latecomers arrive and her heart gave a small jump as her brother-in-law, Jean-Marc, entered. Tall, handsome and rugged, he walked over to where the duke and duchess were sitting. He stayed with them for a short while and, after dancing with the duchess, he came over to where Nicole and Judy were standing. The three Scott-Quettevilles were happy to be together. It was a fabulous ball and they loved being part of it; however, as Judy so rightly suggested, it was not quite their sort of occasion. Jean-Marc quietly explained to Nicole and Judy the reason for the duke's absence and his own late arrival.

"The French have broken through the Prussian cavalry which have had to withdraw. The duke and Colonel de Lancey are preparing the Operation Order for the deployment for battle of our army. The duke will be here as soon as he has finished doing this. He is quite adamant his battle plan is not being compromised by him – or for that matter – the other officers – by being present for a couple more hours. General von

• PART IV – 1 •

Müffling is with him now. To tell you the truth, the duke is being dressed while they are still talking. You know, Mother, William de Lancey is a genius; he is not only able to remember where every unit of every army is, he knows the name of almost every commander."

Nicole told Jean-Marc of their progress at the Dufeus' farmhouse and how important it was to have a surgeon and some trained orderlies there. Judy joined in the conversation.

"Do you think the duke would authorise somebody to help us – not on the battlefield but back at the Dufeus'?"

"Judy dear, you are not only going to need medical staff, you are going to need them soon, within hours rather than within days. By midday tomorrow there will be wounded everywhere. The surgeon-general is over there by those potted palms. I shall speak to him in a few minutes. He will be relieved to know that his almost non-existent medical team is being augmented. When the duke arrives, I can tell him what I have done. I am quite certain he will approve. In any case, I know he wants to talk to you both – particularly you, Judy. He has not stopped mentioning your name since our dinner with him. I shall have to tell François to keep a close watch on you."

"Jean-Marc, I admit that I shall be grateful to have one of his surgeons out at the Dufeu farm; but, apart from that, I have no interest whatsoever in your duke. I have enough fine Scott-Quetteville men to more than fill my life, without having to put up with a philandering Commander-in-Chief."

Laughing at his sister-in-law's comment, Jean-Marc walked across the room to where the surgeon-general was sitting. In less than five minutes both officers returned. After formal introductions, Nicole let Judy explain precisely what they had already done and the layout of their surgical centre at the Dufeus' property on the Quatre-Bras/Nivelles Road.

"This is wonderful, Lady Nicole – and Mrs Scott-Quetteville. Of course I shall have a good surgeon there first thing in the morning. The quicker we can treat battle casualties, and the nearer the battlefield, the greater are our chances of success. Where possible we shall evacuate the wounded you have treated to enable your unit to be kept as uncluttered as possible and I shall ensure that your improvised field hospital is visited regularly to maintain stocks. Once again, Mesdames, thank you for your help – and your courage."

They watched him return to the group of officers with whom he had been talking when Jean-Marc had approached him. Having spoken to one of them for a few minutes, the officer left the carriage house.

About fifteen minutes later, there was quite a hush in the ballroom as the Duke of Wellington, looking every inch the Commander-in-Chief, made his entrance. He shook hands with the Duke of Richmond and kissed the duchess's glove. The remainder of the more important guests in the Richmonds' group having been formally introduced, he danced with his hostess as he had promised he would. A few minutes later he made his way over to where Jean-Marc and his family were sitting.

As he was crossing the room, he was somewhat taken aback to see Prince William of Orange. The heir to the Netherlands throne was in command of a large allied force whose role it was to protect the main body and to give warning of any advance of Napoléon's forces. Although his task was to remain at Binche and send reports back to headquarters, the magnet of the glitter of the Duchess of Richmond's ball and the many beautiful young women who would be present was too much for him. He was dressed in an ornate, regal uniform and looked more like a dashing young playboy prince than an absent without leave commander. The duke was not at all pleased.

"This is indeed a surprise, your Royal Highness. Tell me, has there been any enemy activity in your sector?"

"Nothing serious, your Grace – only a few skirmishes between the French and the Prussians."

"Why then, your Royal Highness, have you not reported this to me?"

"I did not think that these enemy sorties were very significant, your Grace."

If the look the duke gave him could kill, Prince William would have dropped dead on the spot.

"It is my responsibility, sir, to assess the significance of all enemy activity – and it is your responsibility to pass the information to me so that I can do this. You may be interested to know that the insignificant skirmishes to which you refer have, in your absence, forced the entire Prussian cavalry force to withdraw. I am sure you will think it is imperative for you to return to your post first thing in the morning. In the meantime I should get some sleep, if I were you."

His face flushed with embarrassment – and guilt – the crown prince promptly left the ball.

The duke continued walking to where Nicole and Judy were standing with Jean-Marc. He spent some time talking to them about the field hospital they were setting up near Quatre-Bras. When he was informed about the conversation between Jean-Marc and the surgeon-general, he assured the two women that they would certainly have a doctor and military detachment to assist them.

Having heard many stories of the duke's amorous interest in the fairer sex, Judy was a little circumspect when he came close to her and started to tell her that he had been an admirer of hers for many years. She accepted his compliment with a light smile.

"But, your Grace, we met for the first time on Tuesday evening."

"That is true Madame; however, perhaps you might tell me if you have ever known a Major Augustus Fortescue?"

"Why, of course I have. He was a darling sweet man."

"And many years ago, not long after I was commissioned, he was my superior officer."

"The major died nearly ten years ago. It was quite sudden."

Judy did not think that it was appropriate to add that she had inherited almost all of his – substantial – estate. The duke continued.

"I well remember meeting him a few days after he returned to London from the Canary Islands, in the second half of 1787. We had dinner together at our club and he told me how he would have drowned in Teneriffe if it had not been for the presence of mind and courage of a fifteen-year-old American girl. He then told me the shocking story of that bounder Cornish. After having met you at dinner on Tuesday, I asked Sir Jean-Marc how his brother had the good fortune to find such a beautiful wife. No sooner had he started talking about Captain Phillip's voyage to New South Wales, than I realised that it was you who had been the heroine to whom Fortescue had referred in such glowing terms."

"What a remarkable coincidence, your Grace! It is indeed a small world."

Notwithstanding the sincerity of the duke's remarks, Judy's assessment of him as a womaniser did not change.

A few minutes later, with Nicole on one side of the duke and Judy on the other and Jean-Marc leading the way, they walked across the floor to where the Duke and Duchess of Richmond were sitting and together they all went into the supper room.

During the last hour before supper, it had been interesting to observe a liveried servant who, from time to time, entered the ballroom, holding a silver tray on which was an envelope. On each occasion he approached Captain Verner, the officer who had delivered Nicole's and Judy's invitations to them. He apparently knew the names of almost everyone at the ball and, having been shown the name on the envelope, he was able to direct the servant to the officer concerned. These messages were obviously, requests – or orders – to return at once to their regiments as, hardly had each of the messages been read, than the officer concerned would approach Lady Richmond to ask to be excused.

* * *

Early that morning, 15 June 1815, the *Scottbridge,* with François Scott-Quetteville aboard, was edging its way up the river Thames. The Bridge Company's senior executive was returning from New York, where he had been visiting Crocker and Ficket's shipyard, where a team of research engineers were determined to be the builders of the first "steamship" to cross the Atlantic[53]. As the *Scottbridge* passed the Isle of Dogs, although Scott-Quetteville could see that there was much activity going on there, he thought to himself that, within less than a week, there would be much more. Douglas Robinson, a clever young Scot, one of Crocker and Ficket's brightest managers, was standing on the deck with him.

"It was a great pity the British naval experts rejected that *Nelson* ship of yours, on the grounds that the stern-mounted, rotary paddle was too vulnerable. What do you propose to do now, sir?"

---

[53] They did not succeed in doing this until 1819, when the *Savannah* crossed the Atlantic from Savannah to Liverpool in 27 days.

"We will develop a steam power system embodying a horizontal shaft that will protrude from the stern of the ship. This must have under water rotary blades that will propel the vessel – and we are going to start on the project at once. In our family we have a number of important apophthegms that rule our lives. The most important of these is – success is the capacity to survive failure – and I intend to persevere until The Bridge Company's ships are steaming to every country in the world."

"I do not think that your company – or ours, either – is far away from achieving that success."

As soon as the *Scottbridge* was tied up, the two men disembarked and, having first taken his American guest to his hotel, the company's carriage took François to St James's Square, where he became aware that, a few days previously, both his wife and his mother had departed for Brussels. Having been overseas for nearly four months, he had no idea that Napoléon had escaped from Elba and was once again Emperor of France. A note from Judy informed him about the forthcoming battle to rid Europe of the power-drunk Corsican and Nicole's determination to do what she could to alleviate the suffering of the soldiers.

Knowing his mother's obstinately casual attitude to danger, François was more than a little alarmed – and not without reason. Having read the morning newspapers, it was obvious to him that the impending battle was expected to be the biggest and bloodiest ever fought. His older brother was a cavalry officer on the Duke of Wellington's staff and it was inevitable that he would be in the thick of things. However, that did not mean that his seventy-year-old mother had to wander around the battle field saving the lives of wounded servicemen; nor was there any reason for his wife to be as casual with her life as his mother was. Having read the reports from Europe in both *The Times* and the *Advertiser*, he made up his mind that something needed to be done. He threw down the paper and announced to Harvey, his butler, what he thought about it all, what he intended to do about it and what he wanted Harvey to do.

"I am going to Brussels tomorrow to find my wife and Lady Nicole and make sure they are in no danger. Even if I have to get Sir Jean-Marc to ask the duke to order them home, I am prepared to do that. Would you please get a messenger to ascertain where my brother, Mr William is. If he is not in his office, he will probably be with Mr Rothschild."

"Excuse me, sir, could you tell me the address?"

"Rothschild's office is in New Court, off St Swithin's Lane."

François quickly wrote a letter to Douglas Robinson explaining to him that, due to unfortunate circumstances, he had urgent business to do in Brussels. Instead of accompanying him to the Isle of Dogs, The Bridge Company's head engineer would look after all his arrangements for the next two weeks. He then wrote a note to William telling him that he had to meet him that evening as he was leaving on the morrow for Brussels, where it appeared that their mother, Jean-Marc and Judy were trying to rid Europe of Napoléon. Having written these letters, he leapt into his carriage and hurried back to his office on the company's wharf. There he gave a brief report on his New York trip and his outline plan for the new "steamship" project. He explained why he had brought Douglas Robinson with him and that he was to be treated as a helpful colleague and an honoured guest. He emphasised that the American's views on building steam-powered ships – and his advice – should be considered seriously. He called his subordinates together at Bridge House to brief them on his plan to go to Belgium.

* * *

Even as quite a small girl, Ettie loved to go with her grandmother when she visited the three François Quetteville research clinics in Marseille, London and Paris and, by the time she was twelve, she was determined to devote her life to caring for the sick – and the wounded.

It was only natural that this interest – almost an obsession – brought her closer than ever to Lady Nicole. Feeling that it could have been loyalty to her that had prompted her grand-daughter to take up this calling, the countess raised the subject during one of their voyages from Marseille to London.

"Ettie dearest, you do know, do you not, that whatever you want to do with your life, I shall love and respect you just as much. Just because I am committed to my father's work, there is no reason why any of the other members of my family should want to do the same thing. After all

François Quetteville was a great distance back from you – your great-grandfather."

Ettie, even at the age of fifteen, was unequivocal.

"Maman, darling, I just love trying to make sick people feel better. Just watching the doctors in your clinics work and listening to the way they encourage their patients makes me want to do the same. Dr Ledrun in Marseille was wonderful. His patients have so much faith in him that he only has to tell them they will get well soon and they do. And last year when we were together on the *Twinbridge* taking the wounded back from the Peninsula, the way Dr Birchall and you looked after them and helped them made me determined to learn to do the same thing. Do you know, Maman, he told me – 'healers are born, Nicole, not made. Some are doctors, some are nurses and some are just like you – people who feel for the wounded and sick, whose determination and true feeling inspire their patients.' That made me decide that I would do the same things as he did and talk to them in the same way as he did – and it worked. Last year when I stood next to him when he had to cut off a soldier's arm; I nearly fainted; but in less than three days, when I could see how quickly the soldier recovered, I learned how to cope with blood everywhere and the soldiers having to bite on round lumps of wood to stop themselves from crying out with pain."

"He told me about that, Ettie, and he told me how brave you were."

"Not as brave as the soldiers and sailors."

"And what do you think is the most important thing that people like you and I can do to help – apart from comforting and inspiring?"

"I am not quite sure what you mean, Maman."

"My father taught me that infection kills more people than muskets and cannon – and it is true. Cleanliness, cleanliness and cleanliness! Making sure that instruments are boiled for a long time. Keeping dressings perfectly clean. Using spirit and mercurial chemicals to prevent infection; keeping flies from spreading disease, and burning human excrement. If you remember that you will save many lives."

For the next two years Ettie worked on the ships taking the sick and wounded back from Spain and Portugal. It was then that her grandmother arranged for her to work in the clinics in London and Paris. She loved the work and she encouraged some of her friends to follow her example. By the time she was nineteen she was teaching others to do the same things as she was doing.

* * *

Early on the morning of 16 June 1815, on her return to London from Marseille, Ettie was shocked to learn about the impending battle in Belgium. As soon as her ship was tied up she went across the wharf to Bridge House and was thrilled to learn that her father was in the office. She waited until his meeting was finished and the others had left, then she hurried into the directors' room and ran towards him.

"How wonderful to know you are back from America, Daddy."

"And even more wonderful that you are here, too, darling. I only arrived back in England yesterday."

François explained to Ettie how the Napoléon crisis had arisen and that Nicole and Judy had left for Antwerp and that he was equipping one of the company's ships to evacuate the wounded from the battle that was about to be fought near Brussels.

"Trust Mama and Maman to want to be in the thick of it. I certainly hope that I can come with you and join them."

"No darling! I cannot spare you for that. I badly want you on board the floating hospital – that is, if you will come with me."

"Of course I'll come, Daddy."

"Thank you, darling. We have nearly twenty nursing people coming on board and I know they need someone to lead them and teach them. None of them has had any experience in treating battle casualties."

"What about doctors?"

"We have several of them coming with us, but I have not yet met them and I have not had time to know how good – or experienced – they are."

"Who is going to ensure you have enough bandages and dressings – and disinfectants?"

"Now that you are back, I should really like you to do this – that is, if you feel up to it."

"Of course I do. If you, Mama and Maman are going to be there, I want to be there, too."

"Thank you, darling!"

"Well, what is my first task?"

"I should like you to go at once in my carriage to the François Quetteville Clinic and explain my aim to Dr Harmer."

Ettie knew all the doctors at the clinic and she was aware that they had excellent stocks of everything that was needed. Although she was longing to go home and have a bath and change her clothing, she kissed her father and departed.

As soon as his daughter had left his office, François went to the wharf and supervised all the preparations. By the middle of the afternoon Ettie returned with the good news that all the surgical stores would be delivered before nightfall. She asked her father –

"When do we sail?"

"Tomorrow, if possible!"

* * *

William arrived at François's home a little before six o'clock. The two brothers spent the next hour discussing the "Napoléon crisis". François, not having had any idea that he was returning to England to find almost the whole of Europe about to fight a horrendous battle, explained to his brother why he wanted to see him.

"William, I have returned home to find the whole of Europe in turmoil. *The Times*, which is usually quite a conservative newspaper, suggests there will be about one hundred thousand cavalrymen fighting at one time. This means that the battle is going to be both vicious and fluid – and highly dangerous. It is all very well for Jean-Marc to be galloping all over the countryside with the Duke of Wellington. That is only to be expected and, we both know that the pair of them will be in their element. That is all very well; but for mother – and Judy – that is a horse of another colour. In the note I received when I returned home this morning, Judy said that mother believes that there will be dozens of women on the battlefield, trying to care for the wounded and dying soldiers. At her age she should know better than to want to be in the midst of it all."

"You know Judy much better than I do, but I'd suggest that, without the slightest encouragement from anyone, she would want to be there. Do you think you can do any good by going there yourself?"

"I am going to Antwerp with a ship that can bring wounded soldiers back to England – and Ettie is coming with me."

"Don't you think she is too young?"

"She is as bold as Dick Turpin and she is more than capable. The experience she had bringing casualties back from the Peninsula will hold her in good stead. As soon as I told her that mother and Judy had already set out for Brussels and that they intended to treat the wounded in the field, she told me she wanted to join them. When I assured her that she would be more valuable helping me, she agreed to stay on the ship and assist the doctors I am taking with me. We shall take several surgeons with us and some men who can carry stretchers. Our people down on the wharf are already rigging up litters and temporary beds on one of our ships. As soon as I get to Antwerp, I shall try to persuade the army people to help me. I intend to urge our two women to help with this evacuation work and to realise they will be doing just as good – and probably more effective – work on the ship as they will on the battlefield itself."

"Wouldn't Ostende be a better port from which to evacuate casualties?"

"I think not, William. It would involve a much longer road trip to the coast and the shorter the journey by road the better."

"Although I think your idea of trying to involve mother and Judy in an evacuation by sea is a really sensible one, I'm not certain that they will want to leave the battlefield."

"I'm inclined to agree with you. I can only do my best."

"In case you are short of company on the way over there, I would like to come with you."

"What on earth do you mean? You loathe and detest everything to do with war."

"I most certainly do; however, I have a contract with the government to provide the gold necessary to pay the British troops, and also to subsidise the costs of the war of some of the other allies. I have to deliver some £200,000 to the Duke of Wellington's headquarters. Apparently the Belgians, the Dutch and some of the Germans are desperately short of money and they are demanding cash for billeting, fodder and food, as well as paying for their troops and the other materials of war. I shall have a small military escort with me."

François was pleased for William to be travelling with them and he confirmed with him that his team would be ready to sail early the following morning.

They spent the next half hour discussing the forthcoming battle and François's plans to ship the first load of casualties back to England and then to return to Antwerp. When they had finished their conversation, François, who was anxious to return to see how Ettie and the others were progressing at the wharf, suggested that he and William meet for supper later in the evening.

On his arrival at the wharf, Ettie greeted him warmly.

"I am so pleased you are back Daddy."

"And I am equally pleased, Ettie – and you have no idea how happy I am that you have returned from Marseille and can give me so much assistance. Is everything going well down here?"

"Very well! The *Hullbridge* is at least as well fitted out as the two vessels on which I worked bringing the wounded back from the Peninsula. When do we leave for Belgium, please?"

"Tomorrow, as soon as the doctors and the other staff arrive.

Both François and Ettie continued working until quite late in the evening and, although it was midsummer, it was dark before they reached St James's Square. As they drove along the embankment Ettie was silent. François placed her hand in his.

"Have I asked too much of you, Ettie dear? You are very quiet and you have told me nothing of your voyage from Marseille."

"It was very interesting; all the French in Marseille hate Louis XVIII and they worship Napoléon – the fools. But Maman's clinic is doing wonderful work there."

"And the task I have set you. I hope it doesn't frighten you."

"Of course not, Daddy. I feel really honoured that you think I am sufficiently capable to be your lieutenant."

"I have no doubts about that. People like Dr Ledrun and Dr Birchall have told me how well you handle both staff and patients and how proud I should be of you – and I am!"

"I love the work I do and it gives me a thrill to be able to help the wounded."

"You are Maman and Mama over again – and you are the joy of my life."

He squeezed her hand as he lifted it to his mouth and kissed it.

"When they reached St James's Square, William was already there. Ettie was particularly fond of her uncle and, as she had not seen him for some time, they had a long chat before she excused herself and went upstairs to have a hot bath. She was too tired to join her father and her uncle for supper, so she had a light meal and a glass of wine in her bedroom and fell into bed.

* * *

François, William and Ettie were ready to leave London first thing the following morning, 17 June, and by the time they reached The Bridge Company's wharf, the medical staff and the military guards – with their chests of coins – had already boarded and, within less than an hour, they were under way. Although it was a warm morning, the sky was dark and there was a strong wind blowing. Before they had even reached the English Channel the rain had started to fall and it hardly stopped until late in the afternoon when François and Ettie arrived in Antwerp.

As soon as the ship reached Belgium, François lost no time in setting out for Brussels. There he was able to learn the whereabouts of Wellington's rear headquarters. He found the place in turmoil, the most serious problem being a shortage of ammunition for both the artillery and the infantry. This was so acute that some forward units had had to abandon their good positions for want of ammunition. There were reserve formations and units not yet committed to the battle with stacks of all the essentials for which the front line regiments were screaming. There were reinforcements arriving from England who, in spite of the main road being over-congested, had to be moved forward overnight. While staff officers and their assistants were solving these problems, other people were still working on the casualty lists, compiled from the scraps of information coming back from the front line. The constant heavy fighting had taken its toll and the lists of officers and men killed and wounded in action, were long, and included the names of some of the finest soldiers in Britain.

As soon as the ship had arrived in Antwerp, William reported to the British army's base office. The major in charge had been informed that the banker with the gold was expected "on either the 16th or 17th". He arranged for an escort to take the gold from the ship to the bank from where the paymaster-general was operating. As the money for the various allied armies had been already divided out and packed separately, immediately it arrived at the bank the chests of gold and silver coins were passed over to the major and his staff of armed escorts who were ready to move off as soon as the formalities had been completed. All the organisation for this was being handled by Amschel Rothschild who, as was usually the case, had organised everything excellently. In anticipation of the money coming from London he had already paid the Prussians, the Austrians, the Poles and the Russians in advance. This meant that the armed escort moved on to Frankfurt with the gold and silver coins to repay the advance the Rothschilds had made. Amschel and William followed them.

For François things did not go so well. It was nearly ten o'clock before he found somebody he knew who had the time to listen to him. The few medical staff who were there were exhausted from overwork and they were more interested in getting some sleep than discussing a casualty evacuation plan. Eventually, a bright staff officer agreed to meet him at seven o'clock in the morning to see what could be done to implement his plan. His only success was to ascertain the whereabouts of the duke's headquarters. François's difficulty was how to get there.

He checked in to the same hotel as Judy and his mother had stayed. There he was informed of the congestion on the road south to the main headquarters in Waterloo and the advanced headquarters further south in Mont St Jean. It was suggested to him that the only way to cover the ground in anything like good time would be to travel after midnight and to go on horseback. He returned to the army headquarters to leave a message for the officer whom he had planned to meet early next morning. He was still in his office. When François briefly explained his plan, the officer seemed quite uninterested until, in desperation François almost shouted at him.

"I do not think I am making myself clear. I have a ship in Antwerp, with three surgeons on board and plenty of staff and medical equipment. You have thousands of wounded soldiers. I want to help you by taking your wounded to England where there are people waiting to care for them."

The almost exhausted staff officer smiled.

"I am truly sorry, sir; please excuse me! I am very tired and, until now, I did not really get the gist of what you were saying. I now understand clearly how valuable your plan is going to be. If you will be so good as to tell me the name of the ship and its captain, I shall fill your ship as soon as I can move our wounded from here. It will be a godsend – and it will save lives. How many wounded can you take?"

"At least one hundred and fifty on makeshift beds and probably another fifty sitting up. If you can hire carriages and cabs and anything else to get them to Antwerp, I shall pay for the hire. Perhaps a mounted escort might help to clear the road and make the journey more comfortable for your casualties."

It was only when François gave the officer the full details of the ship and his own name that the man realised to whom he was talking.

"I am sorry, sir, you must be Sir Jean-Marc Scott-Quetteville's brother. I should have known – you look like twins and your voices are identical."

"Yes I am Sir Jean-Marc's brother – and I want to see him quite urgently – and for that matter my wife and my mother, too."

"Well I know where Lady Nicole and your wife are. They have opened a hospital not far from Quatre-Bras and the duke has sent them a surgeon and some staff to assist them. The name of the family who own the château is Dufeu. Colonel Dufeu is commanding an artillery unit in the Belgian army."

"Thank you for being so helpful."

"And thank you, sir, for bringing your ship here. Would it be asking too much for you to stay with me until we are able to move our casualties to Antwerp? I am certain things will work quicker and better if you are close at hand until your ship is on its way."

There was quite a silence while François thought. He certainly did not wish to awaken either Judy or his mother in the middle of the night; furthermore, as they were managing a hospital, the chances were that they would be reasonably safe. He wanted to see Jean-Marc, but really that could wait for twenty-four hours.

"When do you propose to begin moving the wounded to Antwerp?"

"The orders will go to the two hospitals at once...We can get the first convoy on the road by five o'clock."

"Good! I shall go back to my hotel and get myself a few hours sleep. You can rest assured that I shall be in Antwerp by the time they reach the port. Could you please send one of your officers ahead and have some space cleared on the wharf so that we can bring our ship into one of the moorings. At the present time we have to use lighters to move people and stores from ship to shore."

"Of course, sir! That will be done before you reach Antwerp."

II

FRANÇOIS HAD SEVERAL HOURS SLEEP and felt much refreshed. He then set out for Antwerp in anticipation of recovering the first of the casualties for evacuation. Even at four o'clock in the morning the amount of traffic on the road was unbelievable: exhausted troops moving back to where they were billeted, limbers laden with ammunition and stores, walking wounded trudging along in the mud at the side of the road – and even some guards taking prisoners as far from the battlefield as possible. However, by the time he reached the port he was surprised – and delighted – that his ship had been berthed in a good part of the wharf. He was even more pleased to see the *Pont de Bandol*, one of the Messageries Maritimes' ships moored nearby.

Having briefed his own ship's officers as to the expected arrival of the wounded, he boarded the *Pont de Bandol* and spoke to the captain. His ship was unloading soap and silk before going on to Scandinavia. François explained what he was doing and asked him to divert to London.

"We have thousands of wounded soldiers who have to receive proper treatment. If you go to Norway via London it would only delay your arrival in Bergen by a day or two. If you can do this, we can take more stretcher cases in the *Hullbridge*."

"You are the owner of the company, sir; we do as we are told. In any case, if it is going to relieve the suffering of the fighting troops, we ought to do our best to assist."

The convoys started to arrive at the port by midday. They loaded the *Pont de Bandol* first and, as there was a good breeze she sailed off in daylight, with ninety soldiers and four medical orderlies. As none of the medical staff on the *Hullbridge* had worked together before, Ettie was particularly pleased that they had that extra half day to settle themselves into their new surroundings. She was surprised but very happy that the senior surgeon on board was Dr Ledrun, under whom she had worked during the evacuation of the Peninsular War casualties. He was as pleased to see her as she was to see him.

Not until the following morning, 18 June, was the *Hullbridge* untied and headed on its way, with instructions to return for a second load, as soon as humanly possible.

* * *

As soon as François had finished supervising the boarding of the casualties on to the *Hullbridge*, he set out for the battlefield to find his family. Having been informed that the whole scene was extremely fluid – and dangerous – he headed directly for Wellington's advanced headquarters at Mont St Jean, where he hoped to find Jean-Marc. It was early afternoon before he approached the village and the nearer his hired carriage came to his destination, the more concerned he became. The coachman had suggested they leave the main road and approach Mont St Jean from the east. He could not have made a worse decision. The noise of the artillery was deafening; there were troops – both mounted and on foot – moving in every direction, and tens of thousands of cavalry and hundreds of artillery pieces. There were wounded being moved back to Waterloo and Brussels and reinforcements coming forward. François had never seen such a concentration of armed forces in his life.

He passed one group of nearly two thousand French prisoners of war, being taken out of the battle area. François was not to know that when these troops approached Brussels, the locals, seeing all the French uniforms marching in formation toward the city, gave the alarm that the enemy was approaching. For several hours, until it was established that they were prisoners of war, there was pandemonium, as civilians started to evacuate the city and the wounded were moved out.

François was disappointed that neither the Duke of Wellington nor Jean-Marc were at the headquarters. A senior officer informed him that the Commander-in-Chief and his staff were on the battlefield. Listening to the British officers he met, he learned that two vital strongholds had been lost to the enemy and that the number of casualties on both sides had been hideous. He became alarmed when he learned that the Duke of Wellington had lost almost his entire staff. An hour later he received a further report that only three had been mortally wounded and a further three had been carried from the battlefield. Distressed that Jean-Marc could be one of the casualties, he hurried on. He was soon to learn that Colonel William de Lancey, a close friend of the Scott-Quetteville family, Colonel Gordon and Jean-Marc were either already dead or were dying. De Lancey had been moved to a small farmhouse and only had an hour or so to live, Sir Alister Gordon had been taken back to headquarters and lay dying in Wellington's own bed and Sir Jean-Marc Quetteville had been killed instantly.

François was quite distraught. Jean-Marc was not only his brother, but also his best friend. As his body had been taken back to the headquarters in Mont St Jean, he made his way there as quickly as he could. When the duke heard that he was there at the inn, he left his room to talk with him.

It was not the first time that he had found himself talking to the son or the brother of an officer who had just been killed. He was well aware that François was next in line for the Scott-Quetteville title. He chose to pay Jean-Marc's brother the compliment to which he was entitled.

"Today might be a victory for England and for Europe, Sir François, but for me it is one of the saddest days of my life. Nobody could have served me in a more devoted way than your brother did. He and de Lancey were hard-working, fearless, and courageous. Furthermore, Scott-Quetteville had a brilliant military brain and he was a great leader. Of course, as far as de Lancey is concerned, the greater sadness is that he has been married less than a week and his bride is back in Antwerp waiting for him to return..."

He paused before reverting again to Jean-Marc's death.

"Would you like your brother's body returned to England for a family burial?"

"No thank you, my Lord. He would not want that and I know my mother would not want it, either. Although he is a soldier, the members of our family are buried at sea."

"That will be done, with full military honours."

He paused, before continuing.

"I met your mother earlier in the week at the duchess's ball. She is a remarkable woman and I have already heard what wonders she is working in her hospital. I met your charming wife, too – both at the ball and also at dinner when she and your mother dined with me in Brussels. May I congratulate you on having such a beautiful and intelligent young woman as your wife."

"Thank you, sir!"

François, more to take his mind off his own loss and to suppress his anger that his brother had been killed than for any other reason, asked the duke about Colonel de Lancey and his bride and how it had come to pass that they had only married within the past few days.

"De Lancey was the most brilliant staff officer I have ever known. His brain worked with the speed of lightning and his capacity to think straight in the heat of battle was phenomenal. He was born in America and he served with me in Spain. His brilliance as an administrator under battle conditions was remarkable and his contribution to the success of my campaign on the Iberian Peninsula was such that I recommended that he be knighted.

"For me, his death is a great personal sadness, as I feel very much responsible. As you are probably aware, only a few weeks ago was I informed that the British government was determined to launch an attack in northern Europe to destroy Bonaparte. As soon as I had been advised that I would be Commander-in-Chief, I demanded – against strong opposition – that de Lancey be appointed as my quartermaster-general. The news of his appointment to this important position did not reach him until last week – at a very inconvenient time. He had fallen in love with – and had just married – a particularly attractive young Scot, Magdalene Hall. In fact they had hardly gone on their honeymoon when he received his orders to proceed to Belgium immediately. He had not been here forty-eight hours when, on the evening of Thursday 15th, because of Bonaparte's advance on Brussels, I gave him my plan for the deployment of the allied forces. Brilliant man that he was, he was able to have the whole field force – the headquarters and the regiments of the armies of each of the countries involved – on the move within hours. And I am not just speaking of the troops but also the cavalry, the artillery, the ordnance stores, the supplies and our medical services."

"That certainly is a great sadness; particularly for his bride. When my wife and I – and our mother – return to Brussels, we shall make it our business to call on her. For a young person such as she is, to be with a family who are also mourning the loss of a loved one, a visit can be quite a help."

The field marshal concurred and once again he referred to the courage and competence of Lady Nicole and François's wife in caring for the wounded, and François's own remarkable effort in bringing a ship to Antwerp.

"There is a further reason why I particularly wanted to meet you, Sir François – to thank you for thinking of the wounded and bringing to Belgium what I call a hospital ship to take our casualties back to England. That is a fine and original gesture. You are probably unaware that I have learnt much about your family from your brother. The way you all live your lives is the epitome of *'noblesse oblige'*. It would interest me very much to learn about your time in New South Wales; but at this moment I am sure that, rather than being detained here, you will want to go to your womenfolk without delay. We shall provide you with a carriage and an escort to ensure that you get there with the least trouble possible. And would you please tell your mother and your wife how genuinely sad and distressed I am at the loss of Jean-Marc. Furthermore, as soon as they can hand over their duties, I should very much like them to stay overnight with me, before they return to England."

* * *

Back in Brussels, the conflicting stories surrounding the death of Sir William de Lancey were nearly driving his bride insane. At first she was assured that he had not been wounded, then, a day or so later, she was informed that he had been killed and then, the following day, she was told that he was lying, wounded, in a small farmhouse. She hastened there to be at his side. There she cared for him for more than a week, doing everything she could to save his life; but he died in her arms.

III

WHEN NICOLE AND JUDY HAD departed from Brussels on the morning of 16 June, at least half a dozen church clocks were striking seven. It amused them that there had been clocks striking from at least five minutes before the hour until five minutes after. Although the military traffic on the road was already even heavier than it had been on the previous day, the coachman managed to get clear of the city quickly.

When they reached the Dufeu château, they were agreeably surprised at how much work had been done on the outbuildings and that they were now functioning as a good hospital. They were even more impressed when, less than an hour later, a military vehicle arrived. It brought a doctor, three orderlies and a wealth of medical supplies and equipment. The senior medical officer, to whom Sir Jean-Marc had spoken, must have issued his instructions almost immediately after their conversation with him at the ball.

They set out at once to where the battle was being fought and had not gone more than two or three miles before they saw formations of cavalry galloping in all directions. At first, all the messages they were getting from officers racing past were that the Prussians were beating the French. Then, an hour or so later, the tide of battle seemed to change as the seventy-two-year-old General Blucher's cavalry had been forced to retire. They treated some of the Prussian wounded, and nearly as many French. Quite early in the day, they came across a deserted French medical post. All the wounded except two had been evacuated. Both men – one a captain and the other a sergeant – had leg wounds. Near them were two mobile litters. These were well sprung and it was not difficult to put the two men on these vehicles and move them to the road where they had left their *chariot*. While Nicole drove the two men back along the Nivelles-Quatre-Bras road, where the Dufeu's vehicle was waiting, Judy attended to some wounded men and she also put down three horses whose injuries were quite shocking. She was amazed at the short period of time it took Nicole to return.

While her mother-in-law had been away, Judy had found a badly wounded French Hussar, lying face down in the mud. She rolled the cavalryman over and to her surprise she found that it was a woman dressed in the hussar's uniform. She could not have been more than twenty. While Judy was cleaning her face and attending to the wounds to her shoulder and right arm, the poor girl kept moaning in French – "Kill me, please! Let me die. My husband is dead and I do not want to live." Judy was quite certain that Nicole, remembering Nicole la Juive, her great-grandmother, would want to talk to her. However, this was not to be. Before Nicole had returned, the wounded Hussar was already dead. During that day and the next, they encountered three more French women among the dead they found on the battlefield.

By nightfall, when the fighting had subsided, they were both exhausted and it was well after nine o'clock when they arrived back at the château. They were surprised to find no less than forty wounded patients there. Of these more than half had been soldiers they had treated in the field. The others had been brought in by the Dufeu family and their staff, or had staggered along the road. The doctor and his orderlies had been busy all day and they were still operating when the Quetteville women returned. Only one of the wounded who had been brought in had died.

While they were having their supper with Madame Dufeu, her husband returned. Although he looked exhausted, he was bright and full of optimism. He gave them all an account of the success his regiment had achieved in a counter-attack. He inspected the makeshift hospital and he was pleased with what he saw. He was charming to Nicole and Judy. He then informed them about the day's fighting at Quatre-Bras. Although the first part of the day had been a victory for Wellington, the afternoon and early evening had definitely gone to the French. The orderly withdrawal from Quatre-Bras and the manner in which Wellington – aided by General Blucher – had successfully contained Napoléon's troops had saved the day for the allies.

What surprised Judy more than anything else that day was the number of tourists and civilians who had been wandering all over the battlefield – with the troops taking little or no notice of them. The French had a well-organised casualty evacuation set-up, with more than one hundred medical staff allocated to each division. In addition, there had been a large number of what Baron Larrey had called "flying ambulances" – litters he had designed to transport the wounded from the battlefield to the hospitals and surgical treatment centres. The Scott-Quetteville women were both angry that the surgeon-general of the British army had neglected to provide anything comparable for the English troops. The only treatment they were getting at the battle of Quatre-Bras was from more than forty women working independently on that part of the big battlefield. It was quite remarkable that all the troops of the countries engaged in the battle seemed to ignore the women and almost certainly this was because, irrespective of their nationality, they were treating all the casualties they encountered.

Having both had a hot bath, Nicole and Judy retired at once and slept soundly until daylight – about four o'clock – when they had breakfast and set out for the battlefield. Although the work they were doing was much the same as it had been on the previous day, they seemed to work better and were able to treat more people; and the Dufeu team were working more efficiently, too; even though there had been heavy rain and there was mud and slush everywhere. If there had been forty other civilians treating the wounded on the first day, there were nearly double that number on the second day. In addition there were wives and mothers of soldiers – relatives who had heard that their men had been wounded and who had come from Brussels and the neighbouring towns to search for them.

By far the most remarkable of these was the wife of a British officer, Lieutenant Deacon. She had walked all the way from Brussels and had brought her three young children with her. The four of them had trudged all night through the rain and slush. She approached Judy and asked her if she had seen her husband.

"Excuse me Madame, but do you speak English?"

"Yes, I am English. Can I help you and your children?"

Although it was raining, it was a hot and sticky day. Even so, the rather plump woman was wearing a long coat and had a big shawl around her. It was wet and covered with mud.

"I was told last night that my husband had been wounded and that he had been left on the battlefield. Please tell me! Have you seen him?"

"If you tell me his name and his regiment, I shall be able to inform you if I have treated him, and my mother over there has a list of the wounded she has treated; at least, those that were sufficiently conscious to tell her their names."

The woman gave Judy the number of her husband's regiment and his name. It was not on her list. Holding the hands of two of the children, Judy walked them over to where Nicole was bandaging the leg of a British gunner.

"Maman dear, may I please see your list of casualties. This is Mrs Deacon and…"

Nicole interrupted Judy.

"Yes! She must be the wife of Lieutenant Deacon. I treated him yesterday evening, quite late. We took him back to the Dufeu château. He had been shot in the arm. I was able to clean the wound and remove all the metal. Although it was very painful for him, he was not wounded badly and he will soon recover. He was to be taken back to Brussels in the doctor's van first thing this morning."

Mrs Deacon was hardly listening to the rest of what Nicole was saying. She was jubilant. She put her arms around the three children.

"Darlings, daddy is alive and is not badly wounded."

The children started to cry and so did their mother. Together they left the battlefield and slowly retraced their footsteps all the way back to Brussels — urged forward by the knowledge that their man was alive. In less than twenty-four hours they found him safe and well in an army hospital. The following day Mrs Deacon gave birth to a baby daughter, whom her parents christened "Waterloo".

As did all the other women who were working on the battlefield, Nicole and Judy continued throughout the day. At times the noise of the cannon was deafening and the small arms fire of the infantry nearly as bad. By late afternoon they were almost exhausted, but as on the two previous days, many more helpers appeared, they were confident there would be some relief soon. Throughout the day they had been working a little way apart from each other so that, if a stray shell or a burst of musket fire came their way, it would not hit them both. When, in a few hours, the light would begin to fade, they would be able to work closer to each other, in reasonable safety.

The area of the battlefield where they were working was quiet – apart from the moans and whimpering of the badly wounded and the dying, and the pitiful whinnying and kicking of fallen horses. In the distance, however, they could hear the thundering hoofs and raucous shouts of the British and Prussian cavalry as they were relentlessly harrying the fleeing French.

Where the British squares had been there were heaps of dead and dying; French cuirassiers lying next to the British infantry whose bayonets had slaughtered them before they themselves were struck down; and there were dead Prussians and Belgians and even Uhlan lancers from Poland. After three seemingly endless days of tending to the fallen of all countries, they had become numb to the horrors of this nightmare, although the stench of human and equine bodies exposed to the elements for days, and the vile smell of excrement and vomit, was even more nauseating than it had been earlier in the battle. They had lost count of the number of wounded they had treated, the number they had passed over to soldiers to carry back to their hospital and the number of the dying for whom they had been able to alleviate some of their suffering.

In the middle of the afternoon the two women trotted their cart into Genappe where they knew there was a Prussian hospital at which they could leave two "almost walking" wounded Prussian soldiers. They were brothers, and one of them could not have been more than fifteen or sixteen. Quite near the hospital there was a commotion as some poor two-thirds naked, quite badly wounded prisoner of war was being dragged, manacled, along the ground. Nicole looked at the poor fellow and, to her utter surprise, she recognised him as none other than the great French surgeon Baron Jean Dominique Larrey, who for a time had worked at the François Quetteville Research Clinic in Paris. She was appalled and furious and rushed over to where a number of Prussian surgeons were busy treating the wounded. She approached one of the doctors and made him aware of what she had seen. As this surgeon had studied under the baron and thought as highly of him as Nicole did, he hurried back with her to where the poor man was lying.

"What is going on here? That man is to be untied at once. I shall send two men to carefully carry him to the hospital."

The huge Uhlan lancer who had captured the surgeon looked sheepishly at the Prussian officer.

"But, sir, I have been authorised to take this French wretch out to be shot like the other prisoners."

"Well you will not be doing anything of the sort – and am I correct in saying that all the things in that bag you are carrying are the clothes and the belongings of this man and that you have taken them from him?"

The Pole looked guiltily at him and remained silent.

"Give me the bag before I strike you down!"

As the Pole was handing over the big sack, another Prussian officer appeared.

"I ordered that all prisoners were to be shot. That is what the French have been doing to our wounded men."

"And I ordered that this man, one of the greatest surgeons living, will be treated with care and courtesy. Until he is well he shall have my bed and I shall care for him, myself."

"He is French and the French deserve death."

"I do not want to interfere with the orders you are giving, Colonel, but this man has been instrumental in saving more Prussian lives than you would believe. Everything I know about the treating of wounds I have learnt from him."

The colonel ordered that the wounded surgeon be released and passed over into the care of the Prussian doctor. Nicole, whose German was quite fluent, tried to calm the colonel's ruffled feathers by saying that the whole misunderstanding had taken place because the Uhlan lancer only understood a few words of German, the French surgeon could hardly speak anything but French and English, and the first officer to question the baron could not understand a word of what he had said.

To be even more convincing, she added that, when captured, Larrey was in the course of treating a Prussian officer who had been bayoneted. Since the Uhlan lancer could not understand a word of what she was saying, there was nobody present who could deny her claim!

Jean Larrey had difficulty in expressing his gratitude to Nicole. He kept asking her if he were conscious or if he were dreaming that she was there. Not only did she reassure him of the reality of his situation but she poured him a generous mug of cognac and held it for him, as he sipped one burning mouthful after another. While Nicole had been involved with the Prussian officers and Baron Larrey, Judy, aided by several Prussian orderlies, had handed over the wounded soldiers and replenished her supplies of bandages and medicaments.

Much relieved, Nicole and Judy returned to the battlefield to their seemingly endless – and exhausting – task. Everything seemed to be going well for the allies, with a constant flow of good news coming from the front. Wellington, realising that the climax of the battle had arrived, decided to commit his cavalry to the battle. In spite of having Prussian, Belgian and even Polish cavalry, the regiments of which had neither fought nor trained together, Lieutenant-General Uxbridge[54], the cavalry commander, had leadership skills of the highest order. Wellington had a great regard for this soldier's extraordinary ability as a senior cavalry commander, in spite of the fact that he personally detested the man for a number of reasons, not the least of which was that both men were more than fond of female company. This had inevitably caused problems – and arguments – over "whose pen should be dipped into whose inkwell". Furthermore, the duke had been furious when Uxbridge had created a scandal by running off with his sister-in-law, and Wellington refused to have him serving under his command.

Notwithstanding this long-standing personal animosity between the two men, as soon as Wellington realised what a vital part the cavalry would be called on to play in the forthcoming showdown with Bonaparte, he changed his mind and immediately sent for Uxbridge – and was both glad and grateful that he had done so.

---

[54] There is often confusion about his name, Henry William Paget. At Waterloo he was a lieutenant-general and was known as Earl of Uxbridge. A week or so after the battle he was created 1st Marquess of Anglesey.

Uxbridge and Jean-Marc were good friends and as one of the latter's main duties at the headquarters was to convey the Commander-in-Chief's orders to the various cavalry commanders, over the past few days they had seen much of each other. As the tide of battle started to turn, Jean-Marc was ordered to ride over to Uxbridge to advise him that the hour had come for the planned cavalry charges – the *coup de grâce* – to be launched. In spite of the total success of these charges, one of the last cannon to be fired by the French totally smashed the general's leg. Less than two hours later, what was left below the knee of Uxbridge's right leg had been sawn off. The amputation took place in a private house which was owned by a Monsieur Paris. The general showed remarkable fortitude in that he sat on the operating table and watched uncomplainingly as the surgeon sawed off the shattered limb. (Monsieur Paris had a coffin made for Uxbridge's leg and he buried it in his garden and placed a memorial over its grave! The tombstone bore the epitaph, "*Ici est enterré la jambe de l'illustre, brave et vaillent Comte Uxbridge*". Years later the Marquess returned to Waterloo as M. Paris's guest and dined with him – at the same table on which his leg had been sawn off!)

As evening approached and the light began to fail, Napoléon's army was in full flight and were leaving guns, ammunitions and supplies lying everywhere. The Battle of Waterloo had ended – a victorious – but costly – triumph for the Duke of Wellington and his army. But for Nicole and Judy there was still much work to be done. They made their way to an area in which there had been several cavalry charges. The carnage was horrific – a mangled mass of dead and dying cavalrymen, mortally wounded horses kicking violently or just lying there, panting – waiting to die.

They continued for some time and, as the light was beginning to fade, they made up their mind to go back to the château for a few hours sleep and to replenish their panniers. They had decided that the soldiers they were treating at the time would definitely have to be the last for the day. Nicole was talking quietly to a corporal as she was bathing a flesh wound on one of his cheeks. As there was gunpowder burn all around the wound, it was evident that his attacker must have fired at almost point blank range. Although he did not even murmur, she knew that he was really suffering.

Having done all she could to his facial injuries and making him comfortable until he could be moved, she was just about to cut away his boot in order to try and alleviate some of the pain where he had been galloped on by one of the charging cuirassiers when, from apparently nowhere, a wounded French soldier appeared, screaming at the top of his voice "Vive l'Empereur! Vive l'Empereur!" As he waved his musket, he lurched at Nicole – and fired. She put her hand out to parry the blow, but it was too late. He had shot her through the heart. The corporal, whom she had been treating, suddenly gathered strength to reach for a musket. He thrust the blade of its bayonet into the face of Nicole's assailant. Judy, who was working no more than ten feet away rushed over toward Nicole, but to no avail – Lady Scott-Quetteville, la Comtesse d'Anjou, was dead.

* * *

For a moment Judy was paralysed with shock. All thoughts of wounded soldiers vanished from her mind. She knew that she must take Nicole's body away from this scene of total carnage, but it was quite impossible to bring their horse and cart from the side of the road. The field was so wet and boggy it would have stuck in the mud before it had gone ten yards. There were two Belgian officers about a hundred yards away doing very much the same work as she and Nicole had been doing. They helped her cover Nicole's body with a blanket and they carried it to the *chariot*. When the Belgians saw the two open panniers, containing a wealth of drugs and medical equipment, they asked Judy if she could let them have some much-needed items. She gave them one of the panniers. Amazed and appreciative, they carried it off between them and went on their way.

As she slowly made her way back to the château, Judy sat on the tray of the vehicle – too tired to move, too distraught to cry – and wishing she was dead. As well as the covered body of Nicole there were four badly wounded Hussars and the soldier whom Nicole had been treating.

In the half-light it was not until it was almost on top of her that Judy saw – or even heard – the Duke of Wellington's carriage and the two out-riders riding ahead of it. Although, when she looked up she recognised whose vehicle it was, she looked away – in case he saw her and stopped. The last thing in the world she wanted was to have him gushing all over her. She had lost her "Maman" – the most wonderful woman in the world and neither the duke nor anyone else could bring her back to life.

The carriage slowed down and then stopped. The door opened and to Judy's utter dismay, it was not the Commander-in-Chief in his brilliant uniform, who alighted – but François. She could not believe her eyes; she thought that she must be dead and that dead people had hallucinations. François ran forward and took her in his arms. She fainted.

* * *

At the invitation of the Duke of Wellington, François and Judy stayed that night at his headquarters in Waterloo. However, as François did not want to further distress Judy before she had slept; it was not until early the following morning, when they were still in bed, that he informed her that Jean-Marc, too, had been killed in action. Although she was devastated to hear the news, Judy, whose soul was already saturated with sadness, took it with only a little or no expression of her feelings. She put her arms around François.

"Jean-Marc was a soldier and I really think that he would rather be dead than have been badly wounded and have to spend the rest of his life as a total cripple – and in pain, but I know what a great loss it must be for you."

"Yes, he was certainly my closest friend. Darling, this morning there is going to be a big breakfast to celebrate our great victory and the end of Napoléon Bonaparte. If you would rather not be there, I am sure the duke will understand."

"Of course I shall be there. As you well know, I am not in a mood to celebrate anything; but Maman would expect me to be present."

"Your first appearance as Lady Judith, la Comtesse d'Anjou."

"I should rather have waited at least another ten years – I loved Maman very much."

"I must tell you something, darling. For more than three months, mother knew she had only a few months to live. Several days before I left for America she was told this by Sir Gilbert Blane[55]. She had been seeing him about her condition for some time."

---

[55] England's leading physician.

"What on earth was the matter with her? I am amazed that she did not tell me."

"She told Jean-Marc, William and me — and she made us promise not to mention it to a single soul. She said that she did not want you to worry about her and she did not want anyone to stop her doing what she wanted to do. During the second half of last year, she had been haemorrhaging from time to time and, just after the Christmas hunt and the ball at Woking Grange, this became more frequent. It was then that Sir Gilbert gave her the bad news. As you know, it was about this time mother asked me to join the board of the François Quetteville Research Foundation. As Sir Gilbert is the president, we saw each other at the clinic. After one of these meetings, I took the opportunity to ask him if any of us could do anything to help. He assured me that, for the little time she had left, it would be better for mother to do exactly as she wished."

"It is going to be an empty world without her."

"Time is a great healer, Judy — and I can tell you something you probably do not know. You and Ettie were the greatest joys of her life. She loved us boys and said she was proud of us. However, on many occasions she told me that the best thing I had ever done for her was to find you and bring you into our family — and into her life. Mother used to think of you more as her own daughter than as a daughter-in-law."

Judy wanted to cry but forced herself to change the subject.

"I think we ought to get ourselves up and dressed so that we can join the others downstairs. Who will be there?"

"Almost all the leaders of the allied army and the senior members of the field marshal's staff who are still living. There will be many people — and much wine — and the duke is sure to make a speech."

* * *

The duke, looking magnificent in a spotlessly clean uniform, was at his very best and, at every turn, he was thanking people for their contribution to what he described as an historic victory. As he entered the room, everyone stood. He asked them to be seated and, before even saying good morning to the generals commanding the armies of the allied countries, he walked over to where François and Judy were sitting. He kissed Judy's hand, expressed his condolences and his sincere appreciation for the work that she had done in the field.

"From what I have heard, Lady Judith, your tireless efforts have saved many lives. Would not your patron Augustus Fortescue have been proud and thrilled?"

Judy was determined not to break down and become emotional.

"Thank you, your Grace, and God bless you for a great victory."

For the duke, as for almost everyone else in the room, there were very mixed feelings: a great sense of sadness and loss for the comrades in arms who had been killed, sympathy for the wounded, and a feeling of relief that it had been a short and victorious war.

Later in the proceedings, standing where he could best be seen by all those present – not far from where François and Judy were sitting – the duke addressed his guests. There was a certain humility in the way he spoke and this impressed everybody present and particularly the foreign army generals. He emphasised the significance of the victory as an example of what can be achieved when nations pull together in the same direction and, having paid tribute to such people as Picton, de Lancey and Uxbridge, he moved behind where François and Judy were sitting and continued. He was standing behind them facing the generals and other senior officers present.

"If there was ever a family – British or French – in which all members lived up to their family motto, then surely it would have to be the Quettevilles of Anjou. In what, in my dispatches, I have chosen to call the 'Battle of Waterloo', I regard myself as being singularly fortunate to have had, under my command, no less than four fearless and capable members of that family. Colonel Sir Jean-Marc and his wonderful mother Lady Nicole, la Comtesse d'Anjou, both of whom have given their lives for our country; and Sir François and his courageous wife Lady Judith – the new Comte and Comtesse."

The duke paused and moved closer to where the Quettevilles were seated. He raised his arm slightly towards them, as he continued.

"And, in the same way as today we are mourning the loss of all the other heroes who have given their lives in this great battle, we are sharing with the Countess Judith and Sir François their own family sorrow. In commencing our victory celebrations I should ask you, not only to drink to our comrades in arms who are no longer with us, but equally to these two heritors of the Anjou tradition, who have already given — as did their mother and their elder brother — a new and deeper meaning to the words that so aptly express the life they live — '*Noblesse Oblige*'."

Epilogue

NAPOLÉON WAS IMPRISONED (in considerable comfort) on the island of St Helena, where he died in 1821.

The Duke of Wellington returned to London a hero and devoted his time to politics. He was Prime Minister of England 1828-1830 and he died in 1852.

Vicomte Paul Barras's public life ended when Napoléon became First Consul. He died in 1829.

Joseph Fouché's (Duc d'Otrante) political career virtually ended at Waterloo. After the battle he was made French Ambassador at the Court in Dresden. He retired to Otrante where he died in 1820.

Baron Dominique Larrey, Comte de Bigorre, continued for many years as one of Europe's greatest surgeons. He died in 1842.

Sir François Scott-Quetteville lived to see The Bridge Company's steamships sailing all over the world and, in 1840, he and Lady Judith who had visited Sydney several times, retired there on their farm and vineyard in the Hunter Valley.

Ettie Scott-Quetteville developed the François Quetteville Medical Research Institute into a great international establishment. Working with Florence Nightingale, she devoted much of her life to working to reform the British army's medical services.

During the nineteenth century the Rothschilds emerged as the world's most powerful bankers:

Nathan in London,

Amschel in Frankfurt,
Carl in Naples,
Salomon in Vienna; and
Jacob (James) in Paris.

Their sons and grandsons were made barons, lords and knights and became financial advisers to the governments of the great powers.

William Scott-Quetteville continued to work closely with the Rothschild family. In 1822 he was knighted for his services to the Treasury.

Bibliography

Anglesey. The Marquess of The Capel Letters. Jonathan Cape, 1955.
Arthur, Sir George. The Story of the Household Cavalry (Vol II).
Ashton, John. English Caricature and Satire on Napoléon I, Volumes I and II. Chatto & Windus, Piccadilly, 1884.
Asprey, Robert. The Reign of Napoléon Bonaparte. Basic Books, USA, 2001.
Bloch, Ivan. Sexual Life in England Past & Present. Oracle Publishing Ltd., England, 1996.
Burrows, (Ed.). The Blue Plaque Guide. Newman Neame, London, 1953.
Cadbury, Deborah. The Lost King of France. Fourth Estate, London, 2002.
Churchill, Winston S. A History of the English Speaking Peoples, Volume III. Cassell and Company Ltd, 1957.
Clark. C.M.H. A History of Australia. (Vol I). Melbourne University Press, 1962.
Cornwall, Bernard. Sharpe's Waterloo. Collins, London, 1990.
Craik, George L., MacFarlane, Charles. History of England, Volumes V and VI. Charles Knight, 1847.
Crook, Malcolm, (Ed.). The Short Oxford History of France – Revolutionary France. Oxford University Press, 2002.
Ehrman, John. The Younger Pitt (Volumes 1, 2 & 3). Constable & Co Ltd, London, 1969.
Evans, Eric J. William Pitt the Younger. Routledge, London, 1999.
Falls, Cyril (Ed.). Great Military Battles. Weidenfeld and Nicolson, Great Britain, 1964.

Ferguson, Niall. The House of Rothschild, Money's Prophets 1798-1848. Penguin Books, England, 2000.

Forssell, Nils. Fouché – The Man Napoléon Feared (translated into English by Anna Barwell). 1928.

Glover, Michael. The Peninsular War 1807-1814, A Concise Military History. Penguin Books, England, 2001.

Grafton, Augustus Henry. Autobiography and Political Correspondence of Augustus Henry, Third Duke of Grafton. Edited by Sir William R. Anson, John Murray, Albermarle Street, 1898.

Hamilton-Williams. Waterloo – New Perspectives. Brockhampton Press, London, 1999.

Hart, Sir B.H Liddell. The Ghost of Napoleon. Yale University Press, USA, 1935.

Hart, Sir B.H. Liddell. The Other Side of the Hill. Cassell and Company Ltd., Great Britain, 1948.

Harvey, A.D. Sex in Georgian England. Pheonix Press, Great Britain, 2001.

Hazlitt, William. The Life of Napoléon (Vol. I, IV, XI). The Grolier Society N.Y.

Heyer, Georgette. An Infamous Army – Heinemann. London, 1937.

Hibbert, Christopher. George III, A Personal History. Penguin Books, 1998.

Hibbert, Christopher. Napoléon, His Wives and Women. HarperCollins*Publishers*, Great Britain, 2002.

Hibbert, Christopher. Waterloo, Napoléon's Last Campaign. Wordsworth Editions, 1967.

Howarth, David. Waterloo – A Near Run Thing. Collins, London, 1968.

Jordan, Robert. The Convict Theatres of Early Australia 1788-1840. Currency House, NSW, 2002.

Levi, J.S. and Bergman, G.F.J. Australian Genesis – Jewish Convicts and Settlers 1788 – 1850. Rigby Limited, 1974.

Loomis, Stanley. Paris in the Terror June 1793 – July 1794. Stanley Loomis, Great Britain, 1965.

Ludwig, Emil. Napoléon (translated by Eden and Cedar Paul). The Modern Library, New York, 1933.

Madelin, Louis. The French Revolution. William Heinemann Ltd., London, 1928.

Morse, John T. Jr. Benjamin Franklin American Statesman. Houghton, Mifflin and Company, 1889.

Morton, Frederick. The Rothschilds. Secker and Warburg, London, 1962.

Muhlstein, Anka. Baron James: The Rise of the French Rothschilds. Collins, London, 1983.

Packe, Edmund. An Historical Record of the Royal Regiment of Horse Guards or Oxford Blues. Parket Furnivale & Parker, London, 1847.

Picard, Liza. Dr Johnson's London. Phoenix Press, 2000.

Porter, Roy. English Society in the Eighteenth Century. Penguin Books, 1990.

Rudé, George. The French Revolution. Weidenfeld and Nicolson, Great Britain, 1988.

Stuart, Andrea. The Rose of Martinique. McMillan, London, 2003.

Thackeray, William Makepeace. Vanity Fair. Daily Express Publications, London, 1933.

Watson, J.N.P. The Story of The Blues and Royals (Royal Horse Guards and 1st Dragoons). Leo Cooper, London, 1993.

Dramatis Personae

In a trilogy it is not always easy to remember, from one book to the next, the names of all the characters. The list set out below, although by no means complete, may be helpful. The characters and lives of people marked thus * have been researched and portrayed as accurately as possible.

Alisha
> An eighteen-year-old London girl convicted of prostitution and sent with the First Fleet to Australia.

Amy
> An eighteen-year-old London girl convicted of prostitution and sent with the First Fleet to Australia.

B, Mrs
> The London madam convicted of managing a house of ill repute and sent to New South Wales on the First Fleet.

*Bailly, Jean
> Mayor of Paris 1789.

Bandini, Cardinal
> Ex-patient of François Quetteville, who saved his life. He gave the beautiful Cellini necklace to François and he was Nicole's attorney while she was away from Marseille.

*Barras, Viscomte Paul-François de
> One of the leaders of the French Revolution and, for a time, Commander-in-Chief of the French army.

Bassett, Lady Hélène (née de Basseville)
> Wife of Lord David Bassett. Daughter of Colonel Roland de Basseville.

Bassett, Lord David
Husband of Hélène. His country estate was Woking Grange. He had proposed to Nicole when John Scott was in America.
Bassett, Nathalie
Second daughter of Lord David Bassett.
Bassett, Rachelle
Eldest of the three Bassett daughters.
*Beauharnais, Général Alexandre de
First husband of Rose (Josephine). President of the Convention and Commander, Army of the Rhine.
*Beauharnais, Eugène
Son of Alexandre and Rose. Adopted by Napoléon and became a brilliant general and viceroy of Italy. Married Augusta Amalia, daughter of the King of Bavaria, in 1806.
*Beauharnais, Hortense
Sister of Eugène. Married Napoléon's brother, Louis (King of Holland). Mother of Napoléon III.
*Blane, Sir Gilbert
Leading British physician 1749 – 1834. Equally renowned in France and the rest of Europe.
Brown, Enid
Parlour maid in the Cornish's household, who had been raped by the major.
Buttrose, Anthony
Lord Bassett's head groom.
*Campan, Henriette (nee Genet)
First Lady of the Bedchamber to Marie-Antoinette. Subsequently opened a girls boarding school at Saint-Germain and was later *directrice* of the school Napoléon established for daughters of the Legionnaires of Honour.
*Coutts, Thomas
One of the founders of Coutt's Bank. Chairman of The Bridge Company.
Creuse, Bernard
One of the leading coach and carriage makers of Paris.

*Dalberg, Baron von
Archbishop-Elector of Mainz. Made Grand Duke of Frankfurt. (On fall of Napoléon he was stripped of all titles except Archbishopric of Regensburg.

*Danton, Georges
Danton was the leader of the Jacobins who instigated the Reign of Terror in 1793. He himself became one of its victims in 1794.

*Dorset, Duke of
John Frederick Sackville, 1745 – 1799. Third Duke of Dorset. British Ambassador to France 1783 – 1789. Considered to be the best cricketer in England.

Earhart, Mrs Doris
Housekeeper of the Cornish family in Bond Street, London.

*Eclipse
(by Marske from Spiletta) 1764 -1789. Britain's greatest racehorse.

Eisen, Herr Wilhelm
Frankfurt banker who worked closely with the Quetteville family – and also the Rothschilds.

Fortescue, Major Augustus
Senior victualling officer to Captain Arthur Phillips on the First Fleet. Returned to England from Tenerife, July 1787.

Freyberg, Enika
Tutor to the Scott-Quetteville boys.

Gerbier, Robert
Nicole's Marseille manager.

Scott-Quetteville, Gerda (Née Hoffmann)
William's wife.

Harvey
Nicole's butler at 22 St James's Square. On retirement he was replaced by his son.

*Hunter, Captain John
Captain of HMS *Sirius* and later returned to New South Wales as Governor in 1795.

*Hunter, Dr John
Famous British surgeon. The eight years younger brother of William Hunter.

*Hunter, Professor William
   Brilliant British surgeon, physician and gynaecologist.
Jennings
   Lord Bassett's butler in London.
*Jouffrey, Marquis de
   Designed and built first steamship for use on River Saône.
Lambert
   Chef de Ménage in Colonel de Basseville's château.
*Lancey, Colonel Sir William de
   Wellington's chief of staff at Waterloo.
*Larrey, Baron Jean Dominique
   Famous French surgeon and Napoléon's physician.
*Lassonne, Dr Jean-Marie
   Leading French physician.
*Liverpool, Lady Theodosia
   Wife of Earl Robert.
*Liverpool, Earl Robert
   Tory Prime Minister, Great Britain, 1812 – 1827.
*Mirabeau, Comte Honoré de
   French revolutionary leader.
Mulligan, Joe
   Convict on First Fleet.
Nicole "*la Juive*"
   Great-grandmother of Nicole (1624 - 1713).
*O'Kelly, Dennis
   Irish immigrant, an upstart rogue, husband of Charlotte Hayes and owner of the great horse, Eclipse.
Partridge
   Major Cornish's butler.
'Paul'
   Code name for the French count whose escape was organised by Major David Black.
*Picton, Lieutenant-General Sir Thomas
   One of Wellington's most brilliant divisional commanders, killed at Waterloo.

Quetteville, Dr François
Son of Jean-Marc, Comte d'Anjou. Father of Nicole.
Quetteville, Jean-Marc, le Comte d'Anjou
Admiral, successful businessman and philanthropist. Nicole's grandfather.
Quetteville, Professor Pierre, Comte de
Nicole's uncle who for many years was known as Professor Pierre Lazard.
Quetteville, Véronique
Twin sister of Nicole. She was murdered in 1767.
*Robespierre, Augustin
Brother of Maximilien and one time close friend of Napoléon.
*Robespierre, Maximilien
Leader of French Revolution. One of the instigators of the Reign of Terror. Executed 1794.
*Rothschild, Amschel
Oldest son of Mayer.
*Rothschild, Gutele
Wife of Mayer.
*Rothschild, Mayer
Father of the great international banking house.
*Rothschild, Nathan
Son of Mayer and leader of the English Rothschilds.
*Rothschild, Jacob (James)
Youngest son of Mayer and leader of the French Rothschilds.
Scott, Charles
Brother of John Scott.
Scott, (Sir) John
Became Sir John Scott-Quetteville (Bart). Nicole's husband was killed in Paris, May 1788.
Scott-Quetteville, Ettie (Nicole)
François and Judy's daughter Nicole had the same first name as her grandmother. Within the family, the younger Nicole was always referred to as Ettie.

Smythe, Gregory
    Son of English farmer convicted for poaching in River Thames. Sent to penal colony in New South Wales. Married Amy.
*Tallien, Jean Lambert
    A leader of the French Revolution.
*Tallien, Thérésia
    Wife of Jean Lambert Tallien. Introduced by Barras to Napoléon but derided and rejected him.
*Tattersall, Richard
    Founder of Tattersalls, the famous bloodstock company.
Templeton, Major
    Retired army officer. Went to New South Wales to supervise François Scott-Quetteville's interests there after the latter and his family returned to England.
*Tuffnell, Colonel
    Retired colonel of Royal Horseguards (Blues).
*Uxbridge, Lieutenant-General (Paget, William, Earl of)
    Brilliant cavalry commander under Wellington. Member of the famous Paget family. Later he was made the 1st Marquess of Anglesey.
*Verner, Captain William
    Officer in the Hussars. Delivered invitations to the Richmonds' ball and assisted at the ball.
Webster, Captain William
    Senior Captain in The Bridge Company's fleet.
*Webster, Lady Francis
    Duke of Wellington's mistress at the time of Waterloo.
*White, Dr John
    Surgeon of the First Fleet to New South Wales.
Wilmott, Captain Richard
    The successor to William Webster as senior captain of The Bridge Company's fleet.

FAMILY TRE

THE QUETTEVILLES OF ANJOU

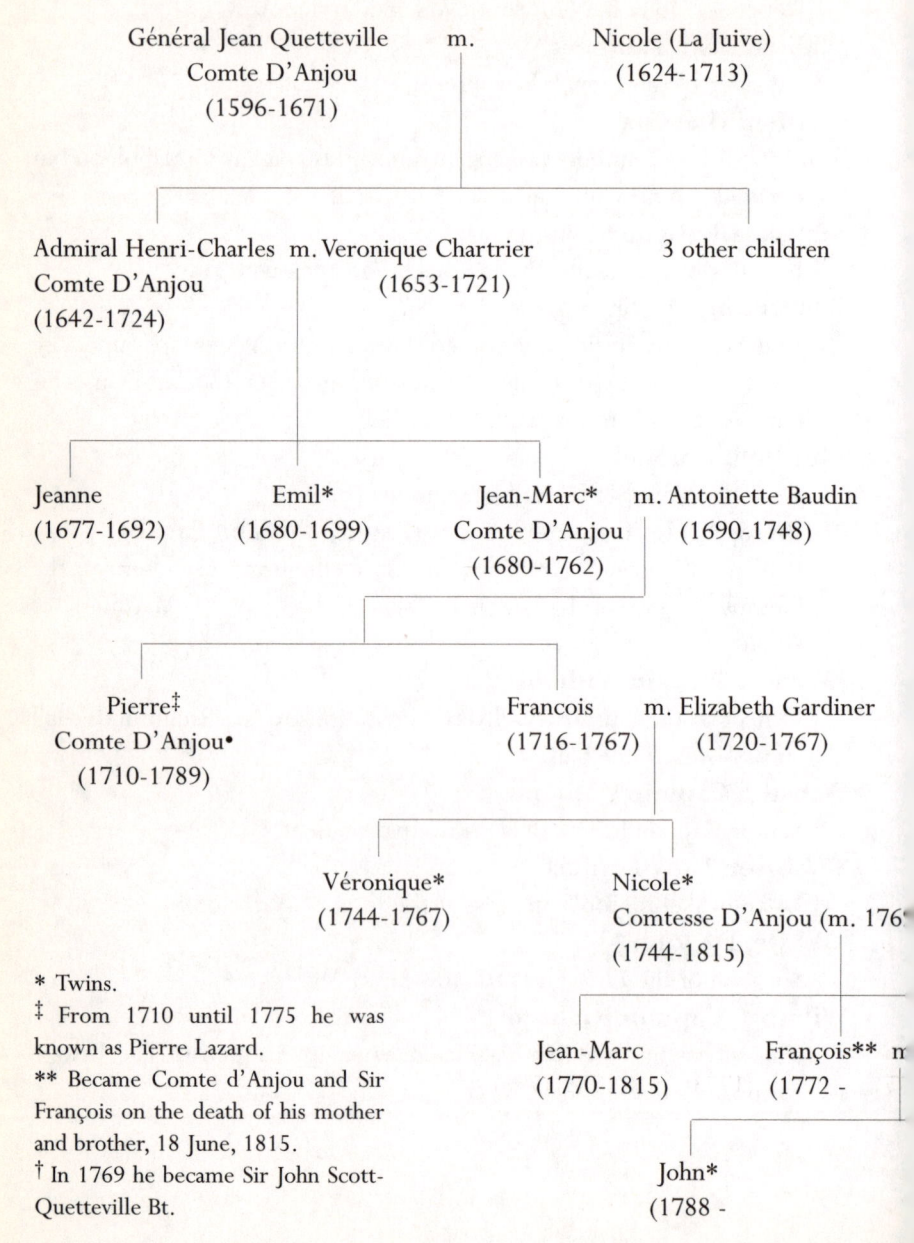

Général Jean Quetteville m. Nicole (La Juive)
Comte D'Anjou (1624-1713)
(1596-1671)

Admiral Henri-Charles m. Veronique Chartrier   3 other children
Comte D'Anjou (1653-1721)
(1642-1724)

Jeanne   Emil*   Jean-Marc* m. Antoinette Baudin
(1677-1692)   (1680-1699)   Comte D'Anjou   (1690-1748)
                                    (1680-1762)

Pierre‡   Francois m. Elizabeth Gardiner
Comte D'Anjou•   (1716-1767)   (1720-1767)
(1710-1789)

                    Véronique*   Nicole*
                    (1744-1767)   Comtesse D'Anjou (m. 176†
                                         (1744-1815)

* Twins.
‡ From 1710 until 1775 he was
known as Pierre Lazard.   Jean-Marc   François** m
** Became Comte d'Anjou and Sir   (1770-1815)   (1772 -
François on the death of his mother
and brother, 18 June, 1815.
† In 1769 he became Sir John Scott-   John*
Quetteville Bt.   (1788 -

19 JUNE, 1815

THE SCOTT FAMILY

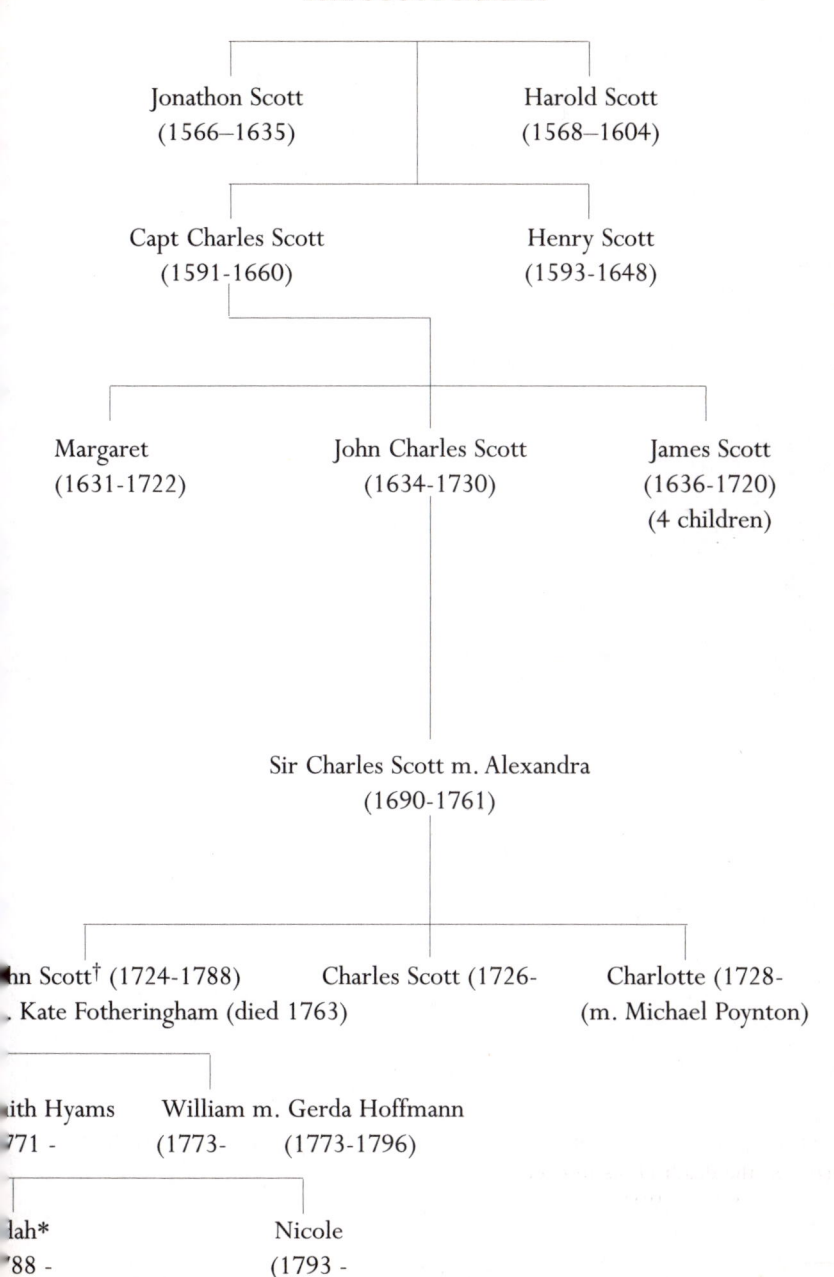

- Jonathon Scott (1566–1635)
- Harold Scott (1568–1604)
- Capt Charles Scott (1591-1660)
- Henry Scott (1593-1648)
- Margaret (1631-1722)
- John Charles Scott (1634-1730)
- James Scott (1636-1720) (4 children)
- Sir Charles Scott m. Alexandra (1690-1761)
- ...hn Scott[†] (1724-1788) . Kate Fotheringham (died 1763)
- Charles Scott (1726-)
- Charlotte (1728-) (m. Michael Poynton)
- ...ith Hyams 771 -
- William m. Gerda Hoffmann (1773-) (1773-1796)
- ...lah* '88 -
- Nicole (1793 -